JUST THE BEGINNING
Book 10

The new Life Series

By

Louise Bouck

DEDICATION

This New Life Series is dedicated to Jesus, and my family, those that have gone before me, those who are with me, and those to come, and all my brothers and sisters in Christ.

†

ACKNOWLEDGEMENTS

It is important to say thank you to all the people who have encouraged me. A special, "Thank you" goes to all the wonderful Christian family and friends who have continued to keep me and this work of love in their prayers.

A note of appreciation goes to Ray Shaw, who patiently taught me to use the technology necessary to create this series and make it available.

I acknowledge God's strength and favor that has helped me to continue to plod along on this ten book series. His precious touch is needed daily. Thank you Jesus.

TABLE OF CONTENTS

6   Chapter 1   The arrival

25   Chapter 2   Telling the Secret

39   Chapter 3   The Village Has Changed

50   Chapter 4   They are Coming

65   Chapter 5   Hard Work and Strong Hands

83   Chapter 6   Ben's Golden Day

105   Chapter 7   Ben's Return

114   Chapter 8   The First of Many

134   Chapter 9   Town Meeting

146   Chapter 10   Do It or Starve

163   Chapter 11   Excitement In the Air

181   Chapter 12   Success and Failure

199   Chapter 13   The Journal

215   Chapter 14   It's a Home Now

233   Chapter 15   The New Camp of the Lion

252   Chapter 16   A New Situation

266   Chapter 17 No More Blue Stones

279   Chapter 18 Pacification with Courage

289   Chapter 19 Building A Future

305   Chapter 20 The Future

340   Chapter 21 A New Way

346   An Invitation

347   Book Titles in The New Life Series

348   About The Author

CHAPTER ONE
THE ARRIVAL

Sarah's heart felt a little heavy as she watched the many young men escorting her mother back to their village. She knew she would see her and the rest of The Blue Stone People in the early spring. She planned to visit. It all was very exciting.

Now with the knowledge of the secret of the large salt Cathedral within the bluff she planned her day so that she could be near the entrance of the cave when the sun hung over the trees. I have to see the image again, she thought. I can't live here so close and be casual about it. The cave drew her like a bee to a flower. She held Pili tightly in her arms and looked at the small hole in the floor where the little wolf had fallen into the waterway. It's strange the way everything happened to give us the knowledge about the underground water and that it passes through Ben's small lake. I can feel you here Lord standing close beside me. Your Spirit moves across this land with the power of your will directing it. I wish that I could understand why we have been given this special knowledge and why you have put us here.

David heard the thunder in the distance and started moving the horses back across the river so they could use the shelter he had built in the trees. It was a temporary windbreak with a roof made of all the branches stripped from the logs that the men had used to build the storage building at their cabin's back entrance. He patted the wide rumps of the work horses as he moved beside them pouring feed into bins that he had made.

"It's going to rain soon," he spoke to them as if they would answer. "You will all be comfortable here. Blackie you and Moon Boy need to move over to make more room for Pretty Mother and Sugar Baby." He pushed on the horse's sides directing their move. "There, that's better. I'm hoping for a good long rain so Sarah and I don't have to carry water to the garden. So all of you just be cozy and think rain." He chuckled at himself and knew that even if they had a long, soft rain; it would be by the good will of God not by anything horses thought.

"Sarah, where are you honey?" She was sitting on a blanket with the baby, facing the front of the cave.

"I'm here. I was waiting to see if the sun would make the image, but the clouds have moved in. I guess I should go fix us a meal and get Pili fed."

"The thunder is loud. It almost scared me in the cave. I thought for a moment that it was the start of another quake. Do you think the vibrations from thunder could start another movement, or make more rocks fall in the cave?"

"No Sarah, I think God controls all that happens around and in this cave and none of it just happens." He helped her up and gathered the blanket over his arm. They walked together to their cozy new cabin and as they entered, the first few drops touched them and brought a smile to Sarah's face. She didn't see the serious look that crossed David's face as he thought of damage that another quake could do to the beautiful Cathedral carved in salt that they had discovered.

The rain came and soaked the land raising the level of the river and watering the garden. By noon the next day David was working on adding to the size of the horse shelter while Sarah scraped two more rabbit hides that she was planning to use for Pili's winter coat.

*****

In Silverville Sam laughed heartily as he checked items off the list of ordered supplies as the men piled them on the bank of the Silver River.

"When spring comes we intend to build a proper dock so that it will be easier for all of us to do this."

"That would be a big help to us and a time saver, too," said Daniel. He waved and smiled at the two young adults that had ridden down the Silver River with him, before he expertly began to maneuver the mail boat; slowly turning it around for the difficult trip back up the unpredictable Silver River.

Sam stood there another moment watching, before remembering his manners and invited the two young people to jump aboard the back of the supply wagon as Matt adjusted the reins in his hands and clacked his tongue to gently begin the slow trip; passing the four fingers of the river and pulling the team to a stop at the front door of Sam's general store.

"Welcome to Silverville," he said as they slid down and brushed the wrinkles from their clothes. The young man nodded slightly to acknowledge the greeting as he pulled their two small bags down. The girl showed no sign that she had heard it.

Several men waited there anticipating the arrival of items they had ordered. It wasn't long before Sam's bundles and barrels were removed from the wagon and taken inside. Matt moved his team to the area behind his blacksmith shop across the street and praised them as he removed their tack and fed them giving each one attention and loving scratches. Matt was glad to be back at his shop. He knew that the two young people that had come on the mail boat would soon figure out that he was the most likely person to be able to help them with transportation or directions. He thought they seemed inexperienced and strangely timid.

Liz, his wife brought out a tray with coffee and a meal to share with him as soon as she saw the horses being released into the field through her kitchen window. He had left at first light and it was well beyond noon. He must be very hungry she thought as she added another biscuit to the tray.

They sat together in the back of the shop and ate and she explained that their girls were with Melanie.

"She is starting a children's choir and wants our girls in it."

"That's sounds like a good idea. It will be fun for them and it will give you a few minutes free of children."

"Matt, who are the young people standing in the street? They look totally lost."

"They came on the mail boat. I don't know their names."

"The poor dears are probably hungry and scared to death." Liz didn't wait for a reply from Matt. She hurried out to the street and introduced herself.

"Hello, I am Liz. My husband Matt has the blacksmith shop. I can tell that you are new here. Is there anything that we can do to help you?"

"Yes, we are new. I'm Mark Moody and this is my sister Lori. We came on the mail boat. We are looking for Benjamin Slater. He is our relative."

"I see, well you are going to need a couple of horses and some directions. Their place is upriver on the Hickory." Matt approached smiling and offered his hand to Mark.

"This is a nice little village," said Lori. "My name is Loraine, but everyone just calls me Lori."

"I hope they are not far upriver. I am ready for a meal and some rest," said Mark to Matt, as they walked into the shop.

"Who are you looking for?"

"Benjamin Slater is my cousin twice removed. We are looking for him. When his letter arrived, our uncle said that we should go to Silverville and find him. That was the start of winter so we had to wait and then by the time we helped with the planting, and then Aunt Velma died and it just took a lot longer than we thought to get out here. I guess we need to get a buggy or some kind of a rig so we can go find him. Now that we are here I am anxious to get to his place and be done traveling." Liz looked at the tired young woman and intervened before Mark could set his plan in motion.

"It is a long ride out there. Let us put you up tonight and then Matt would be happy to ride out there with you. Wouldn't you dear?"

"Come this way Lori and you can have something to eat while we get acquainted." Lori gratefully followed her. She felt welcome as they went up the steps and into Liz's warm and inviting kitchen. "We have two girls. They will be home soon. Mark you can put those bags down anywhere. Come sit at the table and I will pour you both some coffee. "The two small bags looked old and worn that he tucked against the wall trying to put them out of the way. One was made of flowery tapestry, the other dark brown leather.

"This house smells wonderful. I can tell that you are a good cook just by the scent in here."

"Thank you Mark, you can smell the apple pies I have baking in the oven. They should be done soon. While we wait for those, I am going to make you each a sandwich. Matt and I just finished our lunch before I spotted you standing in the street."

"Mark, tell me about what you can do. How old are you?" Matt asked with interest.

"I guess I can't do much, just the stuff I did on the farm back home, but I can drive a buggy. You don't need to waste your time coming with us in the morning, if you will just tell me how to get there, then I will be fine."

"I have horses you can use, but I don't have a buggy." A look of pain washed over Lori's face.

"I don't know how to ride a horse. All we had on the farm was work horses and a buggy horse," she confessed.

"When Aunt Velma died Uncle John sold it all and gave us two tickets for the train and a little money and Ben's letter. I have it in my bag if you want to see it."

"That's fine. I don't need to read it. We all know the troubles that Ben has seen. He is a special young man. He was about your age, Mark when they came out here. He is a married man with four sons now and he and Jed have a growing ranch."

"I'm seventeen and Lori is eighteen. We are old enough to work hard and earn our way."

"Yes, I'm sure you will be fine." Liz was glad for the interruption when the girls came home. It seemed that these two young people were very intent upon becoming independent.

Matt smiled at the excited sound of his daughters as they talked about the choir and who had been there. He stepped outside for a moment and asked Reverend Brown if he could borrow his buggy in the morning. The Reverend had brought the girls home and was just turning his little rig around.

"Yes of course Matt. I won't need it until Friday. How is everything? I heard that two young people came in on the mail boat."

"That's why I want to use your buggy. The girl doesn't ride and they are shirttail relatives of Ben's. I'm going to take them out there in the morning."

"That's nice of you. You can come get the buggy in the morning whenever you are ready."

"Thanks, I know the girl will appreciate not having to ride out that far on horseback."

Matt was glad for a chance to visit at the ranch.

In the morning as soon as the family and their guests were fed, Matt led them across the bridge and they were on their way. Liz had packed them snacks for the trip and one stop was all they needed.

As the big oak came into view, Matt heard the bell clanging and with little effort they were ferried across the river. Matt's horse and the Reverend's were tied where they could reach water and grass and left to rest comfortably. Ben and Jed had both responded to the bell and Beth had come to the crossing with her little wagon. Mary had stayed in her house and was surprised when everyone appeared talking and laughing at the front door. She slid the big roast into the oven and turned around to see new faces as well as Ben, Jed and Matt, smiling at her. Beth and Lily hugged Mary and said they would be back later.

"Well, hello everyone, I heard the bell but I thought that it was for the wagon from the fort to get the milk. He should be here soon."

"I didn't see them but they may have been just a bit behind us," said Matt.

"Mary, I would like you to meet my cousins. I just met them myself. This is Mark Moody and his sister Lori."

"It's nice to meet both of you. Hello Matt, did you bring these folks out?"

"Yes, I sure wasn't going to miss a chance to enjoy your good cooking," he teased, "but you know I always like seeing all of you. Mark and Lori stayed at our house last night. They came down the Silver on the mail boat."

"That explains it. The boat comes on Wednesday and the milk wagon from the fort won't come again until Friday. I had my days mixed up. Matt, we appreciate you bringing them so they wouldn't have to find their way alone." Joshua and Adam came in together and introduced themselves politely.

"Everyone please sit wherever there is room. I will put on a fresh pot of coffee. "

Lori sat down on the end of one of the benches at the table and suddenly she couldn't hold back her tears any longer. They slid silently down her cheeks. She tried to brush them away but Mary noticed and handed her a glass of water and a handkerchief so cleverly that she was the only one that saw it. She pumped a pitcher full of fresh well water and handed a glass to Mark.

"You must both be terribly tired after your long journey. I think that you would probably like to rest before we all get acquainted. Lori, come with me dear and I will show you where you can wash up and then rest until that roast is done."

"Oh, I am sorry; I don't want to be a bother. Really, I will be fine," she whispered but followed Mary into the boy's bedroom. Mary poured a little water into the basin and handed Lori a fresh towel.

"Wait just a minute, I will be right back," she said as she darted into her own room long enough to collect a clean cotton dress and then scooped up Lori's carpet bag on the way back through. "Here, put this on so you can relax. It will be too big but sometimes that can be a comfort. Traveling

14

clothes were never designed to rest in. I will come get you when it is time to eat. No one will bother you." Mary gave the girl a quick gentle hug and closed the door.

As she entered the main room she gave orders that all the men should do their visiting outside.

"I will bring out a tray when the coffee is ready." She was smiling and humming as she added the last clean vegetable to the big roaster and closed the lid.

"Joshua, would you help me with this?" He opened the door wide and then took the large pot of coffee from the tray of cups. Having followed her instructions, the chairs, steps and grass found men and boys seated on them. Mary noticed with one glance that most of the faces wore smiles. "I have the roast in but it will be a while. Mark, are you hungry?"

"Matt and his wife, Liz treated us well, they fed us last night and again before we left. She even sent a snack with us so I am not starving. I can wait."

"I am glad that you were at their house. Liz is a good cook and a sweet caring person. Here Mark I brought you a few cookies to go with your coffee, just in case."

"Is Lori alright? She's not sick is she?" He asked with concern.

"No, she is just exhausted and probably a little overwhelmed."

"Yes, the train was very uncomfortable. It was hot and noisy. No one was able to sleep on it. Some of us tried to open the windows but that let the smoke and soot in. Then when we found the place to get a ticket for the mail boat they said that it only came down to Silverville once a week, so we waited three days just out of sight of the folks there. I bought some bread, some cheese and four apples and we slept in the grass under a big pine tree. The two men on the mail boat were nice and they gave us some stew they had. They also gave us some red wine. Lori was so funny. She kept giggling until she fell asleep with her head on a bundle of supplies."

"It sounds like you had quite an adventure!" Joshua was impressed with anyone that had traveled farther than Silverville. "What's it like where you came from?" Mark's face became serious.

"After our place burned down we lived with Uncle John and Aunt Velma. Our dad died two days after the fire. He got pain in his chest and just fell down. I think trying to save our house was just too much for him. It was mostly gone by the time folks saw the smoke and came to help. My mom that was your cousin Vickie died with the bad sickness that went through. We all missed her so much that we didn't know what to do with ourselves last winter. It was just one thing after another. Then when Aunt Velma died, it took the heart out of Uncle John. I wanted him to come with us but he refused. He sold our land and the crop on it and told us to go while we could.

Mary looked at the faces before her. No one was smiling now. She could see the effect his story was having on everyone, especially Ben.

"Mark, do you remember my grandparents?" Ben asked.

"Yes, they were nice people. Strangers bought that place some years back. I remember visiting the farm when I was a kid."

Jed stood up abruptly and motioned for Josh to follow him.

"We better get started milking or we won't be done before that roast is. Johnny, do the chickens need attention?"

"Yes, I will do it. Come on Adam, we need to clean the pens."

"I can milk a cow. I'll come with you, Josh." Mark followed along looking at everything as he went. He was still wearing his travel clothes. Jed stuck his head in the door of his house long enough to ask Beth if she had some clean work clothes that would fit Mark.

"I am sure I can find something. Come in Mark, and let's see what we have." Mark was soon heading out the back door in bib overalls.

"The cow barn is the one on the right." She pointed and he jogged down the path in that direction. Maybe these kids will be a help once they get used to us and the ranch. Beth had not been there to hear the sad story Mark had related. She looked forward to talking with them and hearing all about their home.

The bread pudding was done and she had added oodles of raisins made from the wild grapes. She stirred the purple grape sauce as it bubbled. This can sit on the cupboard and it will thicken some more as it cools. I better take down a jar with some cream in it, just in case the new kids don't like grape sauce. I wonder if Mary has enough butter. I will take some of that. We were going to have a ranch meeting tonight. I think the men will probably want to postpone that, but I better take down the tablet anyway, just in case.

As she scanned the list of things they needed to accomplish in the coming months, she wondered how they would get them all done.

"Lily, please put this butter and cream in the wagon and the tablet. Make two trips so you don't drop anything. I have hot bread pudding and grape sauce to go down. I will put a lid over them and then I think we are ready."

"Mom how old is the new girl?"

"I don't know, maybe fifteen. She is small but I think she is older than you are by a good bit."

"Hmmm, I think she is pretty. Do you?"

"Oh I didn't notice. We were only there for a moment." As they climbed up onto the seat of Beth's little wagon, they both wrinkled their noses and looked at each other.

"Mom, what is that awful smell?" Beth had noticed it, right away. She stopped the horse and sat looking at the lake.

"The fish are dying, our lake has gone bad! Oh Lily, this is terrible! The horses will get sick! The thoroughbreds drink this water!"

She turned the little wagon around and drove swiftly to the barn where Jed was just finishing the milking.

"Jed, the lake has gone bad! Can you smell it? The fish are dead. The horses will die. They drink the water from the lake!"

His eyes grew wide as he realized what she was telling him.

"Beth this is terrible! Josh and Mark take water buckets from the well to the horses in the barn and block off their lake access right away. I am going to get Orville and tell Ben. Hurry we have to act fast or we will lose a lot of our best animals!" He rode to the mustang field to tell Orville and then sped to Ben's. Jed's heart was racing as he quickly related his story.

Ben was upset, but his mind was more analytical. He was already figuring out what had happened.

"Jed something has happened to the waterway. We know that it feeds the lake. Let's go check the lake where the water comes in."

"It is still coming in; I can see the mud rolling just the way it always has," said Jed. "This just doesn't make sense to me." Ben knelt and scooped water to smell it. Then he licked his hand.

"Salt, Jed! The water is bringing in salt, that's why the fish are dead!"

"What are we going to do?"

"We need to be calm and think this through. Thanks to that poor wolf pup we know this water comes through the cave. We have to let Sarah know so that she doesn't use it for anything. Are you sure that all our livestock are alright?"

"I told Orville to start in my barn with Blaze, Star and then Dash Away. He ran in there and I haven't seen him to talk to him but I know he was putting them in their stalls with buckets of well water."

"Good, that's all anyone can do for them right now. I am glad that it rained. The girls haven't used lake water on the garden for several days. I will ride out for Sarah's at first light. I am going to take Orville and some dynamite with me. I would rather have no water than that salty stuff. Now we better get back to my house. The family is there waiting and worried."

Everyone was talking excitedly as soon as Ben and Jed stepped in the door.

"Ben, are the horses sick? What about the milk cows? Is there milk bad?"

"It's the waterway to the lake; it is bringing in a lot of salt. The animals all seem to be alright but we are going to keep them all away from the lake. You girls should check the milk before we send it to the fort tomorrow. If it tastes salty, don't send it."

Lori came out into the noisy room looking puzzled.

"What is going on?"

"I hope you rested well. Everything is going to be fine, but we have discovered that salt is getting into our little lake and the fish are dying and we had a scare because our animals drink from that lake. It is going to take some work but we will figure it all out. The animals are not sick. I guess Lily's sense of smell saved the day." Lily laughed and pinched her nose.

"It is pretty bad and it will probably get worse before this is over," said Ben. "Mary, I am going to take Orville with me and head for Sarah's at first light. They need to know that the water in the cave should not be used." Just then Orville tapped lightly on the door and came in.

"The horses are all fine but they sure did appreciate the good fresh water. The poor things were drinking and getting thirstier. That's a strange thing how a fresh little lake could get salty like that."

"Orville I need you to ride with me down to see David and Sarah at first light. I think we should eat and then all bed down. We have a lot to do in the days ahead." Beth nodded agreement as she placed the tablet where Ben could see it. The meal was preceded by Ben thanking God for the safe arrival of his two cousins. He thanked God that they had discovered the bad water before any of the animals became seriously ill. He gave thanks for the extra hands to help with the work and then he gave thanks for the food and they all began to fill their plates. Orville gobbled his and asked if he could take his desert with him. He wanted to check the horses in Jed's barn again and then he would go to his cabin.

"I'll meet you at the crossing first thing in the morning," he said to Ben as he took the generous portion of bread pudding that Mary had scooped into a bowl. She slathered it with the grape sauce and covered it with a small plate.

"Careful with that Orville, the plate will slide off."

"Thank you Ma'am." He said politely. No one had thought to introduce Orville to the new people at the ranch.

He wondered but didn't ask. Cousins, he thought. I guess he must have a big family.

The meeting was short.

"Nothing has changed but the lake. Now we have that to deal with. We have to come up with solutions before we lose land and animals," said Jed crossly. "What is the point of having a meeting when all we have is a growing list of problems and no solutions?"

"Jed it helps to face the facts so they are fresh in our minds. We can think about what we should do while we are doing other things."

"You can think all you want to but that won't get the cabins built or that stinking lake cleaned up. We need help and we need it now!"

Jed, calm down. I think we can get help from The Blue Stone People. I plan to go there after we blow up the waterway."

"What? Well thanks for telling the rest of us! I thought that was what meetings were for, Ben. You are supposed to discuss things with the rest of us, not just decide to go do it."

"Yes, Dad, Jed is right. You should have told us what you were planning," said Josh.

"I wasn't planning it exactly, it just came to me that they have men and we need them."

I think I have an idea," said Adam. "Mom could you and all the ladies make us some really big nets? We could pull the dead fish out of the lake and bury them."

"Oh Adam, that would be such an awful job. Yes we could make the nets, but using them in that nasty water might make us sick. I don't know. We need wisdom. Pray about it." They ended the meeting with Jed asking God's guidance and blessings on all of them.

Beth took Lori home with her to sleep for the first night. They covered their noses and all traveled quickly and hurried through the door closing it as fast as they could but still it seemed that the dead fish smell was everywhere.

The windows had been left shut, but when Ben stepped out his back door in the morning, the stench from the lake made him gag. Orville was waiting at the crossing and even Sundown and Tinkle seemed glad to hurry along and leave the smell behind."

"I figure we can test the water at the cave and if it is salty, we will need to go farther upriver before we set the charges. There is no telling where that water is running on a salt bed."

"How are you going to know where to put the charges? You can't see the waterway."

"I don't know Orville. We will just have to figure it out when we get there." Ben stopped at his usual spot and was glad to scoop the fresh river water over his head and neck while the horses drank.

"Ben I think I made a bad mistake riding Tinkle. She doesn't look so good. Sundown was with the horses in your corral so he got river water, but Tinkle was with me in the field with the mustangs. They were all using the water from the channel you made from the back of the lake. Look at her Ben, she is shaking." Just then Tinkle rolled onto her side in the grass by the river. "She is sick Ben. She is really sick!"

"Easy girl," said Ben as he knelt by her head. "Orville make her drink. Pour water in her mouth. She is dehydrated from the salt. Stay here, I have to go back to the ranch. No one mentioned the mustang field. We have got to get good water to them right away. Orville I am so sorry. I can't help you with Tinkle but maybe I can save the others." Ben headed back to the ranch as fast as he could without misusing Sundown. He splashed across the river and rode straight to the channel that carried lake water to the mustangs.

Jed had thought about the channel that morning and had enlisted the aid of everyone to block it and with a bucket brigade from the well they had filled a big trough. They were still pouring water into it, surrounded by thirsty horses when Ben arrived.

"Thank God, you thought of it. Tinkle is sick. She went down when we stopped."

Ben, that is terrible. Orville loves that horse. You should go back but leave Sundown here. He is tired. Take one of the other horses with you for Orville to ride. I put the mares all in your corral. The women have been helping. They are hand feeding the foals with fresh water and very soupy mash. The foals from my barn were starting to get wobbly so we separated them from the mothers and started with the fresh water treatment. The mares have too much salt in their systems. It's coming through in their milk. I hope Tinkle will be able to overcome it. None of the other horses that had lake water have been ridden."

"If anyone can save that horse, Orville can." Ben rode Buddy and took Rusty with him. When he reached Orville, he was standing on the prairie crying like a baby. Ben assumed the worst.

When he looked over where Tinkle had been down she was standing there chewing on a big mouthful of grass.

"Ben she is going to be alright. Her stomach is bad and I think she should stay here while we are gone, but she is going to be fine. I poured enough water down her for ten horses. She probably thinks I have lost my mind, but I think it saved her Ben. I listened to her heart and it was flopping around something awful. It's steady now."

"Orville I am proud of you. You kept your head and I think you did what she needed. You saved her. I want you to ride Rusty back to the ranch and lead Tinkle back slowly. You stay there and help where you can. The foals and mares from Jed's barn are sick and we don't know about the other horses from the mustang field yet. Jed had everybody carrying water to them when I arrived. He put Dash Away in the field beyond Sarah's cabin. That field gets river water. I have got to go now Orville. Tell Mary that I may go to the Indian village. So she won't worry if I am gone longer."

"I will Ben. I won't forget, but Tinkle is still weak. I am going to go very slowly."

"That's fine. Tell Jed that if I am successful, the water should stop flowing into the lake completely."

"That is sure going to change things isn't it? No water in that lake, I mean, it sounds impossible." Ben nodded and rode toward Sarah's. His saddlebags were bulging with sticks of dynamite and coils of fuse. He thought that the lake that Orville described was something that he dreaded ever having to see. He wondered how they would deal with it.

CHAPTER TWO
TELLING THE SECRET

Ben stopped Buddy and tied him near the river. At the church crossing stood a large pair of David's work horses, gladly mowing the grass with every mouthful of their lunch. It was easy to pole across the river and David and Sarah stood grinning ready to give him hugs as he came up the river bank.

"Ben I am so glad you came. We were outside working, and I could see Buddy coming through the trees. His white coat is so beautiful, but why did you come alone? Where are Mary and the boys? They aren't sick are they?"

"No everyone is well but we have some sick horses. The water coming into the lake is salty and it is so strong that it has killed the fish. It stinks worse than anything you can ever imagine. Most of our animals were drinking it. The thoroughbred mares in Jed's barn and the mustang field all used the lake. The milk cows had a channel from it, too."

"Ben, are the thoroughbreds and foals going to be alright? What about Dash Away?" Sarah was so upset that she was starting to shake. She hadn't connected yet that the reason Ben was there, had to do with the waterway and the cave. David's face turned ashen as the reason hit home. He glanced at Ben and saw the set of his jaw. David knew Ben and that look well enough to know that he had already decided on a plan of action.

"The foals were getting salt from the milk of their mothers so the girls have taken the foals separate and they are feeding them fresh water and very soupy mash. I think they will be able to recover. The old corral by the hut has the mares and Dash Away is in the small field beyond your cabin. It has river water. I have come to test the water in the cave to see if it is salty. If it is you shouldn't use it for anything. I brought dynamite and I am hoping that we can change the route of the underground waterway. I would rather have no lake than the dead one we have now."

"Ben you can't do that! You can't change anything about the cave. It is sacred!"

Ben looked stunned. It was then that Sarah realized what blasting near the cave would do. David looked at Sarah and without saying it; he conveyed the thought that they had to explain to Ben. He had to know everything.

They hurried into the cave and dipped out a palm full of water. It was brine.

"David, this is terrible! You must tell him where the salt is. He has to know!"

"Ben, walk with us to our cabin. We have a long story that you have to hear."

"David, I don't want to take the time for a long story. The sooner we can blast that waterway, the sooner I can stop the salt from pouring onto my land."

"Ben I think there is something even more important than your ranch here that we must protect."

"Don't be ridiculous. Nothing is that important! I know you thought that the shadows on the wall above the cave looked like a lion, but you both know what is at stake here. Blaze and Star and their foals are sick from drinking that water! We could lose the ranch if we don't stop this right now."

"Ben, I am about to break a sacred oath. I have to show you what you are about to destroy."

"This time, I am coming, too, said Sarah. It might be my last chance!" She stuffed dried food in a saddlebag and water bags were filled with fresh river water. Pili babbled and talked to Moon Boy patting his neck as Sarah cuddled her close in front of her.

"I don't understand. Where are you taking me?"

"We are going to see something that may be dissolving as we stand here." He had hurriedly helped Ben to saddle Blackie and David was on Thunder in record time. I am taking a lantern just in case."

"Good idea, David, lead the way," said Sarah. They rode single file through the passage he had used with the men of the Lion.

"The opening is behind those huge pine trees just this side of the white streak on this side of the bluff."

"I can see the white on the rocks up ahead. Look up there. There are the trees." David slid down placing Pili in a sling on his back. The walkway is far too difficult for you to carry her. I pushed this sling that you made into my saddlebag as we left." Sarah was excited. She had longed to see the miracle Cathedral that David and the men had seen. She had prayed many times asking God to allow her to see it. Now she was here, trembling with anticipation and a little fear. She had an ache in her chest that would not go away. What if the water has worn away the floor and destroyed the beautiful carved walls. What if it isn't safe to go in? What if we fall through the floor? David was thinking similar thoughts. He broke a strong branch from the old pine and stripped it.

"When we get to the part that is salt, I will test every step. Don't worry." David bent low making sure that the branches didn't scratch Pili as he entered with her. Sarah followed and then Ben. "We may not need the lantern. The quake opened holes that let light in above the walkway," said David. They headed down cautiously. Ben could feel his heart racing. Already he felt the sanctity of his surroundings.

He felt unworthy. Just the fact that this passageway was here and his sister and David had been here guarding it, believing; while he stormed about his ranch and what he needed to do. It made him feel ashamed.

"It is farther down than I pictured. The calves of my legs are getting tired," said Sarah.

"It is even harder going back up," said David. He stopped and tapped the floor. "We can go a little farther but then we should take our shoes off. We can leave them in here." David continued to tap and then he pulled his shoes off and placed them neatly by the wall. Sarah copied his action and so did Ben.

"I can tell we are walking on salt," said Sarah.

"Yes, honey, we are approaching the area behind the huge altar. See there. It looks like a big block of salt. We have to go to the front of the room so that we can see the Lion and The Lamb on top of it."

"David, look at the walls. This is the most beautiful thing I have ever seen." Ben stood silently gazing in awe at his surroundings. David had stopped tapping the floor. He was distracted by the beauty and the strong presence of the Holy Spirit. Ben turned back just as a bright light hit his face. The sun beamed through one of the small holes in the ceiling sending a ray onto the crown's largest jewel on the Lion's head. It shone directly into Ben's eyes. Ben fell to his knees; covering his face with both hands.

"Oh, my eyes, my eyes, he wailed. I'm blinded! I can't see!" Ben cried out. "Take me out of here. Please take me out of here."

Sarah wrapped her arms around Ben and helped him up.

"Listen," she said. "I hear water!" Her voice betrayed the fear she felt. "David we have to get out of here right away!"

"No, Sarah, take Pili. I think I see something. Help Ben and I will follow." Now that she was aware of the sound of the water. It seemed that was all she could hear.

"Hurry Ben, we have to get out of here. She carried Pili and when they reached the part of the hallway with the shoes in it, she grabbed hers and kept going. "Ben, get your shoes and come on." Ben still could not see anything. His world was filled with blackness. She handed him his shoes and helped him put them on and then she slid into her own.

Pili clapped her hands and reached for David.

"Daddy, Daddy," she called.

He scooped her into his arms and shoved his feet into his shoes swiftly.

"Sarah, the water is running under the floor of the Cathedral, but it is way down under. It is crossing the floor of the workmen's chambers that Two Feathers found. I think I know a way to save it all." He hurried ahead of them. Ben continued to rub his eyes. Little by little he began to see shadow-like shapes, but the sun outside was nearly more than he could endure. Sarah finally was able to help by wrapping his eyes with one of Pili's cotton diapers that she had brought along. David led Ben's horse and when the evening came they took the wrapping off. Ben's eyes were red, swollen and sore.

"Ben, I am going to put some salve on your eyes and wrap them again. I think they will be much better in the morning."

"That's kind of you. You are my Ananias."

"What do you mean Ben?"

"In the Bible Saul was in route to Damascus to get permission to put Christians in jail in Jerusalem. I am like Saul, in a way. I thought the ranch was more important than anything that could possibly be here. You remember the story, don't you? It's in Acts 9: 1-9 NIV. Saul was blinded, too. God sent Ananias to him to lay hands on him. Sarah, please pray for me. I lost the fact that everything belongs to God. He has a plan. Pray that God will forgive me and give my sight back. Pray that He will somehow allow me to still have the ranch." She cradled his head against her chest like a child's as he wept, they prayed. Later after they had eaten, she began to worry about him.

"Ben, what are you thinking about? You aren't acting like my brother. You haven't said two words since I bandaged your eyes."

"I guess I have a good deal of praying and thinking to do, but David, I would like to hear your discovery and the solution you came up with. You are right. That Cathedral is awesome. It must be protected!

"Well it is simple really. There is a huge chamber under the cathedral as big as it is. The water pours across the floor of the workmen's chambers and falls in little streams to the bottom of the pit of salt beneath the Cathedral floor, filling it to a point where it now pours out the side, still sliding its way over salt and goes under where it can't be seen. The water on the floor of the workmen's chambers is still fresh. It doesn't pick up salt until it falls into the area beneath the salt chapel. We can divert it so that it flows out the back of the bluff and onto the prairie, it will stop the flow of the salt water to your ranch and preserve the floor of the Cathedral from being eroded if the water level ever rises."

"David, that is fantastic! I don't understand how you can divert the water without blasting away part of the bluff."

"Ben, have you ever used dynamite?"

"We use it just to loosen stumps, and that only takes a tiny bit."

"That's how we will divert the water, a little bit at a time and one rock at a time if we have to. We can't do anything to shake the salt carvings. The earthquake we had must have blocked the course of the waterway and it found a new one across the salt bed."

Ben was thinking that a process that slow would not do much to help the ranch but at least now he understood why it was absolutely necessary.

"I appreciate now why the Holy Spirit brought you and Sarah here. You are guardians of The Lion's Den!"

"It is hard to comprehend, but Two Feathers and Willow are forming a new band of people and will move here for that very purpose, said David.

"I just had an idea," said Ben. "We should use some of the gold we removed from the Hickory River to buy the land on the other side of the bluff. They will need land and maybe if we do it right the water will form a new lake there for them." David and Sarah both gave their approval, smiling and agreeing.

"Ben you have always been generous with The Blue Stone People. Now I think they will be ready to give back. Let's deal with the water and then I will go with you to talk to Chief Dark Wolf. His people will help you." David worked hard from first light until he returned in the evening. His persistent small charges upriver, placed at the base of the bluff began to show progress. Each small vibration caused Sarah and Ben to cringe. Finally by the third day Ben's eyes were nearly healed. He still shielded them from the sunlight, but he could see much better and the pain was gone.

When David returned that evening with wet leather clothing and a wide smile, it was clear that he had broken through to the waterway. Sarah laughed and ran to the cave to check the hole where the wolf had fallen in the water.

"It's too dark. I can't see down there." She took a long stick and plunged it down. Her smile faded when she saw that it was wet.

"That's because the hole I made needs to be widened. Don't worry Sarah. We will be able to reroute all of it. I am certain of it. Oh and don't run over there so close to that hole like you just did. You could still fall through and get hurt."

"I got so excited that I forgot to be careful. You are right." David wasn't taking any chances. He went to the nearest tree and cut a large branch to place across the path to the hole.

"That won't stop us from checking it but it will remind us all to step carefully." Ben agreed. "Ben if you will come with me in the morning, we can place charges in the crack that I have made. That should open up a space wide enough so that more of the water will push through."

"David you have done well so far. I will help anyway I can. Should we go back in to make sure there is no damage?"

"No. If there is we can't do anything about it. I already feel that I did something very wrong taking you and Sarah and the baby in there. Let's just widen the crack and then I will go with you to the village. I need to talk to Two Feathers. Remember Ben you gave your oath. You must tell no one. Chief Dark Wolf does not know. It is not our place to tell him."

"I understand David. I don't give my word lightly." Ben had given his solemn vow and he knew he would have to guard his words when he spoke of these days and their efforts to redirect the water.

The sun was just peeking over the horizon as the two men carefully carried the dynamite and coiled fuse to the area above the crack that David had made in the base of the bluff

"Look over there, Ben. The deer have already found this water. You can see their prints."

"Father, please bless our efforts so there will be more clean water for the animals," said Ben. David laughed and said "Amen."

"If I read the prairie correctly, it looks to me like it will flow over there." David pointed.

"It does look lower in that direction."

"I have this charge in tight. Did you pack the top one?"

"Yes, I think all three are where they need to be. Let's slip behind that big boulder as soon as we light the fuses."

"Hurry Ben, get your head down!" The explosions went off in rapid succession, throwing rocks out onto the prairie and as they landed, they were swiftly followed by a gush of water. The volume was more than they had anticipated. It arched out with force and sprayed into a growing circle.

"You did it David! You did it!"

"We did it Ben, and thank you for trusting me to start it while your eyes were healing." Just then they heard Sarah call to them.

"Is it safe to come out?"

"Yes, but what do you think you are doing? We are using dynamite!"

"I know that silly but I knew you wouldn't close the passageway and I wanted to see. I waited until the booming was done. We were safe in there."

"Sarah, what do you think? Have we made a lake for The People of the Lion?"

"It is flowing hard. It is possible you have made a small river. Who knows where it will go?" They stood there in awe of the scene before them. "Ben I am sorry that you have lost your lake but I know you will do something to keep the ranch growing. Please don't worry. I feel this is the right thing."

"Sarah, I am going with Ben tomorrow to the camp of The Blue Stone People. This time I think it would be better if you would stay here and care for the animals. It won't be a pleasant ride and we plan to move with little stopping. We will each take two horses so we can switch. There is a good deal at stake Sarah. Ben needs help at the ranch right away if he is to save the ranch."

"I understand David. I will stay here. We will be fine. I will pack food for you. You can leave at first light. The cabin is secure and comfortable. You both have business in the village. I will be glad for your return." Sarah turned her horse back into the passageway and rode back to the cabin with them.

*****

Mary fussed about the smell but she was proud of the way everyone had pitched in to remove the poor creatures causing the stench. Even Lori had volunteered to help. Baskets were taken to a hole by the far fence and dumped. Time and again the wagon made the trip taking its awful smelling burden away from their living area. More than once they had all fallen into the nasty slime. It wasn't funny anymore. The unfortunate victim of the slippery mud would simply walk to the river and submerge, coming up scrubbing. Dripping wet they would return to the nastiest of tasks.

Beth tried to dissuade them from doing more than they already were. She took on most of the chores and watched the younger children.

"Nature will take care of it all in time," she said. She cooked inside and kept a huge pot of strong soapy water on the outside fire and near it, stood another tub to rinse the soap from their clothes. She scrubbed them at night and hung them to dry. At least you won't have to put on the filthy stuff from the day before.

"Mary, that slippery part of the mud looks like the clay that Sarah used to make pots. It looks like we are cleaning out the lake to make a clay pit."

"It is clay. The rich red-brown color of it is different. The rest of the mud is much darker. There seems to be a wide strip of it going through the front part of the lake bottom. It could be useful. We will need to show it to Sarah."

"Beth, I am glad that the birds came this morning. They took a large number of the fish and frogs out before we started. We are beyond the mid-point now and if they keep coming back, it will help. Orville said they were swooping down on the pit he dug where we are dumping the baskets. He covered it and that sent them here."

"He is such a good man. He works so hard and always seems to know what needs to be done. I can't understand what set me off when he first came, but it took me a while to get to like him. Now I thank God for him each night and hope he stays forever and I am so glad that Tinkle is getting better."

"Mary, I don't know, but I felt that way too in the beginning.

Right now I am wondering if I will ever be able to eat another fish as long as I live."

"Lori, you have been such a good sport about this. We are not always in such a mess. There is always chores on a ranch this size, but usually things are routine."

"I know. Mark and I are not city folk. You know you all called this a lake but it was more like a pond. That's a good thing the way it turned out. Once we get it cleaned, the men will be able to dike part of it and run river water in here. After a few days, the animals will be able to use it again."

"Lori you are a genius! That would work and it would help the folks that were getting the benefits of the waterway before it went bad. Its hard work now but we will have a useable pond again."

"Look the birds have come back again. As long as we aren't scraping and making noise, they are not afraid of us."

Jed came out of the barn and said he would change out of his clean milking clothes and help them as soon as he had checked on the thoroughbreds. Joshua was with him and Adam and Johnny had helped Beth with some of the chores and they were now ready to get back into their stinky work clothes. Mark followed Jed to Ben's corral and watched through the fence as Jed checked each beautiful mare. The foals are doing well without nursing.

"Beth has done a good job at saving them. Lori was helping her feed them this morning. She sure isn't afraid of work. I respect that," said Jed.

"Jed, now that the water has stopped running, do you think we could try to dig a ditch to channel the river water through here? If we bank the pond down toward the backside, we could dig a channel like you have for this corral. The water would flow out of the pond where it did before and eventually it would wash away all the salt and after a little while it would be useable again."

"Mark I have been thinking about the same idea before you mentioned it. It is doable, but I am worried about the time it would take. We have land that we will lose if we don't dig wells and build cabins on them. There is only so much we can get done. The cabins have to be built by spring when the land office sends the inspector out."

"Gosh Jed, how much of the ranch is in jeopardy?"

"More than half of it," said Jed sadly. That's why Ben isn't back by now. He has gone to see if he can get help from The Blue Stone Indians."

"Are you talking about real Indians? How can people that live in tents help build cabins. That's a strange idea."

"Mark there is history here that you don't know. Trust me on this. If Ben can get them to come, they will save the ranch."

"What about Lori and the rest of the women? We don't want them around Indians!"

"Don't worry Mark. Ben knows what he is doing. He would never put his family in danger. The men of The Blue Stone Indians are honorable." They walked back where the women stood watching nature at work.

"Beth, what is happening?"

"Just stand here quietly and watch. It is amazing. Now that the animals and birds have discovered the empty pond, it is like a huge platter of food for them. I think by tomorrow they will have removed the rest of the fish and anything else edible that is there."

After scrubbing in the river until they felt clean, and putting on a fresh change of clothes, it was nice to sit down all together to a bowl of Beth's chili. Everyone was tired but talked excitedly about starting the dike in the morning.

"We should exclude the clay pit and start the dike closer to the middle and take it in a gentle curve back to the willows. We men will work with pulling the rocks for that right after the milking, if you girls will all do the rest of the chores and then start to make the channel from the river. We will have to build a bridge on the path big enough for the wagons and strong enough to hold horses. Lily would you and Johnny move the goats and their pen before you do the other things? They need a new area."

"Sure Dad, I can do that. The goats like me." Johnny nodded but didn't say anything. He knew that the goats would follow her lead but it was up to him to move the fence that kept them safe and confined.

Jed went out to the edge of the river. He held the hands of Ben's youngest sons as he surveyed the lay of the land.

"We will have to start the channel here and run it across the path about there. The water will pour into the pond there in front of the little fishing dock. We will probably want to move that when we can." They walked the route as he visualized what had to be done and verbalized his thoughts.

"What you going to make Uncle Jed?" Eli asked.

"We need to put new, clean water in the pond to wash it out and make it nice again."

"How you going to clean the stinking stuff out of there and take the new water in," asked Natty?

"We will make a channel and bring some of the river water in there, but first we have to make the pond smaller so it looks more like a new little river."

"I see," he said, sounded much older than he was. "You will have to make the channel bigger than the one to Dad's corral." He stated it as fact and Jed and Mary laughed. He was quite right.

The next few days were extremely difficult ones for everyone on the ranch. Sore muscles and sunburns, blisters and sore hands and fingers were the results of the rocks moved to skids and from trying to dig between ancient trees and through thorny berry bushes. Progress was slow.

The following Monday the wagon came again from the fort and the soldier was glad to taste the milk and said that it was just fine. He was sad about the little duck lake and offered sympathy when he saw all the hard work they were doing; wishing he could help.

CHAPTER THREE
THE VILLAGE HAS CHANGED

Ben and David left early the next morning. David had checked the back of the bluff quickly and saw that a pond was forming in the distance near a clump of trees. I wonder how big it will get before it meanders elsewhere, he thought. Ben had prepared the horses and was ready to go when David returned.

"Sarah has provided each of us with plenty to eat and full water bags. She added two bags of water for the horses for the dry stop in the middle. She seems to always think of everything. She stuffed in a soft collapsible basket to use to give them a drink."

"She is the best woman I ever met and I am glad that she is my wife. I know that it was hard for her to stay behind, knowing that we are going to the village. Most women would have been whining or pouting. She is smart and sensible."

Ben didn't reply, but he was glad that his sister had a husband that loved and appreciated her. It was difficult to carry on a conversation at the pace they were traveling.

"Ben I know that you are eager to get there, but at this pace our horses will tire quickly."

They reined in the horses and slowed to a more reasonable rate.

"I guess I feel driven by circumstances. You are right David. This is better. It will be fun to see where the water goes. I was thinking that when I get back I will have to flush out the lake and see if I can create a channel to take river water to the mustang pasture behind Jed's barn."

"Once you have that done, you should start the well on the Parker place and the pasture piece across from Jed's, before the ground freezes. Once it does digging them will be nearly impossible but the cabins can be built on any tolerable day."

"I wish that two wells were all that we have to do. As soon as we get help from the Blue Stone men, I will take some gold and head to town to buy the land we talked about for The People of the Lion, and check with Tom about all the loads of logs we need right away and where to take them. He will be in a tail spin to get them all ready and delivered. I hope he doesn't disappoint us. He never has before."

"You sure do try to juggle many things in your head. If I were you I would buy a little pad of paper at the store and write all that stuff down. I see a couple trees up ahead. Let's stop there, eat and switch horses. I can tell that Blackie is getting tired."

"It must be past noon. Could it be that you are hungry?"

"I admit it. I could use a meal," David said with a laugh.

As they slowed to a walk the horses stopped in the shade and were grateful for the care they received and the water. Ben took all the tack off of Buddy and scratched him where it had been.

"Aren't you going to tie him to the trees?"

"No, he will stay with me as long as there isn't a pretty female in the area. I am glad that we brought all males. It is always easier that way."

David's cautious nature urged him to fasten his horses to the trees and he did before sitting down on the grass to eat his hearty sandwich and drink from his water bag.

"Ben, how will you explain to Chief Dark Wolf why you need so many cabins and wells right away? I don't think he knows about the laws and rules of the homesteaders. He will think you have gone crazy."

"David, I don't plan on explaining any of it. I am simply going to tell him that I urgently need the help of the People. I

40

think that is a request that he will respond to much better than if I get all tangled in rules and laws."

"I guess you are right about that. He will probably send the men of the night guard. They are the young men that are The People of the Lion. They helped us build our cabin instead of going to the summer meeting. At least they will know what they are doing."

As the sun set they were able to see the big rock country in the distance and decided to stop and rest until morning.

When they rode through the woods along the bluff and entered the camp, David could see that many changes had taken place in the time he had been away.

The first thing he noticed was a new addition to the church. Beside it was a long building with four windows to let light in and view the lake. A door on each end gave those inside an easy way to enter or exit. The wood shingled roof was nailed in perfect overlapping rows. Its exterior was complete.

Father Bob was the first to greet them as they walked their horses to the gate and removed their burdens. They hung their tack and blankets on the fence.

"David and Ben Slater, too, it is good you have come to see the new school." He shook their hands and hugged and slapped their shoulders, while hurrying the horses into the field and watching as they instinctively went to the area where water was available. Father Bob closed the gate quickly and walked in the direction of the school, turning the group so that their backs were toward the men working in the area that had been Chief Dark Wolf's favorite little sitting knoll.

"It appears that this camp is busy. The church is larger. You have kept the men working," David said lightly, while giving Ben a curious look. He knew that Father Bob was not behaving in his usual manner. He seemed nervous. A sigh of relief escaped his lips as he spotted Chief Dark Wolf approaching.

"Ben Slater, my friend and Sharp Knife, I greet you. What wonderful wind has brought you to visit us?" He smiled broadly, but David and Ben read the tension in his body. What are they afraid of? Both men were thinking the same thing.

It is amazing that you have built the school in the few short weeks since your young men returned from helping with my cabin. I am grateful for their help. Each day I thank the Lord for your people and ask God to bless the Blue Stone People."

"Sharp Knife, you are family. We always help family."

Just then Moonflower spotted Sharp Knife standing near the new school with the other men. She hurried to them, thinking that Sarah and Pili had come. She laughed and gave David a big hug and said hello to Ben Slater.

"Where is Sarah and Pili? Why did they not come with you?" Ben chose to be the one to answer her question.

"I am sorry to disappoint you, Moonflower. Only David has made this brief trip with me. We have come to talk to Chief Dark Wolf but she sends her love and I assure you that she and the baby are well."

Chief Dark Wolf motioned to the men working nearby and the work ceased. They all walked to the common area of the camp and then entered the big tent.

"Moonflower, have a feast prepared while we talk. Ben Slater, does this matter require privacy or should the men stay?" The tent was quickly filling with men.

"Yes, allow them to stay since my request will involve some of them."

Growling Bear leaned forward, not wanting to miss a word that was said.

"Our visit is of importance to all of the people. I have need of many good men to help dig wells and build small cabins before early spring. Much has happened at the ranch since you were all there. In order to keep the land that feeds the beef cattle, I must do these things. The large pond that you saw shining clear and clean as the heart of our ranch is now a putrid stinking mess. Many of our animals became ill from drinking its water. David and I found the source of the pollution and have stopped the water that feeds into the lake. By now it is probably drying up."

"What killed the beautiful little lake?"

"Salt, poured in as the underground waterway found a path across a salt bed. My family at the ranch is working hard to help our animals recover. David and I used dynamite to reroute the waterway. It now pours onto the prairie behind the bluff near his land. It is fresh and does not reach the salt."

Two Feathers' face had shown his mixed emotions as he listened and realized the danger to The Lion's Den both from the water and the blasting. David gave him a sudden look that said he would fill him in later. The others that had seen the underground Cathedral all knew instantly that David and Ben had been used by the Holy Spirit to protect The Lion's Den from the water and to change its route to create a new lake for The People of the Lion.

The Chief looked concerned and puzzled.

"David and Ben, come walk with me. The rest of you help your wives to prepare a ceremonial fire for tonight. Prepare an animal for the pit and do whatever is needed. It is the first time that we have been honored by the presence of our benefactor."

Ben felt uncomfortable. He had hoped the situation would be talked over and the Chief would decide quickly who he could part with to help him. He didn't understand that the delay was in itself a way of honoring the request Ben had made. It acknowledged that this was an important decision that required thought and showed respect for the person asking. The three men walked along the outside of the meadow fence for several minutes before Chief Dark Wolf stopped and sat down in the shade of the trees that bordered the north side.

"My men have had an unusual summer, Ben Slater. First they fought a fire and some rode to the summer meeting wearing stains on their clothes and blankets because of it. At the summer meeting two of our men found wives and returned to our camp to pledge their support to Two Feathers who is leader of The People of the Lion. A new band of people grows within my village. It is only a matter of time before they leave and declare their independence. I dread that day. The camp of The Blue Stone People will be reduced to older couples who have grown children. Those children will leave us unless the camp grows from an influx of new blood. Somehow we must keep young people here."

"I am sorry Chief Dark Wolf. You are burdened with worry for the survival of your people. It was not my intention to add another problem."

"No, you were right to come. I understand the need for the cattle and the land to hold and feed them. What I don't understand is why you need to build many cabins before spring. Why is that necessary?"

"The land that my ranch is built on is from homestead grants and part of the conditions to retain the land is that it is parceled and homes be built. If it isn't done by spring when a man comes to inspect the land, it will be sold to someone else and I will no longer have it."

"The laws of the white men are confusing and seem very strange to me."

"Sharp Knife, do you also need to dig a well although the river runs in front of your cabin?"

"Yes my Chief, it is required, but I have not had the land as long as Ben and I have three years before they will come to check my land."

"Then if it is required to keep the land we will build cabins and dig wells. You must not worry about my concerns for the people because the Great Creator has given me what I need to increase the number of people in our camp and perhaps hold the young men here a little while longer. You saw the men working in a pit where my hill used to be. Sharp Knife, didn't you wonder why they were digging there?"

"Well, I must be truthful, yes it did seem odd to me. There appears to be no good reason to make a pit there."

"Our people will soon be trading the blue stones again. During the earthquake, the ground opened its mouth wide and showed me that there are blue stones there in great supply. So you see when the other people at the next summer meeting hear that we prosper, they will want to join us as before. This time we are not naive. We will build a building over the opening in the ground and will post guards again outside the camp. We will be more selective about the people we allow to follow us or come to our village.

When Two Feathers takes The People of the Lion from our village, others will come to take their place. We will ask the men tonight at the fire. They will volunteer to come with you Ben. Do not worry. You will have the help that you need. You are family." His statement touched Ben's heart like nothing else could have. They think of me as family. He heard the words of the Chief echo in his mind.

They talked casually about many things while leaning on the top rail of the meadow fence and admiring the horses. Father Bob joined them when he recognized that their formal private meeting was over.

As the sun moved lower in the sky the camp was filled with wonderful scents and busy people. They had been taken through the expanded church and nearly finished school. The growing flock of sheep was brought back from the prairie and assembled in their pen in an orderly fashion waiting for their shepherds to fill their trough with fresh water from the lake. Ben noticed the rough cut of their growing wool and made a mental note to ask Sam to order several shearing clippers. He would give them to the people as part of his thanks for their help.

He watched as the milk cows were tied in their shelter and given fresh cut grass to eat while women did the chore of milking them.

Morning Dove walked by carrying a basket with a few eggs and a little girl followed her carrying a half grown chicken.

"I hope they are not going to add that poor little chicken to tonight's feast," said David.

"No, I am sure they won't. That girl has adopted that bird and has carried it around with her since it was a small chick. When she sits it down on the ground, it follows her wherever she goes. Somehow it gets plenty to eat. It is bigger than the rest of the chicks born last spring," said Father Bob.

"Father Bob, where is Brother Tim?"

"I saw him earlier teaching and playing with some children at the pavilion. He is good with them and the youngsters all love him. I am sure he will show up when we start the feast. His appetite has increased lately. He has been such a good help to me. I don't know what I would have done if he had not come out here when he did."

Once the people were assembled on their colorful blankets around the communal fire, Chief Dark Wolf stood and invited Ben to speak. He was caught off guard and wasn't sure what he should say.

"First I want to thank all of you again for coming to our rescue this summer, when we needed help to put out the fire. The men of The Blue Stone People are strong and worked hard. You saved my buildings and animals from harm. Thank you for allowing me to visit the camp of the people today. Thank you for showing me your church, school and homes. I enjoyed seeing all the animals." The people applauded courteously. The women had not been informed of the reason for his visit, but the men knew.

Once again I need desperately to ask for help. I need many strong hands to help with necessary work to keep the ranch. I must have the land to feed the beef cattle so that I can share them with you, my friends, in this village. The white men have strange laws and they insist that I build several cabins, and dig wells or they will take much of the land that is the ranch and they will sell it to someone else." Comments could be heard, but many thought that the white men's rules were more difficult than those of their people.

As it grew quiet Ben looked to the Chief for approval. He gave a small nod.

"I need many men to go with me back to my ranch. I can promise you will be well fed, but I also must say that I know you will have much hard work to do. We must get it done before spring. Who will come and help me save our ranch?" Ben wasn't expecting what happened next.

"I will come," said Chief Dark Wolf. "We will all come, but some must stay to care for the women and children and the camp."

"No really Chief Dark Wolf, that isn't necessary. I need a dozen men that are young and strong and the rest will be needed here to do the work they are usually doing."

"I guess he doesn't need all of us. Who would like to go to Ben Slater's ranch to build cabins and dig wells?" All The People of the Lion stood, when they saw Two Feathers and Willow stand. Even the women and children were standing.

"You pick who you need. We will come," said Two Feathers. Soon most of the young men in camp were gathered around Two Feathers as usual. Willow continued to stand.

"Those young women without children, if they are willing to go and cook and help with whatever work needs doing, then they should come. We should take several tents in case the weather turns cold before the work is finished. Tomorrow we will prepare. We can leave the next day."

She sat down and a look of pride crossed Two Feathers' face. He had chosen well. His wife would soon help him lead his people. He nodded agreement and with that simple gesture, the celebration began. Brother Tim stood up and said a quick grace and then Ben and David were both honored by being handed plates that Chief Dark Wolf and Growling Bear had prepared for them.

Father Bob leaned close to Tim's ear so that he could be heard above the drums and singing.

"I think you should go with them. You may be needed there. The rest of us can finish up the school before the snow flies."

"Are you sure?"

"Yes, you are a good carpenter and can fill their spiritual needs at the same time."

"I guess I should go. I hadn't thought of it. To tell the truth, I was wishing I could, but not including myself, as if it weren't possible. Good, then, I will go." He was smiling as he headed back to the food to refill his plate.

Two Feathers sat down on the blanket beside David and Ben.

"If you wish to head back at first light, I will bring my people as soon as possible. I know you are eager to return," he said to Ben.

"Thank you Two Feathers, that sounds like a good plan. I will ask Chief Dark Wolf right now." The Chief heard his name and turned to them. David repeated what Two Feathers had suggested. The Chief smiled.

"I wish I were young again. It seems that adventures are passing me by," he said laughing. "I suspect that the work at the ranch will be taxing even for the younger men. It is good Ben Slater that you have come. We will all benefit from their labors and work here will continue also."

CHAPTER FOUR
THEY ARE COMING

The next morning Ben and David left for home at first light as planned, but it wasn't as early as they thought it might be. The sky was overcast and before long a cold rain sifted down making the trip back to the ranch a cold and miserable one. It continued to rain for three days. Ben was pleased with the progress that had been made at the ranch. He knew how hard the work was and that it had to be done in addition to the routine chores of the ranch.

Orville immediately rushed to assure him that all the animals were doing fine and that the foals had somehow managed to go back to nursing on their mothers and so the chore of feeding soft mash had been eliminated. He thanked everyone over and over and filled them in on the reception that he and David had received at the village. He carefully worded his explanation of the rerouting of the waterway. He had given his word and would stand by it, but inside he was longing to tell them about all that had happened and what he had seen.

*****

Two Feathers and Willow left the village two days later with the volunteers, riding beneath oiled hides leading pack animals with covered bundles.

I think I am being wicked, but it feels good to leave Clover and the children behind for a few weeks. She has become adept at caring for all of them. Willow was thinking as she rode along. She noticed Sylvia Warren riding beside Brother Tim on Jack. The horse he has chosen for her from the herd is smaller than Jack, but looks like him. That mare is docile and a good mount for a new rider. I have ridden her myself.

"They look good together, both the horses and the couple. It is too bad that he is becoming a priest. He would make a good husband for her."

"What are you talking about?"

"I think that Sylvia Warren and Brother Tim would make a good couple." Two Feathers shook his head and grinned.

"Women are always trying to pair people."

Ahead, the men had stopped to rest the horses and they had quickly propped up several hides under a group of pine trees and scrub oaks.

"We will take a little rest here and eat something. The horses are doing well. Everyone has kept up. I think they are all eager to get to the ranch," said Two Feathers to Willow.

"Our people have grown in numbers since our wedding. Have you noticed that?"

"Yes, Two Feathers, we have many people with us, and if you think of the people we left behind, I think we have at least twenty two in The People of the Lion."

"I wonder how long it will take to do the work that Ben outlined. This rain is very cold and I think we will soon see a frost at night."

*****

David had ridden home to Sarah. He didn't like being away from her. He was surprised to see all four work horses on the edge of the river. Each had a pack on its back and Pretty Mother stood close, as Sugar Baby nursed, waiting impatiently. The brown pack horse stood near her with several bundles tied behind Pili's seat and harness. It looks like Sarah is preparing to leave, he thought as he stepped down from Thunder. She came quickly out the door and met him with Pili in her arms.

After a tight squeeze that made all of them laugh, she explained that she was sure that the big work horses would be needed at the ranch and that she had left a note inside the cabin just in case they missed each other.

"Are you hungry, David?"

"Yes I am. I just had a snack along the way."

"Is there anything that we can take to help them that I haven't thought of?"

"It looks like you have packed nearly everything that we own!"

"I tried to think of what they will need when The People of the Lion arrive. I thought of the tools that they would use. They are here on Buck. Joey has loaves of bread and corn cakes and some jars of the wild cherry jam that I made. We will probably think of something that we left behind after we get there. I packed clothes and food for Pili. I don't know how long we will be there."

"If you are serious about this, we should take all the horses. We can't just leave them behind. They can be put in one of Ben's fields. What about Woof, Water Baby and Tip Toe, did you leave them extra food?"

"Yes, they are fine and they are getting very good at providing for themselves."

"Then let's head out as soon as the rain stops." Another lengthy trip was not what David wanted just then, but he knew she was right. The work horses and tools would be needed. "How did you know that The People of the Lion would be coming to help Ben?"

"David, it is simple logic. They have been given the spirit of service. That's what they do, guard, help and rescue."

"Yes I guess you are right. All the young married men will be coming and some of their wives."

"That's good; it will be nice to see them again. I checked their lake and it is growing and beautiful. That prairie will be an awesome home for them when the time comes. I have checked it every day and it is growing in the direction you thought it would. That clump of trees looks like a small island now. I hope they sit high enough so that they will live."

"I guess time will answer that." David said he would be riding Blackie and would attach long ropes to the rest of the horses.

"Sarah, everything here is well done, but would you mind if we leave here after I rest and do a couple things?"

"No of course not, whatever you think is right will be fine with me. We can put all the packs in the lean to; in there the horses are out of the rain and so will the packs be."

After they ate, they went to bed and David slept soundly. He was tired. They rode hard going to the village and came back in the cold rain, she thought as she lay beside him.

The next morning he was up and out before she was awake. The rain had let up but was still drizzling down softly.

"Blackie, there are several things that I need to check on. First I want to see the new lake." The horse's hooves clattered on the rock base of the pass as he made his way through the bluff.

Once they were on the prairie, he stopped and stood in awe at the expanse of water before him.

"Thank you God for allowing us to be your instruments to divert the water." He tied Blackie to the trees at the base of the bluff and climbed up to the big pines that covered the back entrance to the cave. I need to see if the floor is dry in the workmen's rooms now.

When he reached the spot where he was able to look through to the salt bed beneath the Cathedral, he was glad to see that it was all dry. He picked up a piece of rock salt and tucked it into his pocket with a smile.

As he climbed down he was surrounded by the three young wolves, hopping, prancing and wagging.

"Well, hello there. I am happy to see you, too." He scratched their ears and noted that they were not very wet.

"Where have you been sleeping? You must have been in the den. Your mother chose a good place for you. Didn't she?"

When he returned to their land, he went to the area by the cave and stood looking up.

"It won't be long now before your people are here. I feel your presence around us and on our land and this cave. Great Lion of Judah, help us to help Ben." He puttered here and there and it seemed to Sarah that he wasn't doing anything that couldn't be done when they returned. She was frustrated but tried to be patient. That afternoon when the clouds parted he called her name.

"Sarah, come quickly! He took her hand and they walked to the front of the cave, just as the shadows and light reflections from the yellow rocks, formed the Lion above the cave entrance. They knelt and felt His blessing pour over them. As the sun lowered behind the trees David admitted that he had been stalling.

"I don't know why, Sarah. I just had to wait here to see the image before we left. We can go first thing in the morning."

David knew that without a mental burden, they would make the trip and feel refreshed when they arrived.

Sarah suggested two stops. One was so she could change Pili's diaper and feed her.

At that moment she finally remembered to tell David that she had spent the first day he had been gone, picking more gold from the river.

"I got one pan full from our part and then I took a second pan and saw that the river on both sides of the church crossing was sparkling, so I picked that out. I have both bags wrapped double and padded with grass inside. They are on Brownie and Buck. We need to be careful when the horses are unloaded, if people are around. Maybe Ben can use the gold to buy the land behind the bluff for The People of the Lion."

David stood with his mouth open not believing his ears.

"Are you telling me that two of the bundles on the horses I'm leading are filled with gold?"

"Yes, David, I didn't want to leave it there sparkling in the water and once I had collected it, I thought we should bring it and put it with the rest."

"Sarah, sometimes our life sounds like a fairytale. You were right. I'm glad that you made time to do that. I know by the wonderful smell of some of those bundles, that you were doing lots of baking. You are amazing, and I love you so much. I should tell you that more often." Her face brightened with a big smile.

"I know that you love me, but it is always nice to hear you say it."

Their next stop was to take the horses down to the water for a drink while they had a sandwich and an apple. They picked two sacks full of the wild apples, from the trees that grew there.

"These will make wonderful applesauce or apple pies. I am sure they will get used."

"The one I ate was sweet. He pulled two handfuls from the trees and gave one to each of the horses."

As they rode along David was the first to hear the bell. Eli and Lily were on the bluff at the lookout.

"The children make it impossible to surprise them with a visit," said Sarah smiling. She was quite surprised when she saw the two youngsters carefully climbing down.

"I didn't know that you two were allowed up there!"

"We were watching for the Indians. Dad said they will come tomorrow or maybe the next day, but we were watching anyway." Eli was proud that he had finally gotten to ring the bell.

They were greeted with enthusiasm and Ben said that he was glad that it didn't smell as bad now as when he left for David's a week earlier.

"We can see that everyone has been working hard to get rid of the mess," said David. Beth had been working in the kitchen. She picked Pili from her horse and tickled her tummy.

"This little one is getting chubby."

"Yes, she is a good eater.

"Ben, tell us what you are doing here."

"I intend to bring a supply of water from the river through this channel, around the dike we have started there in the lake bed and then let it run out where the water did before. It will be more like a small creek than a pond, but it will bring the water from the Hickory in here and wash away the salt. When it is fresh we will be able to open the channels to the mustang field and the cow pasture again."

Josh and Adam began to help David pull the packs from the backs of the horses. Sarah watched and directed the boys where to take them.

"Put that one off Buck and that one there, in your mom's bedroom for now." Johnny looked puzzled, the last two bags she had indicated, were heavier than grass, but all he could see was the dry grass sticking out that Sarah had stuffed in with the pouches of gold. Joshua took all the leads and rode Pretty Mother, bare back to the field beyond Sarah's cabin where he released them. There they would have plenty of grass and fresh river water. He stood stroking Sugar Baby.

"You are as beautiful as any of the babies on the ranch. Pretty Mother, you have a sweet baby," he said, as he latched the field gate.

"Ben I brought my work team. I haven't any big project going on and I figured you will need them when you start building the cabins."

"We sure will. I have been trying to plan everything out, but I had forgotten about needing a team. Thanks for bringing them. How long can you stay?"

"I am not sure. We haven't anything pressing at our place now. As long as Sarah is busy and happy then I will be glad to stay and help. When are Two Feathers and his people coming?"

"I'm not sure. You heard what he said." Mary came along the path with Natty riding on her horse in front of her. She slid down and gave hugs and said she had large proportions of food cooking. Beth suggested they all come in her kitchen and have a quick lunch so they could get back to the chores they had been doing. Sarah noticed the wide stripe of clay in the empty pond and commented that she could see some nice pots being made from that when time allowed. Lily and Eli had taken a bundle of sandwiches and cookies and jars of milk and had gone back up to the lookout while the rest of them had a quick lunch inside.

Lily reached the bell before Eli and started ringing it as if there was a fire.

"They are coming! They are coming! The Indians are coming!"

Both children were yelling as they came down.

"Thank you children, please calm down. They are coming to help us. There is no need to act alarmed," said Ben.

*****

Two Feathers and Willow crossed the river slowly, riding side by side. Behind them came their band of young followers.

"I would like to have our people back in the village before we get a serious snow. I am also eager to see if there are changes to the bluff near the cave. Too much is going on. It is difficult to keep track of it all," said Two Feathers. She nodded agreement.

When The People of the Lion arrived at the ranch they were greeted with cheers and applause as well as soggy hugs and weather chapped smiles. Faces were redder than they should have been and hands were rougher than usual from the constant outdoor work.

"Ben this isn't as bad as my imagination painted it. I can see the dike you folks have started and the small channels from the lake bottom to the willows to let the rain water wash the soil and carry away the salt. That was a good idea."

"Joshua thought of that and had one done before I got back from the village. He and everyone else here have been working every minute of light to get things back manageable, so we can press on with the other projects."

"You have a good family. The ranch is hard work but it is its own reward. They all realize that. My people will set up a temporary camp here near the work for the dike. We brought small hunting tents and oiled slickers. What were you doing before we arrived?"

"We were carrying stones and packing them into a line in the riverbed. The dike in the Hickory will be just a small finger pointing upriver, over there, and the water will come across there through the trees where the women have cut brush and started a ditch. It will go across the path and tie in with the curved dike spreading out a bit and then go under the willows where the waterway emptied hopefully taking the salt that saturated the soil with it."

"Ben with all of us working, we can have this flowing soon. You will need a bridge wide enough for your wagons over the part where it crosses the path. How do you want that built?"

"For now we have been avoiding digging that part just to save us going all the way around Jed's barn to go to my house. I want to use logs for the base and planks for the surface. I will be taking my biggest wagon to Silverville tomorrow. I plan to talk to Tom. I will make sure he understands the rush on the logs we will need. I will bring back the planks for the bridge and check on my order for everything else for the cabins and wells while I am there. He won't like the haste we are in but he has good men and I know they will do all they can to provide what we need."

Ben was amazed at the speed with which the women had set up a camp under the trees.

Beth, Lori, Sarah and Mary had cleared the main area of Ben's barn and had a small fire going in the fire pit with kettles of chili and stew keeping warm.

As soon as Ben returned and told them that The People of the Lion were coming to help, they started cooking and baking. They had swept the hut and the barn floor and spread any spare hides they had.

"I hope they will go inside at night. There is no need for them to sleep in tents in this miserable weather," said Beth. This barn is cozy and I think I am going to start a little fire in the hut, too." She hurried away to do it.

"I noticed that nearly all the young men here brought women with them. Some of them have pots of food cooking near their tents."

"Lori, we will just do whatever they are comfortable with. After they helped put out the fire, we asked them to sleep inside but they all just curled up on sleeping pallets outside where they had eaten."

"I felt scared when I heard that Indians were coming here, but they have a special aura about them. I don't feel threatened by them at all."

"They are special. They have all been baptized by Father Bob and they believe in Jesus Christ as the Son of God. That tall thin one over there is Two Feathers. He is their Chief and the pretty little woman talking to him is his wife Willow. They and a boy are the last people of the Sentu. He is remarkable and just seems to draw people to him. They are good people and God has used them in special ways already. When we aren't working so hard, I am sure you will hear some of the stories about these people."

"Look, they are starting to work on the channel. Lily, I want you to go to Aunt Mary's house and help her until I send for you and we will go help carry rocks."

"Hello Beth, you look like you could use a rest."

"Brother Tim, I am glad you came. This is Ben's cousin, Lori and the young man over there is Mark, her brother. They arrived just when the lake started going bad. They both have pitched in and have been such a good help." Lori smiled and placed a heavy rock near the dike.

"It is nice to meet you. She called you Brother Tim. Are you a monk or something?"

"No," he laughed heartily. "I am a Jesuit that hasn't finished his schooling. I guess the Bishop thought it was a good idea to send me out west to help Father Bob, until I felt I was ready to make a final commitment."

"I'm sorry. I didn't mean to pry."

"That's quite alright. I'm not sure why Father Bob introduces me as Brother Tim. I guess I am his brother in Christ." He said it with a wide smile putting her at ease as he stomped a stone tightly in place and retrieved another from the pile. "If Ben does all that he says he must by spring, he will need this many people helping him. It is amazing isn't it how the Holy Spirit moves people and puts them where they need to be?"

"Yes, I guess so." Lori noticed a small woman standing in the bottom of the drained pond, with her hand in the clay squeezing it between her fingers.

"What are you doing," she asked?

"I am admiring the treasure they have here. Look at this clay. If it is rolled flat and baked hot and long, it will be like a sheet of rock. They can line the canal with it and it will keep the water from eroding the sides."

"How can we make long sheets of that stuff?"

"I need to think about it, but I know it would work. I'm Sheltah, what is your name?"

"I am Lori. I am Ben's cousin. You must be an expert at making things out of clay."

"I won't claim that title, but I do make pots that hold water and last a long time."

"I would love to learn how to do that. Would it be possible for me to work with you?"

"Yes I would like that, but right now I think we should carry more rocks from the riverbank to the dike." They worked side by side until suddenly Sheltah, said excitedly. "I think I have figured it out. If we roll the clay into sheets and lay it on the sides of the channel and then build a fire in the channel and cover it. That would lock the heat in and bake the clay walls."

"How would you cover the long channels?"

"I haven't got it all figured out yet, but I will." She walked over to Debon where he was working with a shovel to deepen the channel through the trees.

Debon, can you think of anything that I could use to cover the top of the channel? I want to line it with clay and put a fire in there. It will bake the clay hard enough to last for years, but I have to cover it or it won't get hot enough to make the clay really hard."

"If you used the same portion of the channel to make several sets of clay sides, maybe that would work, by baking some, taking them out and baking some more."

"No, Debon, we need big sheets of tin or metal barrels we can flatten. The channel isn't straight. The clay will need to be formed to the sides as it is made. I am going to talk to the ladies that live here."

When Beth heard Sheltah's idea, she knew that it wouldn't be long before she would have a cheese shed with no tin roof.

"We must move all the containers from the shed into the back corner of the barn and cover them before the roof is removed. I don't want to take a chance on one drop of rain or dirt getting on the cheese."

Sheltah and Lori worked hard, standing in the lake bottom, she instructed the young woman.

"Lori, we must dig big wads of this clay and carry it to the grass where we can roll it with a bark-stripped fence post until it is as wide as the channel is deep. By using a sheet of tin roofing under it, we will be able to move it and maneuver it into place. They continued to make the sheets until they had completely lined at least fifteen feet of the channel.

Sheltah motioned for the younger boys to help her and explained that she needed great piles of kindling and dry fire wood piled near the portion of the clay lined channel. Very carefully she started a low fire burning the entire length that was lined. Gently she added wood here and there until a visible color change was taking place in the sheets of clay. More wood was added and then the sheets of tin roofing were placed over the top of the channel to seal in the heat. The smoke rolled out the partially closed ends. The workmen gathered on both sides of the canal to see what was happening. She explained and told them that it would need to burn for hours. I will feed the fire until mid-night.

"If you pass dry wood as you collect stones, I will need it here to keep the fire burning."

"Joshua, Johnny, Adam and Eli, don't forget your regular chores tonight", said Beth. "Johnny, Dad is in the milk barn and could use your help."

"Yes, Ma'am, I am on my way."

"You need to scrub your hands with that gray soap before you start milking, and if you see Orville, ask him to stay away from the cheese in the back of Dad's barn," she called as he walked swiftly away. He stopped.

"I think he knows that because he was talking to Dad a while ago and Dad told him to put Dash Away back in Uncle Ben's field on the other side of Aunt Sarah's cabin, so he wouldn't be near the cheese. Sometimes he wanders in from the field."

"That's good son. Have the chickens been done?"

"Josh did them all and he gathered the eggs. We have loads of eggs Mom. I guess we will use them with all the people here." Johnny took off for the cow barn before she could say anything else. She was proud of her son. He is growing up to be a responsible young man, she thought.

None of them could have imagined that a single egg would sell for as much as twelve dollars in California during the gold rush, an event taking place that they were totally unaware of.

Mary brought the children in the small wagon and bumped across the field and appeared on the path coming from the gate behind Jed's barn. She wasn't sure how the digging had progressed and didn't want to pull up on the path near the lake and find a channel going through it.

Lily climbed down and held Natty by the hand.

"You don't have to hold on to me. I am a big boy now. I know not to get in the water or by the fire."

Mary nodded and reluctantly Lily released her charge.

"Beth, what's with the fire and why have they pulled the roof off of the cheese shed?"

"Come inside and I will explain. Let's take a break and have some tea. The water is hot." Lily stayed near Natty and coaxed him to go with her to feed the goats some grass.

"They need to have their fence moved again. I will ask Johnny to help me when he comes out of the milk barn." They quietly watched the activity and saw the long sheets of clay rolled out on the lawn.

"I don't think we should get near that. It looks like they are making mud walls for the new little river. It looks like a big muddy mess to me, said Lily." Natty giggled and headed toward the sheets of clay lying on the grass.

"No boy, do not touch this! Do not walk here. You go see your mother." Sheltah's voice was firm with authority. Natty's smile faded and he backed up. Lily was shocked.

"He won't hurt it. He just wants to know what you are doing."

"I will show you later. You go to mother now."

CHAPTER FIVE
HARD WORK AND STRONG HANDS

That evening, The People of the Lion had yielded to the ladies coaxing them and had taken comfort in Ben's barn.

They enjoyed the big kettle of chili and ate large slices of the homemade bread spread thickly with fresh churned butter and wild strawberry jam. They bedded down on their sleeping pads around the fire or in the empty stalls made soft by the dried grass.

The next morning, Ben pulled their large wagon to the crossing and David noticed that he had hooked two of his big work horses to it.

"Good, Ben, I am glad they are being used. They don't need to stand around getting fat and lazy. You have Brownie on the left and Buck on the right. They know their names and will respond to them."

Mary stood near Ben on the grass. She handed him a piece of paper.

"Maybe you won't need this, but I thought it couldn't hurt. I have written down anything I could think of that you would need to do in town. Most of it is from the list we made at our last meeting, but I added to the bottom."

"What is that?"

"I abbreviated it. That is essayer's office first and then land office." She spoke quietly so others wouldn't hear her. "Have you got the bags that Sarah brought?"

"Yes, they are here under the grass bundles. That was perfect timing. It saved us from having to go dig up one of the dead horses," he whispered in her ear. They both laughed.

"You have your lunch and water bag and I put a tin of different cheeses in there for Tom to try. If you can make time on the way back through, you should stop at the store and buy a treat for the children. They have all earned it."

"You girls have earned a treat, too. Mary, I don't know how I would manage without you." He gave her a hug before stepping up into place on the wagon seat and pushing his satchel under the seat. He snapped the reins and away he went into the water of the Hickory and across. The wagon sat high, but not quite high enough. The water washed over the bed of the wagon floating the grass bundles and his lunch against the side rails. "It is a good thing that pouch is sealed tight or I would have a wet lunch," he yelled back laughing as the back of the wagon cleared the water and the wagon's contents sloshed against the tailgate. Ben headed out under the big oak, in the direction of Silverville. The steady cold rain of the past few days had raised the water level and with all that he had on his mind, he had not paid attention to it. He felt embarrassed at the reckless appearance of his departure with many people watching.

Jed looked at Mary and laughed.

"He forgot that the water is running deeper. You can't think of everything," he said it kindly. "I don't know how he keeps his sanity trying to keep track of it all. You know he was supposed to pass on some of the responsibility to others, but so far I haven't seen much of that going on."

"You know him as well as I do, Jed. He has to have the reins or he gets worried. This way he is frayed on the edges but somehow, he gets it all done."

"Mary, even with all the help we have here, I don't know how we will get the wells and cabins done. I am heading over to the milk barn with Joshua. Johnny and Lily haven't come out of the house yet, but when they do would you make sure that Johnny helps her move the goats and their pen. Oh, you might want to check on Dotty. I think she is pregnant."

66

"Really? I thought they were both babies because they are small. I don't know much about goats but I will check her anyway. I hope she is. That would be fun for Lily." Jed looked over at the smoke rolling out both ends of what used to be the tin roof of the cheese shed. Most of the people were hard at work, digging and Sheltah and Lori were rolling out a new slab of clay for the next section.

"Thank you, all of you for working so hard this morning, but has anyone here had breakfast? You can't work on empty stomachs." Two Feathers looked up and answered her.

"We have eaten enough. We will eat again tonight by firelight. We want to finish this channel while Ben is gone to Silverville.

When he returns, we will start the wells."

David noticed that Sarah was helping Lori and Sheltah and they were talking excitedly.

"Are you sure that will keep the fire from catching the trees?"

"I can't be positive. Fire is a difficult thing to control, but I think that by molding thick clay against the roots and trunks near the canal, we should be able to line it and do as we have done with the rest of it. After that, only the straight part by the willow trees is still to do. Those poor trees are trying to survive. I think it might be a good idea to line the canal with rocks in that area and not heat their roots."

"Sheltah you are doing an amazing job. I will take some of the men to the willows and see if we can accomplish that. I think I will get one of the work horses and use a wagon to take a load of rocks over there," said David.

"He is your husband?"

"Yes, I am very lucky. David is a good man."

"He is lucky, too. I have heard of your many skills from Sweet Grass." Sarah smiled and helped to gently ease the piece of tin further under the growing slab of clay.

"I would not have thought of making a clay lining. My skills with clay are very limited," said Sarah.

"The Great Spirit gives each person a special talent. He puts us where that gift can be used. I hope that your skills as a healer will not be needed here this time. My husband, Debon, has the ability to learn new skills easily. He can learn a new language in just a few days. I have difficulty with that. He learned to build with the beautiful smooth boards at the church and he will be able to help build the cabins." Lori continued to bring the globs of clay from the lake bottom and had enough nearby for Sheltah to start rolling the next sheet. Sheltah and Sarah carried the finished slab to the next section of the canal and carefully pulled the tin away as the clay settled into place. Sheltah patted and pressed until she was satisfied.

"Let me try to do that," said Sarah. "Who knows, I may have a hidden talent!" The three laughed together at her little joke.

Willow approached and asked if she could be of help.

"Yes, soon we will need to carry clay from the lake bottom to plaster the trees and roots near the canal as it cuts through the trees." Two Feathers came over and suggested that Sheltah come look at their progress.

"We are having a great deal of difficulty digging deep enough so that the river will run into the canal and gravity will take it down into the lake bottom. So far we think we need to go down at least another three feet. We are hitting rocks and roots all the way along here."

"I am glad that the men of the Lion are strong," said Sheltah, giving no hint of sympathy for their difficult labor as she returned to her job on the grass near the clay.

He shook his head and picked up the heavy pick. It rang as the steel hit rock again and again. David looked at the slow progress and wondered if they would end up having to cut the trees that were close and then use dynamite. He wasn't ready to suggest it yet.

Several of the young men came to help load the wagon with large rocks from the river bank as soon as David pulled it up.

"If we can get it all done, except that part that Two Feathers and the men are working on, maybe we can figure out another way to finish it," offered Pine Berry. "We can put the canal across the path and then his will be the last part to do."

Jed came out of the barn and took the milk in the littlest wagon, to the ice house. David spotted him and knew where he was going. He met him there.

"Jed, I have an idea. We should cut the trees on both sides of the canal where Two Feathers is working, and then we can use them to build the bridge supports for the path. If we put a couple tiny dynamite charges in the canal there, it will loosen up the rocks and roots in the way and we should be able to get down deep enough to make this channel work. What do you think?"

"I think you are crazy! I have never used that stuff and it can be dangerous!"

"Well, you are right. It can be, but I have used it and it would only take a little dynamite to do what I'm suggesting. Do you have any?"

"I don't know. I think Ben took it with him when he went to divert the waterway."

"Where did he store it?"

"I'll show you, but that doesn't mean I am agreeing to this!"

"There. Look in that wooden box with the lid on it." David carefully lifted the lid. He saw that Ben had left just two sticks and a short piece of fuse.

"These are old. They are sweating. That stuff that is on them is really volatile," said David as he gently slid his index finger along the dynamite and gathered a drop of the liquid on his finger. "Step back." He flicked his finger at the dirt floor and as the liquid hit a tiny rock it exploded, making a loud bang and a hole in the barn floor.

"Wow, if we can put this in the canal and blow it up we won't have to do much digging!" Jed was concerned.

"David, this isn't stuff we should mess with."

"If you can get the men to cut the trees all around the tough part, I can do this. It would be great to have this project done when Ben gets back. I am going to pack this box full of dried grass and I won't move it to the spot where we need it until the trees are down and pulled out of the way."

A few minutes later, Jed stood talking to Two Feathers and then he went to his barn and returned with a crosscut saw. It wasn't long before Pine Berry and White Grass were pulling the crosscut saw through the trunk of a stately old pine. Ben had made a point of not cutting any of the ancient trees. He said they made him feel comfortable. Sorry Ben, he thought as the first tree fell. Quickly it was cleaned of its branches and the men took turns using Dickey or Joey to pull the big logs to the open area near the path. Two other men took the saw and it seemed that this was a contest. They cut as fast as they could. It went down and a third soon followed. David took a look at the area and said that he felt that was all they would have to cut.

"I want this whole area to myself as soon as those trees are moved out of here. I don't want to put anyone else in danger. Please if you would all go up and sit on Jed's lawn, Jed ask Beth to bring out some cold milk and cake or something. Sarah, Sheltah all you ladies there by the lake, please go up on the lawn by the house."

Sarah was frowning as she took Pili in the house. She had felt the vibrations and heard the boom of the blasts on the bluff near her cabin. She was not happy at all that David had decided to use dynamite again. She had a bad feeling about this. What if he gets hurt? She turned toward Jed.

"I don't want him to do this! Jed can't you make him stop?"

"I tried. I told him I thought it was too dangerous, but he insists."

Mary and Beth had been making pies from the apples Sarah and David had brought. They stopped and served hot coffee, and milk. Beth quickly piled sugar cookies on a platter and pieces of apple cake on another. She cut the pieces small so they could be eaten out of hand.

Although they were all glad for the break, and the snack, the canal area where David was working held their attention. Lily and Eli came in the house. David had sent them there. He had opened the gate and led the two little goats away from the pen they were in. He asked one of the men to hold their leads for a few minutes. He felt their pen was too close. The sound would frighten them. He forgot about the thoroughbreds and foals that had been moved to Ben's corral. Dash Away and the other horses in the fields were a safe distance but the sound would definitely startle them too.

David carefully carried the heavy wooden box to the spot that he had decided to blast. He walked up and back along the canal until he spotted what he was looking for. Two Feathers had chipped away at a boulder, buried in the roots of a tree. He used his finger to remove the debris from the hole. It was deep enough to hold half a stick. That's all he wanted to put there. Further along, he found another place. He had to attach the short fuse to the separate pieces. He had cut the sticks in half wetting his knife blade with every small cut. He was sweating when he packed the charges tightly into the rocks and roots that were holding up progress, and then he entirely covered the bottom of that trench section with dry grass. He said a silent prayer and lit several matches at once. He ran toward the water dropping them into the ignitable grass above the fuses.

Hunkering down behind a huge tree trunk he covered his ears and waited. Then he waited still longer. No explosion came. Finally when his impatience got the best of his good sense, he leaned around the tree to look, just as a huge blast sent rocks flying in every direction. He landed on his back. His ears were ringing as another loud boom shook the ground, then another and the fourth went off. The horses were running around, rearing and trying to get out of the corral.

It was over. I am uninjured, he thought, but his ears were still ringing. He couldn't hear anything else. He didn't hear the men as they cautiously returned to see if he was finished and safe. He could see the men applauding and saw their faces talking and cheering, but he couldn't hear any of it. Sarah came running and wrapped him in a tight hug. She had tears on her face and then he felt her reach up and touch his neck with her fingers. She held them up. They were covered with blood. Both his ears were dripping blood!

He could feel her shaking as she held him and knew that he had done something terrible to his ears. They were beginning to hurt. The men gathered around him talking but he couldn't hear them. Sarah was sobbing as she took his hand and led him back to Jed's house.

"Heavenly Father, I have never had to try to heal injured ears before. I know you are the Great Physician. I know you can heal David's ears. Use my hands and show me what I should do to help him." She prayed loudly and the people that followed them back to Beth's kitchen all said Amen and continued to pray under Brother Tim's direction. Praising God and thanking Him for being there with them. They prayed for David to be healed quickly and they prayed for Ben to do all that he needed to, in town and to return quickly and safely.

Sarah's training as a healer of The Blue Stone People took over and she began to act instinctively. She prepared a pain remedy and Beth brought out her bottle of strong brew she had made from the flowers that fight infection. Sarah could tell by its black color that it was very strong. She poured a small amount into the pan and let it simmer while she prepared a poultice for each side of his head. David held his hands over his ears and said nothing, but his look was apologetic, when he saw the distress on everyone's face.

"Please continue to pray for David, but I think it would be best if the animals were all checked and then perhaps you can all go see if his foolish sacrifice has accomplished anything."

Sarah had cleared the room with one sentence. They knew she was right. They couldn't do anything to help him but pray and they would continue to do that the rest of the day and into the night.

White Grass helped Johnny to move the goat pen farther away from where they were working. The poor things were prancing and nervous. Lily was the only one that could touch them. She put an arm around each little neck and told them that it was all done and they were safe. She sat down in the grass and soon they each settled beside her. She stroked and scratched until she was sure they were alright. Next she went with Johnny to take care of the chickens. They were a flighty mess, skittering around in their pen and one had laid an egg outside the coop right on the bare dirt.

Once again Lily was able to bring comfort and soothing.

"These poor birds were all frightened. They can't understand what is going on." She was discovering her gift. When she and Johnny left the pen, the chickens were pecking at the grain they had scattered and dipping into their fresh water.

"I wonder if they will lay eggs tomorrow after such a scare," Johnny was frowning. Let's take these eggs in Aunt Mary's kitchen and then we should check on our chickens, too. That blasting was so loud that it set the mustangs running and they are farther away."

Orville had been in Jed's barn when the charges went off. No one had thought to tell him what was going on.

"It was terrible, it surely was! I had no idea what happened. I could have told him that you can't cut and divide an old stick like that. It is unpredictable! Is he going to be alright? I'm so sorry. If there is anything I can do to help him, I'll be glad to do it."

Sarah looked up at Orville's sunbaked, leathery face and saw the sincerity there.

"Thank you Orville. I think he has what he needs for now, but if there is anything later. I will be sure to ask."

"Yes Ma'am, Sarah, you send someone for me and I'll come right away." He stepped out the door and went swiftly to Ben's barn to check on the purebred mares and foals. "Dang fools, all of them. Why didn't they move the animals away from the old barn first? Why didn't they ask me for some advice? Young folks today, they all think they know all there is to know about everything. Now that young man may never hear as well as he did. Maybe he won't be able to hear at all. It's a shame, yes it is."

Orville was still yammering away when he let himself into Ben's corral and checked every horse and foal there.

These horses were the most valuable livestock on the ranch. Orville knew it the first time he saw them.

He stroked their coats and looked for any sign that they had injured themselves. They were all fine. "Thank you Lord," he said. "Ben has enough to worry over without these guys being harmed."

Adam stood at the gate waiting for Orville to come out.

"I was thinking I should go make sure that no horses are missing from the field on the other side of Aunt Sarah's cabin. If the noise got them running, I know Buddy and Moon Boy could clear that fence."

"You are right boy, I'll go with you." They strolled along together and were surprised when they had to jump over the start of the canal as it crossed the path. "Did the dynamite do its job?"

"It did more than we had hoped. You can take a look if you want to," said Jed with a smile. They are still cleaning the rubble out of the way but you can see that it will soon be ready for Sheltah's clay sheets."

"That's really good, Uncle Jed." Adam looked at all the men clearing the rock and dirt from the canal and he grinned. "You guys are sure strong and you have worked hard. My dad will be so happy when he sees all this." The men appreciated the praise, even though it came from a youngster.

Sheltah checked the progress on the end of the channel near the willows and was pleased. It looks solid to me, she thought. She added wood to the last section that she had lined and covered it.

"By dark, we will be able to line where they are working. I want to have all the sheets of clay ready so that we can get the fire going in that last section before we eat."

Lori agreed with a nod as she brought out another huge glob of clay from the pond bottom.

"They are building a pile of rocks at the start of it, to make the dike that goes out into the river strong enough to hold against the times when that river gets high and flows fast. I was concerned that the clay would be used up before we finished this job. It looks like there is enough to finish and still make some pots."

"Lori, you have worked so hard. Why don't you take a break while I roll these last two slabs and maybe you could check with Beth or Sarah to see how David is doing? The last I heard, he was sleeping and they had packed his ears with medicine and he was still in pain so she gave him something that made him sleep."

"I'll go right now, but I think you will need more clay for those last two sheets. The canal where he blasted is deeper. They wanted it that way so the water would spill downhill to the lake bottom." Lori washed her hands and arms in a bucket nearby and pulled her mud-heavy shoes off before going up the grass to the front steps of Beth's house. She tapped softly and Beth opened the door quickly before she could tap again.

"Lori, come in. We are whispering because David is still sleeping and Sarah got Pili to take a nap, too. Are you hungry?"

"Yes, but I will wait and eat when everyone else does. I would like to know if there has been any change in David."

"I don't know Lori. He will sleep for a while longer. Sarah gave him a strong sleeping potion. Rest is always a good healer."

Beth offered her a drink of water which she drank and then told them that she would pass the word about David to the others.

The air was chilled and damp, but the trees were still. No wind stirred the smoke that rolled from the canal on both ends of the last section. Sheltah had met her goal and the entire channel was now lined, except the last wider portion by the willow trees where the water would exit.

"Ben will be amazed when he sees what these people have done," said Jed. "Our cows didn't give as much milk tonight as they usually do. I am glad there won't be any more blasting. It was really hard on all the animals. They were frightened."

Mary and Beth had both looked at the area that had given the most difficulty. Now it was covered with sheets of tin and clay had been wrapped here and there where roots outside the canal might still catch on fire as the clay was baked inside the channel nearby.

Back in Beth's house Sarah came out of the bedroom where David was sleeping.

"I need to have everything ready for him. I think when he wakes he will be hurting again." She prepared everything and added more willow bark to the solution she was heating.

"Where do you want to serve the meal? It is quite chilly outside. Maybe we should serve it in the barn and build up that fire a little," suggested Jed. "I will go make room, by moving the animals to the far stalls and put fresh hay in the front ones. Don't try to carry the food. I will come back and help when the barn is ready."

He left quickly. It was early evening. He hooked a lantern up high on a rafter and opened one side of the barn door to invite people in. Mary had loaded the little wagon with all the extras like bread, jam, butter, milk and pies. Plates and bowls were stacked in there, too, held by Lily and Natty. Eli sat in the corner surrounded by cups and glasses.

"Now, I am going to go very slowly and everyone hold on to the things around you so they don't tip and break."

Adam had gone up to the lookout for a quick look to see if Ben was coming, but he wasn't visible yet. He came down and took ahold of the harness of the little tan mare that was hitched to the wagon. With his hand on her he walked along and she kept his very slow pace.

"Thank you Adam that helped. She is full of energy and would like to run," said Mary. Jed stuck his head out of the barn and told Adam to stay with the little mare. He came out and lifted the children down and handed the stacks of kitchen items to many waiting hands.

"Mary, I will bring all the hot containers, you go ahead inside with the people and get the children settled."

"Thank you Jed."

"Hop up, Adam and hang on." Adam was grinning and holding on to the sides of the seat with both hands as Jed turned the wagon back toward the house. Then he smacked the reins and yelled for the little mare to go. She lurched forward nearly unseating both of them. Jed headed her down the path around the back of the lake, passed the willows and around the back of his barn in a big circle. Finally he turned her back toward his house and she trotted with high stepping feet and proud head held high. "This little girl would make a great buggy horse. Maybe we should check with Matt Morgan or the Reverend Brown. She has class."

"Dad has been calling her Queen. It sort of fits her doesn't it?"

"Yes, I like that."

Beth directed the move of the food and made sure everything was still completely covered.

"Take it easy Jed. No more hijinks! You could have spilled all the food."

"That was for her benefit not mine. She wanted to run. None of our horses are getting the exercise that they should have. Orville can't do it all."

"Jed, please take the food over slowly."

"Are you coming?"

"I don't want to leave Sarah here alone in case she needs something when David wakes up. I will eat with her later."

Two Feathers and White Grass stood near the corral gate and helped carry the big pots and platters into the barn. The men had prepared a table to put the food up off the floor and as soon as it was delivered, Tim lifted his hands and began to pray.

"Thank you, Father, for the strong hands that have worked here today. Thank you that the canal is nearly ready for the water to flow through it. Thank you that we know you are the Great Healer and that you are healing David's ears and that he will hear again and we thank you for helping Ben to do successfully all the things he needs to do in town. Please bring him back to us soon, and safely. Thank you for the wonderful food you have provided from your bounty. We ask that you bless this ranch and everyone on it. Amen."

"Amen," they all repeated.

"Please come, fill your plates. There is beef to wrap up in the corn cakes. We have baked beans, vegetable soup, and loaves of bread with butter and jam. For desert we have wild cherry pies and apple pies. We want you to eat until you are stuffed. We have hot coffee and cold milk and this jar has sugar if you want to put some in your coffee." Mary's voice sounded happy and encouraging. She smiled and tried hard not to show her concern for David and Sarah in the house. Beth came in and closed the door quickly.

"The air is turning colder by the minute. Does anyone need anything? I just came to tell all of you that David is up sitting at the table and he has a bowl of vegetable soup and a glass of milk. Sarah changed his bandages and put a new thick wrap on his head. He says the slightest sound causes discomfort but he isn't in constant pain now. He took his medicine and Sarah says that she put more sleeping medicine in it, so he will soon be back in bed. She was smiling when I left and I think that is the best sign of all."

"God is healing him, just as Brother Tim said he would in his prayer." The people were in good spirits after Beth's delivery of the good report. They laughed and went back for seconds.

Tim smiled and offered to help Beth clear up the meal and transport the dishes and food back to the house.

"Let's leave the coffee and that big tin has sugar cookies in it. I guess the rest of this should go back in the wagon."

Jed stood up then and began to transfer the kettles to the wagon. Mary said she wanted everything to be taken quietly around the back path to her house.

"The kids should sit in the front with the same duties they had coming." Soon, plates were stacked and snug under the watchful eyes and small hands that cared for them. The food goes in last. It's not hot now, but I still want it away from them. Beth I won't be back until early morning. Lily can stay with us tonight, if that's alright and Johnny, why don't you hop on the back and come, too. That way, your house will stay quiet for Uncle David."

"Sure, I want to go where the rest of the pie goes," he said laughing. Joshua jumped on beside Adam and pretended he was reaching for the pie. "Hey I spoke for it first!"

"My arms are longer," Josh said, as he pulled a slice from the pan and stuffed half the piece in his mouth.

"You are disgusting! You have pie all over your shirt!"

"That's fine as long as I have cherries in my mouth," he said while laughing and chewing.

"Joshua and Johnny, stop that right now! I have plenty of pie at the house. Son, you look like a two year old. You have pie all over your face!" They were all laughing as they pulled up in front of the porch. The house was dark except for a light glow warming the interior from the fireplace. Mary turned up the wick of the lantern and then helped the little ones out carefully. Josh, take Natty in and light the lantern above the table. I will be working in the kitchen for a while. Oh and rinse off your face and that shirt before it stains."

"Yes Ma'am, I will," he said as he carried his little brother in and tucked him into bed.

Mary was surprised at the time, as she wound the clock and enjoyed its pleasant soft ticking. It is nearly nine, she thought. It will be ten before I get these dishes washed and stacked back in the wagon.

"Joshua, will you please put the little mare in the field for tonight. I will need her in the morning."

She didn't hear a reply.

When she looked in the living area she saw a sight that made her smile. The youngsters were laying everywhere and

Josh was tip toeing between them, doing his best to make sure they were all covered.

"I will go put the mare in the field mom and then I can carry out the dishes as we get them cleaned." He said it softly.

It sounds like he intends to help me do the dishes. I certainly won't refuse the help. I am tired.

"Josh, I think I am going to peel a bunch of potatoes and put them in the vegetable soup and add the rest of the beef we brought back. I think I will add a few more tomatoes and carrots, too. This big pot can simmer slowly and it will be a good thick stew for tomorrow. That's the last of the dishes that need to go out in the wagon. After you take those out, you better go to bed. Thank you for helping me. I'll finish up here. The house feels strange with your dad gone. I don't like to go in the bed alone."

"You won't be alone."

"What do you mean?

"Lily went in there and crawled under your covers as soon as we got here."

"I didn't notice that she isn't out here with the others. Fine Aunt I am!" She said it smiling.

"Goodnight, Mom. I miss him, too. Maybe he will be back tomorrow."

CHAPTER SIX
BEN'S GOLDEN DAY

Ben had scurried first to the assayer's office. He was eager to hear the value of the contents of the little pouch that he laid on the counter. Wisely he had separated a small portion from the rest of the gold.

The man's face brightened when he saw the color of the small pebbles and flakes that he poured out onto a glass plate.

"This looks like the real thing! I've been seeing lots of fool's gold lately. Where did you get this?"

"Does it matter? I need to have it analyzed and a value per ounce please," said Ben.

"You are all business. I'm not going to claim jump you. I will take this little piece and test it. He placed it on a separate little plate and touched it with an acid. His reaction was immediate. It's gold alright and about as clean as it comes. I'd say you are looking at thirty five dollars an ounce and this is close to an ounce and a half."

"Thank you, sir. Would you please give me a piece of paper that says that?"

"Just a minute and I'll write one out for you. There is a charge for my service, and the statement of value. That will be fifty cents."

Ben carefully placed the gold back in his pouch making sure he had every speck back in the little pouch and then he tucked the paper in his pocket. He paid the fee and thanked him for his service. Ben crossed the street to the land office after rummaging under the grass bundles to get his lunch and put it up on the seat.

Next after looking up and down the street and checking windows to see if he was being observed, he casually pulled out the full pouches and put them in the large inside pockets of his coat and buttoned them. He chuckled to think that he probably looked like he had just gained weight. He took a long drink from his water bag and promised Brownie and Buck that they would soon get a break and well-earned food and water. He waited until the man inside was alone and then he entered the land office.

"How much is an acre of land going for these days, Mr. Cantwell?"

"Why Ben, don't you have enough to drive you crazy already? It is good to see you again. How is the family? How is that priest, Father Bob? Fine, we are all fine. I haven't seen Father Bob for a while but his assistant, Brother Tim is visiting my ranch right now. He is a nice man. We all like him. You didn't answer my question. How much is an acre of land?"

"It depends on where it is located and what kind of land it is." Ben stood in front of the map and studied it silently.

"I don't need it to be on a river. Does that bring the price down?"

"Yes it does. Say have you got your wells dug and cabins up on the homesteads your family has claimed? You know they are due for inspection this coming spring."

"Yes, I know and we can talk about that later. How much is this strip of land along behind the bluff where the church land is and Brother Tim's?

"Oh that's still a dollar an acre."

"I want to buy that whole strip, from the curve in the river to the back of the bluff and beyond, all the way to here." He placed his finger on a surveyor's mark.

"Ben you are out of your mind. That would cost a fortune."

"That's a half of a day's ride from your place. Each section is one hundred and forty four acres and you are pointing at five of them. Let me count it out."

"I also want the piece on the other side of David's and the strip that borders the church land and Brother Tim's." What are you going to do with all that land?

"I don't want to do anything. That's the whole idea. I want it to stay the way it is, undisturbed and left for those who love the earth and God and know how to respect it and Him. If I let anyone on it, they will have to be the sort of people that know that it all belongs to God."

"What? That's a strange thing to say. You are the one who will have to pay for it, not God."

"He made it for us to use, not abuse. Take a good look at this town and the area around it, and that bar down there isn't adding anything good to it either. There is trash all over beside his tent and he has lumber piles that are all warping and an eye sore. I don't think he has nailed two boards together yet."

"Calm down Ben. He owns that place and he can do with it what he wants." Ben still stood in front of the map.

"The land between the Parker place and this piece, is all that still open?" Ben asked.

"No, I believe it was bought several years ago. Yes the owners name is Steinberg. I haven't seen him since he bought it. He took all three pieces."

"Is the land across the river from my place still available?"

"Yes, there it is, but it is not cheap. Ben land on the river is going for Two dollars an acre now."

"I want that piece. My parents are buried there."

"Yes I know they are, but Ben how are you going to pay for all this land? You might be able to work something out at the bank. Did you know that there is a bank here now? It is the second building on Third Street."

I will go there as soon as you figure out how much money you will need for the purchase. Ben I have totaled it twice. It comes to one thousand, seven hundred and twenty eight dollars. That is for the piece beside David Sharpe, the piece next to the church land of Father Bob and the piece across from yours. Those are Two dollars each acre. That is three pieces at two dollars an acre, that's eight hundred and sixty four dollars. Then you wanted the piece next to Brother Tim's and the five pieces behind the bluff in that area. That is six pieces at one hundred forty four dollars each, that's another eight hundred and sixty four dollars. So all together that is one thousand, seven hundred and twenty eight dollars."

"That's good so far. How many pieces are left between Sarah Slater's and the others behind the bluff?

"There are four more."

"Please give me the pleasure of marking them all sold on the map," said Ben. He noticed that the man's hand shook a little as he handed him the pen. "Thank you, Mr. Cantwell. Can you close up for a little while and meet me at the bank. I want to take the horses down to Matt Morgan. I will walk back to the bank. It shouldn't take me very long."

"Yes of course, I usually close for lunch. I will just say it was my lunch hour if someone asks."

"That's good. I don't need the whole town knowing my business, do I?"

"No, you certainly don't. I'll bring the paperwork and we can do this properly. I will meet you there."

As Ben closed the door of the land office the bell attached to it made a joyous jingle. He smiled. I feel as happy inside as that bell sounds. It feels like Christmas, he thought.

Ben jumped up on the seat of the wagon and drove it to the blacksmith shop.

"Hi Matt, will you do me a favor and give these boys some feed and a drink. I am going to be at the bank for a while so you can unhitch them and spoil them a bit."

"I know these big fellows," said Matt. "I put shoes on them for David Sharpe. They sure look better now than when he bought them."

"Yes, he treats all his horses with love and tender care."

"Matt, I will be back as soon as I can. I still need to go to the mill and talk to Tom today. I'm hoping to get a load of planks to take back."

"I'll have these guys ready for you."

"Thanks Matt." Ben walked quickly to the bank. It was built of bricks and he noticed the thick door as he swung it open. The room he entered was quiet. He thought that it felt like an empty church. A teller appeared behind a counter, separated from the rest of the room by a metal grate that went all the way to the ceiling.

"Good day sir, May I help you?" The teller was polite.

"Yes you can. I want to exchange some gold for common currency. How do I go about doing that?"

"Yes, oh, of course sir, just a moment sir, I'll get the bank manager." He stepped through a door and was out of sight for a moment and then, a short, well-dressed man with gray hair and glasses came to the end of the counter and invited Ben into his office.

"How do you do sir, my name is A.C. Williams. I am the bank manager. Come right in here. Sit down and make yourself comfortable."

"My name is Benjamin Slater. It is nice to meet you," said Ben as he glanced around noticing the bars on the window and the large safe that stood behind the desk where

Mr. Williams had installed himself with an impression of authority.

"I would like to open an account and use that account to purchase some land that I have chosen. Mr. Cantwell of the land office will be here directly."

"That's fine. Gordon will bring him back here when he comes in. What kind of an account do you want to open?"

"Well, I would like you to have the man from the assayer's office come over here and join our meeting. We are going to need him," said Ben, feeling uneasy in the strange environment. He was more at ease in a barn near his animals.

"We can send Gordon to get him, if we do need him."

"Mr. Cantwell, good day to you. Thank you for coming. I see that you have brought some paperwork for me and you thought to bring the map from the wall of your office."

"Yes, I thought it best, so that you can also record the numbers properly."

Mr. Williams unfurled the map across his desk.

"Which pieces of land are you interested in buying, Mr. Slater?"

"I want to buy several, and pay for them with this," he said, lifting out one of the heavy pouches and gently placing it on top of the map. "That's why I suggested that this meeting include the man from the assayer's office. I showed him this little pouch this morning and he gave me this statement of value for the gold in it. The big pouch holds more of the same."

The banker was smiling as he read the document and then peered into the small pouch. Boldly he reached for the larger one and opened it.

"This is top grade stuff. How do I know it belongs to you? Where did you get it?"

"That is my business. It is mine or I wouldn't be here with it. It needs to be weighed so its value can be established."

"You don't look like a man that would be walking around with this much gold. How do I know this isn't stolen?"

"Have you been robbed lately?"

"No, of course not, but it's too much for someone to just walk in here with and plop it down on my desk!"

"Well, apparently not. I'm here and I just did!" Ben turned to the teller and directed him to get the man from the assayer's office. He moved out the door so swiftly that it amazed Ben.

"I apologize, Mr. Slater. It isn't every day that someone brings in this much gold at one time. Please forgive my bad manners." Ben was wondering what the man would say when he found out that he had another bag of gold in his coat.

After much discussion and testing, weighing and repeating the process, they decided that the gold on the desk was worth one thousand and twenty dollars. Ben was pleased with the sum. He removed the second bag from his coat and Mr. Williams sputtered and shook as the analysis started all over. Mr. Cantwell used the time to prepare the deeds for the properties that Ben had indicated. When everything was completed, Ben had signed his name many times and he held in his hand a small dark green bank book that showed that his account had nearly two hundred dollars in it. Each deed was stamped paid in full and also signed by both Mr. Cantwell and Mr. A. C. Williams. Ben laughed as he held the little book and confessed that he had never had money in a bank before.

"Mr. Williams, I have a small problem. I promised to stop at the store to buy treats for our children but I haven't brought money to use at the store."

"How much money do you need?"

"I think I want ten dollars. I want to take a surprise for some others, too."

"That's fine, Mr. Slater. Let me just adjust the figures in your book and I will get you the money."

When Ben stepped out of the bank it was dark and quiet outside. The street was empty. He could see light spilling onto the street from the open bar. Several horses waited outside it, standing patiently for their owners to go home. Laughter drifted down to him as he walked toward Matt's shop. I wonder how late they keep that up. I doubt if Rose is happy with that near her house.

Matt was waiting for him just inside the door of his shop. He was sitting on a stool and working at his bench, tapping a design in a wide leather belt.

"Well, that sure took longer than I thought it would," said Ben. "Can you imagine doing all that paper work every day for a living?"

"No I don't care much for writing or reading. I read the Holy Bible and that's about all. The newspaper isn't really anything that I haven't already heard by the time it is printed, so there is no cause for reading that."

"What were you doing that takes that long anyway?"

"I bought the piece of land that is across from my ranch. When we first got there, I had to bury my folks and their grave is on that piece of land. At that time I didn't know that I would end up with a ranch on the other side of the river."

"I remember you told me that was their grave under that huge oak tree when we all came to build Jed's house. It's good that you were able to buy that land. That way you will always know that it will not be disturbed. Hey, have you eaten? Liz made a nice meal tonight and there is plenty left. I put your horses in the field out back when it started to get dark. Come on in and eat something and visit awhile. You can stay the night and see Tom tomorrow."

"Thanks Matt. I think I'll take you up on that. I am starving and it will be good to sit and talk with you."

Ben needed a chance to tell someone all that had been happening at the ranch. He, Matt and Liz were good friends and he enjoyed talking with them both. Liz was a comfort and lightened the mood by saying that Ben was the only person she ever heard of that could take a lake and turn it into a little stream. They laughed easily together and it helped to laugh. Ben had not realized how exhausted he was until he sat down with them. The process at the bank had been far more stressful than he had ever imagined. They sympathized over the fright that the fire had caused and also asked how he was getting along with his cousins.

It was late by the time he leaned back on their couch and fell asleep almost instantly. Liz covered him with a blanket and left him there to rest.

When Matt and Liz went to bed, she spoke softly.

"They have been through so much lately, and yet they must be doing well. He said he paid for that piece of land across the river. Land is expensive now. I am glad that they are managing and prospering against the adversity."

"That's a good way to look at it, Liz, but remember, most of his original land is homestead land and I don't think he has had time to put down wells or build cabins. Even Mary's piece where they have the beef cattle doesn't meet the requirements. They had a cabin there but remember the Indians burned it. He is really up against it. Right now time is his enemy."

"Matt, he looks so tired. Isn't there anything we can do to help him?"

"No I don't think he wants our help. If he does, he will ask. He likes to do things his own way. I figured that out the first time I met him. Let's pray for him and the people at the ranch and ask God to bless them all and I know that He will give them what they need."

Liz made a nourishing breakfast and sent the men off with full stomachs and smiles on their faces. She gave Ben a package of dried apple slices and a beef sandwich for later. He knew he still had the lunch that Mary had packed for him and hoped that it was still in good shape. He put the bundle under his seat and filled his water bag with fresh water from the well beside Matt's shop. With the work horses hitched and ready, he said goodbye and thanked them for their thoughtfulness and friendship.

Ben patted his pocket and felt the small green bank book there and the ten dollars in with it. He checked his inside pockets to be sure that all the papers from the bank were safely tucked inside and that the pockets were buttoned. He knew that everyone at their next meeting at the ranch would be amazed. He planned to keep it as a surprise until then, if he could. Yesterday was a story begging to be told, he thought.

Tom waved as he rolled through the open gate and into the middle of the Sawmill grounds. Ben was impressed with the huge piles of logs and lumber, all stacked neatly. Cookie came hurrying over and greeted Ben with a cup of hot coffee.

"Hello, Ben you come to see Tom and buy logs today?"

"Hello Cookie, yes, I have lots of things going on and will need plenty of this stockpile of logs and lumber. Thanks for the coffee."

"You want to eat?"

"No thanks Cookie, I had a good breakfast. I spent the night with Matt Morgan and his wife. She fed me well." Ben watched Tom from a distance as he finished his conversation with a customer. He immediately strolled in Ben's direction and shook his hand with a firm grip.

"Hello Ben. I am glad to see you. I heard about the fire you had out at the ranch. I am glad that you were able to contain it. Lightening is a mystery. Can you imagine what it could do here? Our only fire was when that saw caught the sawdust on fire. We lost that whole building but a least no one was hurt."

"Tom I came here praying all the way that you would be able to accommodate an unreasonable request."

"What do you need Ben?"

"I need most of the logs and lumber that I see piled here."

"What in the world are you planning on building?"

"Well, nothing large and grand, that's for sure. I need cabins and wells so we don't lose our homestead lands. I have to dig three wells and put up three cabins before they come to inspect in the spring!"

"Have you hired some help?"

"No, but I do have friends that are there working right now. They are ready, willing and able. I just need the supplies."

"You tell me where to take them and how many. We will do our part."

Ben handed him the list and Tom whistled. You weren't kidding! I have to tell you this is going to cost you some money. I have to pay my men, you know. They have families to take care of."

"Tom, I can pay you for all of it. How much is a load of logs?" Tom rubbed his chin and his look told Ben to wait a minute. Tom was doing some thinking and calculating.

"Give me fifty dollars for each place. That will get you a small cabin, one room, one window, with a fireplace and a rope and bucket for each well. They will satisfy the improvements stipulation. You can make them bigger and better later on."

"Tom that's very fair! How soon can you get the logs out my way?"

"They can start loading the wagons as soon as Monday morning. This is Friday. We have to take some logs down the Silver for a family way out of town. They are adding on to their place. He started out with a tiny little one room place. I see you brought your wagon. What do you need on that?"

"I want some strong planks to build a small bridge over a ditch."

"That's fine. Look around and tell me what you want and I will have a couple men load them."

"Those stacked right there will do. I don't think I will need more than a dozen."

Tom bellowed a command and soon two strong men were loading the planks for Ben.

"Tom, do you feel like taking a walk?"

"Sure, where are we going?"

"We are going to the bank to get you your money and when we come back, don't let me forget. I have a gift for you from Mary and Beth."

"I won't forget. I bet I know what it is. They baked me a pie, didn't they?"

"No, not this time, they sent you some samples of cheese to try."

Ben opened the door of the bank this time with confidence. The teller greeted both men with a wide smile.

"Hi Gordon," they said at the same time. Mr. Williams heard their voices and came out to shake their hands and greet them cordially.

"Tom, we need to add on for the planks."

"Five dollars will cover those easily."

"Mr. Williams, I want to put one hundred and fifty five dollars in Tom's account," said Ben. He was beginning to enjoy the feeling of having money in the bank. He felt less wealthy when he looked at the page in his bank book later and it showed a balance of thirty five dollars.

"Ben you don't have to pay me all of it now. I just meant that I couldn't extend that much credit for all winter. I know you are good for it. You are an honest man. You have always paid me in the past for anything that you ordered."

"It's alright Tom. I have enough. God always provides what we need and a little bit more." As soon as they had returned to the Sawmill Tom reminded him about the cheese. Ben laughed.

"You are like a big kid."

"Well, everyone likes treats, don't they?"

"Yes they do Tom, yes they do."

Ben's wagon was loaded and the planks were carefully tied to secure the lumber from shifting. He noticed that someone had kindly offered his team drinks from a bucket and each of the horses had a pile of hay in front of them.

"Come have a cup of coffee and some lunch before you leave," offered Tom.

"I will pass on the lunch, but I can take another cup of Cookie's good coffee," said Ben. He talked with his friend about the lake and the salt ruining it. He admitted that he wasn't sure they had completely solved the problem yet, but that they had stopped up the source of the salty water.

"We are trying to channel a little of the Hickory water to use for the back pastures. We keep the mustangs back there before we work with them and there is a field for the cows back there. Jed has a well near his barn and they have troughs that are being filled from his well. That takes a great deal of time and muscle."

"I am sure that it does. Water is heavy. I hope you can get that channel working, soon Ben.

"Thanks Tom, I will look for the wagons with the logs next week. You know where they go. One place is the clearing in the woods on the Parker Place. Please make certain that the men delivering there stay away from the spring area. Slim Parker is buried under the big pine near that spring and Mary and Josh both have voiced their concern about that area. They don't want it messed up."

"I will send my best man to drive that team. He can stop them on a plate of eggs, without breaking them if he wants to. You said the second goes near the river on Jed's pasture, opposite his house and the third has to cross the river and you want it beyond the long pen on Sarah's land. Tell your men that the logs are on the way, and that they can start preparing the land and digging the wells."

"Thanks Tom, I knew I could count on you."

"Anytime Ben, Oh don't forget your list. It looks like the women have something down here at the bottom but I can't figure it out. Thank them for me, for sending the cheese."

"Thanks again," Ben was smiling as he directed the team out of the big gate moving slowly down the main street. He stopped in front of the General Store and went in.

Near the front counter in the store, stood a barrel, full of bright red apples and Ben chose two from the top and carried them out to Brownie and Buck without giving Sam more than a smile. Sam watched with interest as the horses chomped at their sweet surprise.

"Well, hello Ben, have you ever seen apples like those in these parts? They came down on the mail boat."

"They are beautiful. How much are they?"

"I hope those horses appreciate it, because they just ate a nickel each." Ben felt the money in his pocket that he had gotten from Mr. Williams to buy treats. Count them out Sam. I want the whole barrel, but not any with spots on them, and wrap them up so they stay nice until I get home and I will take that jar of candy sticks. Helen came out of the back and smiled at Ben. She had been standing near the curtain that separated the store from their living quarters. Ben had seen her feet behind the curtain and knew that she was there listening.

"Ben, it is good to see you again. How is your family?"

"They are well," he replied. Ben always tried to keep his tongue civil but it had been hard for him since the day she had been so unkind to Sarah. Sarah had forgiven her, saying she just doesn't know me or The Blue Stone People that I came from. It was much harder for Ben. Now that he had Sarah back, he wanted to protect her from everything. That included pain from unkind remarks.

"I have some old newspapers in the back. I'll get them and we can use them to wrap the apples for you," she said. Sam's curiosity was as active as Helen's.

"What are you going to build? I see you have some lumber out there."

"We are just covering an area on our path that needs to be stabilized where we go back and forth. Don't want our wagons to have a problem." Ben could tell that Sam was mulling over his reply. He knew there had to be more to the story. "While I'm here, would you look and tell me how my account stands?"

That redirected Sam's thoughts. He always liked to talk about money. You are ahead by four dollars. You brought all that beautiful furniture and the harvested vegetables this fall, and most of it sold right away. We can take another cradle and rocking chair. You folks can bring in anything you carve. We can always sell the fine things you make."

Ben placed the ten dollars on the counter.

"Subtract the apples and candy, and I better take three lanterns and some wicks, three tins of lamp oil, three coffee pots, three tins of coffee, and I could use several shovels if you have any."

"I have four."

Good, I will take all of them. Now, what do I owe you?"

"It comes out even Ben. Your account is paid and you have a nickel toward next time."

"That's good. Let's leave it like that. I'll just get these carefully loaded up near the front where I can watch them and then I have to get going." Sam packed the glass globes of the lanterns in a crate cushioning them with more papers and some straw. The rest of the order went in another crate to stabilize them.

"There, that should do it. Thanks for stopping Ben. We will see you again soon I hope," said Sam. Helen waved but didn't say anything. She turned to go in the back, but stopped to look at Sam for a moment.

"He is an odd man, isn't he? He doesn't seem to want to share any news about his family at all."

"Helen, maybe he doesn't want to share it with the whole community," Sam said it unsympathetically and then added, "I'm going for a walk. Watch the counter."

"You needn't speak to me like that Samuel! Where are you going?" She didn't get an answer. He was walking down the center of the street and didn't look back.

Sam turned his head to the side when he noticed bright white sheets flapping on the line. Melanie is late doing her wash this week. She usually does it on Monday, he thought. He could hear the bell-like sound coming from Matt Morgan's hammer as he worked on some horse's shoe. Rose was playing the piano quite strongly. She sounds angry. The sound she is making isn't her usual soft lovely music. It must be something in the air. I feel angry myself. He walked faster passing the mill and two more houses. I haven't been down this way all summer, he thought.

Finally he slowed and stopped under a big oak that invited him to sit down beneath it. Be noticed that it was the only tree in the area with its leaves still in place. The big bronze and tan leaves sheltered a rich harvest of acorns for the forest creatures, one of which he could hear above him scolding for Sam's intrusion into his territory.

"Alright, I'm going," he said with a chuckle. He got up slowly and turned back toward the store but didn't feel ready to go back to business as usual. His feet took him to the front of the tent that held the promise of a few minutes of escape. The canvas of the tent had yellowed during the summer and rain had splashed mud up the sides. The doorway was tied wide open. Lucas Donner smiled too brightly and spoke too loudly.

"Come in. Come in and sit down. What can I get you?" Sam looked around. He was the only customer.

"I'll take one drink," he said quietly.

"I know you. You are the storekeeper down at the corner." At that moment Sam realized that he had no money with him.

"I'm sorry; I have to change my mind. I didn't bring any money, maybe some other time. I will come back some other time."

"Here, Storekeeper, here's a drink on the house. I'll have one with you."

Lucas Donner poured two drinks and downed one of them swiftly. He held the other out to Sam.

"No thank you, really. I don't know what I am even doing in here."

"You think you are too good to drink with me. Don't you?"

"No, I just changed my mind that's all." Sam stepped toward the opening and felt himself jerked back with force. A fist slammed into his face before he could defend himself. Sam fell backwards and landed with his head under one of the tables. He was knocked unconscious.

"Sleep well; you stinking, little, sugar coated Storekeeper! I know your type. You have your vices. You probably cheat every person that comes in your store!" He was shouting at the top of his voice. His face was blood red.

"What have you done, Lucas? That is Sam from the store. He is a nice man. Why did you hit him?"

"Shut up woman, what are you doing in here? I told you to bring me some food."

"I did Lucas. I brought your food. See it's there on the counter."

"I said shut up, Hope! Don't talk to me about what you brought. You bring the same stinking thing every day! I want beef!"

"I can't buy beef. You didn't give me money to buy beef. We are lucky to have any food in the house! You are drinking up the whiskey. Soon this place will be closed. You won't have anything to sell!"

He swung at her and the blow knocked her out of the tent and onto the street. She scrambled to her feet and ran to their house crying. Lucas started to follow her. He looked like he wanted to kill her. Sam opened his eyes just in time to see Lucas hit his wife.

When it became clear to Sam that Lucas was going to follow her and maybe seriously injure her, he knew he had to do something immediately! Sam reached out with his foot and tripped Lucas.

As Sam rolled over to get up he felt an empty bottle that lay on the floor near him. Without a thought, Sam grabbed it and brought it down hard, hitting Donner above his ear. The bottle shattered and Lucas lay still. Sam got up slowly, still feeling the results of being hit hard with a fist. He hurried to the mill shouting and yelling to Tom to come quickly. Several men followed Sam back into the tent. Lucas was sitting up rubbing his head.

"We need to lock him up! I'll explain later. Where can we secure him?" Sam asked.

"Go empty the tool shed men."

Two of the lumberjacks took hold of Lucas, one on each arm and headed him across the street in the direction of the mill, to the shed. The rest had gone back and were carrying tools out of the shed and into one of the other buildings.

"Put him in there and make sure he doesn't get out," ordered Tom. They shoved him in the shed and slammed the door. His pounding on the door and hollering could be heard all over the camp. A heavy log was rolled by two men, against the door. There was no way for him to get out.

"Sam, tell me what happened. You have a mark on your chin and your face is swelling. Did he hit you?"

"Yes, but I think it is because he is drunk. I started to leave and he spun me around and hit me. I didn't see it coming."

"Sam, I have never known you to drink. What were you doing there?"

"I had to walk off some frustration so I walked through town and sat over there under the trees for a few minutes. I had never stopped in his tent so I thought I would look inside and that was a bad idea. His wife, Hope, brought his lunch in and he yelled at her and knocked her clear out of the tent. She ran off crying. I think we should go see if she is alright." They walked quickly to her house and knocked on the front door.

"Mrs. Donner, are you in there?" Tom and Sam could hear sobbing inside. She didn't come to the door immediately. They tapped again gently and asked if she was going to be alright. Her son Mark opened the door just wide enough to see outside.

"Where's my dad?"

"He isn't here. I had the men put him in my tool shed until we could sort this out. You are safe Mark. Please let us in."

Hope sat on a kitchen chair holding a wet towel against her face. She rested her forehead on the table.

"Hope, let me see what he did to you." Sam spoke softly and she lifted her head. The right side of her face was red and turning purple. Her eye was starting to swell shut.

"Does he do this often?" Tom asked.

"Mostly when he is drinking," replied Mark. "He gets awful mad and sometimes I can't figure out why he is yelling. I go into the woods and stay there until I know he is asleep. He hits my mom more than me. He blames her for everything!"

"Mark, would you do something for me? Would you go tell Cookie that I said to put two steaks on the fire and I want him to bring one out of the ice shed but leave it raw."

"Yes Sir, I will go right away." He looked back at his mom and crossed the short distance between them and placed a kiss on her forehead and then went out the door still looking back at her.

"Tom, it looks like you have this situation under control. I think I better go back and help Helen. I have been gone longer than I intended. If you need anything, just let us know."

Tom nodded, and said that Lucas would be spending the night in the shed and that he hadn't thought past that yet.

He wrapped a blanket around Hope's shoulders and picked her up as if she were a child.

"I think you need to come to our camp and get a little care. Cookie knows a little doctoring and he will know what to do to make you more comfortable. Mrs. Donner, would you consider selling all the rest of the whiskey to me? I think I have a plan." She nodded yes, and snuggled close as he carried her. She was feeling safe for the first time since Lucas had erected the tent and started drinking.

Helen was in an angry snit when Sam returned, until she saw his injured face.

"Oh Sam, What on earth happened to you? You poor man! Come in the back and lay down and I'll make a compress for that. Does it hurt much? What happened? Did you fall?"

He wondered if he should tell her or let her wait to hear it second hand from someone else. He hesitated and then said that he was going to tell her what happened, but she had to promise to never mention it to a soul!

"Sam, why would you ask such a thing?"

"Helen, you are a gossip! I want you to promise me that you won't say a word or I am not going to tell you!"

"Why would you say that? I just talk to folks to be friendly. I care about people and try to show it."

"Helen, you are not going to tell stories about people anymore, not even if they are true, and neither am I! Do you understand?"

"Sam you really shouldn't talk to me like that!"

"Promise or I am not saying a word."

"For heaven sakes, I promise. Now tell me!"

Sam told her the whole story, stretching it out to even include the chattering squirrel in the oak tree. He said that she need not fear because he was sure that Lucas Donner was going to be dealt with by Tom and the lumberjacks. Sam closed the store for the rest of the day and they enjoyed a family meal in the back without interruption.

Henry noticed the injury to his father's face and asked what had happened.

"Do you want to tell him, Helen," asked Sam?

"Oh, it's nothing dear, accidents happen," she said, flashing a look at Sam. He smiled and took a big bite of his meat. He figured the best thing he could do was to keep his mouth full so he wouldn't burst out laughing at her.

CHAPTER SEVEN
BEN'S RETURN

Ben rode along the trail beside the Silver. His wagon moved easily over the well-worn trail. He thought about the good feeling that it gave him to have the deeds to all that land in his possession. Then he thought how good it felt, to see Mr. William's expression when he produced the second bag of gold. That is a man that loves money, he thought. He chuckled at the scene. That was quite an experience, but I hope I never have to do it again. I can see how something like that could get into a man's soul and pull him. I know the Holy Bible warns us about that somewhere in Timothy, chapter one. I should look it up when I get home.

"Boys, when we get across the river, we are going to stop and have something to eat."

Brownie and Buck trotted along as if the wagon was empty. The planks were not a heavy load for them. He prepared himself as the team drew near the crossing. "Hey there boys, you know what to do." He said it loudly and snapped the reins as he yelled their names. "Go Brownie, Go Buck, let's get this wagon across the water so we can rest and eat!" The energy in his voice carried to the horses and they leaned into the harness with their strength. The good care and generous supply of feed had put them in prime condition. They crossed without incident and Ben pulled them up close to the trees. Praising them, he unhitched them and let them drink and then rubbed them down with the tall dry grass in the area. You guys can eat all you want. It's all free. He tied their long ropes to the trunk of a tree and sat down.

I think next spring we should make it a point to come in to visit folks. We haven't had the time. We need to make time when the weather breaks.

Ben had no idea of the harsh reality of the things going on in the little town he had just left. He opened his lunch that Mary had packed. She had wrapped it well and then put it in the sealed satchel. It was still eatable. His foolish start had not ruined it. He had hard boiled eggs, cheese, dried meat and bread with butter and jam made into a sandwich. In the bottom he found a pack of two big sugar cookies. He took a drink from his water bag and then crunched a big bite from one. Both horses turned their heads in unison.

"Why do I get the feeling that you boys know what I am eating?" He stood up and offered half to one and gave the second half to the other. "What do you think? Can we move on now?" He talked and patted as he hooked them back up and soon he was cutting across the late fall prairie. He traveled another hour of light before he stopped for the night. The wind was cold and he couldn't help but wonder if all his scurrying was in vain. "God please help us to get all the work done that we need to do before the cold of winter makes it impossible." Ben prayed for protection for the ranch and everyone there, and then he felt compelled to pray for Tom and all the people at the mill. At the last, he asked a blessing on the people of Silverville, because he didn't want to leave anyone out. He made a nest of soft grass under the wagon and spread out his bedroll on it. For some reason he felt vulnerable. Maybe it's because I haven't been out here alone, for quite a while but I can't shake the feeling that I am being watched. He pulled his rifle down from under the wagon seat and placed it beside his right hand. Finally, he slept.

At first light, he was already hitching up the team and soon underway. Adam saw him coming a long way off and gave the three expected clangs of the bell. Everyone knew that it was Ben before Adam said that he could see him coming.

"He has lumber and some other stuff on the wagon. He doesn't even have a full load, but he took a long time." Work had stopped and the early warning gave time for the whole family and The People of the Lion, to be there at the crossing to greet him.

Jed had the big raft ready and tied to the bank when Ben pulled up. They ferried the wagon across and the team waded through the water and easily pulled the load to the spot for the new bridge. Arms were first busy with hugs and then unloading.

"Leave the crates on there for now. I want to see the canal! You have all worked so hard! It looks finished."

"We waited for you. All we need to do is unplug the last few stones from the barrier and the water from the river will start to flow. We thought you would want to be here to see it."

Jed and Two Feathers put some effort into removing the last large obstructions that fortified a sheet of slate holding back the river water. As they removed the slate the water gushed into the channel they had made.

"Wow, look at that canal fill! Look at the embankment you made. It is taking the water right where we wanted it. I am puzzled by the lining. What is that? Where did it come from?"

Two Feathers explained that Sheltah had gotten the idea to line the canal with baked clay and that she and Lori had done most of the work.

"Ladies I know everyone worked hard, but this had to be strenuous! Thank you so much. Thank you, all of you for working so hard while I was gone." They all stood near the canal, watching the water spread out in the back area where the wall had curved to allow the small pool to form. It is amazing!"

It was then that Ben saw Sarah standing back, holding Pili. He glanced around and suddenly realized that David wasn't in the group.

"Where is David? Sarah, what's wrong?" He could see that something serious had happened by the look on her face and everyone else's when he asked the question.

"Ben he used dynamite to move rocks to make the channel deep enough. He told us all to go up to the house but he stepped out from his cover just as it started exploding. He has damaged his ears. I have been keeping them covered and giving him pain medicine and sleep medicine so that they will heal. Any sound causes him pain. He is asleep in Johnny's bed." All the joy drained from Ben's face.

"I don't understand. Where did he get the dynamite?"

"He used the two sticks that were left in the box and cut them in half to make four blasts." Jed was looking like a child that feared he would be punished.

"Jed, I left them there because they were too old to be stable. They should have been put in a bucket of water until the wrapper dissolved and then sprinkled in the river slowly or buried. Sarah, it is my fault. I should have gotten rid of it. Then this wouldn't have happened."

"No Ben, you can't blame yourself. He is a grown man and he was told by Jed that it was too dangerous. He wouldn't listen. He decided to do it and that was it. He didn't give us time to move the livestock away either. The mares and their foals were in your corral at the time. He scared them really bad and the chickens, too."

"We took my goats up by the house but they got scared anyway. It was awful loud, Uncle Ben," said Lily. He picked her up and held her so tightly that she could not breathe. He asked her if she had been scared. "Yes, I was a little bit, but not like the animals."

"I am so sorry. Was anyone else hurt?"

"No, he insisted on doing it alone," replied Jed.

Orville joined the group then and shook Ben's hand.

"I am glad you are back, Ben. Your plan for the water is working I see. That's a handsome piece of work by the ladies. I have never seen that done before. I guess we will be putting a new roof on the cheese shed." Ben was surprised when he looked in that direction. He hadn't been home long enough to take everything in yet.

"Yes, Orville I guess we will. We can add that to a long list of things that we will be doing. Mary, where have you and Beth been feeding all these good folks?"

"We built up the fire in the old barn and we have been taking the food in there so we could all eat out of the wind and cold. Two Feather's folks have been sleeping in there."

"This big crate can go in there but leave the rest of this stuff until tomorrow."

Joshua and Johnny each took a side of the crate and carefully carried it into the barn.

"This smells so good, I can't wait to bite into one of these apples," said Johnny. Let's don't tell him that we know what's in there. It will spoil his surprise. I wonder if he brought some candy.

"I don't know, but it looks like we will be eating earlier tonight." Dishes and food in big pots and on trays were being transported to the barn. Ben and Jed stood together watching the water as it poured through the canal.

"How long do you think it will take to get rid of the salt residue?"

"I don't know, but I think it will be fine. Jed after we eat, we are going to have a meeting and include everyone."

"You mean Orville and the Indians, too?"

"Yes, I mean everyone." Jed looked at Ben with questions written on his face. "Trust me. It will be alright."

Everyone gathered around the food and The People of the Lion had gotten comfortable with Brother Tim asking a blessing and the ladies opening the kettles to reveal the good food inside.

"Tonight, I have a few surprises from Silverville plus news, so as soon as we all finish our meals, I will help Jed and Joshua with the milking and Johnny and Lily and Adam can take care of the chickens and goats. Orville, I know that the men will help you feed the horses in the barns and get them taken care of. That will give the ladies time to put the food away and lets all meet back here as soon as our work is finished." Ben headed for the milk barn knowing that the women would be done much sooner than they would.

With the milk in the cold storage, Ben smiled as he entered the barn. Orville and several of the men followed him in.

"We checked the horses and everyone has been fed and they have clean stalls in both barns," said Orville. He settled himself comfortably against the wall of an open stall. He didn't know that he had been the focus of a discussion between Ben and Jed while they were milking.

"Mary and Beth, would you step outside with us for just a moment please?" The women looked surprised but went quickly out the door. When they reentered, all four of them were smiling.

Ben stood very formally.

"This meeting will come to order. Heavenly Father, we are here tonight to thank you for all that you have provided for us. We ask you to guard us from injury as we work together in the coming weeks to complete the projects that we plan to do. We thank you for all the good things that I have the privilege of telling my friends and family that you have provided."

Ben paused and said quietly, Sarah is coming and bringing David. Please do not make any loud noises while he is with us. David stepped into the barn with Sarah and Pili. His ears were padded and his head wrapped many times to hold the padding in place. David's appearance was joyous, but at the same time sad. His friends were glad that he was up and able to come, but sad that he had been severely injured. He received gentle hugs and smiles. The little family snuggled into the soft hay near others in the front stall and Ben continued.

"I cannot share with you yet, how this came about, but God has provided money for the logs, to build a cabin on the clearing in the woods of the Parker Place. Josh and Adam, it will be very small and there will be a well with just a rope and a bucket, but it will be what the law requires to keep the land for generations to come." The boys stood up and would have cheered but instead they each grinned and gave their dad and mom a hug. The wagons with the logs were to be loaded this morning, so they are on their way right now. They will bring logs near the river on Jed and Beth's pasture land, across the river and Orville, a third pair of wagons are coming and they are for a small cabin to be built the other side of the long pen. We have talked about it and we, as a family, feel it is time that you settled down and had a home. It will be your home for as long as you want to stay."

"Well, if that isn't the most generous thing I have ever heard in my entire life, then I don't know what is. You mean you want me to stay here permanently? What about when I get old and can't work no more?"

"We want you to be part of our family and to stay here no matter what."

"That's more than I can take in. I love this ranch and all the folks on it and the horses. I'm not so fond of the cows, chickens and goats, but I would like to stay. It's a good place to spend the rest of my days. Thank you for wanting me." He said it softly, and walked to the door and went outside where he let out a very loud, "Yahoo!"

Inside the barn, everyone had to work to stifle their laughter. David had his hands over his ears and was also trying hard not to laugh out loud as Orville came back in the barn grinning.

"David and Sarah, I have a deed for you and it is paid in full, for the land on the side of your place."

David looked at Sarah, and she was grinning. She had already been told that the gold she had plucked recently from the Hickory river; had been spent for land. She was glad.

"Brother Tim, I have a deed for you, for the piece of land on your right, and because of the curve of the river, you now have water running on your land. This deed is for Father Bob. It is for the piece next to his. Don't forget, you both still have to build on your first piece and somehow put down a well."

"Thank you Ben, yes, I know and the well is going to be the more difficult of the two. This is amazing. Thank you."

"Last, I have five pieces of paper for Two Feather's and Willow. These papers say that The People of the Lion may

112

live on the land behind the backside of the bluff, the prairie, and the new lake that is forming there and some of the forest behind it. It is a very large portion of land. When your people are ready, their home is waiting for them. The land is in my name so no one can make you leave it or take the land from you."

"How can this be? We have prayed for a way to live near David and Sarah. We feel we have been given a sacred commission. Now it is becoming possible. You are a blessing to our people Ben Slater. Thank you for our new home." Two Feathers held the papers in his hand knowing that the Lion of Judah had been at work to make all this possible. "If it wasn't dark outside, I would say, let's go dig those wells and build the three cabins!"

The people could no longer restrain themselves. They applauded and cheered and David was clapping right along with them. David stood and looked around. His face was red and beads of sweat formed on his forehead. Ever so slowly he removed the wrapping over his ears. Everyone waited silently to see what would happen next.

"I can hear! It doesn't hurt and I can hear!" he shouted. Sarah's face showed her joy as tears flooded her eyes.

"Thank you Jesus, Thank you Lion of Judah, said David. Brother Tim stepped forward and placed his hands on David and began to pray. Others did the same. "Thank you Jesus, Thank you God, We claim this healing in Your Holy Name. Thank you Lord," they said over and over.

"God has been at work with these folks for a while now," said Orville. "They are my family, all my family now."

"I think this is "JUST THE BEGINNING," said David.

"I feel like we have all taken the first step on another new and exciting journey," said Ben.

CHAPTER EIGHT
THE FIRST OF MANY

The people gathered there in the barn were so excited that long after the beautiful apples had been eaten and the candy sticks given to Mary to treat the now sleeping children, they continued to talk and plan. They saved the apple seeds with hopes for a future orchard holding a harvest as sweet and red as the fruit they had just enjoyed together.

Two feathers knew that his destiny was in the making and that he and Willow would one day soon, lead their own people. Without saying it, he was almost certain that after helping build the cabins on Ben's ranch that his men would want to build cabins for their own families. We will build them close to the back of the bluff, where we will be protected from the wind and be able to secure the opening to the cave, he thought.

In the morning, the roosters were crowing loudly with much effort and little success at rousting the people from their sleep.

Finally when Beth slowly opened the barn door and sat down a fresh pot of coffee, near the embers of last night's fire, the scent of fried potatoes, scrambled eggs and fresh bread brought the people in the barn fully awake. Jed added wood to the fire and coaxed it alive with a gentle blow. He carried in a tray of jam and butter, sugar and milk. The plates were there on their temporary table, ready to be filled. Bowls were there to hold the oatmeal with raisins and cinnamon. David popped his head in long enough to greet everyone with a big hello and smile.

"I feel great this morning. No ear pain, at all and I am starving! Sarah laughed at him and fed Pili some of the eggs and watched as Eli managed to put some on his own plate. He took a glass of milk and sat down beside Sarah in the hay.

"Daddy says we are going to start to dig a well today."

"Yes, I know about that well. Do you think you and Natty would like to help start making the bricks for it. We have the forms ready and we need to pack them with clay and then bake them hard as rocks."

"You know I have chores to do, don't you?"

"Mom said that after Adam and I do the chickens, we can go up to the lookout and watch for the wagons of logs."

"Natty and Lily are going to feed the goats and then they are going to help Mom bake some cookies."

"All of those jobs sound like fun to me," said Sarah.

Just then the door to the barn was flung open and Lily came in crying.

"Aunt Sarah, come quick, something is wrong with my goat, Dotty. She is crying and I don't know what the matter is!"

Sarah handed Pili to David and followed Lily out the door and to the pen where the two goats were. There in the grass lay a new baby goat. Dotty was licking and nudging it. Sarah stepped into the pen and helped the little one to stand and find where it was to nurse.

"There you are Lily, now you have three goats! I think that sound she is making is just happy singing because she has a baby. Oh, my look at this. Plop and as quick as a blink, a second little goat lit in the grass. She has two babies!" Sarah rubbed the second baby with grass and showed her where her twin was nursing and then, Dotty let out a bleat that really did sound like a song of joy.

"She has two babies! She is so special." Lily was crying.

"Why are you crying now, Lily?"

"I am crying because I am so happy. Tell everyone to come see my babies. I don't want to leave her. Dotty is a mother now, but she is still little." Sarah stuck her head in the barn and told everyone that Lily's goat has just had twin babies!

"This is really wonderful. Look how proud she is of them." Dotty was licking first one and then the other. "Is it alright to leave him in there?" Beth looked around but no one seemed to know.

"I am going down to the cow barn to help Joshua and Johnny. I will take the new dad with me and put him in the empty calf pen for a while until we see how it goes." Jed was grinning as he led the little goat away.

"Mom, they are so little and cute. I didn't know she could make babies. Did you?"

"Yes, I thought she might someday, but I didn't know that someday was now."

"Is it alright if I stay here with her until Johnny comes out to help me move the pen?"

"Yes of course." Beth felt a little overwhelmed as she hugged Lily. So much was happening and God was using double scoops of blessings. You are an awesome God. Thank you for the little goats and all the blessings you continue to give us. Thank you for Lily's love for animals. She will always enjoy being here on the ranch. She continued to pray as she walked into the house. Thank you for showing Sarah the gold visible in the river. The two bags paid for the land. Again you gave us double and we were able to buy the land for The People of the Lion. She was humming as she started to cook a big kettle of chili and was making the dough for the cookies.

Mary pulled up with the little wagon and Ben helped to carry in the big trays.

"Beth I hope you are alright here; if I take Mary down with me. I want to check the clearing and make sure there is room for the team and wagon of logs to pull in without damage to the spring area. I am going to round up all my boys, and take them with us, so you don't have to worry about watching them. You have worked so hard. Don't think that I don't know it."

"I will be fine. Why wouldn't I be? There are folks here that are willing to help me if I need it." Mary and Ben rode out side by side on their saddle horses and Joshua sat tall with Adam on the seat beside him. He was driving the little wagon and Natty and Eli were sitting on hay inside it.

"This is fun Dad," yelled Josh over the sound of the rattling wagon. When they arrived, they quickly checked the fence and determined that the beef cattle were securely contained. Ben opened the channel and allowed water to pour into the pond that they used for drinking.

Mary led the way. The path Slim had made to the spring was overgrown with weeds and brush, but she could still find her way through. She stopped at the big pine tree that marked his grave.

"The wagon can't come in here. There isn't room but maybe it could angle in closer to the river." Ben walked the route to the clearing and noted that it would take a full day's work to clear a path wide enough for the team pulling the load of logs. He marked several trees with his knife. "They will have to go."

"Ben, where should we put the well?"

"Josh, what do you think?"

"I think that the men should start working here, since this place is closest to town they will probably bring the first load of logs here. If we put the well over there, then the cabin can sit in the clearing and the team could come in, turn around, put the logs at the back of the clearing, and then pull right back out."

"Josh, you are right. That means we only have to take out these three trees and clear the brush from the back where we want to pile the logs. That's excellent son, let's head back so I can get some men and tools. We can start on this place first, maybe this afternoon."

The men at the ranch were surprised at Ben's quick return. They had started to dig a well just a short distance from the long pen. Jed had staked out a small rectangle for the little cabin. Orville was showing an interest and sat on Tinkle, smiling and watching.

"I am going out to check on the mustangs. Do you think that I can open that channel to their field for a bit? I'll watch it. I tasted the water this morning and it seems fresh to me."

"Sure Orville, go ahead if you think the water is clean of salt now, that's good enough for me." Jed walked over close to Ben and spoke softly.

"He has been grinning and acting like he just bought this little cabin."

"Good. I am glad that it has made him happy," said Ben. "I know that when he is old we will have to care for him, but that's what I intended. He doesn't have a family and we will be his family now. Was this his choice for location?"

"Yes, he said if we didn't mind he wanted it to face toward the river and that way he isn't looking at your house and Sarah's cabin. He said he didn't want anybody thinking that he was being nosy." They laughed at that, knowing full well that somehow he usually knew what was happening.

"I think it would have been a help if he had known that David was using that dynamite! He was in my barn when the charges went off. No one thought to tell him. He is usually out in the pasture with the mustangs or somewhere out of sight. He covers lots of ground in a day," said Jed.

"Did you know that the women are planning on making bricks for the wells?" Ben looked puzzled.

"That is not practical. I think when the men come with the first load of logs; we should tell them that we need them to bring some bricks for the three wells. I never thought of that and it wasn't discussed at our meetings."

"Ben, were you planning on taking a crew down to the Parker place?"

"Yes, I need to clear a path for the team with the logs to enter. It has to be big enough for them to turn around to get back out. I may take a tent and some food and stay there until we get the well dug."

Mary knew just by Ben's expression when he had headed back to the ranch that he would be immediately taking some men back to remove the trees and start the well. She and Beth had already anticipated this part of the project. Beth used Queen to pull the wagon out of Jed's barn and parked it in front of her house. They had stacked half of it full of tools including the big crosscut saw and 2 shovels. She packed two hunting tents in the bottom and used them to support several packs of food and solid water jugs. In the corner she padded one of the new lanterns and a tin of lamp oil, along with a pack of matches in a glass canning jar to make sure they stayed dry.

Beth brought the new coffee pot and coffee and then smiled as she added a jar of sugar and a few spoons, forks and two knives. Mary added a stack of blankets and Joshua's bed roll. She knew he would want to be there from the start. She debated whether to include Adam but decided against it. Maybe later on, she thought.

"Mary, pray with me." She reached for her hand and they bowed their heads. "Please, Father, bless all the men that are going to work on Mary's land. Keep them safe. Be with them and help them to accomplish all they have planned. Please hold the harsh winter weather off long enough so they can get done what they need to both there and here. Give us all your blessing and allow the work to continue safely. Thank you, Father, for I know you hear my prayer. Thank you for healing David's ears. You are a good and caring Father. We give you the praise and glory, for all we have we owe to you. Amen."

When Mary lifted her head, Beth could see that there were tears on her cheeks.

"Mary, why are you crying?"

"I'm not sure, really. I was fine when I was down on our place earlier, but now I feel terribly sad. Beth, don't mention to Ben that I was crying. He wouldn't understand. I love him very much, but right now I am missing Slim something awful."

She hurried into Beth's house when she noticed the men coming down the path. Several men had been working all morning putting the planks in place and nailing them securely. They would be able to cross the canal on the path with confidence. It was strong and secure.

Mary placed a jar of milk in beside the sugar when she came back out.

"If you keep that in the river water, it will stay good for at least a day or two," she said trying to hide that she had been crying. Ben could tell with a glance. He knew her well.

"Ben, I want you to take Joshua with you and include him as much as is safe. I think Adam should stay here for now, maybe he can come later on." Ben walked to her and wrapped her in his arms. He didn't acknowledge the all too bright look in her eyes, or the redness of her nose. He just held her close knowing that she was doing her best.

"Don't worry about us, we will be fine. I will make sure that Josh stays safe."

"Dad, I am going to use a different horse to pull the wagon. Mom hitched up Queen, but she is high strung. Uncle Jed said she would be perfect for a buggy. This big guy needs some exercise." Joshua made the exchange of horses smoothly and Sundown stood in front of the little wagon while Queen was led back through the gate and into the pasture. "Is it alright if I take the wagon across Dad? Is there anything else we should put in it?"

Several men rode up on their horses, with bedrolls and saddlebags packed. The group included Mark, Ben's cousin, Debon, White Grass, Soren and David.

Ben looked at David and asked to speak to him privately.

"David, I would appreciate it, if you would stay here and help Jed with getting things going on both the other wells. He will need help with the regular chores, too. Depending on when they bring the logs, we need to have things marked out on his land across the river. You experienced the teams bringing in your logs. You know what has to happen to be ready for them at both places."

"Well, if that's what you want, I will stay. I want to help anyway that I can."

"Thank you, David; I know you are someone I can count on to do this for me." Ben swung up on his horse and looked at Joshua, grinning from the seat of the wagon. "Josh, I want you to pull up to the big raft. We will ferry that load across. No sense taking a chance on getting things wet like I foolishly did when I left."

"Oh, Dad, I guess you are right, but it would have been fun to let Sundown take it through the water." Josh walked the big horse and wagon across the bridge on the path for the first time and the men that had worked on it applauded. Ben praised their work. It was stable and strong. They had used the logs from the three trees they had cut to make the supports. The base was durable and would last for many years.

Once the wagon was across the river and back hitched to Sundown, the men going with Ben began to head along the trail to the location of the first cabin. Joshua was enjoying his position as supply wagon driver. Ben made sure they had shovels on board. Getting that well dug was very important. He was glad that he had bought extra shovels before returning with the planks.

Meanwhile Two Feathers and Willow had talked to Jed and he went with them to see what they were talking about.

"Jed, if you put the little cabin here, facing the river, you will look out the window at the river, framed by those two big maples. Think how beautiful that will be in the fall."

"That's fine Willow, whatever you think. Yes, that would be a nice view in the fall when they turn red. I wish they were that color now, but the leaves are down. That tells me just how late in the season it is." It was easy to see that the pressure of the late season and so many projects was distressing him.

"Where do you want us to put the well, Jed?" Two Feathers asked.

"Stick it close to the river. It may be easier to hit water that way," said Jed looking up at David. "What are you looking so disgruntled about?"

"I am fine. I just wonder why Ben made such a point of me staying here. He didn't want me to go with them to the Parker land."

"Is that all that is bothering you? I think it is pretty obvious to all the rest of us. He didn't want you sleeping out in the open. Here you are under a roof. I know that God did an amazing miracle on your ears, but you still went through a terrible ordeal and should take care of yourself now and be careful not to get hurt again. Sarah and Pili need you. I think it is a case of Ben still trying to protect Sarah in his own way."

"Alright, I get it now. Thanks Jed. I didn't look at it that way."

"David, how are they doing on the well down there at Orville's?"

"You better stop saying it that way. He is already acting like he bought the place. They are down about six or seven feet but no water so far. At least it is far enough from the bluff that I don't think that digging it will be terribly hard. The men are taking turns and they made a ladder this morning."

"That all sounds good David. Take a look at the view that Willow pointed out to me. If we put this little cabin here, when we look out its window, there will be a maple on either side framing the river."

"Willow, you picked a good spot. I like that. Jed, do you want to mark the corners?"

Two Feathers broke a branch into pieces and they paced off a small rectangle marking the corners with the sticks.

"Where will you have them put the logs?"

"Well if we are digging over there, let's have them put them on this side. That way we won't be in each other's way."

David nodded and got a pair of large branches and made an X with them, placing a heavy rock on top. With another stick he handed Jed the honor of drawing the circle for the well.

"There we are folks, now all we need to do is make it happen."

"Don't worry Jed it will happen."

They were heading back to the crossing when they spotted the army milk wagon coming. None of the children were at the lookout to sound the bell. The private looked disappointed. He joked with Jed.

"Don't I deserve two rings anymore?"

Jed chuckled, and said he would be glad to help load the cans full of milk and a large wheel of cheese that the women had ready. Two heavy tins of butter were also ferried across and placed against the ice and then covered with straw in the wagon. The soldier signed the paper showing what he had received and then carefully turned his wagon around.

He sat on the seat looking across the river at all the activity on the ranch.

"I passed Ben and some men down by the field of steers. It looks like you folks have a whole lot of work to do. I sure hope the weather holds for you. I noticed where you staked out the little building. That's a good spot. Well, Jed, I'll see you again. Thanks a lot." He pulled slowly away making sure that the full cans of milk were tied in place and stable. He had secured them with ropes. As usual he had returned the empty cans in immaculate condition.

The ranch was buzzing with activity. The children had all been assigned chores. Pens needed cleaning. Animals needed to be fed and eggs gathered. Mary was hanging a large wash on her lines and Natty was handing her the clothes pins. Orville strolled over to the fence near her and asked what the ladies were cooking for the evening meal tonight.

Mary smiled after he walked away. He seems more at ease since our meeting. He would not have asked me that before. He is a good addition to the ranch. I am glad that it was decided that we should adopt him. She was still watching him as he worked with a mustang mare, when she finished hanging out the wash. He rode over to the fence and told her not to be dumping those big tubs of water that he was coming through the gate to do that for her.

"Thank you Orville. They are heavy." He emptied the tubs and returned them to the pegs on the back of the house where they hung when not in use.

"Whatever you need, just let me know," he said returning to the mare. "My lady is waiting," he said laughing as he approached her and slid on and off while scratching her neck and ears.

"I wonder what Beth is doing, Natty. Do you think we should go see?"

"Yes, I want to go play with Lily's babies."

"Thank you for helping me with the wash, Natty."

*****

At the Parker place, when Ben and the men had the path cleared for the wagon and team bringing the load of logs, they didn't have to wait very long. Joshua worked at the spring and cleared the path trying to make it look as he remembered it had years earlier. The three trees had carefully been cut low to the ground so the wagon could pass over them. They had been cleaned of their branches and rolled to the back of the clearing where it had been decided the rest should be unloaded. Josh and Ben had paced off the location for the cabin but hadn't driven stakes in the ground, knowing that the team would have to turn around in that area. Ben had drawn a circle for the well and the sod was already removed when they heard the wagon coming. Jake was driving the team and smiled with recognition when he saw Ben.

"Good to see you Ben. Where do you want me to take these?"

"If you don't mind hopping down for a minute, I'd like to show you." Ben walked him down the path they had made that left the trail in a big arch and ended in the clearing.

"Well, that will get me in there but I don't see a path leading out." Ben looked at him with disbelief.

"Hey, you are no rookie! Come in here and make a circle. You have room to go back out the way you came in." The men were trying hard to look serious, but they knew Jake was just teasing him. Jake started laughing and soon they were all laughing.

"Jake, I needed that laugh as much as the logs. Let's bring them in. With the logs off the wagon, Jake was ready to head back to the Sawmill. Ben finally remembered at the last minute.

"Jake I need bricks to line three wells. I know someone in town can get them because the bank is built with them. Can you bring me a load?"

"No, I can't, not really. They make those down river at the clay pits. That's about a day's ride from the edge of town. They have been there about two years now and Tom and Donaldson don't get along at all."

"How can I get them here right away?"

"That's probably not going to happen. You need to go talk to Donaldson with money in hand and take your own team and wagon. That's the best advice I can give you. I have got to get back. Nice seeing you again Ben. Come visit sometime. Tell everyone I said Hello." He started to pull out onto the trail and stopped. He pointed to draw Ben's attention to the second and third loads moving slowly across the prairie toward the ranch as Jake pulled out and waved goodbye. He would go down the route to the bridge by Sam's store now that his wagon was empty.

The men had already started driving stakes to indicate the four corners of the cabin. Two men were standing in the circle of the well and digging. Ben swung up on Buddy and told them that he wouldn't be back to help until he solved the brick problem. They nodded and understood. Ben headed home and soon rode beyond the wagons. The bell clanged three times, as he rode up to the group of men where Jed was working on his pasture.

"Jed and David, I need you both to come up to the house with me." Once there he quickly explained to them and the women that he needed the work team and the big wagon and more importantly he needed enough gold to pay for the bricks.

"The clay pit where they bake the bricks is a day's ride down river from the edge of town. I don't know how long I will be gone. Jake said the owner is a man named Donaldson and he is hard to deal with. David, are you well enough to come with me?"

"Yes I am fine. I'm perfect, but you should wait until almost dark to get the gold."

"You are right. It will be hard to get it and not be noticed with so many people here. Beth and Mary, would you be able to serve the meal just before dark? That will keep everyone else busy in my barn while we dig the gold up behind Jed's."

"Beth laughed and said sure, but which poor horse are you going to disturb, Goldie or Chum?"

"I don't think it matters as long as we are trying hard to do God's work. It all belongs to him," answered David. "Sarah, you agree don't you?"

"Yes of course I do, but since Father Bob isn't here to agree, please use Goldie, so there is no possibility of a problem about it later."

The next morning David and Ben had hooked Brownie and Buck to their biggest, strongest wagon and headed across the river just as the sun was rising.

"Joshua would have liked to be driving the team just then. He seems to want to take a team through the river," said David, "He told me that just before you left with the men for the Parker place."

"I know he wanted to do that with the supply wagon. We will be able to check to see how things are going on our way into Silverville." The new bridge is strong enough for us to go across now, with an empty wagon but I am sure we will have to go the long way coming back."

"I think you are right. Look at the progress they are making on Jed's pasture cabin. I can see the outline."

Two Feathers was smiling when he saw the two men jump down from the wagon and check out what his crew, had already accomplished.

"We will put the window as close to the door as we can. I know that Jed intends to turn this into a shelter for horses after the inspection"

"That's a good idea. He will be making a double barn door next summer and the window will move to the end I think," said Ben. "I don't care how you do it for now. Who knows? He may change his mind and leave the little cabin and build a barn. I just want to thank all of you for all the hard work you are doing? Two Feathers is there anything that we need while we are in town? We have to go right through there to buy the bricks."

"No, I can't think of anything; unless the store has more of those wonderful apples. We all enjoyed those." The men nodded agreement.

The well was already getting deep enough that the two men stood shoulder deep in the hole and the dirt they were throwing out would soon need to be lifted out on a rope contraption they had put together.

The logs in that load were all nice and long. It would be a beautiful square cabin. Ben thanked God silently as he rode along.

David had gained confidence and expertise at handling the team. His work at the reins seemed effortless.

"Ben, can you hear that?"

"What are you hearing?"

"In spite of all the noise the men are making, the trees are full of birds. I will never take any of my senses for granted again."

"Yes, I can hear them. You are right David. God is a generous and good God."

"I can't imagine not regaining my hearing. I would miss so much." They rode along quietly until they could see the fenced field full of cattle.

Approaching the area was Chief Dark Wolf and some of his senior hunter, warriors.

"We have come to buy cattle, Ben Slater. We have many blue stones to pay you." He said it proudly. "These men will take the beef back and put them in our field. The women are eager to do their part in preserving some of the meat for winter. Sweet Grass says that snow will come soon. I hope she is wrong, for your sake. How are you doing with the cabins and wells?"

"Chief Dark Wolf, your men work very hard. Come, ride with us into the woods and let us all see how they are doing."

His invitation brought smiles on the men that had ridden from the village. They were glad for any diversion. None of them were eager to deal with the cattle. They had taken part in the drive several times and it never seemed to get any easier.

Ben acknowledged Growling Bear with a nod and several others that he recognized from the battle against the fire. These were good men. He was proud to know them. Strangely he still thought of his parents and their wagon at that moment. He couldn't help but wonder if any of these men had actually taken part in the raid. He really didn't want to know. I must forgive them and try to forget it. They are not the same men that did that. They are saved and baptized. They are my brothers in Christ.

"Ben, did you hear me?"

"I am sorry Growling Bear. What did you say?"

"I said that you should have some of the lazy work horses that graze with our herd. They are fat and need to do something."

"Yes, we could use at least four, to pull the logs up the ramp. Maybe brother Tim would bring us some." It was then that David and Ben both realized that Tim had not been seen at the ranch since the evening meal the night that David's ears were healed.

"I haven't seen him. Where did he go?"

"He came back to the village yesterday," said Growling Bear. He said that he wasn't needed and that he missed the children of the village." Chief Dark Wolf laughed out loud.

"I think it is someone else that he was missing."

"Standing Bear go back to the camp and have Brother Tim bring work horses, old enough to be wise and young enough to be strong."

"Yes, my Chief," he replied and rode quickly away. The men laughed at the Chief's remark about Brother Tim and then turned their laughter to the men digging the well and offered a hand to pull them out but they didn't accept, saying they were where they needed to be for now, but later they would need a ladder. The comment had not escaped Ben and David's ears. They wondered if the Chief was right. Was Brother Tim getting involved with one of the women in the village? Sylvia Warren seemed the most likely candidate for his affection, but she was at the ranch. He had seemed to give her no notice once they arrived. She had been helping with the cooking, baking and washing of pans and hadn't been out of the house except to help the children do chores. She seemed to be happy doing whatever needed her hand.

"This will be a big cabin," said Debon as Ben walked over to appreciate their small overnight progress. Ben knew that The People of the village all lived in tents much smaller than this cabin would be.

Even the Chief could imagine the room inside when it was finished and knew that it was larger than his tent. Only the communal tent was larger. The Chief was beginning to plan.

Chief Dark Wolf handed Ben a pouch filled with the blue stones and said that if it wasn't enough, he would send someone with more. Ben and David were amazed at the size and beautiful blue-green color.

"Chief this is more than enough. These are truly beautiful. I will take two pieces for each animal you want. How many will make a comfortable food supply for the people this winter?" He thought for only a moment.

"We will take half the field and you will take all the stones. I want the cattle to multiply so that we do not have to come buy grown animals. If we buy many, it will happen. Our men have prepared a field for them to live and grow. Does this seem like a fair trade to you Ben Slater?"

"Yes, my friend, very fair."

They studied the field of cattle standing near the fence, side by side for several minutes, until the Chief pointed at one large animal that appeared to be all white. I must take him. He will live long and have many wives. White is a sacred color to the people. When he dies of old age, his hide will hang on the wall of the communal tent. He will be respected and revered. He will bring prosperity to the village."

"No." Ben's reply was like a knee jerk response. "He is not to go with you for that purpose. You are a people that know where your provision comes from. You must honor God and thank him and respect and revere him only. He is a jealous God. There is only one God. That animal is not a spirit. He is just an animal that happens to have a white coat. You may not take him and lead your people away from the God that blesses all of you. Father Bob would be disappointed in your words, as am I."

"You are right. The old ways die hard. We are a new people with a new name. We are The Blue Stone People. We will leave him here to do with as you see fit. He is just an unusual animal."

"Thank you Chief. David and I will help you move half of them out of the pen." Joshua stood wide eyed watching as his father and David on horses belonging to Soren and Debon rode into the pen. They eased the cattle toward the chute that led to the back gate of the field. Ben bravely slapped the flank of the white bull and headed him away from the others as seventy were sent out onto the prairie.

Most were full grown but some were young spring calves. Ben waved goodbye and laughed at the antics that the old hunters were going through, trying to bunch the running cattle and slow them down.

"Wow, Ben I was afraid that the Chief was going to get really angry when you said no so abruptly. He isn't used to people telling him no."

"David, he knew what I was saying was right. He will always have to fight the old ways that he was raised with, but I surely wasn't going to provide him with an animal that would be a stumbling block."

CHAPTER NINE
TOWN MEETING

Within five minutes of the Chief and his men leaving with the cattle, Ben and David were back on the wagon and heading to town.

"You know something weird is going on with that all white bull, Ben."

"What do you mean?"

"How many times have you checked their fences and filled the water hole since you got that last batch of beef?"

"I don't know, probably dozens, why?"

"Had you ever seen him before today?"

"Now that you mention it, I don't think I ever noticed him. Now every time I look at the field, I think I will see him first. It is strange. He is so different. Why didn't I see him before today?" Ben didn't say it but he thought maybe God put him there to test me. He wanted to see if I would speak up. I am glad that I did. They rode along not talking. Each lost in their own contemplation.

They could hear the ruckus at the mill as soon as they pulled onto Main Street.

"What in the world is going on here? Look Ben. All the shops have closed signs in their windows."

"We will know soon enough. It sounds like the whole town is at the mill!" Buggies and single mounts were left tethered along the edge of the Hickory River opposite the mill. Some folks had found things to sit on but many of them were standing. Tom was taller than most men but he had stepped up onto a log to be seen and heard.

"Folks please settle down. This is just to let you all know that we need to build a jail and I plan to send for the Marshal when the mail boat stops tomorrow. We have a man locked up in the tool shed over there. I have witnesses that saw him hit his wife and injure her. He had too much to drink, but that is no excuse.

I don't think any of us wants to be responsible for keeping the law here and since Silverville is growing we thought you would all like to have a say in how these things should be handled."

"String him up yelled one old woman."

"Hit him the way he hit her, an eye for an eye," yelled someone who was obviously aware of what happened. Mr. Williams, from the bank, stood up and waited for silence.

"I think it is time that Silverville has a permanent sheriff in town.

"What if someone robs the bank and takes all your money? Who is going to catch them?"

After that question everyone started talking again.

"Quiet please. We can't settle anything this way," said Tom. "Mr. Cantwell, is that piece of land beside the saloon still for sale?"

"Yes, it is. No one wants to build next to a saloon."

"I make the motion that the town should use that piece of land to build a sheriff's office and jail," said Tom.

"I second the motion," said Sam. "That's a perfect place for him to see what's going on around here."

"Is anyone opposed?" No one said a word.

"That's fine. Mr. Cantwell will draw up the paper and anyone that owns land in Silverville should sign the bottom.

"You can't just keep that man locked up until a U.S. Marshall comes here. That could take months, offered a man that Ben didn't know.

"We are working on that. I will let him out tomorrow and he can work for his meals, but I am not taking my eye off him until I know that his family is safe."

"Well that sounds fair." Several men agreed and nodded.

"If any of you would like one drink, you can come with me to the saloon. I bought the place, land, tent, and barrels. I need some men to help me pour the liquor into the Hickory. There are going to be some surprised fish as they swim by," said Tom joking.

The crowd followed Tom across the street. They weren't thinking of a drink but wanted to see if he really was going to smash the barrels and pour away his money.

"Reverend Brown, if you can use this tent for a big church meeting or something, you are welcome to have it at no cost."

"Well I am sure that we can use it. Thank you, Tom.

The lumbermen had a grand time splitting open the kegs and rolling them to the edge of the water as they spewed their contents.

Ben and David found themselves standing near the man that had asked about keeping the man locked up. He was Frank Donaldson and not at all pleased with the way things were going in this town. His personal opinion was that he would rather do business after a man had been drinking. It gave him an advantage. He didn't say it, but that's what he was thinking. He shook Ben and David's hand and introduced himself. Ben said they would be out his way to get a load of bricks as soon as they could. But first they had some business in town with Mr. Williams.

In his office Mr. Williams said he was pleased that the good people of his town had seen things his way. He was eager for the security of a sheriff nearby. That's when it really hit Ben that the money in the bank was not really as safe as it was resting with Goldie and Chum.

"Mr. Williams, I need this gold appraised."

"Mr. Slater, where are you getting all the gold you keep bringing to me? You know don't you that you have to file a claim on the spot where you are mining."

"I am not mining and have no desire to do so."

"Should I add this to your account?"

"No, I prefer to convert it to paper money. Do we need to get it appraised again?" Ben asked.

"No, that shouldn't be necessary," he said as he poured the small pebbles, flakes and nuggets onto the scale. "You have fifteen ounces here Ben. That is worth five hundred and twenty five dollars. Do you want me to add this to your account?" He asked a second time.

"I want paper money Mr. Williams. I want to take it with me."

"Do you think that is wise in a town with no sheriff? You should put it here in the safe."

"Not this time, I need to buy some bricks and I hear that Frank Donaldson prefers cash in hand."

"Yes, I have dealt with him. He is a most untrusting man."

Ben and David left the bank with the money carefully tucked in their coats in the inside pockets. They headed the team out of town, following the trail down river.

"I wish we had time, I would really enjoy one of Cookie's steaks and fried potatoes right now," said David.

"That sounds delicious, maybe we can manage to get one before we leave town. Right now I am eager to see this wagon stacked with bricks and headed toward home." They moved down the trail following the Hickory River out of town.

"Well, let's see what Mary and Sarah have stashed in this lunch satchel for us," said David as he pulled out a note from Sarah and chuckled. "Listen to this. David, please take extra care to cover your ears at night. I know you well and unless I remind you, you will forget."

"She is looking out for you, David. She knows God did his part, and now she just wants to make sure that you do yours. Right now it is not ears I am thinking about. It is my stomach," said Ben. "What did they put in there for us to eat?"

"It looks like we have a variety. Here let's start with the butter and jam sandwiches."

They stopped for the night, pulling the wagon into the trees along the Hickory. Brownie and Buck were happy to be done for the day. They drank from the river and munched the sweet grass near the edge. Ben took them each half of a sugar cookie and they happily crunched them, too.

"It is getting cold tonight. Do you think we should start a fire?"

"No, I don't for two reasons. I think we should hitch up and move on. A fire would let the guys that are following us know exactly where we are."

"What are you talking about Ben? I haven't seen anyone."

"I did, a while ago. I kept waiting for them to catch up, but they never did. They are hanging back until we camp and go to sleep. Someone must have seen us in the bank, or talked to Gordon or Mr. Williams."

"Ben those men know better than to say anything about the transactions."

"Well maybe someone heard me telling Tom about being here to get bricks. It stands to reason if we haven't got the bricks yet that we must have the money on us to buy them." They traveled along slowly, letting the team follow the trail in the moonlight.

Each man had a rifle on his lap.

"If they shoot us in the back, it won't do us any good to have these. I still haven't seen any sign of someone following," said David. Ben moved into the back of the wagon and pulled his small hunting tent forward. He rolled it up and put his hat on the top, jamming it down tight on the seat so that it would stay.

"Meet your new traveling companion. I want you to keep going until you hear a shot. Then you can come back and pick me up." Before David could object, Ben jumped off the side of the moving wagon and disappeared into the brush.

"This is not what I signed up for!" David said it softly to his team. He gently slowed them but kept moving. His heart was racing. What if they spot him? He said he saw two men. He can't stop both of them.

*****

Back at the ranch Sarah was pacing Beth's living room.

"I know something is wrong, I can feel it."

"Sarah, you are just worrying over David because he was injured and you aren't with him. He is fine now and Ben is there. They are just buying bricks. How hard can that be?"

"I am telling you Beth, something is very wrong." She placed Pili beside her on the big bear skin and knelt placing her folded hands on the seat of a chair. Beth knelt beside her. Jed had been feeling uneasy. He came in and found the women praying. Without a word, he joined them. They stayed there together for several minutes. Finally, Sarah stood up, tucking the corner of a blanket over Pili.

"Whatever it was is over now. I feel empty inside. Someone may be dead!"

"Sarah, don't say that! You can't know that."

"I know that something terrible has happened and it involved David and Ben. I am leaving for Silverville at first light."

"I'm going with you," said Jed. He walked out the front door and found Two Feathers approaching.

"What has happened?" He asked. "Willow and I have discerned serious trouble.

"I don't know, Two Feathers. Sarah and I are leaving at first light. She is sure that something bad has happened. I will send Joshua back here to help with the chores. Please oversee the building of the cabins and digging of the wells for us until we return."

"I will, and Willow will help, also. We will make sure that the work here continues. Just bring your men back safely."

Jed walked quietly to his corral and brought out three horses and saddled them. I will need to leave one with Josh so he can ride back, he thought. He found Orville in his bedroll, down near the start of the new cabin by the long pen. He explained as well as he could what was going on and asked him to let training the mustangs go until he returned.

"Just make sure that all the normal chores get done and that the animals all receive what they need. The women will need you to help with the chores and anything heavy. Please take good care of them. They are your family too, now."

"I will Jed, I promise. You know I will."

"I trust you, Orville. Go back to sleep now, until morning. You will probably be working harder than usual until we return."

Mary had come down, riding bareback, to see what was going on.

"I heard you ride by," she said to Jed. "What is going on? Has something happened? Why are you up at this hour?" He tried to explain but since he had no information, it was difficult to make it sound sensible.

"Sarah is frantic. She is sure that David and Ben have been involved in something terrible. We are going to ride out for town at first light.

"What about Pili?"

"Right now she is asleep in our living room. I guess she will leave her with Beth."

"Jed, this is like a nightmare! Sarah is so different. Sometimes she scares me. She seems otherworldly. I hope she is wrong, just this once."

Beth had scrambled around and packed bags full of everything she could think of in the way of food, and extra clothes. Sarah had not slept. She had been busy preparing a traveling pharmacy, with bandages and every possible medical aid that she could think of. They headed out under the oak as soon as they could see enough to keep the horses safely on the path.

When they left, all the adults at the ranch were up. The youngsters slept on. They were unaware of the drama taking place around them.

*****

That morning in town it was business as usual. Hope and her son, Mark Donner, were preparing their luggage for a long trip. With part of the money from Tom's purchase of the whiskey and their saloon, she bought two tickets to ride up the Silver on the mail boat. She quietly told Helen that she was going back east to her parents. She apologized for her husband hitting Sam. She secretly hoped that Lucas would hear the story and if he did try to pursue her it would be in vain. Helen would of course spread the story adding details, but making sure that Sam was not around when she did it.

"He can have the house and all that's in it. I have what I need. As long as I have my son and we are safe, that's all I want." She told Helen sincerely. "I removed only the most essential personal things. I want to put him and all this behind me."

"You poor, poor dear, I hope that everything works out for you," said Helen in her most sympathetic voice. "You shouldn't concern yourself over Sam. He is fine."

Hope and Mark boarded the mail boat and handed the man their tickets.

"Since a few folks have been traveling with us, I have tried to provide a more comfortable area," said Daniel. If you feel the need, you can sit inside there and use one of the blankets. There's not much room but we can all make do as long as we get back to the dock at Langford before the weather changes." Sam watched the boat turn around and then went back to his store. He had received very little supplies and only one piece of mail. I guess I should be glad that I got so much last week. This could be their last run until spring.

*****

Ben crouched in the bushes, silently waiting and watching for any sign that someone was on the trail. He had nearly given up; thinking he had imagined the whole thing when he heard a small sound behind him.

When the two men had figured out that they had been discovered they decided to circle around and stop the wagon on the trail ahead. At the last minute one of them spotted Ben as he jumped from the wagon. They crept up behind him and hit him hard on the head just as he jerked up hearing their approach.

His finger yanked the trigger of his rifle as he fell.

"Dang it, now the other one knows for sure that something has happened!"

"Never mind that, just see if he is carrying the money."

It's not in his pants. Maybe it's in his coat. Well look here. He has wads of money all in his coat lining. What do you think of that?"

"Just hurry up and get it. Let's get out of here before the other one comes back."

"Are you going to shoot him?"

"No, he can't know who we are. He didn't see us."

"Well, I did! Put your hands up. Toss your guns out on the trail with two fingers." David sounded much more in control than he felt. "Sit down where you are and take your boots off. Throw them out on the trail."

"We can't do that! How can we walk around with no boots on?"

"Where do you think you are going? Do it now!" They struggled to pull their boots off and finally did throw them onto the trail. "Where is the money you took?"

"We didn't take any money. We found this poor man like this. We were trying to help him."

"Sure you were. Take your pants off! Take them off, both of you!"

"What kind of man are you to tell us that? It's getting cold out here! We can't be out here standing around in our long johns!"

"I can fix it so you won't ever feel a thing again. Is that what you want? Do it now!" They wiggled around pulling their pants off, spilling money from the pockets. "Well look at that, you just happen to have all his money in your pockets. Stand up, and keep your hands up above your heads. We are going for a walk."

"Ouch, oh, this hurts. I can't do this. My feet are going to be all cuts and bruises."

"Alright, I have a better idea." David pulled his knife from his belt and cut one of the pairs of pants into long shreds. The two men stood looking bewildered. "Sit down with your backs together and hands together. David used the shredded pants to tightly secure the men's hands.

He walked over and carefully checked Ben.

"You hit him so hard that he is still out." He gathered the money from the grass and stuffed it into one of the men's boots. David had pulled both belts from the pants. He stood there holding one of them by the buckle with the leather wrapped around his fist. "I am going to get my team and wagon. If you move, I will use these belts to whip you until you are bloody. If you stay put, I will give you a ride. He slid on to one of their horses, taking their guns, boots, belts and the other pair of pants with him and led the other horse down the trail to where his team patiently waited. It was difficult, but he turned the team and wagon around on the narrow trail. The trees encroached from the trails little use.

When he returned, both men still sat where he had left them. He lifted Ben carefully onto the wagon and turned him on his side. The back of Ben's head was bleeding and he still hadn't moved or made a sound.

David had placed the boots in the front of the wagon under the seat and folded the second pair of pants and put it under Ben's head on top of a pile of grass he had hastily gathered. He covered him with his bedroll.

"If you want a ride back to town, get up on the back of the wagon." They strained and complained that it was cruel the way he was treating a couple of good Samaritans, but finally they managed to climb up. He refused to help them. Their horses were following along just a few feet behind the wagon, fastened to the ropes that David found on their saddles. He drove slowly, fearing that he might add to Ben's injury with every bump. He was keeping a watchful eye on the men he had captured.

CHAPTER TEN
DO IT OR STARVE

It was dawn when David arrived at the Sawmill. Cookie was just beginning to cook breakfast and Tom instinctively knew that something had gone dreadfully wrong.

He dropped his first cup of coffee on to the ground and ran to the approaching team and wagon.

"What happened? David, is Ben dead?"

"No, but he is seriously injured. He has been out like that ever since one of these men hit him over the head."

"How did you catch them? Where are their clothes?" I took their pants, boots and guns. They are not going anywhere!" Cookie knew that Ben needed his attention more than anything else. He yelled at the gathering men.

"Go get ice from the cold house. Hurry! He is hurt bad! How long has he been like this?" Cookie asked.

"I am not sure. It was totally dark. I don't know. We were going to buy bricks. They followed us. Ben spotted them following and got off the wagon with his rifle. He thought he could stop them, but they circled around and caught him off guard. He shot once and I came back and caught them taking the money from Ben's coat. I made them take off their boots and pants so they couldn't run away. I ruined one pair of pants to tie their hands before I thought of the ropes on their saddles." Tom kept shaking his head in disbelief.

"I can't believe how this place is changing! No one is safe anymore," said Tom. The lumberjacks had gently transferred Ben to a folded blanket near the fire where Cookie was doing his best to gently pack the back of Ben's head in ice.

"Let Lucas Donner out of the shed and cut these two loose and put them in. Send Lucas Donner over here, to me."

Ten minutes passed before Lucas walked over hesitantly.

"This is your lucky day, Donner. I am going to give you a job. If you try to leave, the crew will hunt you down. You work hard enough and I'll see that you get fed. Do you understand me?"

"Yes Sir, Tom, I understand, but I'm no lumberjack. I don't think I can do this kind of work."

"You will do it, or starve!" Tom's face was red with anger and anxiety over what had happened to Ben, his friend. He was also still furious with Donner. "David, go get Gentle Fawn. Maybe she can assist Cookie in helping Ben." David jumped on the back of one of the thieves' horses and rode swiftly down Main Street. Gentle Fawn was up and busy when David knocked loudly on her front door.

"Gentle Fawn, please come quickly. A man is injured at the mill." Helen sat next door, on the front porch of the General Store sipping a cup of coffee.

"David, what has happened at the mill?" she called.

"Hello Helen, would you tell Anne and Stormy? I need to take Gentle Fawn right now."

"Yes, of course, but can't you at least tell me what has happened?" Gentle Fawn grabbed the handle of a bag she kept prepared for emergencies. David boosted her up in front of himself on the horse and away they went with no further conversation. Helen soon found out that the twins were fine and they made it quite clear that they were big enough to survive their mother's absence for a while.

Sam stepped out to the porch of the store, and when he saw Helen coming out of Gentle Fawn's front door he wanted to know what she was doing there.

"David took her to the mill. Apparently someone has been injured. I was just letting the children know that their mother would be gone for a little while. Have you noticed how tall Stormy is? He is nearly as tall as you are.

"Well, I hope it is not serious," said Sam, taking the closed sign from the window and getting the broom to sweep the porch.

Ben moaned but still hadn't opened his eyes. David was worried. He busied himself with retrieving the money from the boot and stuffing it in his food satchel. That's when he realized that he was also standing guard over the bag of blue stones that Chief Dark Wolf had brought to exchange for the cattle.

"Tom, I will be back in a few minutes." He climbed up on the seat of the wagon and headed toward Matt Morgan's shop. These poor tired boys need a little attention, he thought. He was glad when Matt stepped out where he could see him as he pulled up.

"Hi Matt, I have an exhausted team and I have to get back to the mill, but I need to share a few things with you first."

He sat down in the shop and told Matt the string of events that had left Ben unconscious and him at a worrisome state of mind. I don't want to put the stones or the money in the bank. Matt would you be willing to put them somewhere safe until I can sort all this out. I don't want to borrow a team and go out of town to get the bricks until I know that Ben is going to be alright."

"David, you have been up all night and you probably haven't eaten. Come over to the house and let Liz fix you something. I'll just turn these big boys into the field where they have plenty of feed and water. There you go boys," he swatted them on their huge rumps as they gladly walked through the gate. They were comfortable here. They had been here before and had always been treated well.

Reverend Brown pulled up in his buggy and David was glad to see him. Matt would it be alright if we invite Jim in for a few minutes? I would like him to lead us in prayer for Ben."

"What happened to Ben?" When he heard, Jim was immediately concerned. They gathered together and prayed intensely for Ben to recover. "I have a member of our church that is ill and I told them that I would come out, first thing this morning, so I must go now, but I will be back this afternoon and I will continue to pray for Ben as I travel. God bless you, too, David. You did the right thing by bringing him in as soon as you could. I will talk to you all later." He drove away slowly.

David stayed for a few minutes, and Liz managed to get him to eat a little and drink a cup of coffee.

"I have to head back. I have to know how Ben is doing." Matt followed him out the door and told him to take the little brown horse.

"She is a good little girl, she will let anyone ride. Just treat her gently. Her name is Betsy."

"Thanks Matt, I will." David slid up on her with just the reins and a blanket over her back. She trotted along as if she was happy to be of service. David put her near the river and tied her to the backside of the railing. It was there for that purpose. He wanted her to be able to reach both grass and water. He noticed that the two horses he had brought in were there and their saddles had been removed. David hurried across the street and into the gate of the mill. Many people stood around Cookies fire. Ben was still where he had been.

"How's Ben? Didn't he wake up yet?" David's voice had a sound of panic.

"David, do not yell. He opened his eyes for a few minutes and was able to tell us some of what happened. Now he is sleeping. I gave him a strong medicine. He should be moved to the sick tent. We will care for him there."

Gentle Fawn's voice was soft and soothing. She was reassuring in the way she spoke.

"I want two men to bring a cot. We will put him on it and move him that way." Tom immediately made it happen. She was his wife and he of all of them knew how well she used her healing skills. He had felt relief as soon as she arrived. "Do not let his head come up. Keep him level when you lift him on and also as you carry him." She directed the strong men as if they were boys. They did as she had instructed them.

Once Ben was placed in the tent, deep in the trees, it was much cooler. She covered him with a light blanket and then ripped a strip of cloth from the edge of a sheet. She wrapped it around his head, securing a poultice she had made from herbs and soft willow bark from her bag. Then she pulled another strip off and used it to wrap under the cot and after rolling him on his side she wrapped the cloth over his head and back under again and tied it. She did the same for his chest and then each arm. He was totally secured. I don't want him to be able to sit up. He needs to stay flat for a while." She folded a piece of cloth and slid it under his head as a thin pillow.

"Thank you Gentle Fawn, I will stay with him," said David.

"He will sleep for many hours now. When he wakes he needs someone to explain to him that he should stay flat. He may fight the bindings if he doesn't know."

"I will stay," said David, "he is family. I don't want to leave him."

Tom nodded to David and walked with Gentle Fawn back to the fire. Another cot and blanket were brought for him and David rested beside Ben with his hand on Ben's arm.

It was not long after, that Sarah and Jed rode through the gate of the Sawmill. They had stopped at the store just long enough to ask about someone being hurt. Then they left Helen standing with her mouth open.

"How could she possibly know that someone in town was injured when she was way out there at the ranch?"

"I don't know Helen, but I am going to go down there to see if we can offer any assistance," said Sam.

"Yes of course dear, and find out what is going on and who was injured. No one has stopped in here with any news at all today"

"Yes, I wonder why," he said it under his breath, but she suspected he had made some remark. He walked down Main Street feeling very disturbed.

Sarah, and Jed, rode swiftly stirring up dust. They both felt urgency in their spirits.

When David heard the added voices at the cooking fire in the center of camp, he glanced out of the tent.

"I am so glad you came to town. I was praying that somehow you would know that we needed you and you would come."

"David, are you alright?" Sarah wrapped him in a tight hug. She was glad to see that he was alright.

"Yes, I am fine, just tired. Ben is the one that took the blow to the head. Gentle Fawn has been aiding Cookie in caring for him."

"Thank you both," she said. "What have you been doing for him?" They quickly related that he was not awake when he arrived and that Cookie had used ice on his head.

"He came awake for a few minutes, but I wanted him to stay flat, so I gave him some strong sleep medicine. It is bad, Sarah. His head is still bleeding and there is nothing else that I know to do."

"It's alright Gentle Fawn; I am glad that you were here. I will take over. Where is he?"

"He is in the sick tent. I was with him until you came," said David.

"David, ask Cookie to measure two cups of water in a pan, and then add these. Boil it down to one cup" She handed him several small pouches. Bring it to me when it is ready. Leave all the herbs in it and I will use them. He should somehow drink the strong solution. Ask Cookie if he has any whiskey that I can use to sterilize the wound."

"You aren't going to believe this. Tom and the men poured nine barrels of the stuff into the Hickory."

"I certainly hope they saved some of it for me to use!" Tom handed her a bottle soon after and she asked if Gentle Fawn could come back in the tent with her. The two women talked and decided to do what needed to be done. They put a razor in the boiling water and a sharp knife. "I will need a needle and thread," said Sarah.

They gently rolled Ben to lay on his right side. The bindings were tightened again.

"If he moves at the wrong time, it could kill him."

"We should hurry. We can't allow him to wake up during it," said Gentle Fawn.

Sarah poured the whiskey over her hands and then over the back of Ben's head. She shaved a large patch where he was bleeding.

"Now we can see what has happened." Sarah cut the scalp away and peeled it down. Blood flowed. "His skull is cracked. We need to make a little hole so that the blood and fluid can drain away. I will need to drill and we need more whiskey."

Gentle Fawn returned quickly, still scared of the proposed action. She had never seen such a thing. She wondered if Sarah had.

"It will be hard to go through the bone and not touch his brain. I am sure that it is swollen. Put both your hands on his head; put one on the temple and one on his jawbone. If he moves, this will kill him. Hold him still no matter what, Gentle Fawn."

Sarah had been told by Singing Lark, but she had not seen it done either. She was not going to admit her inexperience now. Once again she poured the whiskey over the drill bit and the wound. Ben moaned.

"We must do it now. There is no time to think about it. Hold him still." Sarah pressed the drill against Ben's skull at the base of the crack and slowly turned the smooth, handle. The bit was small. She wondered if it was large enough to do the job. What if the blood plugs the hole right away, she worried. "Holy Spirit, you brought me here and I have been given knowledge of this process for this purpose. Help me, My Counselor, and give me confidence to do this right." The start of the third slow turn of the wooden handle produced a slight droplet of water and blood as she reversed the turn of the drill. "It is out. The fluid that is pressing against his brain is draining out. Look Gentle Fawn. We did it! With God's help we did it!"

Sarah and Gentle Fawn stayed with Ben through the night and into the next day. Many times Sarah inserted the tiny drill bit into the opening to make sure it stayed flowing.

She filled her mouth with the dreadfully bitter medicine and placed her lips over Ben's mouth while stroking his throat to force him to swallow. He slept on as she had intended.

Evening came and Tom insisted that the women come out into the night air. He sat down beside his friend on the cot and nearly screamed when he saw the shocking open wound on the back of Ben's head. The bright red tissue and exposed skull bone was almost more than he could accept. Then he noticed the little hole that seeped fluid.

"What have you done to him, Sarah? How can something that grotesque help a man to live?"

"I don't know Tom, but I believe it will help him. It has to work. There is nothing more any of us can do for him. I need to go talk to Cookie. I will be right back. I don't think he will stir, but if he does, place your hand here on his temple and keep him from moving."

She stepped out into the chilled night air and wished that she could enjoy the short, brisk walk to the campfire, but her mind was too troubled. David saw her approaching and jumped up to wrap her in his arms. Not until that moment had she allowed her mind to accept that this was Ben. Not just an injured hunter. Not for an instant had she allowed herself to think that she might lose the brother that she loved so much.

Her hands shook and her legs felt weak. She felt sick as the nausea brought up the portion of the medicine that she had unwillingly swallowed.

Cookie handed her a cup of water to rinse her mouth and then he handed her a cup of coffee that was rich with cream.

"Your stomach needs something in it. I saved food for you and Gentle Fawn. You take the coffee and I will warm up the food."

"Sarah, it took all the strength I have to keep his head still as he came awake. He understands that he must stay still. He is overwhelmed with pain. Hurry Sarah, do something," Tom shouted.

"Sarah, tell me what you will need and I will prepare it," said Gentle Fawn.

"Make the purple flowers into a strong potion that numbs the skin, and the infection fighting flowers, in a second batch, with the white ones that cause sleep and lots of willow bark. The willow bark will thin his blood and it will keep the hole dripping. That is what we want for now. David, please help her and bring them as soon as they are ready."

Cookie handed a quart canning jar to Sarah.

"I boiled this earlier. It is strong willow bark solution. Also, I have this made with the infection fighting flowers."

"Thank you Cookie. That will speed things up. Give them to Gentle Fawn. She knows what to do with them." David had water heating in two small pans. Sarah sat on the floor of the small tent with her hand on Ben's cheek.

"Ben, I am here. I will help you. God will heal you. I know He will. Ben I know it hurts terribly but you must endure it just a little while longer. Lay perfectly still. You must not move.

"Sarah? Sarah? Is that you? I thought they took you away. Sarah, they killed our parents! I couldn't find you, Sarah. I walked and yelled your name, but I couldn't find you. Where were you Sarah? Why did you hide from me?" He closed his eyes then and slept. Sarah's sobs could be heard outside the tent. She wasn't sure if he was sleeping naturally or from the medicine they had given him earlier, or worse than that, was he back unconscious? She knew that it was common for a person with a head injury to be incoherent, but his ramblings had been filled with such real grief and agony. She understood now how alone and frightened he had been that day.

Gentle Fawn and David both appeared at the opening to the tent. David held the tray that carried the medicines, bandages, a clean cup and spoon and the needle and thread she had asked for. He had placed the needle and thread in the liquid while it was boiling. Gentle Fawn had a wash cloth and towel for her and a plate of scrambled eggs, fried potatoes and a glass of cold milk.

"Sarah, you should eat before you do anything more. It will steady your hand and give you strength," she said. "Sit here and eat at least a little."

Sarah washed her face, hands and arms and dried them as if she were performing another procedure, and as she did, all signs of her raw emotions disappeared. She sat on the end of the cot and ate a small portion of the food, before handing the plate to David.

"I will eat later, when this is finished," she said.

With the excellence of her training, she sponged the back of Ben's head, again disinfecting it, and then numbed it with the solution that Gentle Fawn had made. With a steady hand, she sewed the scalp back in place, making a tiny slit at the bottom where she had drilled through the bone. She packed the external area with the soft herbs from both solutions and wrapped his head and bound the poultice in place.

"David I need him to drink some of each of these medicines. Let's see if you can wake him."

"Ben, Ben, wake up! Open your eyes. You need to take some medicine." Ben's eyes didn't open but he spoke quietly.

"If you promise me that you put some sugar or honey in it, I will drink it."

"Oh Ben, I am so glad that you are awake. I will spoon the medicine in your mouth. Don't try to sit up," said Sarah with a smile.

"Ben, how do you feel?"

"David wasn't smiling, his expression was grim and Ben noticed it right away when he finally opened his eyes.

"I have a horrific headache and my ears are ringing. What happened to me?"

Sarah took the opportunity to spoon the medicine in Ben's mouth while David kept him distracted with an answer.

"I don't know what you remember, but we were on our way to buy the bricks for the wells, when you figured out we were being followed. Do you remember?"

"Yes I think so. I got off the wagon with my rifle, but I can't remember anything after that."

"That's because they got around behind you and knocked you out. They hit you so hard that I was beginning to wonder if you were ever going to open those blue eyes of yours."

"How long have I been out?"

"Too long," answered Sarah. "Here take a little more of this before you fall asleep again." She quickly spooned more of each medicine in his mouth. "Cookie made you some beef broth. Take a bit of this and it will help to remove the bitter taste of the medicine."

His eyes closed slowly and he was once again in a sleep brought on by the medicine. She checked the back of his head and made sure that it was still draining.

"He will sleep like that the rest of the night. I think he is going to live," said Sarah softly. She placed a kiss on his cheek and noticed that his skin was very hot.

"He has a fever. The Willow bark will help bring that down."

Tom left the fire and talked to the men in the shed without opening the door.

"It looks like you won't be charged with murder. The man you hit over the head is going to live. I guess you will be able to tell the judge that you just assaulted and robbed him."

"What judge?"

Tom returned to the fire glad to see Sarah sitting there beside David.

"What you did in there Sarah, was amazing. How could you learn to do such a thing?"

"Singing Lark and Talking Mountain were good teachers. He made the drill that I used and the Holy Spirit guided me the whole time. I thank God for his presence in there. I couldn't have done it alone. Thank you, all of you for helping me."

"What else has to be done so he will get well?"

"Jed, I am sorry, I didn't mean to ignore you. I didn't realize that you were here still. Thank you for coming with me and believing me. He will need more of the medicines especially the willow bark solution and now he can have soup. He needs to eat to get back his strength, but I want to still keep him flat for another day or two, and I want to make sure that his injury continues to drain so that pressure isn't on his brain."

"You weren't ignoring me. You have been a little busy. Do you think it would be alright if David and I go get the bricks tomorrow? They will need them at the ranch. It is hard on Beth and Mary to have all of us gone. I think at least one of us should take the bricks home and let them know what has happened."

"Yes, you are right, of course. Mary is probably frantic. Tell them that I will bring him home when he is well enough to travel. You should go get the bricks and go to the ranch, both of you."

"David, we need to go get the team from Matt and the wagon so we can pull out at first light and not disturb his family then."

"I will come with you." They retrieved the money, wagon, and team, but asked Matt to hold the blue stones until they came back through with the bricks.

At first light, they discovered that Tom had asked one of his crew to ride along with them as an escort.

"It doesn't hurt to be extra careful."

"Thanks Tom, but how many men like those two could be in Silverville?"

"I hope no more but it will make me feel better if he goes along and rides flank."

Cookie had taken care to see that they had more than enough provisions and they were underway after a quick check on Ben to be sure he was improving. Sarah was in with him and had changed his bandage and given him some rich broth and another big dose of the medicines.

"His fever is less than it was. I am going to keep him flat yet today, but maybe he can sit up a little tomorrow," she said. "Be careful and stay safe."

Jed and David felt that Ben was slowly recovering and they were glad that someone with Sarah's skills had been there when he needed her. David respected her and loved her. He knew what a special person his wife was.

When Frank Donaldson came to greet the two men, his hand shake was firm and his smile was friendly. They walked with him admiring what he had achieved in the two years he had been there.

"Your prices seem fair," said Jed. "I have never purchased bricks before, but I can appreciate all the work that goes into their making." Donaldson asked if they had a crew that was coming to load the bricks, and whether they had another wagon and team on the way.

"No, we were hoping that we could get some help from you and the men here."

"Well, I pay these men to work for me," he said. "If they are going to work for you, you will need to pay me."

"How much do you charge?"

"Three dollars each man and since you only brought two horses, you are going to only be able to take half of that order. Bricks are heavy and there is no use breaking a horse's back to haul a load that's too heavy. I have another wagon and team you can rent if you want, but I charge by the day."

They turned away and talked privately for a moment.

"I think we are running into the side of this man that Tom said was difficult to abide," said Jed quietly to David.

"We will rent the extra wagon and team and I'll pay one of your men to drive it and bring it back when it is unloaded."

By the time they had the bricks loaded and were on their way, Frank Donaldson had proven to be a very shrewd business man. He had a fee or price on everything. Tom's crewman rode shotgun on the second wagon and as they traveled along, he found that Mr. Donaldson treated his men and animals the same way he treated his customers.

They rested along the trail and moved on again at first light.

When the wagons of bricks were across from the mill, they were stopped by the Hickory and the teams unhooked so they could eat, drink and rest. The men were delighted to see Ben, sitting in the shade on a chair with a tray on his lap. He was having a small bowl of Cookie's wonderful stew.

Sarah was sitting on a blanket near him watching his every move. They could see that his movements were slow and measured. He was eating with his right hand but his left hand was just hanging beside him. He gave them a small crooked smile as they approached.

"I didn't make it all the way back yet," he said. "Half of me didn't wake up yet."

"Sarah what is he talking about? Is something wrong?"

"He has no feeling or control in his left side." The tray on his lap started to slip and she quickly adjusted it. He can't feel half the tray, so he has trouble keeping it on his lap. I don't know what to do to fix him. I don't know how to treat this!" A tear made its way slowly down her cheek. She took the tray and walked away. Both men sat down on the grass next to Ben.

"Ben, we have the bricks. It took nearly all the money. Tom was right. Frank Donaldson is a hard man to deal with."

"I am sorry," he said. "I can't help with anything right now. What will happen to the ranch if I can't work?"

"It will be there when you are ready to work and well enough to do it. Don't think about anything but getting well. The men are at the ranch and our women and Orville are watching over everything. The work is all getting done. It may not be exactly as you would have done it, but it will be good enough to satisfy Mr. Cantwell or Mr. Williams when they come with the inspector. I promise you Ben. It is going to be fine."

Tom greeted them cheerily.

"I just offered Frank Donaldson's driver a job. He accepted. He will take the bricks to the ranch and return the man's horses and wagon and then he is coming here to work. Stubby, is going back and ask for a pay raise and when he doesn't get it, he says he will come back here and work for me." Tom said it with a smile.

Sarah approached the group of men and said that she had borrowed the Reverend's buggy and she and Ben would be going to the ranch in the morning.

"That's great Sarah. We want to leave at sun up with the bricks. We have to go the long way."

"I will get Ben ready. He will be home by late tomorrow afternoon." They noticed that she had the buggy seat and back padded with blankets and she had asked Matt to fasten a long, wide strap and buckle to secure him in place. "I might not be able to keep him from falling if he tips. The strap will prevent that," she explained.

"That was a good idea Sarah. Is there anything we can do to help you?"

"Just pray that he can overcome this. Thank you, all of you for your help and prayers."

CHAPTER ELEVEN
EXCITEMENT IN THE AIR

The Chief was glad to see the last of the purchased cattle enter the gate as he sat on his horse and watched. They circled, milling around the fence enclosing them but soon settled down realizing that one fence was much like another. They were tired from their journey.

"It is good to see many cattle here. I hope they will multiply fast. I don't like trying to keep track of them and bring them across the prairie," said Growling Bear. "I wish he had sold us the white one. It was beautiful, but I understand why he didn't."

"I noticed when he turned it back that it was not completely white. It had a small patch of brown on its back leg."

"Growling Bear, I was wrong and it is good that Ben was not afraid to speak up and say so. We don't need or want symbols of the old ways. We are The Blue Stone People now, and once again, because we honor the Great Spirit, we prosper."

Brother Tim had returned to camp a day earlier. He had spent all his time since his return, under the shade pavilion, with the children, the story mothers and Clover.

"I have to leave again in the morning. I will be taking our big work horses to the ranch. They need them to move the logs to build the cabins. I won't be back until the cabins are built and wells dug. I will miss all of you." He included everyone in his statement, but he was looking at Clover when he said it.

"We will all miss you, too," replied Clover.

As he walked away, one of the grandmothers giggled and murmured that it was too bad that such a handsome man was married to the church.

"Clover, guard your heart. It could get broken by that one."

"Yes, I know, it already is hurting."

*****

The trip from the Sawmill was long and stressful.

The men with the wagons loaded with bricks were not able to use the bridge across the Silver. They had to take the long way. At the last minute they realized that David should ride Jed's horse and accompany the buggy. Sarah needed his help to lift Ben down into the shade of the trees along the Hickory when they took frequent breaks. Moon Boy, The horse that she had ridden had been waiting for them at Matt's. Now he followed along behind on a long lead. They had stopped there briefly to keep Matt informed and to collect the pouch of blue stones.

"The ranch is going to have to pay for extra rent on that wagon and team. They are moving slowly. They looked too old to be pulling any load. Maybe we will be buying some more misused work horses. What do you think of starting a retirement home for old work horses?"

"Are you serious?" Sarah was smiling.

"I was kidding when I said it, but you know it would be a good thing to turn them out on that extra piece of land Ben bought for us. They would keep all the grass and brush down and maybe they would have a foal. I could put some farm fence around it and make a shelter."

"What makes you think they are females?"

"I heard him say that they were. He was fussing about them being cantankerous females, when he was hitching them up."

"It is something to keep in mind. If you want to try to buy them, I wouldn't object. The poor old girls may be too old to have a foal."

Ben woke up with a yawn.

"What did you say about a foal? It is the wrong time of year for foals."

"Yes, Ben it is. I have been thinking about Blaze and Star though. You bred those both with Dart Away. Dash away is the son of Blaze. You can't use him to breed with any females we get from her or star. You are going to have to find another thoroughbred stud somewhere for them."

"Jed said that he saw one at the rail in the fort that was pretty nice. He hasn't had time to do anything about it."

The Parker place came into view and the men came out of the trees to greet them.

"Ben, you have been gone longer than we thought you would. We are ready for those bricks. We hit water yesterday and the hole is about half full."

"How far down is it," asked David?

"I am not sure but it is at least the height of two men and a little more. The water is muddy now, but once we get it lined it should clear up."

"I am not sure how that is done with water already in it. Does anybody here know how to lay bricks under water?"

They all started laughing and didn't stop until Ben asked how they were doing with the cabin as he struggled with his right hand to balance against the buckle supporting him.

"Please pull the buggy up where I can see how the cabin is coming along." Joshua rushed over and gave him a hug.

"Dad, I didn't know you were hurt. What happened to your arm? Are you alright?"

"Yes, I have quite a story to tell when we have time. When did you come back down here?" Sarah asked.

"I came just this morning after chores but I will be going back soon to help with the milking."

"That's good, Josh. Look Sarah, look David, the cabin is more than halfway up. I am amazed! You men have done such a good job. The corners are perfectly aligned and the logs are marked for the fireplace and the door and window. You are either very fast or I have been gone longer than I thought!" David shifted his feet showing his discomfort at the comment.

"We are glad that you are pleased with the work Ben, but we are sorry to see that you are injured."

"I will be fine. Have you still got enough provisions?"

"Yes, Willow came down yesterday and brought us food. We like the cheese and the beef they brought to put over the fire is nice and tender. All the women at the ranch are good cooks. They made sure we are well fed."

"That's good," said David. "I will be back as soon as I can and try to help all I can." They moved away slowly.

As the men watched the buggy make a circle they realized that Ben's injury was not what they could understand. His words had been understandable but he didn't sound quite the same. Now they observed the down turn of his mouth and understood the limp arm and strap that held him safely on the seat. Joshua jumped on his horse and followed, riding beside David.

"What happened to Dad," he asked quietly.

"We got robbed, heading out to the brick yard. He got hit on the head. He was unconscious for days. Thank God Sarah sensed it and came or he would be dead."

"I meant what happened to his arm and face."

"I don't know Josh. I am sure it has to do with something inside his head being damaged. I am hoping that with time he will get his feeling and control back." Ben had fallen asleep again and Sarah had eased a small pillow under the side of his head so it could rest on his shoulder. They traveled along without conversation for a while as Joshua absorbed what he had been told.

Shock showed on Joshua's face as he tried to deal with the news.

"Did you or Jed catch the guys that did this?"

"Yes, I did. They are being held in a tool shed at Tom's lumber mill. He has sent for the Federal Marshall. The people voted and they are building a jail and plan to get a sheriff."

"That's good, but it won't help Dad. What about the bricks? Did they get ordered? Is the man sending them soon?

"Yes, we got the bricks and they are so heavy that we had to rent a wagon and team to bring the second half of the load.

They have to come the long way, but they should be here tomorrow. Jed is with them, and they will stop here first. You and I should help with the morning milking and then we can come back here."

"That's sounds like a good plan to me," said Josh.

As they made their way across Jed's pasture, they stopped just long enough to check on the progress of that well and see the cabin. Two Feathers had done as much as he could by measuring the logs and cutting them the right length to accommodate the window and the door. He had sent a man to get Calvin Briggs and the fireplace was already taking shape. The additional work horses from the herd at the camp arrived the day before and Tim had left two with him. He had the medium size wagon and took two horses to David's and brought back the log ramp. He and Pine Berry had arrived with it, just two hours before they did. The women had sent them to get it. Beth was sure it would be alright to bring it down where it was needed. The bottom row was in place, but now they were looking a little hesitant as to how it worked. David said he would be right back.

"Take a break and have something to eat. I will help get this thing in motion and we will work until dark." He said it with a smile.

"I can see the oak ahead Ben. You are nearly home," said Sarah to wake him.

"I'm not eager to get there," he said dejectedly. "I don't want Mary or the kids to see me like this."

"Ben they will be so happy you are back that they won't care about your problem. You know you will get better. Just keep saying that, to them and yourself."

They heard the bell clang loudly three times.

"That's a happy sound," said Ben. Sarah pulled the buggy up under the oak tree and lined it up to the spot where the big raft waited. David unhooked the buggy horse and Josh helped him maneuver the buggy onto the raft. Josh rode across the river on his horse leading the Reverend's buggy horse and Moon Boy. The buggy horse reared and Josh found he had all he could do to handle him in the water.

"I guess he prefers dry land," he said. They all chuckled. Mary watched as the horse was backed up to the buggy and hooked back up.

As soon as the buggy was up on the dry path, everyone converged on Ben, giving hugs and kisses.

"Ben, when Sarah and Jed left here in a hurry, we were all afraid that you or David had been killed. We have been praying all the time you have been gone. Thank God you are alright."

Ben looked at her with sad eyes.

"Mary, I am only half a man! My left side doesn't work! I can't feel it. I can't touch you or hug you with it. I can't walk!

He started to cry and so did she. She held him close and whispered so only he could hear.

"I will help you get well. You will be whole again and I have you back and I will hold you tight until you can hold me with both arms again. I love you so much Ben. Thank you for coming back to me." She stepped up onto the buggy and sat on his lap, and wrapped her arms around him. It was then that she saw the bandage on the back of his head. "My poor darling, I am so sorry that this happened to you."

"Take us home, Sarah. My man has come back to me!" Joshua rode ahead to open the front door. David came up beside the buggy to help Mary back down. Sarah hopped down and came around to help. The children had all followed the slow moving buggy, filling the air with giggles and happy sounds, talking loudly. It was a celebration of sorts. Ben needn't have worried. His families' love would overcome his handicap, whether temporary or permanent.

As strong as David was, it wasn't hard for him to take Ben up the steps and into the house.

"Where would you like to sit down Ben?"

"Put me by the window so I can see the third cabin. David would you go find out how they are doing with the well and tell Orville, that I am home."

"Sure Ben, are you fine there until I come back?"

"Yes he is," answered Mary and Beth at the same time.

They brought him a wet cloth to wipe his hands and brought him a tray of meat bites, cheese, and bites of bread and butter. A glass of milk was set on the window sill where he could reach it with his right hand. David and Orville came in and Ben announced quite formally, we are going to have a family meeting right now. I know you all have questions. I am willing to answer them if I can." Eli, Natty and Adam sat on the floor as near as they could. Johnny and Lily sat near their

Aunt Sarah. Lori and Mark settled on the floor with Joshua pulling up a couple benches to accommodate the rest. Mary produced a pencil and paper and handed them to Beth. She handed them right back.

"Here, you are better at this than I would ever be."

"This meeting of the S and J Ranch will come to order," said Beth with a smile. "Ben was there something you wanted to talk about?" She said it with a teasing smile.

"In spite of a few setbacks, we are going to get our projects done!" Everyone cheered and applauded. "The lake area has proved what hard workers everyone here is and how willing we all are to fight adversity. The water flowing through the canal is fresh river water. Thank you David, for your help with the dynamite to turn the water away from the salt bed, and Thank you God for healing his ears, when he got injured blasting the rocks to open the canal here. Thank you, all of you for working so hard while David and I were gone to buy the bricks. The wells and cabins will be done before the ground freezes and the bricks are on the way. We had a bit of trouble on our way there and two men thought they would rob us of the money we were carrying, but David saved the day and took them to Tom's and they are in a tool shed locked up until a marshal comes to Silverville. I did get hit on the back of my head by one of them and unfortunately I took a rather long nap as a result. Sarah came and did her best to get me well, but as you can see only half my brain is able to tell that I have a hand and arm that need to work so I have to show patience while the rest of it heals. I am not hurting. The back of my head is tender and that bandage is just to protect it so I don't bump it. Now are there any questions?"

"I have one," said Johnny. Do you and Dad think it would be alright if we ordered a manure spreader?" We talked about it but we didn't get one."

"Yes, we talked about that. We definitely need to get one. If we can get our order on the mail boat before it stops its route for the winter, we would probably get it first thing in the spring."

"When are we going to go to the fort to see if we can buy a new mate for Blaze? I would like to go along," said Adam.

David spoke up then and said that he thought maybe that should wait until their next meeting.

"Let's all get back to our chores now. I promised Two Feathers that I would come right back. That was a long time ago. If it is alright with Ben, this meeting is over."

"It's not alright," said Ben. "Mary, please bring me the Bible. We have all lost track of the days. We have allowed ourselves to be too busy. The Bible has a great deal to say about stewardship and I think we are losing sight of why we are doing all this. In Exodus 25: 1 & 2 NIV "The Lord said to Moses, "Tell the Israelites to bring me an offering. You are to receive the offering for me from everyone whose heart prompts them to give."

"God has given us so much. I want each of you to pray about what we should be giving back and how, and also to please pray for me. Now back to the chores," he said with a small chuckle directed at David.

The house emptied like the plate of fresh baked cookies that Mary had placed on the table as they all arrived.

"Mary smiled at Ben and asked if he wanted to lie down or sit out on the porch with her for a while. I think I would like to go out and spend some time with you. I have missed you, Mary, and if we sit out there we can watch them work on the cabin."

"I will just stir this big pot and then Sarah and I will give you a little help. Sarah stepped out onto the porch and padded the bench with a quilt. It has a high back on it and arm rests. That should work for him. The two women snuggled close to him and locked their arms behind him and across his chest. They eased him up and took him out, finding it very difficult. They sat with him until the sun lowered enough to be in their eyes. Mary went in and brought him out a wide brimmed hat.

"This may be too tight across the bandage, so let's put it just loosely on top of your head to protect your eyes. There, is that alright?"

"It's fine Mary."

"We have a few things to finish up for the meal in the barn. The people will be coming soon. Here is a cup of tea, Ben. I will put it on this stand by your right hand so you can reach it easily. Are you getting tired?"

"No, I think I will be fine. Go do what you need to."

When they got in the kitchen, Sarah finally had an opportunity to ask Mary if somehow she had found out about Ben's condition before they arrived.

"Yes, Calvin came to the ranch and told all of us what happened and what Ben was going through. He was really good about talking to the children and explaining to them that they should just love him and not ask questions about his arm or leg and that in time maybe it would get better. He told them that the more they loved him and prayed for him, the sooner he would be well."

"You were all so good, and no one seemed shocked so I thought that possibly somehow you had been told. Calvin is a good man. The way you greeted Ben was the best medicine possible. I am going to get one of the men to help take him to the barn. I think we should include him in all that he can handle." Sarah hustled down the steps and told Ben she wanted to go see her third cabin. He laughed.

"You better move back into the first one so you can stay here and baby me!" He yelled it so she could hear him. She was laughing, too. There is no way we are going to baby you, She thought. You will walk again. You have to!

Two Feathers left the pasture area and rode down to the Parker Place to compare the progress they were making with that of the other locations. He knew that the arrival of Ben in his physical condition would require David's time for longer than just a few minutes. He was amazed to see two men standing in chest high water, in the well, dipping buckets and sending them up quickly on ropes to be emptied.

"Hello down there," he said with a laugh.

"Hi Two Feathers. We are emptying this thing as fast as we can but it seems to be filling up almost as fast as we dip it out."

"Debon, how full did it get before they started?"

"It got up to ground level during the night. They have been trying to get it empty so they can make a base with river rocks. That's what the pile nearby is for. The water is coming in about a foot from the bottom they are standing on and oddly it is coming from the north. I thought that it would start trickling in on the side of the river, but that's not what happened."

"That is good. They have hit an underground stream that flows to the river. The water will be cool and good," said Two Feathers smiling. "You must be very cold. Come out of there. I have an idea." Gladly the men climbed out without being urged. "We need to do in this well, what you did in Ben's lake. We need to give the water somewhere to temporarily flow, while the rest of the well is bricked. Then we will remove the pipe and let it fill naturally."

"There is a pipe over there against the trees just outside the cattle fence. It was to be inside the chimney of the cabin that burned. It is six or eight inches across. Is that too big?" Debon asked.

"That should work. You two go get dry clothes on and let me think a minute." They gathered near the small fire and soon Two Feathers had retrieved the stove pipe. It was rusted, but would work for his temporary need. He jumped into the well swimming down to the bottom with the pipe. He could feel the slight stirring of the incoming water. His lungs were screaming for air! With his last bit of willpower, he pushed the pipe into the hole before coming up for a gulp of air. His second try forced it further into the soft mud surrounding the flow of water. Up he came again.

"Is there any more pipes?" After searching in the grass, they found a second section and it was forced over the first part. Finally a greased hide was used to channel the water coming up in the pipe to the shoulder of the well and that channeled it away in the grass. A loud cheer met Two Feathers as he managed to climb up and out. Calvin looked at the well full of muddy water and wondered what they planned to do now.

Once again two men with buckets plunged in and the ladder was removed to give them more room to work. This time they could see constant progress as the water level dropped around the pipe.

"You have done a good thing Two Feathers! I would not have ever thought of that," said Calvin.

"What do you intend to do when it gets empty?"

"I will let them figure that part out. They said the bricks will come tomorrow. By then they will probably be ready for them. I am going to go work on the fireplace." He strolled away smiling as if he had a secret. He was thinking that Two Feathers was the cleverest man he had ever met.

"I am heading back now. I just wanted to see how you are doing," said Two Feathers. He rode Friend at a steady pace and was back at the pasture work site before work had seriously begun with the log rack. David had two big work horses there that Tim had brought and was trying to get one of them to understand what was needed.

"Tim, this big guy just doesn't understand that he has to hold the log there long enough for us to peg it. As soon as we let him stop pulling forward, he backs up from the pressure on the ropes."

"Let me try," said Tim. He coaxed the horse to move the log into position as before but then Tim grasped the harness and scratched while whispering in his ear. With just a few spikes in place, the ropes were released from the log and he had done what was needed. "Let's use this one just for moving the logs up the ramp. The other one can pull them into place at the bottom. That way neither of them has to learn the whole process. I wish I knew his name," said Tim as he gave him a small piece of sugar. Tim had gotten in the habit of carrying lumps of sugar while training Jack, his own horse. Now it was just something he did. Every once in a while it proved useful.

"We are ready if you are," said one of the men and once again Tim led him gently moving the log in place, but this time as he held near the bit, he gave him the smallest sprinkle of sugar in the corner of his mouth, which entertained him until the ropes became slack. They managed to get the second row of logs in place without a problem. It was then that Tim happened to glance down at the feet of the horse he was working with.

"Stop, don't make them do another thing until we have Matt fix their feet. Look at this poor guy's foot." When the men gathered around they could see that he had a split hoof and one foot had two nails but no shoe on at all. He checked the other horse. It had shoes, but they were loose and not properly seated.

"I am heading to Silverville to get Matt Morgan. Please don't use these horses until he has been able to come and do what he can for them. We need him to look at the other work horses, too. We don't want to be cruel."

Two Feathers patted the big horse's neck and led him to the edge of the river and tied him there. He asked them to do the same with the other one.

Tim rode across to tell Ben what was happening.

"Please check the feet of the horses that they are using at the Parker place as you go by," said Ben. "I never thought about the fact that the horses that are at the camp are not being worked by farmers that know how to maintain them."

"That's just it Ben, they aren't being worked at all. I will take the Reverend's buggy back to him for you if you want me to. I just came over to let you know that I was going, in case there was something else you needed.

"I will make sure all the horses get checked. I am glad that you are home, Ben. I am really sorry about what happened to you."

"Thanks Tim."

David felt disgruntled when he saw that work on the cabin had come to a sudden halt but he understood.

"Let's concentrate on the well. The bricks will come tomorrow and until then we should be able to use one of my horses to work on the cabin. They have had good care and they are wearing good shoes. Meanwhile we can gather river rocks for the fireplace and chimney. There is plenty to do without misusing those big guys."

"I guess we could use one of the bigger ranch horses to move one of the wagons." Just a few minutes later the men were working at gathering smooth river rocks and two of them were digging in the well while still another was bringing the available wagon to haul the rocks for the fireplace.

Matt was pleased when he heard Tim's request. He had wanted somehow to help but didn't want to go to the ranch with so much going on if he wasn't needed. He loaded his Ferrier's tools into a supply wagon and together he and Tim were able to load a small but very heavy anvil on the back. He placed a box filled with horse shoes in varying sizes beside the snack that Liz had provided for them and they were quickly on their way.

By nightfall Matt and Tim pulled into the circle of light that the fire provided at the Parker place.

"The progress you have made here in such a short time is amazing! That's going to be a snug little cabin."

"Yes and the men have hit water in the well and the flow is strong. We had to put a pipe in there so that we could contain it until it is bricked." Tim rinsed a coffee cup and filled it with the water flowing from the pipe and drank from it.

"This is good water. These wells will be worth more each year as people build along the river. Who knows what is being poured in upstream? Not everybody pours in barrels of Kentucky whiskey!" The men nodded and laughed. All of them settled close to the fire, anticipating hearing a good story. Matt told it with relish and embellished the tale making the barrels emptying into the river, the main theme.

"I am glad that Tom bought that man out. I thought that saloon would be trouble when I heard about it," said Matt. The men sat quietly for a moment listening to the sounds of the night and the pleasant crackle of the fire.

"The nights are growing colder. I am glad that we have the tents to crawl into to break the wind," said Soren.

"I doubt if any of us will sleep late," but be warned, "I will be putting shoes on any of the horses here that need them before we pull out. It is a noisy process. I will check the shoes of all your horses in the morning. They will fare much better this winter if their feet are in good shape. You don't need to worry about paying me either. I am doing this for Ben. I wish I could do more to help him." The men nodded.

"We appreciate it. We all feel that way. I don't understand what happened to him. Do you?" Mark asked.

"No, not completely, but I know that thief hit him so hard that he cracked Ben's skull. He damaged his brain and if he ever can move his hand or walk it is going to be because God listened as lots of people prayed for him every day."

"Well I have been praying and so have my sister Lori and everyone else at the ranch," he said sincerely.

Tim asked them to pray with him then before they turned in for the night. The dark sky covered the moon with heavy clouds as he quietly sent their petition to God.

"Also, please Father God, hold off the winter snows until the wells and cabins are done." The men added a loud "Amen" to that and then quickly got into their bedrolls. Matt and Tim were glad that Liz had insisted they take heavy bedding. With most of the tools set on the ground, underneath, they made a bed in the wagon. The sides of it helped to block some of the cold wind that made them shiver.

*****

Matt and Tim checked all the horses and were well on their way to Jed's pasture when Tim said he wanted to tell Matt something but he didn't want him to tell anyone else.

"Promise me that you won't say anything to anyone."

"Sure Tim, I promise. What's bothering you?"

"I have been praying about this for months and I think I have decided. I am not going back to the seminary. I am going to ask one of the women of the camp to marry me and I want to go with Two Feathers and Willow."

"Tim, are you sure? That will be a big change for you! Does Father Bob know what you are thinking about?"

"No, I don't think he has any idea, but I think Chief Dark Wolf suspects."

"Tell me about the woman. She must really be something special."

"Matt, she is strong, and beautiful. She has three children; one of them is just a baby that she had after she got to the camp. She is one of the women that were rescued by The Chosen. I know that you know about that because you made the shields for the men that went."

"Yes, I do Tim, and I am so happy for you. I think God moves people where they need to be to do his work. It is wonderful that he brought you all the way out here to give you a wife and three children. She survived for a reason. Maybe you are the reason."

"I never thought of it that way. Thanks Matt."

"Look Tim, I can see Jed's pasture already. This ride has seemed short. I was well entertained by your news. I promise again, that I won't say a word. Whatever you decide, I want you to know that Liz and I will be praying for you."

"Thanks Matt." Tim was smiling when he jumped down from the wagon and approached the working men. He felt so much better now that he had been able to tell someone, and his news was met with approval.

"Matt and Tim, we are glad to see you. We haven't used the horses since Tim noticed the condition of their feet. We sure will be glad to have them ready to work. Thanks for coming out here Matt."

"David, I am glad to be able to help. I am so sorry about Ben. Liz and I have been praying for his healing ever since we found out."

Matt walked over to the first big horse and led him away from the water, up onto the prairie sod where it would be easier for him to work. With his fire going and a man helping to keep it hot, soon the sound of his hammer on metal shoes could be heard. Matt reinforced the cracked hoof with a metal band and put on a set of new shoes. The next big horse was a little easier. Matt pulled the two nails out and ground down the hoof before fitting him also with four new shoes.

"Now give these guys until tomorrow morning to get used to their shoes and they will be happy to work." He checked all the horses and found several from the herd of the people that were without shoes. He explained to Two Feathers the importance of what he was doing and that they would need replacing from time to time, depending on how much they ran on rough ground and rocks.

"These shoes are at no charge to you. I am doing this for Ben, but bring your horses to Silverville and I will put on four new shoes for one small blue stone the size of my nail." He indicated his index fingernail.

"It is good. We will do that," said Two Feathers.

CHAPTER TWELVE
SUCCESS AND FAILURE

The men worked hard with the cold hurting their fingers and toes as the days went by. Calvin was pleased with the well the men had finished on the Parker place. The river rock bottom and brick sides left safe margins for the water to balance out its pressure and continue on its way underground to feed the Hickory River, but in the well, with the stove pipe removed, it filled the space three quarters of the way up. The support posts were inserted and the crank attached. The rope and bucket were put in place and Calvin lowered it for its first official fill from the new well. A cheer went up as each man dipped a cup into the very cold water and took a sip. Calvin praised their work and said he could not have done better. That was high praise.

Debon and Soren walked over to their bedrolls and scooped them up at the same time.

"We may not have the roof completed yet, but the walls of the cabin make it warmer in there. Calvin, let's put a fire in that little fireplace you built and we can sit in there tonight."

"Just remember, that the rocks could explode if you get generous with the wood. That fire must stay very small until all the rocks dry out."

"We know that, but even so, I think it will be warmer." The men all took their bedrolls in and arranged them as close to the little flame as possible. Soren said he was glad that they were nearing the end of their job. "I want to take Cumae back to the village and see Obona. We have been gone a long time."

"Yes, we are all eager to finish and go home. You know that our tents are going to feel small inside after working on the cabin and being at the ranch in their barns; and the houses are so big."

"I am thinking that Two Feathers will be glad to be back in our camp, too. He has a second wife and children to miss," said Debon laughing. I have been missing Sheltah. She is a good wife. That was a clever idea she had. The women worked very hard making the sheets of clay for the canal."

"The woman that worked with her, they call Lori. I think she would make a good wife," said White Grass.

"Be careful, where you look, White Grass. She is a white woman and full grown. She would make you learn her ways. Things are changing fast. I think the women of the Lion are all going to want to have big houses like this cabin. We may just be learning how to build these so we can make some for our own use." They couldn't see the frown on Mark's face in the dark room. He was not pleased to have his sister the subject of their conversation.

The other crews had accomplished similar progress. Matt and Tim worked on the horses at each cabin site

"I wonder what Chief Dark Wolf would think if we started building cabins?" Night Hawk was kidding, but some of the men had been thinking the same thing. Night Hawk was older than the other men that followed Two Feathers. He didn't consider himself one of Two Feathers' men and yet he found himself here working beside him. He thought of himself as just being supportive and helping get the work done for Ben. He didn't know that Two Feathers held him in high regard and thought of him as his wise council.

"When work is finished here and we are free to leave, I would like you to ride with some of us to the land that Ben has represented on these special papers," said Two Feathers, carefully pulling the deeds from his satchel.

"I would be much honored to go with you to see the land," said Night Hawk but I think all of the people that came with you, will want to go to see it."

When the horses had been carefully examined by Matt and their shoes repaired or replaced, work quickly resumed on the cabin on Jed's place. The bricks were placed in the well as the men dug down. No one had to endure the freezing water until the last day, when the river rock bottom was installed and the ladder aided the last man out of the filling well. Their efforts were met with applause and cheers and Jed lowered the bucket for the first fill. He was glad to be back and to see the men expertly building the last rows of the walls of his cabin. Jed had asked Josh and one of the men to go to the Sawmill to ask Tom to send the planks for the roofs and the wood shingles right away. Josh was accepting more responsibility and he didn't disappoint.

Once the needed supplies were on hand, all three cabins were finally finished within the next few days.

Adam came racing with the good news that Orville's well was done and the water was good! David had worked on the fireplace for Jed's cabin in the pasture, and he and Jed finished Orville's the same day that the crew arrived from the Parker place. They announced that they thought the place would pass anyone's inspection. Ben wanted to see it. Jed had not had time to think about accommodations for Ben's condition, but Orville had made the time to build a small wagon with high wheels and a seat with high armrests and a back and seat that were padded. He had attached the leather belt to secure Ben in place.

During his visit, Matt had helped with adapting the wheels of the medium size wagon to the frame of this new cart. It sat high enough that Ben could cross the river with it, as long as he went slowly. Getting up on the seat was solved by Orville. He built a ramp that Ben could pull himself up by resting his side on a padded rail while swinging his left side forward. Once he was up in the seat, with a minimum of help, he could move about the ranch and all the property. His attitude was good and he grew stronger. Queen turned out to be the best horse to use. She was patient and enjoyed moving about the ranch pulling Ben's cart.

Sarah and David had taken temporary residence in her original cabin. Pili, was walking now and busy getting into everything that she could reach. Sarah encouraged a rugged exercise routine for Ben, knowing that it was his only chance to regain the muscles that were not responding. She made him sit in hot tubs of water, before and after the sessions. He objected, saying that no man in the history of the earth ever took so many baths but he did it, because he knew she was doing all she could to help him.

One day, nearly a month after he had returned home, he yelled for her to look at his hand. He was moving his left thumb! As the days went by she didn't see any further progress although they faithfully followed the routine.

One evening, Orville brought in a big bottle of horse liniment and asked if he was willing to try it, Ben said he would.

"It's strong, and it might sting. It will bring the blood to the skin and surface muscles, Ben."

"It won't sting, Orville, I can't feel that side at all. Oh, my, wait a minute. It's hot Orville! Ouch! Oh, it is hot and stinging. I can feel it Orville! Quick get Sarah. She needs to be here." Ben sat in his living room wearing only trousers that they had hastily helped him pull on, with Josh and Mary near him. Adam and Natty and Eli were on the floor by his feet, when Sarah and David rushed in with Orville. She plopped Pili in Josh's arms and took both of Ben's hands.

"This is it, Ben. This is why we have been working so hard! Children move. Stand up Ben! Stand up now and feel your feet on the floor and your hands touching mine. Do it Ben, stand up and thank God that you are getting well! Take a step Ben. Take a step," she shouted. His Body was shaking as she pulled and lifted him from the chair, forcing him to step forward on his right foot to keep from falling forward. Then slowly he dragged the left one to support himself. "Step with the left one Ben. Do it now!" She could feel both his hands gripping hers as he moved his left foot forward and then his right. "Again, again, do it again, Ben." Everyone held their breath as he moved forward. "Ben, you are walking and you are holding my hands."

"Thank you Jesus," shouted Orville. "Who would think that God would use horse liniment?" Mary took Sarah's place and held Ben's hands as he slowly shuffled around the room.

"Ben, you are well! Hold me Ben. Hold me with both arms!"

He wrapped his arms around her and everyone in the room was feeling tears spill onto their cheeks as Ben rocked from left to right, holding Mary tightly and thanking God.

"It is a miracle to hold you and feel you against me again. Mary, I am getting well and I will do the exercises and baths and not complain anymore. Thank you, Sarah, for not giving up on me. Thank you Orville, for caring enough to try that horrible liniment! I need a bath! That stuff stinks!" He was laughing and crying at the same time and so were the rest of the loved ones in the room.

*****

The projects were finished and Ben, Jed, Beth, Josh, Adam, Mary, Sarah, David and Orville all rode together to visit all three new cabins.

Ben was using his little cart, but soon he would feel comfortable riding on Buddy again.

Many of The People of the Lion that had worked so hard rode with them and after they had visited all three places, the women announced that there would be a celebration in Ben's barn as soon as they could get it prepared.

Both kitchens were full of women cooking, baking, laughing, and talking. Lori and Sylvia had become good friends with the young women of the Lion and dreaded the thought of them all returning to their lives in the village. The time at the ranch had been exciting and stimulating. It had opened their eyes to many new things.

The barn was warm and filled with people and good food. The fire burned in the pit, keeping huge kettles hot while lanterns hung high to light every corner.

"You all know that we must leave in the morning," said Two Feathers. We have finished what we came here to do and now it is time to go back to the village before we are plowing our horses through snow drifts. God has been kind and he has held off the snow so that we could finish our work without that hardship. Ben, we are all joyous that you are healing and getting strong again. We praise God that David has also received his healing touch. We all thank the people of this ranch for allowing us to work with them and become lifelong friends. Ben I will be going with David and a few others to see the land you have given us, before we go to the village. We thank you for it and we know that it is where God has chosen for us to live, even now before we see it!" Two Feathers sat down and placed his hand in Willow's. It was strangely quiet in the barn. "You will come with me to see our land won't you? I want you always at my side, Willow."

"Yes, of course I will come. I think all of The People of the Lion want to come with you." Many nodded or said yes.

"Then it is settled. We will all go to see the land that will be home, now let's rest. We will gather our belongings and head out as soon as we can in the morning."

Sarah and David quickly cleaned the little cabin and prepared also to leave. She clung to Ben and reminded him that even when he felt well he should continue the exercises. He promised that he would.

As usual Mary and Beth had packed huge quantities of leftover food from the feast that included extra loaves of bread and jars of jam.

At the last minute Lori and Mark both announced that they wanted to go with them to see Sarah and David's place and to see the land that would be home to the young men and women they had become friends with.

When Tim heard that David had expressed a desire to raise work horses, he suggested that the team from the village that he had brought should also go with them.

"We can pack all the bundles of food on them," he said laughing. "Any other horse would be greatly burdened. Mary and Beth you are very generous."

When the People moved out, they formed a column, much like the one that The Blue Stone People formed when they traveled to the summer council. Sarah noted the only difference.

"It seems that the women of the Lion prefer to ride beside their men."

The people on the ranch were sad to see them leave but they knew that they would see all of them in the spring.

"I am late getting the milking started this morning," said Jed.

When he entered the cow barn he was pleasantly surprised. Johnny had two cows done and was milking the third.

"Thanks, these old girls expect us to be on time. I appreciate you getting started." Johnny looked up at Jed and smiled.

"Did you see how excited Lori was? Ben told her she could take his little wagon and go with them. He got off and she threw her satchel in the back and just waved at me. She still hasn't learned to ride very well but she wanted to go with them. She and Sylvia Warren headed out together. Is Sylvia coming back here to spend the winter?"

"I don't know Johnny. That must be something the women have worked out. We can ask your mom when we get finished here."

The column moved along at a comfortable pace and Sarah found herself riding beside Willow when Two Feathers moved up to talk with David.

"Willow, this will be an interesting winter for you. After you see your new land you will all be able to plan how you will use it. It will be a safe place to raise a family."

"Yes, I remember the bluff and the image above the cave. It all seems like a dream of the past. I am glad that I will get to see it again. Are you comfortable in your cabin now that it is finished and you have lived there a little while?"

"Yes, it is wonderful. I love the location and the ground in our area is rich. My garden was put in very late, but still it produced plenty of good food for the winter. My storage room has many baskets of dried vegetables. I have some of the apple seeds from the store apples that Ben brought. I will treasure them and plant them early in the spring. I hope they will grow."

"I have some, too. I was thinking I might put them in the ground and cover them up with leaves near the new lake they have been talking about. It would be fun to come back in the spring and see them sprouting."

"I wonder if the new lake will get fish in it. I guess if fertilized eggs wash in there, they might hatch and grow. I guess it depends on where the water comes from. It will be interesting to see," said Willow.

The column slowed to a stop at midpoint and Two Feathers rode back along the people and suggested they get down and rest their horses and have a snack. He pulled several withered apples from the trees that marked the spot and fed one of them to Queen. Lori and Sylvia were puzzled at the prospect of getting her to the water until White Grass volunteered to unhitch her from the little cart and take her to the edge of the river. He talked to them politely and brought the horse back and tied her in the sunshine where she could graze. They offered him a piece of meat and bread and he sat in the grass near them. His eyes studied every hair of Lori's head.

"How is it that you came with us?"

"We both just wanted to see where Sarah and David live, and see the land that The People of the Lion will be moving to in the spring. I am glad that it isn't too far from the ranch. We will all be able to visit next summer."

"Yes, maybe you ladies will come and help us build our cabins," he said jokingly.

"I don't think I would be much help with that, but we might do other things." Two Feathers waved at them and White Grass knew that it meant to prepare to move out. He hitched Queen back up and held Lori's hand as she stepped up into place.

"Thank you White Grass, now that we have watched you do it, I think we will be able to manage releasing Queen, when we arrive," said Sylvia smiling. White Grass knew that her comment was a dismissal, but he wasn't going to be discouraged that easily. He rode up closer to Soren and asked if he was glad they were on the way home.

"Yes, I am. I want to see our future land. This is exciting. Isn't it?"

"Yes, it feels like everything is changing, as if we are moving into a new world. I think when I can; I want to build a cabin to live in. I liked the ones that we built. They were strong and solid. I don't think I will ever be satisfied with a tent again."

"White Grass, you need a wife to build it with you. To make all the good things inside that make our tents comfortable."

"I am working on that."

"I saw you back there talking to those two women. I think you are looking for trouble!" They laughed together and rode along enjoying the restful day of sunshine after the hard work and cold nights they had endured for more than two months at the ranch.

It wasn't long after, that Sarah and David, Two Feathers and Willow turned their horses into the trees of the church land and rode across the river and on toward the back door of the cabin.

"It is good to be back here. David, we have been gone much longer than I ever thought we would. I hope everything here is alright."

"It looks fine," said David as he opened the door and carried Pili in. "This little girl has been so spoiled by her Aunt Beth and Aunt Mary, that it will take a firm hand to bring her back to reality." He said it laughing.

"She has been loved and given everything she wanted. She is a lucky little girl to have her family near her."

David wondered how hard it had really been for Sarah, when she was young. He knew the reference was to her childhood not Pili's.

With all the bundles pulled from the workhorses, Two Feathers asked David where he would like the big horses put.

"I had thought I would put them on the new piece that Ben gave me, but it isn't fenced yet. Let's just fasten all of them near the river where they can eat, drink and rest."

David looked in amazement at the eight big horses. If I get those two from Donaldson, this could turn into something pretty special. He thought. If the weather holds I can use them to pull some trees over there and build them a shelter and start a fence. I plan on working with them so they don't get lazy. His mind was busy and he didn't hear Sylvia's comment.

"David, I don't think you heard me. I asked where you were going to put all of those big horses for the winter."

"I guess they will have to help me build a shelter." She smiled and nodded. The answer satisfied her. She followed Willow and Lori inside and soon the small cabin was warm and crowded with excited people.

Two Feathers suggested that they go through the passage and see their land now while it was early afternoon. If we don't stay too long, we can be back here before dark. I want to head for the village in the morning."

They rode out in single file and David and Sarah went with them. They wanted to see just how large the lake had become.

As each rider cleared the passageway and entered the prairie behind the bluff, they moved out toward the small lake and stopped. It was big and clear and beautiful. The water still poured with force through the opening that David and Ben had made. The flowing water had formed a moving stream on the other side and they could see that it followed a low area into the far woods.

"It is good," said Two Feathers. "In my mind I see us building many cabins here along the bottom of the bluff. I see the women planting corn over there beside the water and I see our men entering the trees to hunt. We will have room for many and welcome any who wish to join us. It is here we will live."

The people cheered and applauded. He turned his horse and rode slowly to the Hickory where he crossed and tied his horse on a long rope for the night. The others did the same, using David's little raft to ferry back and stay dry.

All their tack and bundles were placed in the mouth of the cave where they spread their sleeping furs. David lit a fire for them in the same place he and Sarah had used. Sarah brought food and they all ate together and the talk was happy and optimistic.

Both David and Sarah were watching the sun lower in the sky. Two Feathers led his people out and walked to the cluster of tall pines in front of the cave. He looked up, waiting.

As the sun lowered over the trees, the image of the Lion appeared above the cave. It was better-defined than the shadows of the trees on the ground. Silence, awe and tears, wrapped the group in a sacred embrace, as each one knelt. They had been given a welcome home gift that they would never forget.

The next morning The People of the Lion wished they could stay. They planned to return eagerly in the spring. Sarah thought of Moonflower, Snow Star and even Chief Dark Wolf and how they would feel when these young men and women pulled their tents from camp and left. It will be a sad time for them. I will go there early enough so that I am there when they leave and then I can return when these people come back, she thought. It will be a happy time here.

As the caravan left, Sarah was smiling.

"What are you thinking about Sarah? David asked.

"I was thinking of the joy when they all return."

*****

Sylvia and Lori had ridden double on Moon Boy to see the new home of The People of the Lion, but now they were hooking Queen up for the trip back to the ranch. They were both of a quiet nature, but since they had seen the image of The Lion, they had said even less. They had made their beds on the floor in the cabin and whispered to each other after the others slept.

"Lori, are you asleep?"

"No, I can't! I keep thinking of the image above the cave. I have never seen anything like that before. Have you?"

"No, of course not, now we know why they call themselves The People of the Lion. The rest of the camp is called the Blue Stone People. We know about that, but this is mysterious!"

"It is more than that! It is sacred and special. I felt like I was in church in the front row."

"Me, too, but we better get some rest. We can talk about it on our way back to the ranch."

*****

The morning was cold and clear as the people headed for the village. They could see their breath before their faces and before the noses of the horses. Lori and Sylvia got in their small cart and said goodbye, thanking David and Sarah for letting them come.

"You have a very special place here," they said in unison as they drove away smiling.

"It's going to be a long winter. I am eager for spring already, said Lori, as they moved along.

"You are not thinking of White Grass are you?"

"Maybe, why shouldn't I? He is single, handsome, strong, and I think he likes me."

"Well for one obvious reason, he is an Indian and you are a white woman. There are so many problems in this territory between the Indians and the whites that it wouldn't be wise to get involved with one."

"I'm not. I just think he is kind of cute. That's all."

"Lori! Stop thinking like that."

"You can't tell me where to look. You rode all the way to the ranch, beside that brother, priest-guy Tim!"

"Yes, but riding is all we were doing. Most of the time, he was talking about the village and the people there. I think he is in love with one of the women, but he was clever and never gave me a hint as to which one. I don't think he will ever go back east and finish becoming a Jesuit Priest!"

"That's interesting."

"I can hear the bell clanging. One of the kids has spotted us."

Jed helped to take them across and they were surprised to see Ben coming slowly on a huge, old horse.

"Ben, I hope you are alright on that big horse. We came right back so that you can have your cart to use."

"Thank you ladies, but I think I will stay on Big Boy until lunch. He is a good old friend and seems to be glad that I have chosen to ride on him today. Did you have a nice time at Sarah's?"

"Yes we did and the land you gave The People of the Lion is wonderful. We saw the image above the cave! It was awesome! I feel special. Have you seen it Ben?"

"Yes, most of us have seen it and we feel that it is accompanied by a blessing when it appears." Beth and Mary rolled up with a wagon filled with household goods and the smaller children. Josh was just entering Jed's barn. He waved and disappeared into the interior.

"Girls, we are all so happy that you are both here. You have proven your willingness to work ever since your arrivals. We have been working on a little surprise for you. Follow me," said Beth. She crossed in front of them and drove slowly to the little cabin by the lake. It was farther from the flowing water now, since all the changes to the lake but it still had a pleasant view of the willow trees and the water in the canal edged with red clay.

She pulled up near the front door. "Orville moved out of here just yesterday, so there is still some cleaning to do, but we have swept the bedroom and Jed and Orville switched the new single beds in here from Sarah's cabin. I took the curtains down to wash. They are on the line. Josh has swept and scrubbed this floor for you and we wiped out the cupboards and put in fresh supplies. The coffee pot is clean and that jug is filled with well water. Here is a tin of coffee and a jar of sugar. There are shelves in the bedroom for storing your things. This lid lifts up and it is dried meat and there are baskets of dried fruits and vegetables in the back storage. In the floor back there is a tiny cold storage, with milk and a few things. It's best to keep an eye on the stuff in there because if it turns warm it won't last long, not more than a few days and if it gets too cold, it could freeze. I didn't put fresh meat in there. You know that we all eat the evening meal together so no need to cook separately unless you feel you want to. We will all be having supper at sundown at Mary's house tonight. Mary started laughing.

"Beth you didn't give them a chance to get a word in since they got here," said Mary. "Beth thought of this early this morning and wanted to surprise you. We all thought you would be more comfortable if you had a place of your own to stay in. Orville invited Mark to bunk in with him and he accepted, so I guess we have a girl's cabin and a bachelor house. If we have forgotten anything please tell us and we will do our best to get it for you."

"This is wonderful," said Lori. I appreciate you letting me stay in Lily's bed but I didn't like putting her on the floor. This is a good solution."

"Lori, Ben said he will keep Queen in Jed's corral or the field next to his barn so she will be handy for you to use the little cart. Sylvia, the horse that you rode when you arrived, belongs to the herd of the Blue Stone People. It is in the field right there. Lori, Jed says that they intend to teach you to ride soon and that both of you will have other horses available for your use also."

Sylvia looked at all of it and felt very grateful.

"We both feel very fortunate to have such a warm and comfortable place to stay. Thank you for all the work you have been doing for us."

"You have both done so much here at the ranch. We feel lucky and blessed to have you. Now we are heading to Orville's and Mark's to see what else they might need to be comfortable. We will see you at supper. Your satchels are in the corner in the bedroom. Unpack and get acquainted with the place. Your wood for the fireplace is down on the side next to the porch. Josh will be cutting more and bringing it for you."

After Mary and Beth left, the girls stood in the middle of the cabin and hugged.

"I guess we are roommates. This is so nice of them to let us live here."

"Well, we are family," said Lori.

"I'm not. I don't have any family. I was rescued by the Chosen."

"Don't look sad. You have family now! I am your sister, and it is pretty obvious that they have all adopted you."

"In that case, I get the bed by the window!" Sylvia ran into the bedroom laughing and sat in the middle of the bed.

"That's fine. I would rather have the one near the doorway anyway. It will probably be warmer."

A tap on the door stopped their laughter as Joshua came in carrying clean bedding from the line.

"The basket on the porch has curtains and two rag rugs for the floor by your beds." Sylvia brought it in and spread the curtains out on the beds so they wouldn't wrinkle.

"Thanks Josh. we will see you at supper."

"Do you want me to stay and help put the curtains up or anything?"

"No, I think we can do that," said Sylvia. Josh placed a small log on the dying fire and fanned the embers until it caught. You will probably want to add some wood to that before you come to the house to eat. You don't want to have it go out before you get back. I am going to bring you a load of wood tomorrow and pile it on the side. We need to stock up. I think snow will be here any day now."

"Thank you Josh, I think you are right and we will appreciate having the wood here when we need it," said Lori. She wanted him to leave so they could feel free to look around in the cupboards, make a pot of coffee and put the curtains up.

"Let's start by hanging the curtains and making our beds. After that we can take the stuff out of our satchels," said Sylvia. The rods slid into a hem at the top of a simple piece of blue cotton. They were a bit faded but the fabric felt strong. "Maybe we can dye these darker," she said. The rag rugs on the floor were many colors as were the quilts they placed on the beds. There were more heavy quilts than they thought they needed for now. Together they folded the last two and put them on one of the big bottom shelves.

"I don't have very many clothes," said Lori as she pulled the contents of her carpet bag out onto the bed.

"You have more than I do. I have the dress I am wearing and one more, plus a set of leather shirt and trousers that Snow Star gave me. I know I will need those when it gets bitter cold. I don't have a coat or boots. Beth has been kind to let me wear her sweater."

"Can you sew?"

"Yes, and I can knit, too. Maybe we can get some things in town if they go. I don't have any money. Do you?"

"No, I think Mark might have a little, but not enough for buying clothing."

"They did say to tell them if we need anything."

"Lori, I think she was referring to household things. I think somehow we should figure out a way to get our own clothes."

"Don't be silly, how are we supposed to do that?"

I don't know yet. I am still thinking about it."

CHAPTER THIRTEEN
THE JOURNAL

After a few days of a more normal routine, Ben sent word to Beth and Jed that after the evening meal; he wanted to have another meeting. Adam was glad to dash off to the meadow where Jed was working with Orville and Mark. He loved being where he could watch them work with the mustangs and usually wasn't allowed near them.

He wasn't there long before Jed thanked him for the message and told him to be sure Beth and the rest of the family knew. Adam headed out of the field and rode to the gate but didn't exit immediately. He was watching them work with a brown and white filly. She pranced and backed up and then bunted Orville's hand. I think he must be holding treats for her, Adam thought as he watched. She sure is pretty. He let himself out of the gate and latched it making sure it was secured before heading to find the rest of the family.

The newly created waterway flowed and sparkled in the cold sunshine. There was an edge of ice here and there. He wondered if it would freeze over.

That evening as they sat together Ben reached for the Bible that he had laid on the table.

"This meeting will come to order," said Beth

Ben looked at her and smiled.

"This is a meeting for thanksgiving to our Lord. He has given us the help we needed and the supplies to do what we had to do. He healed our bodies and our spirits when we got discouraged He lifted us up." Amen everyone said. "That's funny" he said, "I wasn't really praying. I was just saying what was in my heart. I was thinking that with all that has gone on the last two years we haven't written anything in the Bible since Pili was born. I think we should use this extra notebook that we bought as a journal to record some of the important things that happen here at the ranch or with our family, sort of a record of God's blessings every day. What do you all think?"

"I think it's a good idea, Ben."

"First you should all be pleased to see this," he said with a grin. "This is a bank book and it shows that we have thirty five dollars in the Bank at Silverville! We don't need to record that in the journal, but I thought you would all like to see it." Each person looked inside and handed it to the next until it had made its way around the table. Each one appreciated it.

"Let's start our journal with The Blue Stone People helping us to put out the fire along the river," suggested Jed.

"Mary your writing is much better than mine. Would you do it?"

*****

† Journal

The Blue Stone People were on their way to their summer council meeting and Father Bob and Brother Tim were with them. They saw the smoke and Father Bob recognized that it was coming from the area of our ranch. Chief Dark Wolf had just said that he would like to meet Ben Slater someday when they realized that we needed help. The men of the people came and worked hard for several hours until a sudden hard downpour helped to put the fire out. All their women and children came to the ranch and after the men's clothes and blankets were cleaned as much as possible, Beth and I fed them and they spent the night. They slept on blankets and hides outside and wouldn't sleep inside the barn or hut.

Because David had started a cabin on his land the people stopped to see it and visit with Sarah. The young People of the Lion stayed and helped them build their cabin while the rest of the people went on to the summer meeting. Sarah and David had been living in the front of the cave on Brother Tim's land next to theirs.

David and some of the men explored the cave and felt that the area was sacred.

Above the cave entrance as the sun started down above the trees; the shadows created in detail the perfect picture of the Lion of Judah! The cave became known as the Lion's Den. To this day if the sky is clear and no clouds block the sun, the image can be seen for just a few moments before the sun lowers behind the trees.

After David and Sarah had moved into their cabin, an earthquake closed the front of the cave. It is open only for about thirty yards now, leaving room to camp but impossible to go explore. †

"That's good Mary. What should we put in there next?"

"I would like you to put in there that we adopted Uncle Orville Baker," said Lori, smiling and linking her arm through his. He chuckled, feeling a little embarrassed.

"Uncle is it? I'll take that title!" They laughed with him and Mary noted his addition to the family.

"We need a note that our cousins, Loraine and Mark Moody came this summer," she said. Everyone agreed.

"Next we need to tell about the lake going bad and Ben and David rerouting the waterway so that it didn't reach the salt bed in the bluff."

"Should I write about the wolf falling in and coming out here?"

"It is an interesting part of the story, just leave room and you can add it later," said Ben. "We need to tell about the lake going bad and at the time that we were trying to build the cabins and dig the wells so we could keep the homestead land. We need to record that the young men of the Lion of Judah all came here and built the cabins and helped dig the wells.

Tell all about David's miracle on his ears and about my trip with David to town to get the bricks and getting robbed and hit on the head and how Sarah and Jed knew to come and help me and now God has healed me. I am almost as strong on the left side as I was before it all happened."

"Ben, do you really think I can write that fast? It is getting late. I think I should work on this journal tomorrow."

"You're right, as usual, but I want to read from the Bible before we adjourn this meeting. We have neglected our time with the Lord and if you remember I asked you all to think of how we were going to give God the ten percent that he tells us to tithe, any suggestions?"

"Well Ben, I have been thinking that we should give Queen to Reverend Brown and Melanie. She is a good buggy horse and doesn't mind a rider on her back. She is a good all-around horse," said Jed. "They only have their buggy horse and they need a second one.

"That's a good beginning. I agree."

"We have people here that have needs. Although, they have worked very hard right alongside us during all our trials, Mark, Lori and Sylvia have not received a thing from us. They all need winter clothes and I think Uncle Orville could use a few things." They laughed at Ben's use of the name Uncle. "I think you ladies should plan a trip to town, with Mark and Orville, while the rest of us do the chores. You will be able to take Queen with you and one of our best milk cows. I want you to give them both to Reverend Brown. At the store you ladies will be able to buy some things and material and yarn to make others. The last time I was in there, I noticed a rack with coats and some hats up on the wall. You can get what you need and look at the catalog that Sam has. See if there is anything else that you need. We can talk more about that tomorrow, but now let's read a Psalm of praise. Psalm 103 1-5 NIV. "Praise the Lord, my soul; all my inmost being, praise his holy name. Praise the Lord, my soul, and forget not all his benefits- who forgives all your sins and heals all your diseases, who redeems your life from the pit and crowns you with love and compassion, who satisfies your desires with good things so that your youth is renewed like the eagle's." Ben looked up at Jed, will you close with prayer?"

"Our Father," Jed prayed softly as others joined him in saying the prayer. "This meeting is adjourned," he said.

"It seems when I am around this family for very long, I always feel like I have been to church," said Orville. "Are all you folks going to be alright going back to your cabins and house? Have you got enough light to see the path?"

"Yes, we are fine. Thank you Uncle Orville," said Sylvia laughing. "We have a beautiful full moon to show the way."

Ben saw that Mary was very busy writing.

"Honey, are you ready to come to bed?"

"I think I want to get some more of this written while I can remember all that was mentioned."

"Alright, but don't stay up too late."

"I won't." She poured another cup of tea and returned to her journal. She finished with the sentence that they were all eager for spring and the return of The People of the Lion.

"Sylvia Warren is spending the winter with us. She is one of the people rescued by the "Chosen. I hope she will stay with us permanently."

The next morning the ranch had a slight dusting of snow that quickly melted.

"Orville, I would like you to go with the women and leave very early tomorrow. Mary and Beth will need to go to the bank first and then to the store. You and Mark can take Queen and the milk cow to Jim, while they are in the bank. Tomorrow is Saturday. I want you all to go to Cookie's Café for a meal before you head back, so they will need to hurry their shopping so they have time. If it gets too late, go as far as the Parker Place and use the new cabin. Make sure everyone takes a bedroll, and keep an eye on Mark. He will need a coat, boots and whatever you see that's practical. He could use a new work shirt and pants. Get whatever you need. Don't hesitate. It's part of your wages. If by chance they have more of those apples, you can buy the whole barrel. Get some candy for the children, enough to last the winter. I figure that you are the oldest so you will be in charge. Let the women buy what they need and I want them to have a good time. They have earned it, Orville."

"Yes, they have worked hard. What about the young'uns? Are you keeping them here?"

"That's my intention, so the women can relax once. Even if it snows they will have an experience to talk about. It's nice to have that little cabin and know that any of us have a place to duck into to get out of a storm if one would come when we were in town. We can eventually dig a cache and put dried meat and stuff in there for a kettle of stew. Tell the women to get three kettles from the store and leave one at the cabin when you come by."

"That's a lot to remember, Ben, but I'll do my best to keep it all straight."

"Orville, I know you will. I trust you with my family. There are very few men in this world that I would choose for that job."

Ben wisely had a similar talk with Mark hoping that together they would manage to remember to do what he asked.

With the bank book in hand and a small pouch of gold to exchange at the bank, The women had decided to take the small, cart to bring all their purchases home. Instead of the cart, Jed had hitched a sweet mature, brown mare to the medium sized wagon. Its large wheels had been reattached, now that Ben no longer needed his cart. It was easy to pull and not bad to ride on. By using a skid for a ramp he was able to load the cow in the wagon. He placed the skid upright and tied it against the side rail so that it couldn't fall and frighten her. He knew they would need to use it to get her back down. He placed a large roll of hay on either side of her to support her and keep her safe after tying her lead to the front of the wagon. He knew the brown mare and knew that she would respond well to the inexperienced hand of the woman driving the wagon. Beth and Lori were on the wagon moving slowly and Queen followed. She seemed to dance her way along.

"I don't care if it takes a very long time to get there. I want this cow in good shape when she arrives," said Mary. The girls understood. Mark and Orville rode ahead of them and Mary and Sylvia rode behind Queen.

"It feels like we are all an honor guard for that cow," said Beth, jokingly.

"Yes, but I know that Jim and Melanie will be excited to get her and Queen. So many people in town have helped us through the years that it is time that we give back when we can."

"Yes, you are right. I am looking forward to seeing what we can find in the store. I think I want to stock some of the basics in the new cabins, too, and I hope we can find some nice things for you girls. Neither of you have very much and yet you never complain," said Beth.

"You said that as if you are adopting Sylvia, the way we did Uncle Orville."

"Lori, I never thought about it, but it just feels right having her around on the ranch. She is like Orville in the fact that she has no family. I wonder if she will stay. Next spring when The People of the Lion move, she may want to go with them."

"Lori, I wouldn't stop her, but I am not sure that would be the best thing for her. Lily acts like she is a big sister. Oh I measured Lily before we left. I thought if I saw something at the store, at least I would be able to tell if it would fit."

"Do you think Mark will stay with us now that he knows about The People of the Lion?"

"I never thought about it, but I don't think Mark would want to go with the Indians and I am sure that he wouldn't let me go without him. He is very protective of me," said Lori.

"Well, knowing some of your story, I guess that's a good thing. We all can use a knight in shining armor. Jed is mine, just as Ben turned out to be Mary's."

"It's time to stop for a break, ladies," said Orville. I think the cow will be glad to stop jiggling for a few minutes. I will get a bucket of water from the river for her and Queen." The girls sat down on the grass and had a snack and a drink of water while the men made sure that all the animals were cared for before they had their sandwich and then everyone was ready to move on. They were excited for their adventure in town.

At the bank, Mr. Williams was polite and invited Mary and Beth into his office.

As soon as they said they were from The Slater and Jones ranch, he knew that they were family of Ben Slater. Ben had left a lasting impression on him, with his two large pouches of top grade gold.

"I am Mary Slater, Ben's wife, and he asked me to have you convert this small amount of gold; to paper money so that we ladies can shop at the General Store." He took the little pouch and poured its contents onto the scale without a close examination.

"I know if Ben sent this, that it is good. You have seventy dollars' worth here Mrs. Slater. He left the room for a moment and returned with seven ten dollar bills and counted them into her hand. "That's a lot of money. Keep your purse close at hand. We had a man robbed here this fall. I will be glad when that jail is built and the new sheriff is hired."

"Thank you, Mr. Williams. I am sure that this will be more than enough to buy what we need."

"Thank you, ladies, be sure to say hello for me to Ben."

Mary and Beth hurried down the edge of the street, glad to be on their way to the store. Lori and Sylvia sat on the bench outside the store window waiting for them.

"He doesn't even remember that it was Ben that was robbed! I think all that man cares about is money!" Mary was very disturbed.

Orville and Mark had taken Queen and the milk cow to Reverend Brown and hadn't returned yet with the wagon. Mark had been instructed by Ben to take the mare to Matt's shop for care, while they were shopping. The four ladies entered together, giving Sam a reason to get excited. He hadn't had that many people in the shop at one time for a very long time. Helen came out of the back rooms immediately and started talking and laughing as if they were there only to see her.

When things calmed down, Beth said she wanted to start with finding warm coats for the girls. They had sizes that fit, but there was little selection in styles. The coats were long and made of wool. Lori chose tan and Sylvia found a dark brown one that fit.

The boots were oiled leather and laced up the front all the way to the knee. The girls were delighted with them.

She chose two more coats, one for Josh and one for Johnny, referring to a slip of paper with measurements. She measured sleeves twice making sure there was room for growth. Beth and Mary found a soft cream colored coat that was just right for Lily. Boots for her were not available.

"I think we can make her some, Mary. Maybe, hers are still good from last year. She is small like me. She hasn't grown much taller."

Mary glanced around the store and moved to the bolts of fabric.

"I will take this white flannel, the blue with the flowers and the white cotton. The whole bolts, Sam. We will need ten spools of thread and give us the box of skeins of wool and eight pair of knitting needles, four pair of size five and four pair of size eight." Beth could see Mark and Orville coming across the street smiling.

"Sam, please fit each of these men with a work shirt and pair of new work trousers and each of them will need a warm winter coat and boots."

"I think we can do that for you. Are they staying with you at the ranch?"

"Yes, they are family."

"Helen do you have any cooking pots?"

"What size do you want, Beth?"

"I would like them big enough to hold a large stew. That looks good, Helen." She judged the cast iron pot's size as the heavy vessel was pulled from the shelf. "Do you have three, with covers?"

"Yes, there are just three left in that big size."

"Let me see what else we can use. I don't see them but I am hoping that you have some spoons and forks and dinner knives."

"We just have these. They are made of tin ware. I think they are meant for men on the trail."

"They are good enough. Helen, please give us six of each. We can use some tins or jars that will hold sugar. Have you got anything that will work?"

"Would the canning jars be too small? I have some two quart size in a box in the back."

"Those will work fine. Give us three and their lids. We can take that twenty five pound bag of sugar, and some beans, five pounds should be enough. That little sack there will do."

Mary spoke up and said they should get some of the tin plates.

"Yes, six of the plates, Helen, and three wool blankets."

Sam said he might have to close his door after the ladies finished shopping.

"Sam is the mail boat still running? Ben said we could look at the catalog and place an order if we saw something that we needed in there."

He handed her the catalog and continued to write down items on his pad that had been selected.

"We can't say for sure if they will come. They said that it might be their last trip when they came last Wednesday. They watch the weather and don't want to get caught by a storm."

"That's understandable.

"This is what I was looking for Sam. We need one of these manure spreaders."

"You know that I never noticed those in there. That's an unusual item for a woman to order," he said laughing. "You can have Ben pay for those when they come in. I have been adding this up and I will do it again, but it comes to quite a lot of money. How much do you want to pay on it?"

"What's the total Sam?"

"I am adding this again just to be sure." He labored silently and looked at her with concern. The total is fifty four dollars."

"That's fine Sam. Orville and Mark, do you need to get a hat?" Orville walked around the store with his new wool coat all buttoned up, and glanced at the hats on the wall.

"No, I don't. I just got this one broke in so it's comfortable."

"Mark, do you need a hat?"

"No, I like this one Jed gave me. He said he made it. That makes it special."

"Ben told me to ask if you had more of those beautiful apples that he bought last time."

"No, I am sorry. I received only that one barrel and he bought all of them," said Sam grinning. "I added this up three times and it still comes to fifty four dollars Mary. You can pay half if you want to."

"Thank you, Sam but I have sixty dollars here. Can you give me the change?"

"I forgot to show you the new candy we have. It is taffy and each piece is wrapped separately. Maybe you should take some and put it away for Christmas."

"That is a good idea, Helen. Also I need a can of cinnamon for holiday baking. Take the candy and spice from my change Sam.

"That gives you back an even five dollars, Mary." Just then Orville and Mark each started to smile.

"Sam, we will be back with the wagon after these ladies have had lunch at Cookie's Café. Ben told us to take them there as a special treat!"

"Sylvia giggled and whispered to Lori. "This is the most fun that I can ever remember having!"

As the six people filed out the door and it clanged behind them, Sam looked at Helen with amazement written on his face.

"Look at this pile of goods on our counter, Helen. This is the biggest sale we have ever had. They just about bought us out of business!"

"Yes, that ranch sure seems to be making money. I wonder where they get it," she said with a questioning look on her face. Do you think they have found gold on the ranch?"

"Now Helen, don't go letting your imagination take over. Ben probably sold some more horses to the army or something."

"No, he didn't. We would have seen him bringing them to the fort like we did last time. You know he is the one that got robbed. He had money on him and he paid Tom for all those loads of logs we saw go out of town. He has struck it rich Sam, and he isn't telling anyone!"

"Helen, I warned you about storytelling. I am not telling anyone. I just was having a conversation with you. For heaven's sake, Sam, do you have a better explanation?"

"No, not at the moment, but it's not our business to speculate either. They always pay their bills and that's good enough for me." Helen wrapped the bolts of fabric in brown paper and pushed the yarn down in the box and tied it with string.

"This is a pretty little coat they bought for Beth's daughter. I always hoped we would have a girl," she said.

As each bundle was prepared, the stack grew outside their window on the walkway. Sam carried out the cast iron pots and lids, and the sugar. The rest of the items were placed in crates and paper was stuffed between them to cut down on the rattling on their journey home.

"You know the things they bought are nothing extravagant, Helen. The women didn't buy themselves anything but some cloth. They are frugal. It just seems that they always have money for what they need."

Cookie was delighted to see his friends from the ranch. He brushed the crumbs from the big round table in the corner and asked them to sit there.

"What do you like? Never mind, I will bring coffee and you can read sign up there." He pointed and then disappeared for a moment coming back with six cups and a huge coffee pot. He managed somehow to hold all the cups like a bouquet, with fingers through the handles. Expertly he filled them and distributed them around the table without spilling a drop. "You know what you want?"

"I want a steak and the fried potatoes and some milk for my coffee," said Mark boldly. "Everyone else wants the same." He stated it as if he were in charge. The women nodded agreement, and Lori grinned.

"Mary and Beth, do we have enough money to pay for all that?" Orville asked.

"Yes, I am sure we do." Cookie returned with a platter of sliced fresh bread with a pot of butter placed in the middle of the platter. He placed silverware at each place with a napkin so quickly that he was gone again before they could say thank you.

They watched as he delivered sizzling plates with potholders to a pair of cowboys in the corner. Beth leaned over to Orville and quietly asked if he had ever seen them.

"No, I can't say that I have, but I was new to the town when I met David and followed him out to the ranch." He stood up and slowly unbuttoned his coat. "This is the warmest coat I think that I have ever had. Thank you for it." He carefully placed it on the back of his chair. Soon all of them had done the same.

"It gets warm in here from all the cooking," I think, observed Lori.

Cookie came out carrying four sizzling plates, and swiftly returned with two more. He refilled their coffee and promptly disappeared into the kitchen again.

"Thank you God, for this wonderful food and this whole trip and the provisions we have. Thank you most for my new coat," said Orville. "Amen," they said laughing and taking big bites of the meat. They commented on how tender it was and Beth said how nice it was to sit and have someone else do the cooking and clean up.

They lingered over the coffee, not wanting to budge.

"I am so full that I think I will have to waddle like a duck to move," said Sylvia. Everyone laughed at her.

Cookie returned and asked if they wanted pie.

"Miss Rose makes six apple pies every Saturday morning for me." Mark groaned.

"I can't believe it, Cookie, but I am so full that I have to say no thank you." Mary discretely handed the last ten dollar bill she had to Orville and asked him to pay the bill.

"One day soon, you come with Ben and Jed, too. You should bring the children. They like fried potatoes. I will give you free pie," he said as they left.

"He is a nice man," said Mark. "He sure works hard. He needs help in here." Sylvia stored that thought away. She felt that she was a burden to the people at the ranch. She wished that she was a relative like Lori and Mark.

CHAPTER FOURTEEN
IT'S A HOME NOW

"After that heavy meal I don't think I will need to eat again until tomorrow," said Orville as he slipped the change from the ten dollars into Mary's hand. "I left a half dollar tip on the table. I hope that was alright."

"Thank you Orville."

The wind was colder as they walked to the sidewalk in front of the store. Mark brought the wagon around and Mary crossed the street to the blacksmith shop while the goods were being loaded. She greeted Matt and was happy to see Liz standing in the back. She gave them both a hug and handed Matt a dollar. Ben said to give you this and these. She pulled four marble sized blue stones from the bottom of her purse. He said they would look nice on the wide belt you were making when he was here. He grinned and brought it over for her to see his work. That's beautiful Matt. It will look nice on you."

"Tell Ben I said thank you."

When Mary looked up she could see that her family was ready to leave. She hurried back and they left town moving slowly over the bridge. Mark shifted his horse back beside Beth and Lori after they were on the trail out of town.

"You should have been there when we gave the cow and horse to the preacher and his wife. She started crying. She said she had been praying for a cow for months. She hugged Queen like she had been sent from heaven. You can't imagine how much those animals meant to them."

"I am glad. Thank you for telling us, Mark." He moved up to his place beside Orville. "I hope one of them knows how to milk a cow," said Beth. "Well if they don't, when she gets full and uncomfortable, she will start bawling and they will have to figure it out."

"Melanie knows enough about farms that she should know what needs to be done," said Mary. They rode along quietly, each one cuddling deeply into their coats.

"The turn off for the Parker cabin is right ahead. Lori if you keep the horse on the outside of the circle you will be able to pull right back out without a problem," said Mary.

They all dismounted and the few things that were purchased for the cabin were taken inside. Mary smiled as she set the heavy, black kettle near the fire place and stacked two plates, and two sets of utensils in it. They quickly filled the two quart jar with sugar and placed it beside the coffee pot. She put the bag of dried beans inside the kettle and put the lid on.

"Mark I don't see any signs of little creatures getting in here, but let's hang this blanket up somehow. So it's not on the floor and easy to chew on." He tossed one end up over one of the ceiling beams and it stayed.

"Mary, I think we better get moving. That wind is getting colder and there are flakes of snow in the air."

"Thank you Orville. Come everyone, you heard Uncle Orville, we need to get going and at a decent pace, too. I don't want to be riding in snow drifts." The snow stung their cheeks and fingers but didn't seem to be piling on the ground. It was just sundown when they heard the bell clanging. It rang three times and then after a pause, it rang three more clangs.

"Sounds like someone is glad we are home." Sylvia had said it without thinking. Home, she thought. It is a precious word.

Jed and Ben and all the children braved the cold to greet the returning shoppers. Jed helped to ferry the wagon across on the large raft and then hooked the mare back in place to go to Beth's where the wagon was unloaded and then Mary and Ben took their boys home.

"It was a marvelous day Ben, thank you for thinking of it. I would not have thought to plan a day like that. The meal at Cookies was marvelous. He is so fast! And everything was so good." Natty stood on one foot stacking his second one on top of the first. With his thumb in his mouth he stood clinging to her with his other arm wrapped around her. "You missed me, didn't you?" He nodded. "Did you have a good supper?"

He yawned and said they had jelly sandwiches and milk and cookies.

"Ben, that sounds like a lot of sugar."

I let them have what they wanted. Josh and I had stew and Adam and Eli ate with Jed, Johnny and Lily. I don't know what they had."

"As long as everyone got fed, I guess that is what matters." Mary tucked her two youngest sons into bed and changed into her flannel night gown. I am glad that we made it home before this snow really got started. Look outside now."

Ben stood at the window gazing at the falling snow.

"I think you got back just in time. The family is going to need their coats tomorrow."

Lori and Sylvia had hurried to the little cabin using a lantern that Jed lit for them. One of the men had thoughtfully placed wood in their fire pit and it was still burning. Sylvia put another log on the fire and wrapped her arms around her coat as if giving a big hug.

"Lori, can you believe it? We were talking about winter clothes two days ago and wondering how we would be able to get them. Look at us now!" She held her hands out to the fire.

"It is amazing. This ranch just seems to be able to provide whatever is needed."

"Lori, this ranch isn't the provider, God is. The people here honor him and that's why they have what they need and enough to share."

"I think they have found gold! No one is coming to this ranch bringing them money. She had a load of money at that store and she bought all kinds of stuff."

"What are you saying?"

"I am saying that the army buys milk twice a week and that money adds up. They train wild horses here and sell those don't they? There has to be an explanation for the cash around here. Ben got robbed because of his cash. I didn't hear about anyone else in town getting robbed. Did you?"

"No, Lori I didn't, but Ben had cash on him because he was on his way to buy bricks for the wells. Did you ever think that he might have borrowed it at the bank?"

"You are probably right. It just all seems like things come their way. I am going to bed. I am tired. It has been a day I will never forget! Goodnight Sylvia."

"Goodnight Lori." Sylvia turned the lantern down low and pulled an extra quilt from the shelf. "I think we will want these on our beds tonight." She spread one on the bottom of Lori's bed, where she could easily pull it up and added the second one on her own bed, before putting the lantern out.

"Thank you God, for everything," Sylvia prayed quietly lying in her bed. "I can't make my mind up which I want to make first, a long flannel night gown or a pair of mittens. My hands were so cold riding home that they hurt. I need a hat, too."

The wind had whipped the snow into small drifts and had blown so fiercely that parts of the path were bare. The girls pushed the snow away from the front door and swept off the steps as they went.

Bundled in their new coats and boots they headed for Beth's kitchen, knowing that it would be warm and food would be available. Besides they wanted to find out which project they would work on first. They were disappointed. Beth had gone to the barn to check on the cheese. She didn't want it to freeze.

"Jed are you sure that the tin will still hold up after being used to cover the fires in the canal?"

"It seems plenty strong and I know it looks different but I think we can nail it back in place and if we get a few nice days maybe we can put a new layer of tin right over it. For now the cheese is fine and staying clean right where it is."

"I like the way you turned part of the corral into a goat pen. They even have a cozy little shed. Who found time to build that with all that has been going on?"

"I am sure that it was Orville." Just then Jed and Beth both started laughing. Lily came crawling out the door of the goat shed.

"What are you doing in there?"

"Just visiting," she said. "They like it when I come here to visit. No one else pays much attention to them. You are right. Uncle Orville built the goat house, so they would be warm this winter. I asked him to do it, because I was worried about the babies being in the snow."

"You were right Lily. They did need a place to get in out of the cold. They will be cozy there, and when you feed them I think you can give them a little extra when it is this cold. Did their water bucket freeze last night?"

"No, it looks good but it sure is cold out here. I think I am ready to go in now. All the animals have been taken care of, and I am hungry. What's for breakfast, Mom?"

*****

"Sarah, are you sure you don't mind?"

"I told you that I didn't. It sounds like a good plan to me. He will be glad to be rid of the old girls. He won't use them during the winter and he will still need to feed them. It is perfect timing."

David had been working the last three days to complete ample shelters for all his horses with room for the two old female work horses he wanted to buy from Donaldson at the brick yard. They had plenty of standing grass and they had cut a crop and rolled it into huge bundles late in the summer. Now the grass had replenished itself and would be standing feed for grazing.

"Sarah, is there any reason that you don't want to go stay with your family at the ranch?"

"Yes, David there is. We were there for a long time and now that we are here, I want to work on projects for our home. We can't take all these horses with us every time you need to leave. That reminds me. Stop and get enough gold from Ben to order box fence. If you take our team and Ben's big wagon, you won't have to worry about it being delivered. If you run into bad weather, you can stay at the Parker Place or Jed's new pasture cabin. We don't have to worry about a storm stranding you in the open with those along your route."

"As usual, you are right but I will miss you. If he sells the females to me, I can lead them on home on long leads on the back of the wagon. I may have to be gone quite a while. The brick yard is a long ride farther. It is west of town."

"David, if you have changed your mind about this, I will understand."

"No I haven't. I guess I am just worrying over nothing."

Sarah began to pack large quantities of dried vegetables and meat. She put a package of sandwiches in the top of his satchel and added cheese and cookies and a pouch half full of sugar candy.

"That is treats for the horses. I put a large bunch of crackers in that pack, too. I know that you will want to get acquainted before you head home. I was also thinking that you should borrow a shovel from Ben on your way into town, so that if you stay at the Parker Place, you could start a small cache. Here are enough mats to line it, if it isn't large." She rolled the mats and tied them. I know you will probably start out with Blackie, and these packs can be carried by our work horses until you borrow the wagon. Leave all these dried foods in the new cabin cache."

"Woman, you know that the women on the ranch will stock those cabins. You don't need to do it."

"I know. I just want to, because they did so much for us. I was thinking that you could probably get a couple of pieces of leftover planks at the ranch to use for making a lid quickly."

"Sarah, I don't know if the weather will allow me to even stop there and you have me staying there doing projects!" David was thinking that things always became more complicated than they should have been. I just wanted to go get a couple horses and bring them home. Now I am stopping for a wagon and gold. Going to the bank and buying fence, digging a cache and making a lid. I'll probably get stuck halfway in a snow storm and won't even get to town. He was frowning as he brought his team around and put his saddle on Blackie.

"David, you know you don't have to do any of this if you don't want to. The fence can wait until spring. We won't be able to put much of it in place during winter anyway, and you are right about the cache. Maybe Josh and Adam want to do that."

"Well, it is a sure thing that I won't starve to death with all this food along. I think I will take a slicker, just in case it does snow and I already rolled an extra blanket in my bedroll. The exercise is good for our team and I know it should go fine. Maybe, I'll take Josh or Johnny with me. Those boys have worked really hard. They deserve a change." Sarah noticed that he had deliberately changed his attitude. She was glad. She didn't want him to think that he had to do things her way to keep her happy. He smiled at her and walked close wrapping her in a tight hug. He kissed Pili on the cheek and then kissed Sarah. "Daddy is going away now. I will be back as soon as I can. Daddy loves his Girls," he said. He led the team across the river and out of sight through the trees. Sarah held Pili's hand and took her to the horses to visit. She sat her on Pretty Mother and let her pat the gentle mare's neck. Next they visited Moon Boy and Sugar Baby.

"You are really growing, little girl. I am surprised at how tall you have become." She scratched the foal's ears and Pili squealed with delight as the foal nuzzled her tummy.

As they returned to the cabin, they found themselves surrounded by three nearly full grown wolves. Pili laughed with joy as Sarah placed her down in their midst. She received licks on her face and fingers and Woof jumped against her and knocked her down onto the grass. Pili seemed to know that he was playing. She giggled and grabbed him by the neck hugging him. "Woof plays hard," she said. Sarah picked her up and brushed off the grass. She went to the little room by their back door where she kept a sack of bones. She distributed the treats and gave scratches. The wolves were happy to take their new bones to their den. Sarah wondered as she looked up at the sky if she had made a mistake, by encouraging David to buy fence and stop to dig a cache. I think the weather is changing and not for the better. She could feel the temperature dropping.

"Pili we need our coats on. We are going to bring in wood for the fire. I think that it will snow tonight and we will be glad that it is inside."

Pili grinned and looked cute all bundled in her coat and hat. Sarah loaded her arms with wood and placed it near the fireplace. Each trip in, she gave one small piece to Pili to carry. This kept her busy and safe at Sarah's side.

When they finished and their coats were off, Sarah fixed them a bowl of soup with crackers. Pili finished hers and asked for a cookie.

*****

David talked to Ben and they decided it would be a good idea to keep a bag of gold available without having to dig it up each time there was a need. David took a pouch and tucked it into his coat and hitched his team to the large wagon. He told Ben what the shovel was for, but not the boys. Ben and Mary said they thought that if he was willing, they would like him to take Josh and Adam. He agreed that they would probably enjoy the adventure and before an hour had gone by, the three of them were on their way, with David's big team pulling the empty wagon. David and the boys were all on the seat. Blackie trotted beside the wagon until the trail narrowed and then he followed comfortably.

Adam was so excited that he talked constantly for the first part of the journey. The clouds hung low over the trail and David was sure that they would be breaking a trail through snow before this trip was over.

*****

In the village of The Blue Stone People work had been increased to produce as much raw blue stones from the new pit as they could. They used the few lanterns in camp and worked around the clock.

Word had come by a fast riding messenger that two of the camps that had been at the summer meeting had been displaced by soldiers, forcing the people to move from the land they had lived on and hunted for generations. No one knew where those that had survived had been taken or if they had survived at all. These were people that had fought hard against the influx of white people into their land. Chief Dark Wolf knew that it was only a matter of time before the soldiers would come to the camp of his people.

"You have all been asked to come here to our communal tent tonight, not for a celebration or games. We must all hear the terrible news that this young man has brought to us. It is not for my ears only." He sat down signaling for the young scout to stand and address the people. As he related the events of the last few months, tears filled the eyes of many listeners. He tried to spare their hearts but he knew that the experience and wisdom of the older ones was filling in the blanks of things left unspoken. The scout finished and Chief Dark Wolf thanked him for his brave service, knowing that if the soldiers saw him riding swiftly across the land, he might be killed.

The Chief spoke.

"People of the Blue Stones, things have changed drastically. You must pack everything. We will be moving and taking all our belongings with us. Our people will leave here at the new moon, not at the soldiers bidding, but on our terms!"

The following day, he called a meeting with Two Feathers and all the men.

"Two Feathers, you have seen the land that Ben Slater has marked for The People of the Lion. Is there room there for all our camp to live there? With a sincere heart I ask that you allow all our people to come. If they do not, I believe they will die soon."

"All are welcome, My Chief. When do you think we should move? Winter is in the sky. It will be difficult now."

"If we wait, it will be worse with the soldiers forcing our people to walk through snow with burdens on their backs and our little children starving because they don't allow us to stop or forbid us from taking our food supply. This the scout did not say to our people. He wanted to spare the women. We must move as soon as we feel we are ready. In the meantime, we will dig as much of the blue stone as we can. We will use Father Bob's wagon and the biggest horses in our herd to move the stones."

Father Bob had been listening but not wanting to believe what was happening.

"Yes, of course you may use anything that I have. I can't believe this is happening. We just built the school! The children have not had a chance to enjoy it. How can this be?"

"Father Bob and Brother Tim, will you come with us?"

"I will go where my people go," said Father Bob.

"I will go," said Brother Tim with tears in his eyes. He knew that all he was hearing was true. He felt the pain deep in his soul.

"You must pull as much of the blue stone from the ground as you can and then cover the pit and drag the building out to the middle of the meadow. Leave no trace of the mine's location. The stones that you take will become more precious with time. One day they may be all that stands between the people and death," said Father Bob. "Chief Dark Wolf, when do we leave?"

"I told Moonflower that we would leave here at the new moon. That is less than ten days. Our women are industrious, and they will weave large sacks to hold the supplies in our food caches. Our herd is large. The horses will all have to work, but this entire camp can be moved. I want to leave nothing for the soldiers, not even a worn out slipper or broken pot."

Between sobs and hugs the women created large utility sacks to hold the dried meat and other foods. Every loose hide in camp was stitched into some form of a container.

The communal tent was taken down by the men not working in the pit. Seams were opened and sections were created that were manageable by a team pulling a large skid. Each family was responsible for packing and moving their own tents and its contents. Some were easier than others. Sweet Grass distributed the furs from the floor of the big tent, taking one or two, to each woman in camp. She did the same with the cups and bowls that had been used by everyone at the communal meetings. They would be collected again once the tent was resurrected in its new location.

She looked at her many bundles of dried herbs and finally decided that trying to keep them in their current condition as bouquets, was impossible. She set to work making pouches for each herb and drawing a symbol that perhaps only she would understand, to identify the contents. Then with great resolve, she crushed the bouquets and stashed them in the many pouches. She ran an extra seal of wax across their seams and those of the dye containers she had and stuffed them into a large loosely woven sack. Her clothes and jewelry were all stuffed into large containers. Her cooking pots for medicines were stacked neatly. She sighed deeply as she looked at the raised area covered with dry grass. It was all that was left of what had been her home. Her sleeping pad, with an extra warm blanket, water bag and rifle lay nearby in the grass. Chief Dark Wolf had sent word that all the adults that could shoot, were to carry an available weapon on this journey. Sweet Grass decided that if they were leaving and not coming back, that she would glean from the area any healing plants that she could find. She walked the woods and dug the sleeping plants carefully, making a mental note of the conditions where they had been growing. It was her hope that she would be able to transplant them as soon as she arrived, in similar conditions to insure that she would have them growing in the new area. Her hand shook as she carefully wrapped the roots in a moist cloth and gently tucked them in the woven sack she had made for them.

"Great Spirit, Sarah said that I could talk to you and you would answer. My heart and head are so disturbed that I am not sure what I want to ask you. I really want to know that you approve of this relocation and will continue to watch over our people and protect and provide for them. It scares me that we are moving away from the blue stones and that the soldiers are going to come here looking for us. Are we going to a place that is safe? Are you putting blue stones there for us? I don't understand any of this. Great Spirit, please help us." She had prayed silently. She wasn't aware of her prayer. It was just thoughts in her mind, but she had directed them to God and He had heard.

Chief Dark Wolf had sent Growling Bear and Roaring Water to study the terrain. They were to find a route that the people could take without leaving a trail to their new location. They returned to see their tents being dismantled and the support posts made into skids for them.

"Chief Dark Wolf, we have a plan," said Growling Bear. "We will follow the path of the white men's wagons to Ben Slater's field of cattle, then with our cattle behind us, we will use the trail he uses along the river they call the Hickory until we come to Father Bob's church land. There the ground has been trod and teams have brought logs for Sharp Knife's cabin and those of Ben Slater's. We can enter there and use the passage to the new camp. Our trail will be undetected after the lightest snow."

"You have done well my friends. It is a good plan. It makes our trip longer, but they will not know where we have gone. Growling Bear, do you think you and the hunters are able to move our cattle so they will go where you want them?"

"Yes, we will. If they step off the trail, it is a cow print, not a trail of our people. It will work. The shepherds will sing their song and move the sheep. Two of our women have volunteered to care for the milk cows and Father Bob said that the few chickens we have can go in crates on top of the big wagons. He has good crates made already, with a door that opens. I am so glad that he has those wagons now."

Their last night in camp, Father Bob held mass near the center of the dismantled camp. He too had packed all he could. The empty church was a sad structure. The cross that had traveled across the land with him would travel again and stand at the new church on the Hickory. He spoke to the people bravely.

"Tomorrow we will leave here, moving to a new home. We ask God to bless us as we travel and bless the new land that we are going to inhabit. We thank him for his bountiful provision. He has given us so much that it is hard to pack and take it all. Look around you and know that you are blessed. We are well. We have horses to carry our burdens and us, and you travel with your homes with you. Rejoice People of the Blue Stones, your God goes before you."

Although their hearts were heavy and their minds fearful of the unknown they cheered and clapped at his words.

At first light, Chief Dark Wolf walked the camp and rousted the people to action.

"Load up! We are moving out!" He shouted and smiled and clapped his hands. He had decided that as long as this had to be done, he would try to make it as comfortable for the people as he could.

The men had worked hard pulling out the beautiful blue stones until two days earlier, when the Chief had asked them to bring out what they had loosened. Then he simply asked two men to bring a couple of big work horses and they tied ropes around the little shed that covered the mine entrance.

"Take it to the middle of the meadow and leave it there. Go very slowly so you don't frighten the horses in the field." He stood watching. "Good, you have done as I asked. Now take every shovel available and fill the pit. Level the ground and scatter the dirt widely. Bring sod and place it here where we started digging. Water it all until the dirt is settled. Pack it down so that it does not settle into a dip where our pit was." The men worked hard following the instructions. They carried dirt and water until quite by accident they had recreated the little knoll that had once existed there. When they realized it, then they knew it was time to stop.

Now as Chief Dark Wolf looked around the area that had held the tents of his people he saw that they had done what he asked. Anything that the people had chosen to discard had been buried. Broken pottery was a common site at the edge of the lake. It was now pristine. There was not a hint of the people.

They rolled their sleeping furs and tied them in place on the horses they had chosen to ride.

When the loaded wagons and wide travois had cleared the path and turned onto the wagon trail, and the last person headed out from the path beside the bluff, the first of the big cattle soon followed from the path in the big rocks. Oddly enough, the men had less trouble moving them. It was as if they thought that the moving caravan ahead of them was showing them the way they should go. Chief Dark Wolf and Two Feathers rode side by side, walking their horses slowly in the early morning light. The air was very cold. They could see the breath of the horses and people in the air. The women of high status rode together.

Moonflower worried that this trip was not good for Snow Star. She was heavy with child. She worried that the snow would come and they would not be able to make it to their intended destination. She worried that all these pressures would cause Chief Dark Wolf to become ill. She worried and worried until she began to appear ill. Her face should have been red from the cold, but it was as white as frost. Father Bob noticed it before anyone else. He rode up beside her and softly said that he had a message for her ears only. He leaned as close as he could and whispered softly.

"God says to trust him." Then he rode back to Brother Tim before she could reply or ask any questions. When he saw her face a few minutes later, it was as rosy as everyone else's. Thank you, Jesus, he said silently. The people rested briefly, when it was necessary but their stops were short. Their journey continued.

When Two Feathers and Chief Dark Wolf saw the field of cattle in the distance, they knew to cross the prairie and ride close to the fence. They were aware of the mud bog and stayed well away from it. The cattle in Ben's field surged near the fence and the big cattle they brought with them seemed to want to go back in with them. They walked along with the men not giving cause for concern.

At the Hickory, the people stopped for a short rest. The horses and cattle drank from the river and ate the brittle winter grass grateful for its nourishment.

As soon as the women were able to make the children comfortable again, they urged their men to start moving. Johnny was on the bluff for a quick look when he spotted the slow column. He started to ring the bell and then stopped before he had sounded the alarm. He knew these people. They were not enemies.

"Dad I didn't ring the bell because they are moving so slowly and quietly that it is as if they want to go by without us knowing they are there." Jed went up to the look out, and came away with the same conclusion. I think they would prefer it if we don't acknowledge them. They have all the women and children and so many pack horses and even Father Bob's big wagons are in line and they are loaded. Where can they be going? It is so cold out. They must be suffering. I wish I knew what to do. He was thinking all the same things that Johnny was, but for some reason they couldn't explain, they let the people, horses and cattle move slowly down the trail without acknowledging their presence.

When Jed and Johnny told Ben what had happened, at first he was angry because they had not properly greeted the Chief and his people, but when he had crossed the Hickory and stood watching the people, their belongings, and even their cattle moving slowly away in the distance, he had to agree.

"Something terrible is going on. Where can they be going?"

He didn't expect an answer. They were as puzzled as he was.

When he told Mary and Beth, they didn't seem as surprised by it as the men had.

"Ben I think they are going to the new home of The People of the Lion," said Mary. Beth was stirring a steaming kettle on Mary's stove. Lori and Sylvia sat together on the big bear rug encouraging each other with each stitch. They were knitting. Mary reached for her journal and began to record what the men had described.

"I don't understand why they would want to move when it is this cold. The only warm place on our ranch is near a fireplace. I sure hope the snow holds off for their sake and David's. He has our boys and I know it won't be fun if the horses get bogged down in deep snow."

"Beth you are a worrier. If the people have decided to move now, I am sure they have a good reason. Chief Dark Wolf and Two Feathers were leading the column. They know what they are doing."

Mary looked up with a smile.

"I just thought of something, can you imagine how surprised Sarah will be when the whole camp of the Blue Stone People, show up there!"

She isn't expecting them to come until spring and then not all of them, just the young ones that follow Two Feathers."

CHAPTER FIFTEEN
THE NEW CAMP OF THE LION

David had stopped once for the boys to take a break but he continued on through Silverville as if it wasn't there. He wanted to reach his farthest destination and get back to town without snow. The horses were doing well. With no load on the wagon their strength was untaxed just walking along the trail. David shuddered when they crossed the spot where Ben had been attacked.

"This is where those men jumped your dad. I don't like even being on this trail."

Adam's eyes grew wide with concern.

"Do you think someone might come out of the trees and attack us?"

"No, those men are locked up and I just meant that I don't like remembering it."

They slept in the wagon bundled in their bedrolls after eating a hearty meal from the satchels provided by Sarah and Mary. Finally, at early afternoon the next day, the brick yard came in view.

Uncle David, do you think he will let you buy the horses? What will he think when he sees that you already have four work horses?"

"Josh, I am hoping that he thinks his old girls aren't worth much and that I am foolish for buying them."

They laughed together as he pulled his team into the yard and David climbed down.

"Hello Mr. Donaldson. How are you? Do you remember me?"

"Hello Mr. Sharpe, of course I remember you. How is Mr. Slater doing?

"He is improving every day. I will tell him you asked about him."

"You can't be here to get more bricks. The brick yard is closed until spring. What can I help you with?"

"Well, Mr. Donaldson, I came all this way thinking I would buy some box fence from Tom, but then I thought about that pair of old female work horses you have and thought you might not want to keep feeding them all winter. Would you be interested in selling that pair to me? We live on the edge of a tall stand of wild grass and a couple more horses grazing out there might be a good thing, if the price is low of course."

"Well, I don't know. I will need them come spring and they are not that old. They pulled a load for you, didn't they?"

"Yes, they did, but they were exhausted by the time they delivered the bricks and my team got impatient and passed them when they got on the open prairie. You need younger, stronger horses for hauling bricks. With the money you will save by not having to feed them all winter, you can get a better pair in the spring."

"How much are you willing to pay for them?"

"How does an ounce of top grade gold sound?"

"Gold, I don't deal in gold. I like cash!"

"Are you going to tell me that you would turn this down?" David poured one tiny pebble into his palm and held it out for the man to examine." He rolled it around on his palm and mumbled that it should be tested.

"It essays at thirty five dollars an ounce. This is the cleanest ore in the territory! I will give you two ounces, for the two horses."

"How do I know that it is real?"

David shook his head looking disgusted.

"Never mind, I just thought you were a good business man. I don't have time for this."

"I'll take it!"

"Where are the horses?"

"First give me the gold." David was trying not to be obvious. He was pouring gold from the pouch into his inside coat pocket. He felt the pouch. It was still half full. He poured a little more out.

"This is more than two ounces, but I want to be sure that you will tell all the men you know, that I am an honest man."

"Your old nags are on the other side of that building," said Donaldson pointing. I'll get you a paper saying you bought them and take full responsibility for them."

That's a strange way of putting it, thought David as he waited in the cold for the man to come back. He returned with a carefully printed paper and both horses on long leads.

David tied them to the back of his wagon and turned his rig around heading back toward town. Luckily, quite by chance he had placed them with Blackie on the outside by the younger of the two.

Josh and Adam were huddling under a heavy blanket on the seat. "Uncle David, are you sure you want those old horses. They look like they are all skin and bones."

"Easy Josh, you don't want to hurt their feelings. They are girls you know."

"Uncle David, I think they are more like grandmothers." He laughed and then they all laughed.

Later, David pulled the horses into the trees to block some of the wind and took them to the river for a drink. He tied them under the trees near the trail where the grass had gotten the sun and still looked fresh. They spent the cold night again in the wagon with their bed rolls and blankets up to their chins.

"Josh would you take Joey and Buck down to the water for a drink? Adam here is the line for Blackie and I have got my two and the ladies.

As soon as they are satisfied, we can hitch them up and be on the way." A few minutes later, David examined the two females as he tied them to the back of the wagon. "I think this one is older than the other one. He felt compassion for them. We will go see Matt and leave them there while we talk to Tom. He will make sure they are healthy and give them new shoes if they need them. They probably do." Once again they plodded through town without stopping.

"Matt, how are you today? I have adopted a couple of old ladies. Do you think you could check them over while I go buy some fence from Tom? See if they need shoes."

"David, what are you going to do with these old girls? They are about ready for the bone yard."

"See if you can figure out how old they really are. I will be back as soon as I can."

They could hear him talking to the two horses as they turned around and went back toward the lumberyard.

"Hello Tom."

"Hello, David, I see Josh and Adam came, too; it is good to see you all. It is very late in the year to be building anything David. What do you need?"

"Sarah talked me into getting a load of box fence, since I came to town to buy a pair of old work horses from Donaldson."

"I hope you didn't buy that pair of old females of his. They are cranky and the oldest one bites any horse she can sink her teeth into. She is a mean one."

"She didn't show any sign of that while we were traveling with them. They are at Matt's shop."

"He knows her. He will tell you all about her."

"What about the other one?" That is her daughter. She is alright I guess."

"I hope they aren't a problem to me. Should I pull the wagon back there where the rolls of fencing are?"

"Are you going to want some posts and tethering wire?"

"Yes, I suppose so. Let's load that first so it can ride underneath."

"I doubt if I will get much of this done before spring, but I would like to fence a section off for the big guys to graze so they don't have to be tied."

"Any horse you own is a lucky creature. If you ask Matt, he can tell you about a special mix to feed those females to fatten them up a bit. It will make a better winter for them."

"Let's just put a double layer of posts in the wagon and then we can hoist those rolls on the top. They are pretty heavy. They will stay put without much tying. It is a good thing you brought all four of your work horses." Cookie rang his bell announcing that the noon meal was ready.

Tom insisted that they come eat. As soon as he noticed who was approaching the cook fire, Cookie inquired about Ben's condition and David assured everyone that Ben was recovering nicely. Cookie smiled broadly as he handed two empty cups to Josh and Adam.

"You hold these and I will make something delicious for you." Each cup received a teaspoon of bitter cocoa and a heaping spoon of sugar followed by a stream of very hot coffee and after stirring it madly Cookie added some milk. The drink was hot and delicious just as he had promised. Josh smiled broadly as Cookie handed him a plate with a steak and beans on it. A large slab of fresh bread and butter rested on top of the steak.

"Wow, Cookie, this is heaps of food. Thank you."

"Adam, here is a plate for you." It was also overloaded.

"David and Tom, you take your plates. I will pour coffee."

"Thank you Cookie, this steak is tender and juicy. Tom we appreciate the hot meal."

"Well, I appreciate your business."

"Tom, I have a little problem."

"Is it something I can help with?"

"I don't know. I poured some gold into my inside pocket when I was at the brick yard, but I have a hole I didn't know about. The gold is now in my coat lining. Where can we go to lay my coat down so I can remove the gold without it ending up on the ground?" Tom laughed at the look on David's face.

"Is that all? We can go in my office and do it on my desk. Finish your steak first and then I will help you get it out."

By the time David and the boys headed with their full wagon of fencing supplies to pick up the two old horses it was late afternoon.

"Matt, how did it go with my ladies? You should have asked me about these two before you went out there. This one is the old gal. Her name is Nibble for obvious reasons. She is nasty to other female horses. Keep her away from Sarah's Pretty Mother. She acts like everything is fine one minute and then takes a bite out of the neck first chance she gets. Sarah would have a fit if she gets marked up. Nibble doesn't bother Bell. That's because she has always been with her. Bell is her daughter."

"Thanks for telling me. Did they need shoes?"

"No, I did all his horses about a month ago."

"Tom said to ask about a special feed to put some fat on these girls."

"Just stir this in and give them a big scoop of grain every night. As long as they have all the hay, they can eat; they should start looking a little better by spring. I don't have bags of feed for them. I sold the last I could part with more than a week ago."

"I think Sam might have some left in his shed out behind the store." David talked a little while longer with Matt, telling him that Ben was recovering and that they had managed to get the cabins up and wells dug, then he pulled the team closer to the store and went in. Sam stood out back smiling as David pulled the team around the corner and he and Sam managed to pack six huge bags of grain on the top of the loaded wagon where it would stay dry.

Josh and Adam were both thinking that the heavy wagon would be difficult to take across the Silver River when they reached the crossing. David's mind was on the treat he had in his pocket for the boys when they stopped on the other side of the river. His team was strong and their good care showed in their ability to perform when called on to do it.

When they neared the crossing, David began to talk to his team. Using their names he started telling them to muscle into the straps and dig in their heels. He whistled and told Buck and Brownie that he needed them to work.

"Take this load across boys, do it now!" He shouted. Josh and Adam were laughing and hanging on to the seat with both hands as the heavy load dug into the mud beneath the moving water causing spray to fly high on both sides of the horses and wagon wheels. The whip in David's hand was for sound, not pain as he shouted and cracked the whip over the horse's heads. "Go, Go, Buck, Go Joey, Go Brownie, you get going Dickey, let's take this load home! Good Boys, Good Boys," he said more softly as they pulled the load up the graded bank and onto the prairie. He directed them to slow as they moved near a grouping of old cherry trees, and then stopped. The sides of the horses were heaving and they were breathing hard. It wasn't until then that he had time to glance back at the two females, tied to the back of the wagon with Blackie. The poor things looked as if they had been pulling a load, too. Their heads drooped and they were breathing hard.

"That water is like ice. Let's do what we can to dry them off. We don't want sick animals. David jumped down and gathered great handfuls of dry grass and started rubbing his team. Josh and Adam went back to do the same for the old girls. Adam approached Bell and talked to her as he dried her neck, belly, legs and back. Josh did the same for Nibbles but when he was rubbing her side, she turned around and bit his shoulder so hard that he cried out in pain.

"What happened? Did one of them kick you?"

"No, she bit me! Josh unbuttoned his coat and pulled his shirt and sweater away so he could look at his shoulder. "It is purple already but she didn't break the skin. All the layers of clothes protected me. She's a bad horse Uncle David. You are going to have to keep her away from Aunt Sarah and Pili. My shoulder really hurts!"

"I am sorry Josh. I should have done the new horses and had you guys help with my team. They are good boys and appreciate any care they get. Adam move away from them. If you guys will finish Buck and Brownie, I will deal with these two."

David was angry.

"I bought you to spare you mistreatment! Is that anyway to behave? He was holding tightly to Nibbles bridal and looking square into her eyes." It was then he realized that she was as angry as he was. "What is the matter with you?"

"Uncle David, I think she didn't like it going through the water behind the wagon. It probably frightened her. She couldn't see ahead."

"Adam, I think you are a wise young man. I think you may be right. Josh is your shoulder going to be alright?"

"Yes, it hurts, but I will live." He laughed a little and said that he had a good story to tell when he got home. "Uncle David, don't worry about my shoulder. I am so glad that you let us come with you. This has been fun. We are both having a good time."

"Well, I am glad that you both came. I am enjoying having time to be with you. Josh, if you aren't afraid of her, I would really appreciate it if you would come back beside Nibble and talk to her and give her a couple treats while I dry off Blackie. Sarah packed some sugar candy and crackers in this sealed pouch. There they are." He pulled it out from under another satchel and was happy that they somehow managed to stay dry. Adam would you like to give Bell a treat? She seemed to be responding to you rubbing her dry."

"Sure, I would like to do that," Said Adam. Josh walked up to Nibble as if nothing had happened, but she backed up as if she thought she was going to get hit.

"Here girl, I am not angry. You were afraid and we know it now. See what we have for you." Josh scratched her ears and fed her a small chunk of the sugar candy. He reached in the sack and got another piece. When he approached her this time she didn't back up. "There you go girl. You were just trying to let me know that you didn't like being dragged through that water. I don't blame you a bit. I wouldn't like it either." He gave her more scratches and said that he thought she was settled down now.

"Adam, when you walk away from Bell, you should be sure you don't turn your back on her and walk away from her front not her back. I don't know if they kick. No use taking a chance."

"Uncle David, do you always stop after a crossing to dry off your team?"

"I always do in the winter, but sometimes I don't if the weather is warm." They fed candy and crackers to his team and offered them drinks from a bucket he kept under the seat of the wagon. "We better get moving. I want to get as far as the Hickory before dark."

David urged the team forward and swung wide enough to avoid the mud bog. He was puzzled by all the hoof prints. "I think the cattle must have gotten out. Look at all the prints."

"Dad and Uncle Jed and Orville must have had to round them all up. I bet they were mad. I wonder how the cows got out."

"They must have pushed the fence down somewhere. It looks good now. They probably had to repair it."

Josh and Adam both grinned when David turned the team right instead of left, toward home. They knew right away that he was heading for the new cabin on the Parker Place.

"Wow, it looks huge to me," said Adam.

"Thanks Uncle David," said Josh laughing. "I was wishing that we could stop here." They climbed down and David lifted all their bundles, satchels, bed rolls and the shovel down to eager hands. It was then that he remembered that he had not asked Ben for a couple pieces of planks to make a lid for a cache. We will have to improvise, he thought.

"We have to care for the horses first. They led them to the river for drinks and then took them to the side of the cabin where it blocked the wind. David took special care to give pats and scratches to each animal as he settled them for the night. He opened one of the bags of grain and poured some into the big cooking pot left by Mary and Beth. He found another big pan left behind by the men when they had been working there. "This will do," he said. Before he went in to see to his own comfort, each horse had been given a measure of grain and he had stirred the special syrup into the portions for Nibble and Bell.

Josh had started a small fire and he had their bedding folded so they could sit on it near the fire.

"This is a really nice cabin. It is small, but we can add on to it if we want to."

"I think it is nice, just the way it is," said Adam. Josh nodded in agreement. They sat looking at the fire and David decided he would give them their treat before he put them to work.

"I bought each of us a big piece of maple sugar candy when I was in the store. I figured after that big steak, we probably wouldn't be very hungry."

"Oh, boy, I love this stuff," said Adam. "Thanks a lot."

"After we eat this, we have some work to do. Your Aunt Sarah thought you guys would want to dig a cache in here and she sent some mats to line it. She even sent dried food to put in it, but I forgot to get some planks to make a lid. Do you think we can do this?"

"Sure it will be fun!" Adam was always enthusiastic. Josh picked up the shovel and went to the far corner.

"I guess it should be away from the fire. Is this corner alright?"

"It looks like a good spot to me," said Adam. "You start and then I will take over. We can take turns. Mom will be surprised!"

David slipped out and brought in some more wood for the fire and some extra branches that he thought they could use to fashion a temporary lid.

"The horses are huddled together up against the wall of the cabin. They are out of the wind there, but it sure is getting colder. I was thinking that maybe we should bring them in here."

"I wouldn't mind. Jesus slept in a stable with sheep and a donkey, so I guess we could sleep with work horses. The only problem is that they are so big that if we bring them in here we won't have room on the floor to lie down," said Adam seriously. David and Josh started laughing.

"I was kidding Adam, but you are a good sport. They are fine out there." David encouraged the boys to get the job done and they piled the dirt on an old oiled hide that David had gotten from under the wagon seat. It was there to use if the driver was caught in the rain. We can drag that out in the morning. No point in holding the door open now and letting all the heat out. That's a fine job. He patted the mats in place and then the sack of dried foods was placed in the cache. "Once we dump that hide we can pull it over the top and pile wood on the edges to make a cover. That is a good job. Now if anyone gets caught in a storm or is too late to continue to the ranch, they can stop here for the night and the supplies are here to make a hot meal."

"Thanks for bringing us here Uncle David," said Josh. "I know that this is not the cabin my dad built, but it feels as if he is nearby and approves." David smiled, but didn't reply. Adam yawned and got into his bed roll. He pulled his extra blanket up over his chest.

"Thank you for bringing us Uncle David, this is fun. Thank you Jesus, for this cabin and everything." Soon all three were cozy and asleep.

During the night, the snow fell. It was not heavy, just enough to cover the grass and create a pristine landscape. They headed to the ranch with David's horses happy to be moving. He had greeted them with scratches and a big bundle of hay, while he and the boys had wild strawberry jam sandwiches.

"I am glad that Ben had the idea for us all to pile that cut grass under the trees for the cattle in case they have a harsh winter with deep snow. My big guys and gals are enjoying some of it for their breakfast."

It wasn't long before they were underway and once again Adam was talking nonstop.

"This has been so much fun, Uncle David. Thank you for taking us and for letting us see the brick yard and lumber mill and it was so nice to eat there with Tom and Cookie. Your ladies seem to be in a better mood this morning. I still don't think I would trust that old girl. She might just decide to bite again. How is your shoulder, Josh? I am glad she didn't bite me."

"My shoulder is fine. It is just a little tender."

"That's good. I can't wait to tell Mom and Dad about the cache we dug. Uncle David, it was a good thing that you put that ball of screen in the chimney. We wouldn't want mice inside the cabin. They would chew on everything. That is a pretty wool blanket Mom and Aunt Beth put in there. We wouldn't want holes in it already!"

"Take a breath, Adam. We are almost home. I can see the oak up ahead."

"Oh Josh, I can talk if I want to and you can't stop me."

David started laughing and then both boys laughed, too.

"I have enjoyed having you boys with me. I am eager to get home so I am not going to come to the ranch today.

Please hug everyone for me and be sure to take the shovel and bedrolls. Grab anything that is yours."

Jed saw the wagon and came across on the small raft and tied it to the trees. He talked with David for a few minutes and looked at the two skinny mares.

"I hope you have a lot of feed for them. Donaldson didn't break his budget buying them any, did he? I know you will take good care of them and when I see them again they will look a lot better, the poor things."

"Thanks for taking us," yelled Josh, as David pulled slowly away.

"Uncle Jed, we had a great time and last night we stopped at our cabin and Josh and I dug a cache. We didn't have the right tools to make a proper cover, but we put some dried food in it and pulled an oiled hide over it and piled some branches on all the edges. Uncle David climbed up on the roof and stuffed a wad of screen that he got from Tom, in the chimney so mice can't climb down in there and chew things. It was fun. Josh has a sore shoulder because that old horse bit him."

"It sounds like you boys have had quite an adventure!"

"We did!" Mary spotted the boys, struggling with their bundles on the path and ran to greet them. She hugged and laughed and helped carry some of their things the rest of the way.

"Are you hungry? Sit at the table and I will fix you some eggs. Tell me everything you did."

*****

The travel worn, weary people brought their caravan onto the church property and crossed using the raft to keep their tents and belonging dry. It was a slow process. The intention of Chief Dark Wolf and Two Feathers was to continue to the new camp site without stopping, but when

Sarah saw them all coming, she bundled in her coat and quickly wrapped Pili in a thick blanket and rushed out.

"What has happened? Why have you all come now and not in spring?"

"Sarah, go back inside! I will have your mother and Snow Star and some of the others with little ones come in while we get some tents set up. We are all here to stay. We can talk later."

Tears filled her eyes as she wrapped her arms around Pili and her mother at the same time. She motioned for others to come and led the way, hurrying them out of the bitter wind. Snow Star came and Clover, but others sent just their children as they continued on through the passageway knowing that Sarah would give their young ones good care. They had to get their tents up and fires going as soon as possible.

Chief Dark Wolf saw immediately that the layout of the new land was a mirror image of the old camp. The lake was to his left instead of right. Woods framed his view in either direction in the distance, with beautiful prairie grass beyond the lake and to his right. Ahead of him was a slight knoll, just a gentle roll in the land, before the trees became thick and blocked easy passage.

"Two Feathers, this is your camp. Where would you have us set up the tents?

"I am a sub-chief in the presence of wisdom, but I would suggest that you ride with me to that knoll and look around."

When he stopped his horse and turned back toward the passageway, Chief Dark Wolf smiled.

"It is good," he said. "It feels much like home. All that is missing is the big rock country."

"I will put my tent here," he said. "I like this little rise."

"I will place my followers there, at the bottom of the bluff. They will be close to guard the passageway," said Two Feathers. He and Willow directed the placing of family tents as they had been before, using Chief Dark Wolf's as their point of reference.

As the horses were quickly unloaded, they were led to a spot where the little river ran wider and slower. Each horse required nothing but a gentle nudge to get it to cross to the long stretch of inviting open prairie.

It was amazing how quickly the tents were put up. Women had small fires going inside with kettles of water warming for tea before the hour was up. Several men helped Chief Dark Wolf to erect his tent and Rising Eagle's just to his left.

As before the communal tent would stand to his right but it would not be put back together until family dwellings were completed and people had a warm place to rest. The women took provision sacks and quickly cut dry grass and stuffed the bags to carry back for insulation between the two walls of their tents. Young men and women were sent to gather stones to surround the fires and the outer edges of each tent.

Father Bob and Brother Tim decided that for now, they would put all their things as far back in the mouth of the cave as they could get. They stacked the many cases of books as a windbreak and lit a fire in the same place that David and Sarah had used. Together they worked as a team, bringing in the altar and their beds, all the pouches of supplies were brought near. Finally they were down to the layer of leather sacks containing the blue stones. White Grass and Pine Berry came to unhook the large teams that had pulled the heavy loads. Father Bob gave each of the horses some scratches and a lump of hardened sugar as they were led away through the pass to join the herd. Singing Wind sat on a downed tree and played softly, giving the people and horses the sound of home. His efforts were appreciated and rewarded.

As soon as others had their tents up they came and lifted his tent and brought grass to insulate it. A patch of grass inside had been scraped away and a tiny fire was lit to warm the leather so that it would smooth out to its full size and fasten down against the wind that rocked it. The people soon discovered that the best place to gather pieces of rock was at the base of the bluff. It was a long way for the exhausted people to carry rocks back to their tents, but they had mercy on their fatigued animals and managed to do it without hooking their horses to skids.

The older couples that Chief Dark Wolf honored, once again were placed near the area of the communal tent. When it was back up, it would shield them from the wind and lessen the snow that would inevitably blow across the open meadow.

Chief Dark Wolf made the effort to go himself, instead of sending someone. He tapped on Sarah's door and was pleased by the warm reception he received from her and all the women and little ones inside the cabin.

"If you will bundle the little ones and put on your own warm clothing, it is time for you all to come to the new camp." He said it smiling, but his heart was heavy. He knew that others that he loved and respected in camps that he saw at the summer meeting, were not blessed with a private, safe place. As he held the hand of one of the little ones, and led the way, his heart pleaded with God that his people be safe here for generations yet unborn.

Moonflower was pleased with the location of her tent as soon as she stood in front of the flap and looked to her left and saw that Snow Star was nearby. She knew that the large open space on her right would be the spot for the communal tent as soon as it could be put back together and the area built up and prepared as before. The camp exterior gave the impression of some order, but inside each tent was a mess. Moonflower encountered satchels, sacks, and quickly made containers piled everywhere. She knelt in the middle and as she tried to make room for their sleeping furs, she thanked God that they had arrived safely and, she hoped, undetected. As she located things she put them where they had been before. It wasn't long before she had a kettle of stew cooking on a small fire inside her tent. She had stacked their clothes when she packed so it was easy now to remove the sacks and place their clothes against the back wall. As each sack was emptied she stuffed it between the walls for further insulation. Then she changed her mind and pulled several out and spread them on the grass under their bedding to stop the cold of the ground from creeping up. When I have time to pad them with dry grass and more hides, then the sacks can go in the walls, she thought. All her cooking utensils were put in the front, right side. She located her favorite tea container and filled it from the lake. With chamomile and mint sprinkled in, she was able to sit down on her furs. With two bowls, two spoons and her favorite, well-seasoned, smooth cooking stones set near the fire, she felt comforted.

Sarah and Pili came in and sat with her.

"I see you are cooking stew and have a pan of tea steaming. I think every tent in this camp has the same things on their fire. It will go well with you mother. Do not worry about anything. You are safe here. Everyone is safe and welcome."

"Thank you Sarah, for taking care of the children; while the tents went up. It is nearly dark, you should go back now with Pili. I just realized that I haven't seen David. Where is he?"

"He will be back in a day or two. He went into town to get some things. He will be surprised that you are all here when he returns. Goodnight Mother. Sleep well." She touched her mother's cheek, wiping away a small tear.

Sarah shivered as she hurried through camp back to her cabin carrying Pili. She stood Pili on her feet and handed her a piece of wood for the fire. Sarah filled her arms and they entered the back door. She added wood to the fire and then put Pili to bed. With a cup of tea in one hand and her Bible in the other, she sat down at the window and stared out at the dark scene. The partial moon gave just enough light to tell that the sky was filling with heavy clouds.

"Please Father, don't allow it to snow a lot until David gets back and the people are better settled. Thank you for bringing them here safely." She opened her book to the Psalms of praise and read until her eyes grew heavy. She readied herself for bed. It's strange that I don't feel comforted knowing they are near. I must find time with Father to talk where others are not listening. There is a feeling of uneasiness in his spirit. I must know the truth, she thought as she pulled the covers up close to her chin. "Father God, please watch over David and bring him back to me safely."

They all woke to a sparkling white world. The sun was bright and the snow would soon melt. She showed Pili the scene out the window and taught her the Winahatah word for snow. With winter clothes and boots she took Pili to check on the horses.

CHAPTER SIXTEEN
A NEW SITUATION

Lori and Sylvia laughed and stomped the snow from their new boots as they hung their coats and hats on the hooks by the back door of the little cabin.

"The chores went quickly this morning. I am glad that Beth and Mary don't need us until later. We can work on our knitting."

"Did you see how long this scarf is getting? I think I will give it to Mark for Christmas."

"I wonder how they celebrate Christmas here. I know they are conservative, so they probably make all their gifts. Mary bought a bag of taffy and put it high in the cupboard to save for the holiday."

"I think I am going to pick out a horse and make sure they know which one I like. Maybe they will give it to me as a gift."

"Lori, they sell the trained mustangs. That's how they make their income. You can't ask for a gift that valuable!"

"I won't ask for it. I will just let them know which one I like the best and maybe Santa will give it to me."

Sylvia shook her head at the way Lori thought. I don't understand her. They have already given us a roof and food and warm clothes. What more does anyone need? She thought. She poured them each a cup of tea and added milk to hers.

"Are there any more of the cookies left?" Lori asked. Sylvia placed the tin of cookies on the little table and took her mug of tea to the window where she stood looking out.

"Even with the little lake altered, this is still a nice view. I wonder if the water will freeze solid in the canal. If it does, it may break the baked clay walls."

"Yes, nothing ever lasts, does it? Did you see Jed up on that ladder while we were doing chores? After they finished the milking he and Johnny were putting the tin sheets back on the roof of the cheese shed. I wonder how long they will last after being used to cover the fires. They may not be strong anymore."

"I didn't mean it like that, I just wondered if the freezing and thawing would crack the clay."

"Well Sylvia, I guess we will have to wait and see. The water will still run through unless they block it off and if they do that, they will be back carrying water to the animals."

"It seems like there is endless work here but the end result is for the ranch, not the worker."

"Lori, that's not true. Look around you. This is the result of your work. When you arrived you had that worn little carpet bag. You didn't have a home or even money to buy a good meal. If I were you, I would be very happy that I have this big family. They love you and Mark. You have a place here forever."

"I don't plan on being here forever. Do you want to stay here and do farm chores the rest of your life?"

"I'm not sure what I want, but I don't mind working to earn my keep. I think Mark had a good idea when we were in town. He pointed out that Cookie needs help. I think there might be others that could use help but I would need to inquire," said Sylvia

"Are you planning on moving to Silverville?"

"No silly, I just meant there are alternatives to making a living on a farm, that's all. We need to learn as much as we can here. Skills like cooking and cleaning and even washing clothes when it is freezing outside, those are valuable. Mary and Beth are both good bakers. We should ask them to teach us."

"You are giving me some ideas!"

"Look, I have finished a row and it is even. When will they teach us to color the wool?"

"I think that will be in warm weather."

"I can't wait that long, because I want to make this scarf brown for Mark for Christmas. Do you think they would be able to do it in the house?"

"I don't know but I do know that if you put wool into hot water it shrinks. You will have to make that a lot longer."

*****

Ben sat at the table with a ledger beside his coffee. Mary patted his shoulder as she walked near to check on Eli's printing.

"That's good, Son. You can go play now if you want to or you can sit with Dad and I will give you some numbers like his to learn."

"I want to go help in the old barn."

"Alright, but bundle up. It is cold outside."

*****

David pulled the wagon close to the church crossing, but was puzzled by the presence of two large wagons on the other side of the river standing in front of the cave. Before crossing the water, he released the three horses on the back of the wagon and slowly led them to the shelter he had expanded before he left. With a little adjusting of positions, he was able to put Nibble on the far end and Bell beside her.

"There you go girls, here is hay and water and no need to cross that cold water right now. He gave them attention and pats and tied Blackie under the trees near the river. With his team back alert he urged them forward across the river and on to his property to the back where he passed the passageway and the large outdoor fire pit that Sarah had used earlier in the season. He continued on slowly, trying to

254

get the wagon as close to the area that he planned to fence as he could.

"That should do it boys." He unhooked his team and led them to the river for a drink and then he tied them in the tall grass on his new land. "Dinner is served." He laughed at the team in the tall grass with stems sticking out of their mouths. Eat all you want. You earned it. After a quick rub with a burlap sack in each hand, the horses were dry and comfortable." David smiled as he looked at his team. He had grown to love these big animals.

With satchels in hand he made his way through the trees and brush to the back door. He could hear voices inside.

"Hello, I am home." He called as he stepped into the warm cabin. Sarah met him with a hug and Pili ran and grabbed his leg with her face turned upward, beaming a smile at him.

"Daddy, Daddy."

"We have company David. Actually they are our neighbors now. Father Bob and Brother Tim have moved into the front of the cave until they can get a little cabin built."

"Really, what prompted that? The Blue Stone People will miss you."

Father Bob greeted him with a hug and a slap on the back and Tim did the same.

"We have a long story to tell you. The People are here David. Last night was their first night here. They are still trying to make order of their camp!"

"This is a big change from what you had planned. Did something happen?"

"Yes, much has happened and I fear there is more to come. Tim and I were not sure what we would do when the followers of Two Feathers came here in the spring, but now there was no decision to make, because the entire village is here."

"David, give me your coat and sit down at the table. I will fix you a plate while we talk. Father Bob is considering going back and taking the church and school apart board by board and bringing them here."

"That would be a huge undertaking! I doubt if the men of the village will be able to help you for a while. They will be busy rebuilding their camp. They will need fences and shelters for their animals. They will probably want to put that big tent back up. Did they bring that too?"

"Yes, they brought everything and they traveled a long route so their tracks wouldn't immediately give away where they went."

"When I pulled the wagon around, I didn't hear a thing. I had no idea. I saw your wagons and wondered about that."

"As soon as they unload the leather sacks of stones, Tim and I will be going back to the village to get a load of boards. We have no need to hide our tracks. I got this land for a church by the river. I told the man that at the time. If we are questioned by soldiers we will tell the truth. The People left us behind and we have decided to build our church here."

"Soldiers, what are you talking about?" Sarah explained.

"Soldiers came to two villages of people that were at the Summer Council. They forced them to move. They made them walk in the snow and with few provisions. Many died! That is why Chief Dark Wolf has brought his people here now. They are on private land that Ben bought. The soldiers can't make them leave, even if they find them."

"Why would they do that? It doesn't make sense." David was standing and angry. He started to pace. "We have to do something!"

"Be calm David. Something has been done. The people are safe here. "What about the others?"

"At this time, I have no knowledge of where they were taken. The scout that brought the news rode swiftly in fear for his life."

"I am going to talk to Chief Dark Wolf," said David. "Sarah, stay away from the new horses. One of them is dangerous. She bites without provocation. She bit Josh and will bite any horse that she doesn't know. It is best that you and Pili stay away until we get her figured out." He pulled his coat on and was out the door quickly. Sarah was about to ask if Josh was alright, but she didn't get a chance.

"Sarah, Tim and I are going to get the men to move the sacks from our wagons, so that we can use them. We will be leaving here as soon as possible." They both pulled their coats on and went out the back door also heading for the passageway.

"Tim, while I talk to Two Feathers I would like you to get us some horses for our wagons."

"I will. Do you think we will need two or four?" Get four for each wagon. When we return, I intend to have those wagons fully loaded."

Father, how do you think that the two of us can take apart two buildings that it took many men weeks to build?"

"I don't have all the answers, but I know they won't get here by themselves." The young men came, bringing big horses. They loaded the sacks of stones on skids and walked them to the bottom of the bluff as Two Feathers directed. The sacks were placed against the bottom of the bluff and the horses were again walked back to the wagons until the wagons were unloaded.

Two Feathers abruptly interrupted a conversation that David was having with the Chief.

"Chief Dark Wolf, I think it is time that you know why the Holy Spirit has put your people here." Two Feathers stated it as fact and David stopped mid-sentence. "In an hour the bluff will stand in shadow. We will go then. David I would like you and Father Bob and Brother Tim to come, also Rising Eagle. One day he will be responsible for the Blue Stone People. He needs to know just what an extraordinary responsibility it is.

As we climb, we will each take as much weight as we can carry. Each of you should get a leather satchel from your tent to use. All the stones need to be moved before our location is discovered. We have no way to know when that will be."

The men nodded and scattered to get the pouches that would be needed. No one questioned his authority, not even Chief Dark Wolf. He felt it in his spirit that something unbelievable was about to happen. He was right.

The young men that had been with Two Feathers when the salt cathedral was discovered knew what was happening and they came to help transfer the stones. They stood in a line and handed the sacks up one at a time.

When Two Feathers and his group that included Chief Dark Wolf approached the clump of old pine trees, the rest of the men stopped, waiting for instructions.

"Bring them inside and carry them to the workmen's quarters. Each satchel must be up where it will always stay dry and hidden." The men responded and others came to the bottom of the bluff and were turned away. Men that had mined the stones came, wanting to see where they were being taken. They were asked to step back down. They were puzzled and a couple of them felt angry wondering if they were no longer trusted.

The men proceeded down the slanting floor of the entrance until it split into two tunnels. The men carrying the stones went right But Two Feathers led the others on down further, stopping to light two lanterns. It felt strange. They heard the footsteps and voices of the others grow faint as they proceeded. David felt concern. What if there is damage? What if I wasn't careful enough with the dynamite? God, please let everything be as beautiful as I remember it.

Two Feathers slipped his knee high laced leather boots off and asked the others to do the same with their foot wear. Some of them had felt an urging to do it before he spoke. Father Bob was physically affected. Instinctively he stepped out of the tunnel, drawn to the massive altar. He knelt and was unaware of the tears streaming down his face.

"Who am I that you honor me with your great presence?" He asked the question softly, but it bounced from the walls echoing back to him.

The Lion leapt from the altar and landed silently. He walked slowly to the huge doors that stood at the front of the room. The light that they carried was nothing compared to the light that emanated from Him. He turned and looked at the carving of the lamb still lying on the altar.

"You have honored the Son, so I honor you. Your people will live and thrive in the meadow of peace. No harm will come to you there, as long as you believe and trust."

The vision was gone like a breath in the cold air. When they turned around, both Lion and Lamb were on the altar as before. The men looked here and there, left and right, trying to absorb the grandeur and perfection in carved beauty that surrounded them. No one spoke, but they all understood that it was time to leave. They moved slowly to the tunnel and put their shoes back on. The strenuous incline caused their legs to tire and ache. Chief Dark Wolf leaned against the wall for a few moments to rest.

"How long have you known about this?" He asked the question humbly. Two Feathers smiled at the question.

"He has brought us here each in the proper time. You are here now and we all will protect the entrance with our very lives if need be. But somehow I know that it is the Lion that is doing the protecting. We must speak not of this to anyone. Sarah has been told. We all agree that she is no ordinary woman. She is the only woman that knows of this. Let it remain so." The six men nodded to each other accepting his word as a vow. They stepped out through the branches of the huge pines and with the help of the lanterns; they descended to the meadow without a misstep.

There in the center of the new camp the people had gathered wood for a communal fire. Chief Dark wolf was delighted. Two Feathers was pleased by something else. He could see that all the pouches of stones had been transported to the workmen's chambers and were out of sight. He also noted that his followers were spacing their tents along the bluff just thirty yards short of the spot where the water spewed from the opening. Both sides of the passageway would be guarded by his alert young men.

Moonflower walked close to the group of men and turned her attention to Chief Dark Wolf.

"Some of the people ask since we have moved here who is their Chief? I told them that you are Chief no matter where we live. Like in old days our people moved with the seasons. Their Chief remained the same and status remains the same. They should know that by the positions of the tents."

"You did well, Moonflower. Have the women cooked special foods expecting a communal fire?"

"We were hoping that it would be tomorrow night."

"That is good. You may pass the word that our first communal feast here will be tomorrow at sundown."

She walked away proudly smiling. This camp is a good new camp. All will be well her body English said as she stepped with more energy than she felt. She scratched on Snow Star's tent and was quickly ushered in.

"How are you feeling tonight, after that ordeal of moving? Is the baby active?"

"Yes, he is moving. We are all well mother."

"Good, God has blessed us. Please pass the word, that we will have a communal fire tomorrow night and I want it to be a celebration for our new camp! I know that all of us still have work to do, but we have to cook anyway. We may as well make a lot of one thing and share with each other."

Clover came near but didn't speak to the men. She waited patiently to be noticed.

"Clover, how are you doing at getting settled?" Brother Tim smiled broadly at her as he inquired.

"We are all doing very well. Our tent is in order as much as is possible. We will try to start digging the food caches tomorrow. The sacks of dry food are crowding us but I don't think I want to put them outside where something might happen to them."

"Yes there are many projects to do. Father Bob and I will be leaving with our two big wagons tomorrow. We are going back to the old campsite and we plan to take the church and school apart and bring them here. Now you must admit that is an ambitious project!"

"How many men are going with you?" Her voice was filled with concern and fear.

"None, we don't want to have them out where the soldiers will see them. We will stay and work there and when our wagons are loaded, we will return to empty them on our church land."

"You brought all your supplies and tools with you. Remember to take back what you will need," said Two Feathers.

"May I make a request?" Clover spoke hesitantly.

"Yes of course you can ask. We will do anything for you that we can," said Father Bob.

"I loved the big willow trees around our old lake. I think if you cut branches and wrap them in wet sacks just as you leave, they will live. We could push them into the mud near the water here and soon we can have our willow trees again."

"Clover that is a good idea, we will do it. I promise I won't forget," said Tim.

"Father that is a huge job you are undertaking. I could come with you. I am known in town as David Sharpe now. I don't think I would have a problem if the soldiers came."

"You have plenty of work lined up for yourself here. Sarah will need help. You brought a load of fencing. She can't put that up."

"That's true, but I think the men here would help her with the care of the new horses and as long as they have water and feed, they are fine. Besides, I can unload my wagon and bring my team, too. With three wagons maybe we could bring the entire project at one time."

"You are tempting me to take you up on that offer David. However, I think you should discuss it with Sarah." said Father Bob. Night Hawk, Debon and Soren stood on the fringe of the group. Wanting to hear someone say what Chief Dark Wolf's initial reaction was to the Cathedral of Salt. It wasn't mentioned.

Instead, David asked them to follow him to his place so that they could help him empty his wagon of fencing, posts and rolls of wire. It was quickly done and David thanked them and then headed toward his cabin's back door. He stopped abruptly.

"Do you think these big rolls would go through the passageway if they were rolled on the ground?"

"Yes, I think it is wide enough. Why?"

"If the three of you will agree to make a separate area to hold my two female work horses that I bought and a shelter for them, I would be happy to let the men of the people use this fencing. It would help to get things started. I know it isn't enough for all the animals but it would help contain the beef cattle."

Then he turned around and asked them to come with him to see the couple of old horses he rescued. Night Hawk said he would like to and so did Debon, but Soren walked away, saying that he needed to help Cumae for a bit before they could sleep.

Night Hawk thought that Bell was a usable horse if David fattened her up with some good food, but he said he thought Nibble was going to be nothing but trouble!

"Once a horse starts biting other horses or a human, it is extremely hard to break them of it." Night Hawk was knowledgeable about horses and David was beginning to regret his decision. I will take you up on the offer of the fence David," he said. "Will you be going with Father Bob and Brother Tim?"

"I think so but I haven't talked to Sarah about it yet. That's why I need a separate area made for these old girls, so I know they are where they won't hurt her while I am gone."

"We will take care of it and keep an eye open to help her if you go. Don't worry about it."

"Thank you, Night Hawk. I really appreciate it." They parted company smiling and David entered his back door.

He discussed several things with Sarah. One of them was Nibble.

"I think I need to put her in an area by herself and let her eat and rest for a while. Maybe once she is rested and lonely, she will appreciate attention and care."

"David I know that you are concerned about that horse biting me or Pili but I have control over that and I can tell you right now that it isn't going to happen. I think there is something else bothering you. What are you thinking about?"

"You know me well. I feel bad that Father Bob and Brother Tim have to go alone to the old village and dismantle the church and school and bring them back here. They have worked so hard, always with The People of the village in mind. Now when circumstances have caused this situation, they have to pay a huge price. It will take them a long time to do that much work and it is winter."

"David, why don't you just say that you want to go help them? Didn't you think that I would agree? I don't like it when we are separated, but I will survive. The people are here now and if I really need help, they will help me."

"So you think I should go help them?"

"Yes, David I do, but I would like it if you could solve the issue with Nibble's care before you leave. Other than that, I will be fine and I can care for the rest of our animals."

"Thank you Sarah, for understanding. I am the only one here that the town knows as not an Indian. They know that we live here separately, so if soldiers come while we are working, we can explain it that they moved away and they don't live with us. That's true enough, isn't it?"

"Yes it is true."

"What's wrong Sarah? I can feel it."

"Do you really think they will look for the people? Since they became the Blue Stone People; there has not been war with the wagon trains. Why would they want to harm them now?"

"I don't have the answer to that or many of the other questions that the people are asking, but I do know that the sooner we get the church and school here, the sooner we will all feel a little better about it."

"When will you leave?"

"In the morning, at first light, I plan to head out, but I am going to the ranch first to see if Jed and Josh can come with me to help."

Sarah nodded, but didn't reply. She felt that her two worlds were on a collision course and she could not do a thing to stop it.

CHAPTER SEVENTEEN
NO MORE BLUE STONES

The winter started out a dry one. That was a blessing to everyone. Jed and Josh returned after being gone three weeks. They were tired but glad that they had helped. Father Bob, David and Tim went back a final time and when they left, it was as if The Blue Stone People had never lived there. Their last chore was to take many cuttings from the willow trees. They wrapped them in wet sacks and tucked them in between the posts and split rails of the fence that had surrounded the horse herd. Just rows of piles of rocks where the posts had been confirmed the hard work the men had finally finished. All three big wagons were full again, this time with fencing.

*****

Earlier, Tim had come up with an idea for marking the pieces of the buildings so they knew where each piece came from and they hoped that it would go back together like a big puzzle. They decided as they traveled along that the school should go in the meadow near the children. They planned to put it back together in the spring. Father Bob came up with the idea to build the church in the mouth of the cave.

"We can start immediately. Weather won't hold us up if we are working in there. We can do it Tim and it will be a unique tribute to the Lion of Judah. We should build the church and our residence first and then put the school together wherever the people would like it."

*****

It was late afternoon and they sat with a cup of coffee on a bench the men of the Lion had made and placed under the pines where the face of the cave could be observed.

"I will help you all I can, you know that, but I need to tell you something. I have been giving this decision a great deal of thought and prayer. I am not sure how you will take it," said Tim.

"What is it? Are you leaving to go back to the seminary?"

"No, just the opposite, I have decided that I want to ask Clover to marry me."

"Tim, marriage to Clover would be taking on a great deal of responsibility. It may be more commitment than the priesthood. Are you sure? How long have you felt this way?"

"I think I fell in love with the children first. She is good and caring and is doing such a wonderful job with them."

"Tim that is not enough to base a marriage on. You could say the same thing about the story mothers. They love and take good care of the children. There has to be more. Tell me about her."

"Clover is sweet, and gentle and beautiful and I can't stand it when I am away from her. When I close my eyes her face is there in the dark. She is the reason I came back from the ranch. I felt guilty with all the work there was to do but I couldn't stop myself. Father, I haven't said a word to her and if you tell me that I am wrong I think my chest will explode!"

"That's rather dramatic isn't it?"

"No, that's how I feel!"

"You haven't told her that you love her and want to marry her?"

"No I wasn't sure what I should do. I wanted to tell you first."

"Tim, you don't need my permission. You know your heart better than I do. You won't be breaking any vows. I guess the bishop knew what he was doing when he sent you out here. You have my blessing Tim, if that is what you want to do then I am glad for you, but may I make a suggestion? You need to let it be known that you have decided not to finish your training to be a priest. Everyone thinks of you as they do me, that you are not allowed to take a wife. You should think about building a small cabin and let it be known that you are preparing to take a wife. You know that she may not feel the way you do. While you are building that cabin, you may want to spend a little time courting her."

"See I knew there was a reason that I was supposed to talk to you first. That all makes good sense; I don't have a place to live! How can I take a wife? I am going to take a walk and I want you to help me pick a place for a cabin and a well. I have to do it or we lose this land, I am so excited that I can't think straight. I was thinking that I wanted it over there near the river but I can't do that, I have to put it somewhere on the homestead piece. Help me find a good spot."

Father Bob started to chuckle and then he was laughing loudly and Tim started laughing too.

"Your laugh in contagious but why are we laughing?'

"I am laughing because I am happy! Tim I love you as if you are my little brother. I can't express how pleased I am that you have found someone special. I can't wait until those kids call you Daddy!"

"Hey stop that! One step at a time, let's find a place for the cabin."

"Look Tim, if those big pines can find water here so could you. If you put your cabin near them, you will be able to put the well here and look out at the cave and maybe the church if we build it in the entrance. If you face it this way, you will not be invading David and Sarah's privacy at all. They will not see your cabin because of the thick trees. What do you think?"

"I feel that it is perfect! The stone from the bluff comes down here almost to my front door, but I would dig the well in back of it anyway. I can't wait to start! I want to tell somebody! Come with me!"

Tim hurried to David and Sarah's back door and tapped lightly.

"Can you come out? I want to show you something." Father Bob and Tim were both grinning. Sarah quickly wrapped a blanket around her shoulders and tucked Pili inside it.

"Where are we going? It isn't far is it?" David asked.

"No, just far enough, to be on my homestead land," said Tim. "I am going to build my cabin here, facing toward the cave and dig the well behind it, about here," he said it digging his heel into the soil to make a mark."

"That's exciting Tim. It looks like there will be room there. The trees are old and it won't take much trimming to keep the branches off your roof."

"I like the spot you have chosen Tim. It is a good one. The trees will block some of the wind and snow, too."

"I hadn't thought of that. I can't wait to get started."

"We are thinking of building the church inside the front of the cave. We will be able to work on it even if it is snowing!" Father Bob was excited.

David's expression didn't change as he said that Sarah and Pili should get in out of the cold wind.

"Come over for supper and we will talk." The little family hurried back inside.

"That was a little strange. It was almost as if they didn't like where I have chosen for the cabin. I hope that isn't going to be a problem."

Tim and Father Bob walked the front of the cave, measuring the space and rejoiced to see that the church could be reconstructed in the cave with room to spare. When they finished, they were feeling very cold and were looking forward to a warm reception and hot meal at David and Sarah's cabin.

When they tapped and stepped inside, they were surprised to see Two Feathers, Debon, Soren and Chief Dark Wolf there already.

"We are happy to see all of you," said Tim, "but we didn't know that you were having a meeting tonight. Maybe we should visit tomorrow."

"Father, we have been waiting for you. This meeting is about your plans," said David.

Two Feathers stood and turned to face them where they stood.

"I am not sure how to say these words. It is not my intention or anyone's here, to offend either of you in anyway, but we all feel that it is important that you leave the cave as it is. We don't want you to build in it, or near it. The cave is sacred and special just the way it is. We ask that you honor our request."

"Two Feathers, I don't think you understand. I have to build on that piece of land and dig a well just as Ben had to, or I will lose it. The spot I picked for the cabin is as far back as I can put it and still be on the homestead land."

"We know that and we are not troubled by the building of your cabin. It will be fine there. It is that you two were measuring the cave with the intention of building your church inside the entrance. We don't think you should do that."

Chief Dark Wolf had listened quietly but now he spoke up.

"Father Bob, my men have become good builders and as soon as we have fences and shelters made for our animals, to keep them safe, we will be glad to help you build your church in the center of your land where you originally intended to put it. They will be able to shape the new church so that it settles between the ancient trees and beckons travelers on the prairie. We know that it is your calling to teach many about the cross and the Son of God. Please allow us to help you all that we can." Father Bob looked around the room, feeling grateful and stunned at the strong reaction he had caused.

"I accept your offer of help," said Father Bob," I will do as you suggest."

"Sarah, I think I smell a batch of chili? Are you intending to feed all of us?"

"Yes, I have made plenty and I just want to say that I am glad that you have all felt comfortable enough to speak up and resolve this quickly. I also would be sad to see anything man made in or near the cave. I don't want it to change either. Now, let's give thanks and eat. Father Bob, would you please say the blessing?"

"Father God, once again you have given me good counsel. This time you spoke through my friends. I thank you for them and we all thank you for the opportunity to be here in this sacred place. Thank you for the protection that you give us and the many blessings, in particular this wonderful meal. Amen" Sarah served the bowls of steaming chili, and crackers she had made. She gave them hot tea and they lingered long after dark enjoying the warmth of friendship and comfortable feeling of being able to express their thoughts without hurting others.

Tim finally got up the nerve to say what he had been thinking about all evening.

"Chief Dark Wolf, I have been praying and thinking long about something, and I have decided not to return to the seminary to finish my schooling to become a Jesuit priest. I would like your permission to court Clover. I intend to ask her to marry me, when I have my cabin built. I would appreciate your approval."

"Tim, this is not a surprise to me. Many have detected the attraction between you two young people. You may court her, but know now that her bride price will be high. She has three children and is a worthy wife with a family." Tim grinned and told the group how much he cared for the entire family and said that he had to admit that he hadn't thought about a bride price. There is time for that, he thought, while I am building our cabin.

Snow finally came and blanketed the land in deep drifts. All thoughts of building anything further had to be set aside for a while. The shepherds took their sheep into the trees where the snow was not as deep and the animals were able to find something to eat. The other animals had shelters hastily made as soon as the tents went up. The chickens cuddled in their open crates placed between two tents with the top covered by oiled hides. They were happy with the mixture of wild grain and cracked corn the people offered in an area where the snow was tromped down. Cumae and Obona made sure they were well cared for. The milk cows were also safe in the edge of the woods. The women had cut great bundles of dry grass and had stacked it under the trees. Now the cows were enjoying it. The beef cattle plodded the prairie behind the tents and with their strong horns and wide hooves they scrubbed the snow away and grazed on the rich grass beneath it. The herd of horses was also doing fine.

David made sure that his animals were cared for and took the feed with the rich syrup mixed in it to the big mares. They acted glad to see him and stepped closer. He fed Nibble first. Talking to her and scratching.

"You and Bell are going to realize soon that you are with people that care for you. You won't get mistreated here." He patted Bell and scratched her ears and then Joey came wanting attention. David backed him up and found a new spot for him where he could see the new ladies, but not get in biting range. The wolves came bounding up as David headed in the back door. "I know what you guys want." He gave them each a big piece of dried meat and then tossed three big marrow bones in the path where his boots had packed the snow down. He scratched ears and rubbed furry faces laughing.

As he entered the cabin and took off his outdoor clothes he could feel the tension in Sarah.

"What are you thinking about, Sarah? I can feel the storm cloud clear over here."

"I'm sorry David, I am not angry, just worried. I was thinking of the way Ben has put the ranch in the middle of the war! I don't think he can keep from taking sides forever. He is white. Everyone at the ranch is white. They make a living gentling the mustangs and selling them to the soldiers. How long can he keep doing that? He bought land for the people to live on. The records have his name on it even if he did give the papers to Two Feathers. When the soldiers at the fort figure out that The Blue Stone People are living on his land there will be trouble. You can be sure of that."

"Sarah, sit down here with me, by the fire and have a cup of tea. I want to tell you what happened when Two Feathers took the last group of men with Chief Dark Wolf into the Cathedral."

They talked for quite a while and when the conversation was over, the tea was cold and Pili was napping in the sun on the bear rug, with her two middle fingers in her mouth.

"All of this tells me that the people are safe here, but what about Ben and the ranch. He has got to stop helping the soldiers."

"Sarah, I don't think so. God has used Ben and the ranch several times. He believes and trusts, doesn't he?"

"Yes, I know he does."

"God continues to bless him. Look at the ranch; it is big and growing."

*****

Josh and Lori sat on a roll of dry grass giggling as Jed entered.

"Josh I can tell that you are as glad to be back here as I am. Hello Lori, I see you appreciate good horses. That young girl you are stroking is the granddaughter of Ginger, our very first horse that Ben pulled from the bog."

"Yes I remember the story of Ben rescuing Ginger. He told me about it one day in his old barn when I was in there helping. How old is this little girl?"

"She is a yearling. I brought her in here to help Ben put shoes on her."

"How long will it be before she can be ridden?"

"Probably next spring she will start carrying a light bundle. She hasn't gotten her full size yet. We won't start her out with a heavy weight. She is not totally developed yet."

"That's interesting. Is it alright if I walk back to the mustang field and just watch the horses for a while? We have all been so busy that I haven't really seen all of them. They are so beautiful. I love all the horses."

"Yes of course you can go anywhere you want to."

"Well, it would be a lot easier to get around if I had a horse to use." She headed out the back door of Jed's barn stepping through the snow. Josh followed her like a puppy. He was smitten. He was experiencing his first crush.

On the other hand, she barely knew that he existed. She was working on her own agenda, which included getting a horse of her own. Jed watched the two walking down the path to the gate of the mustang field and was thinking that she should have a trustworthy horse to ride. They hadn't had much time to teach her to ride properly but she seemed to learn quickly. At least she isn't afraid of them, he thought.

Sylvia always seemed to be involved in one chore or another. She was helping Beth fold the cold clothes from the line.

"I never would have thought of freezing as a way of drying things. The sheets are so smooth that they look like they were ironed."

"That's because I went out and pulled on the seams when they were just starting to freeze."

"Beth you know so many things! I hope you don't mind teaching me."

"I don't think of it as teaching, I just appreciate the help, Sylvia."

"Are you going to be doing any ironing today?"

"No, none of this is going to get ironed. It's mostly work clothes. Jed wouldn't know what to do with an ironed work shirt!" They laughed together and enjoyed each other's company. "Sylvia, I was thinking I should make a cake for our meal together. Do you want to do it and I'll watch to make sure you do it right. I was thinking we would put some cherries in the bottom and then turn it over quick when it comes out of the oven."

"Yes, thank you. I would like to try but you better watch closely. I have never followed a recipe."

"Aw, it's not hard, once you get the hang of the fractions and know to grease the pan, you can make almost anything."

"Fractions, I knew this was going to be hard!"

"Never mind, it just sounds hard. Here is a quart of the cherries and we will use the juice in the jar as part of the liquid in the recipe. We are all going down to Mary's tonight. The men want to have another meeting. You can carry in the cake and say you made it."

*****

As the family gathered at Ben's house, he and Jed had been working on putting shoes on Silk and a spirited yearling from the herd of mustangs.

"Actually she is probably closer to two years old Ben. She has filled out and full size. Orville said he has been putting light bundles on her for a while now. That's why she was so gentle. He has been spending quality time with her."

"Jed what do you think of that brown mare?"

"I think the stallion stole her from a settler just the same as Angel was stolen. She is likely been ridden. She didn't mind us handling her and stood still for the shoes. I checked her all over to make sure she doesn't have a brand or tattoo in either ear. She doesn't. Maybe we should keep her for breeding and the women can ride her once we make sure she is gentle."

"I like her a lot. She has good lines and strong muscles. She is worth keeping."

Orville came in behind them and removed his boots and tossed them near the row along the wall.

"It sure smells good in here," he said with a big smile for Mary.

"You are smelling fried rabbits and other good things. Beth is bringing desert, so I don't know what that will be. Go ahead and wash your hands Orville and I will pour you some coffee. The rest of the family will be here soon."

Mark and Josh followed him in and then the rest of the folks arrived. Johnny came in saying that he had gone up to the lookout and that they had an all clear.

"It sure is hard climbing up there when we have a bunch of snow. I hope that the cattle are alright. I think we should ride down there in the morning and make sure they have grass they can get to and we need to break the ice on their water pond if it stays this cold." Jed smiled at him.

"You are right son. All the animals need a little help now and then. They are pretty smart though. They know to go under the trees for shelter and they can get to the grass easily there. I will ride down there with you, if you want to go, or maybe you and Josh would like to go. We can talk about it in the morning."

Sylvia proudly brought in the cherry cake she had made and it was perfect. Beth had given her instructions but she had done it all herself.

"That looks delicious Sylvia. What's in the bowl?"

"We made whipped cream to put on top."

"Yum," said Adam, definitely appreciating Sylvia's new skills. Lori was the last one in and it was obvious that she had been napping. Her cheek had a crease from the pillow.

"Lori, how are you, dear? You look tired," asked Mary.

"I am tired. Our cabin is a long way from here to walk in the cold and snow."

"I didn't know that you didn't have a ride. I guess I thought that you would be helping Beth and come when she and Sylvia came in the wagon."

"No, after I walked back from the mustang field, I had a headache so I laid down for a bit. I am hungry after all that exercise though. Everything smells wonderful."

"Is your headache gone now Lori?" Mark asked with true concern.

"Yes I am fine now, but I do want a ride back to our cabin when we are done here tonight." It didn't take a minute for Sylvia to figure out what game Lori was playing.

CHAPTER EIGHTEEN
PACIFICATION WITH COURAGE

Chief Dark Wolf had many things that troubled him. The communal tent needed to be reconstructed. It was lying in the snow.

"The snow will melt and cause damage, Moonflower. We have to get that tent back up soon."

"The people made it in the rain. I don't think the snow would stop them if you told them they had to do it. Besides we need it up. Spring is a long way off. We can use it to get out of the cold." The Chief motioned for Bending Grass to come to him.

"Bending Grass, today you will be my messenger. I want you to tell all the men to come here to the communal tent. Go now and tell everyone that is not already working to come here and to bring shovels."

"Yes, my Chief."

The young man hurried away, pleased that he was chosen to spread the message. Soon most of the men of the village were heading in the direction of the big tent where the Chief stood. It looked sad buried in the snow.

Night Hawk came near and asked if he should go get a pair of the big work horses. He had already figured out what the Chief was planning. Chief Dark Wolf nodded. Night Hawk had already considered what it would take to put the big tent back up. He had his favorite hunting horse near his tent. With a handful of grain he greeted him and rode across the shallow part of the water to the herd. It wasn't long before the tent was cleaned of snow and dragged closer to the site where it would be erected.

"The ground is frozen," they complained. We can't dig dirt to raise it up."

"Do you think it is frozen under the ashes of our communal fire? Scrape it back and as you dig a big cooking pit, put the dirt where the tent will sit. How many of you still need to dig a cache in your tent? Put the dirt on an old hide and drag it here. We can do it," he said.

The Chief took a shovel and began to scrape back the warm ashes from their communal fire. Moonflower walked over and observed the activity for a moment and then casually suggested that they start by digging the caches.

"It will be a help to all the women to be able to get the sacks of dried food put away.

"Also, my husband," she said quietly;" Look at the layout of the camp. The wind that blows across the meadow will bring the smoke of the cooking fire into our tents. If you would put the cooking pit on the other end of the communal fire, it would be a little better." She smiled at him and ducked back into their tent. Sometimes, I think she is the real Chief, he thought.

Moonflower seldom asked anyone to help her. She led by example. Soon many women had joined her in her efforts to gather grass to cover the dirt of the raised tent floor. The snow covered most of it, but even a thin layer of grass would help to keep their furs clean. They found a stand of grass on the south side of bushes and inside the trees where the cattle hadn't been yet. Some had been protected by boulders at the base of the bluff. They cut what they could find and were glad to have it.

The men had brushed the snow from the tent and were lacing the heavy sections back together. Growling Bear told Chief Dark Wolf that he would take some help and get the new poles they would need. He had gotten the original ones and knew what size was necessary. Night Hawk went with him and with the help of some willing work horses, the poles were dragged into camp.

As the sun lowered behind the trees, Chief Dark Wolf was pleased with the progress they had made.

The next day they had a relief in the cold wind and by nightfall the communal tent was up. Skids were used to bring rocks to hold the bottom and a fire was lit in the center to warm the leather. Soon it was smoothed to its full size with many braces in place.

Each woman returned the furs and dishes she had transported. They would have to wait for the snow to leave and the grass to dry, but the walls would be packed with grass and the tent once again would offer comfort to many people.

Sweet Grass had been staying in the tent with Chief Dark Wolf and Moonflower, but now she was able to take her many bundles inside the big tent. She made her back corner as cozy as she could. She watched as the men moved the big rolls of fencing that David had given them, through the passageway. The first thing they did was to place a row of posts between the tents and the herd of beef cattle. No one liked the idea of the big cattle being able to amble into camp unhindered. The fence was fastened and pulled straight, marking the start of their field. They did the same for the back of the meadow that held the horse herd. Gray Cloud and Singing Wind appreciated that. It made their job a little easier. Each day they dragged branches to the edge of the tree line and little by little the horse herd was contained. It wasn't the pretty split rail fence of their old camp, but it did the job of making it difficult for a horse to wander off.

Night Hawk, Debon and Soren had kept their word to David and made a cozy shelter for Nibbles and Bell. They had cut some trees and large branches and created an ample surround that allowed access to the edge of the river at one spot. One of them checked the big female work horses every day until David got back with his wagon loaded with parts of the church. The men of camp were unaware of the reason that Father Bob, Brother Tim and David made the last trip back to the old camp. David had added a large sledge hammer to his gear before leaving.

"Four days, Sarah, I promise it won't take more than that, maybe five at the most. We have it all planned how we will do it." She gave him a hug and held Pili's hand as they walked slowly to Moonflower's tent.

"Sarah, it is good you are here. We were just talking about you and wondering what you would think of all of the women pitching in to make things for Brother Tim's cabin. Did you hear that he has decided to stay with the people and not go back to be a priest?"

"Yes, mother, I heard that. I think it would be a fun thing to work on projects together, in the big tent. Let's go over there now. I want to look inside and check on Sweet Grass, too."

"She is fine. She has been sleeping in our tent until we can get the grass back in the walls of the big tent."

"Hello Sarah," Sweet Grass was happy to see her. "I am glad that our new camp is close to your cabin. It will be a good thing if I ever need help. You are a good teacher, Sarah. You were always patient with me. I can't thank you enough. I have everything back in here the way we had it before the move."

"In time the damp and cold will be gone and you will be cozy again," said Sarah, allowing Pili to sit down on the furs.

"Cold snow," said Pili in the language of the people. Moonflower was delighted and all the women laughed.

"I am glad that you are teaching her our words, Sarah."

"She learns quickly. She has your gift of learning new words easily. I think this summer I will ask Clover, Sheltah and Cumae to teach us the Abalinah language. It is always good to learn new things. Besides we never know when it will be useful." Her suggestion was met with murmurs.

"Please if any of you need something or just want to come to visit, come tap on my back door. When you decide on a project for Tim's place, let me know. I want to help." Sarah led the little girl back to their cabin and they both carried in some wood. It had become an automatic ritual. "Pili, I wish your daddy had not gone back to the old camp. Something about it is troubling me."

"Daddy said he will come back soon, Momma. Don't worry." Pili stood on the tips of her toes looking out the front window. "Oh, Look Momma, a big man on a horse is coming." Sarah hurried to the window to see what Pili was talking about. A column of soldiers had stopped at the river and Sarah could see that the one in charge rode across the water and approached her cabin. She picked up Pili, unsure of what she should do.

He knocked loudly. When Sarah opened the door; he boldly stepped inside uninvited.

"Is your husband home Ma'am?"

"No, David has gone with our team and wagon to help the priests. They are moving their church here near the river." She felt that the truth was the best. He looked around almost rudely. She felt invaded.

"Why are you here? What is it you need?"

"We are looking for a tribe of Indians that the priests lived by. They have moved and since the priests are moving here I think the Indians are probably nearby.

"Sergeant, you can't possibly think that they are here living with us! My cabin is small as you can see. If they were here there would be tents all over in the trees wouldn't there?"

"I suppose so. You better put a bolt on your door. The Winahatah are vicious!"

"Is that the people you are looking for?"

"Yes, they all packed up and have moved their camp, but don't you worry. We will find them!"

"I don't think you will. They don't exist. They were a tribe that lived in the land of the Blue Stone People. Have you ever heard of them? The Jesuits took that whole people to the cross. They are gentle Christians and traders. They mine turquoise and sell it. I heard that they have a trading spot along the wagon trail somewhere and people stop and swap goods, food or money for the things the Indians have. They polish the stones and make jewelry. That can't be the people you are looking for."

"I don't know anything about any trading spot or Christian Indians. Where did you hear all that?"

"I talked to the priests. They are building their church about where your poor, cold soldiers are standing. The Blue Stone People moved away when they heard about raids on other villages. Were you involved in all that?"

"Young woman you seem to have a lot of knowledge about the Indians."

"You didn't answer my question. Were you one of the soldiers that marched the Indians away from their lands in the snow?" He didn't answer. He was glowering at her.

"As you can see, Sergeant, there are no Indians here, so you may leave now."

"I say when I leave."

"Do you intend to make war on me, too, a white woman and child?" He turned to the door and left, walking slowly to his horse. Sarah could see that he was very angry. I hope he doesn't come back, she thought. I wonder if I said the right things. She watched as he turned his men back toward the prairie. They headed out across the church land, avoiding the huge piles of logs and lumber brought from the old camp.

*****

David headed back with his loaded wagon first.

As he glanced back, he could see Father Bob kneeling on the bare hill. He had done the same thing on the first day that he had arrived.

"Father God, that first day I was filled with naive enthusiasm and joy. The weeks and months that followed were an education in humility. I am leaving this hill as barren as I found it, but I know now that I have a congregation of Christians waiting for me. Back then I had found a village of people that didn't know you.

As we continue our work please bless us and the people we serve. Thank you for the amazing Cathedral and the visit from the Lion of Judah and your promise of protection." He stood wiping tears from his eyes as Tim pointed at the column of soldiers coming toward them. Father Bob climbed up onto the seat of his wagon and sat there waiting.

"Go ahead Tim; pull out slowly toward the soldiers."

"Halt," shouted the soldier in charge. "What are you men doing out here?"

"We are gathering the last of the useful wood. The Indians left it behind so I thought I may as well put it to good use."

"Who are you?" The soldier asked gruffly, showing disrespect.

"I am Father Bob and that young man is Brother Tim. This was our church until we were left behind by the Indians. We took our church apart and I have a piece of homestead land on the Hickory where we are going to rebuild it. You and your men are welcome to come to Mass there anytime. I will be holding it outside of course until we can get our church put together. I doubt if I will do much building before spring though."

"That doesn't look like lumber for a building."

"No, you are right. It is fencing that the Indians used to hold their herd on the meadow. I am sure that it will be useful."

"Where are the Indians, Father?"

"I told you already that they left us behind. It snowed the day they left. By the time we prepared to leave, we couldn't see their tracks."

The soldier scowled.

"I saw a man with a wagon just on the other side of the trees heading out on the prairie. Is he with you?"

"Yes, he is David Sharpe. His land is near mine and he offered to help. He is a good man."

"Father, I think you know exactly where the Indians are and when I find them there will be hell to pay!"

"Why do you seek The Blue Stone People? They are peaceful Christians that trade with the white men?"

"Peaceful is not a word I would use to describe what I was told! They burned cabins and killed families. They attacked wagon trains and killed everyone. Do you call that peaceful?"

"No of course not, but how long ago are you talking about? I have not heard of such atrocities in many years. Like I said the people that lived here were converted to Christianity. They are not the people you seek. Now if you don't mind, my work here is finished and we want to go build our church by the river." Father Bob moved the strong team with a simple clack of his tongue and a tap of the reins on the horse's backs.

"Have a good day gentlemen," he said as Tim pulled ahead and they rolled into the trees moving slowly down the trail beside the bluff.

Inside, Father Bob and Tim were both shaking but they didn't show it on the outside. The soldiers stepped down from their horses and took a break beside the lake that the people had deserted. One tiny shard of pottery was revealed as an ensign scooped the snow away to fill two coffee pots with water from the lake. He smiled and tucked it deep into his pocket.

"I don't believe a word he said. He knows where they are. Look at this place. You would never know they were here. When they clear out, they really take everything."

"Well what the Indians didn't take the priests did. They even took the fence," offered the man making coffee.

"Sure they built a fence, to keep in their stolen horses!"

"I don't know about all this. Maybe we were given bad information. Any Indian I ever saw was riding a pinto and most white men don't have those." The soldiers entertained themselves with theory and conjecture. Much of it was a deviation from accuracy. "Stories change as time passes. What if the priest was telling the truth?" After their rest and food, the column of soldiers rode back along the bluff and out onto the prairie turning their horses in the direction of the fort at Silverville.

*****

When David arrived with the load of split rail fence, he had made up his mind to tell Chief Dark Wolf and Two Feathers about the soldiers. As he pulled near the church land he was met by two young men on horses that escorted him in all the way to the crossing. Bending Grass and Big Frog had been told how to conduct themselves and they were excited to report to Two Feathers that they had been on guard and brought Sharp Knife back home. He praised them and sent them back to finish their time at guard. A third young man was enduring the cold day at the top of the bluff. He had been the first to alert the camp that someone was in the area. He soon signaled that two others were coming. He of course was seeing Father Bob and Tim approach. They too were escorted in and again they reported to Two Feathers. Since the visit of the soldiers to David and Sarah's cabin, the guards had been put in place. Sarah had watched and when the soldiers were far enough away, she had gone to Chief Dark Wolf and told him what had happened and what had been said.

CHAPTER NINETEEN
BUILDING A FUTURE

A brisk wind and temperature change to the high forties diminished the snow and a few more days of mild temperatures removed the rest. The women were quick to take advantage of the opportunity to gather grass for insulation. Rolls of grass were placed in the trees for the animals.

The men worked hard moving the fencing through the passageway, on skids. They were thrilled to have it here to use. David was surprised to see Two Feathers and several of his men laying out a fence along David's property lines.

"As soon as the ground allows it, we will dig holes for the posts. David, this is our way of saying a big thank you for the fencing you gave us and for helping to bring our church and the priests here," said Two Feathers. "Tell Sarah, that our women will not visit unless they have checked with the guards first. She is welcome of course to come to the camp anytime she chooses, and so are you." David felt the authority in Two Feathers, but there was not a hint of self-pride. I really like him, thought David as he entered his cabin to talk with Sarah.

The following morning a parade of work horses made a slow trip to an area near the clump of pine trees. Each time they came, they were dragging a log for Tim's cabin. Each log measured and hand cut, they were piled neatly ready to use. Tim's anticipation for all that spring promised grew with the delivery of each log. He still had not figured out what to offer as a bride price for Clover.

Father Bob had marked trees that stood in the way of his church and two days were spent cutting them down and they too became logs and piles of firewood.

One day Father Bob announced that he was going to be leaving in the morning to go to the S and J Ranch to visit. He said he would be gone several days and not to worry about him. Sarah immediately started preparing bundles for him to take. When he left, she had covered a pack horse with Christmas gifts for her family. He had offered for her to come with him, but she said she felt she should stay home this time. She thought about that word," Home". This is my home now. I am happy here. Just knowing that they are safe and well is enough for right now.

"Tell them that they are for Christmas and they shouldn't open them now." He grinned mischievously as he rode out. As he rode along he thought of the first Christmas he had celebrated with the people. It will be wonderful for the people this year. The tent is big and warm. We will have mass in the tent for the start of the day. I need to unroll the two paintings that the girls made, so they will hang nicely. He allowed his mind to continue to plan until Macho abruptly stopped.

"What is it Macho?" He didn't see anything at first, but then he heard a soft sob. In the trees, close to the Hickory was Lori and lying in the snow beside her was Mary's palomino.

"Lori, what happened?" He shouted as he ran to her. Lori continued to sob as she explained. I argued with Sylvia and left the cabin. I walked as far as the porch at Beth's and when I saw Mary's horse there, saddled and ready, I grabbed the reins and rode out. I wasn't planning to go anywhere, but once I left the ranch I thought I would keep going and go talk to Sarah. I knew the horse was tired so I rode her down to the water for a drink, but she stepped onto the edge of the ice and her foot went through and it cut her leg pretty bad. She is bleeding and I don't know how to help her!"

"We need to get her up. It is not helping her to lie on the ground. Help me coax her to stand up." Finally after a lot of patting and pulling she stood, with a drooping head and a front foot held off the ground. "You poor girl, you have cut that leg deeply. Let's see if I can do something to stop the bleeding." His saddle bags held a bit of everything. He placed a slice of wheat bread over the cut and wrapped her leg with white strips of cotton and tied it firmly in place.

"I have never seen anyone use bread before. Why did you do that?"

"Lori it is all I had. I am hoping that the salt in the bread will slow the bleeding, but it doesn't seem to be doing much. Take my horse and go get Sarah. Leave the pack horse. Just go get Sarah."

Lori got up on Macho hesitantly.

"This is a huge horse. I am not that good of a rider."

"Just go. Macho knows what to do, Lori, just come back as quick as you can!" She rode along feeling frightened and so sad that it was her fault that Mary's horse had been injured.

When she finally rode into the trees where David and Tim were working, she was surprised to have two young Indian men stop her.

As she told her story quickly to David, they moved slowly away and disappeared into the passageway. He listened and saddled Moon Boy and Pretty Mother knowing they would be needed. Sarah came out bundled in winter clothes and carrying her large bundle of medical supplies.

"I saw Lori out the window. Who is ill?" David looked at her and gave her a quick hug.

"Your patient is Mary's palomino. She has cut her leg on the ice about halfway here. Father Bob is with her."

"Lori, get on Pretty Mother, I will take Moon Boy and leave Macho here. He has done all he can today." Lori nodded and pulled her own tired muscles up onto another unfamiliar horse.

"We must go. Lead the way." Sarah wondered just how deep the cut was. She had seen horses that had cut tendons. They could never run again. Walking was painful.

Sarah jumped off Moon Boy and ran to the horse that was once again down in the snow.

"You poor girl, let me see what can be done for you."

Father Bob and Lori watched as the trained hands of Sarah worked to save this beautiful animal. She poured dark liquid from a jar directly into the horse's mouth. Then she asked for a fire to be made. With care she sponged the entire area of the wound and waited for the numbness to allow her to closely exam the damage.

"The tendon is good but the ice cut into the vein. If I can sew it shut, she will live." Sarah removed a tiny bone sewing needle and thread made from deer tendon from her bag. She poured solution over the wound again and over the needle and thread. "Father Bob, hold her head down and pray for her please. If she moves I could do more damage. Lori, sit down here and wrap your legs and arms around her leg. Don't let her move it. She may kick you if she feels what I am doing. There is no other way." Lori did as she was told holding on with all her might. Sarah asked God's help as she quickly stitched the vein with tiny stitches. As she worked the blood flow decreased and finally stopped. Sarah sponged the entire area again, and then stitched up the slash that the ice had made on the outside. The poultice was soft in the pan of water on the fire. Sarah scooped it out and held it in the cold air to cool. When the leg was finally wrapped and the bandage in place, Sarah asked her companions to back away from her. She will wake soon and you don't want to be in her way when she gets up. She won't feel the injury until the medicine wears off. It is packed in willow bark. We need to take her back to my place where I can care for her. Sarah adjusted the packages on the pack horse so that Father Bob could ride him.

"Let Mary and Ben know what has happened. Thank you Father God, and Thank you Father Bob," she said with a little smile, as she started slowly back toward Sarah's cabin leading Mary's horse.

Sarah offered Lori no concern as they traveled along. She remained quiet. Sarah knew the girl was exhausted. She could see it in the way she sat on Pretty Mother. She is not an experienced rider. She will be very sore by the time we get there. By the time they saw Tim riding toward them, they were near the church land and Mary's horse was starting to limp.

"Tim, I wish I had a barn to put her in tonight."

"She can bunk in with me. I put down an area of hay for her already and the fire has been going in there. It really isn't that bad. I thought you might bring her back here to care for her for a while."

"Thank you Tim, we have to take her across the river and that will wet her bandage. I wish there was another way."

"There is. Wait here." Tim ran to the edge of the river stomping at the ice, wading and stomping on the other edge. "Don't come yet. He ran to the cave and returned with a leather pouch that was soft and sealed at the seams with resin. It had been oiled many times. "This was my first attempt at making a case for my rifle. It was too loose, but if we slip her foot in it like a boot and tie it at the top, it should keep her bandage dry."

"Tim you are a genius!"

"If we ride on either side of her and move slowly, it will reassure her." Tim's horse, Jack, didn't mind sidling up to the beautiful palomino to get acquainted and Moon Boy moved close as they entered the water. Step by slow step, they crossed and walked her directly to the cave. Tim and Sarah removed the sleeve and Tim had been right. The bandage was still dry. She limped over to the pile of hay that Tim had provided and laid down. Sarah dosed her again with the strong medicine in the jar and soon she slept. Only then did Sarah swing up on Moon Boy and take Lori to her home.

David came out to transfer Sarah's bundle of medicines into the cabin and to put the horses in the shelter and give them some care. He had made some deer stew and it was hot and ready with a pan of tea pulled to the side.

"He is so thoughtful," said Sarah as she washed her hands and placed three bowls on the small table, with three big spoons and three mugs of tea. She got out a tin of crackers she had made the day before, just as David came in the back door.

"Well, this is cozy," he said.

"Thank you for making the food David." Sarah bowed her head and waited. David prayed a blessing on the food and then added a blessing on Lori and the injured horse.

Sarah looked at Lori to see silent tears creeping down her cheeks.

"Lori, you are welcome here any time and you are loved. Your legs and back must be painful. The most experienced rider would be sore after all the riding you did today. Let me put something in your tea to ease your discomfort."

"Sarah, it is not my body that hurts as much as my conscience. Oh, I am such a fool. Sylvia tried to tell me that I was loved and that God would give me everything I need, but I didn't want to wait. I wanted a horse now. I just don't get it. You people pray over your food, your work, your sleep, everything. Do you really think that there is a God somewhere out there that waves his magic stick and wham, bam, there is my horse? Well I don't think so. I think we have what we take. You have to be clever in this world or you get nothing! I am sorry that Mary's horse got hurt. I didn't mean to do that, but I just don't get it at all!"

While Lori had been talking, Sarah had heated Lori's tea and doctored it for her discomfort and raw nerves too.

"Lori, you will be here a few days. Let's enjoy our meal and then rest. We will have time to talk about all of this tomorrow. We will start at the beginning."

"Sarah, I saw you peek in the bedroom when you were fixing the tea. Pili is with her grandmother. I took her right after you left," said David.

"That's good. They will both enjoy that."

*****

Ben was just finishing his second cup of coffee. Father Bob had arrived just at dusk and after they had eaten he had talked long into the night, filling everyone in on what had been happening with The Blue Stone People and their new camp. He made a point to explain that their location was not to be given to the soldiers for any reason.

Then he moved on to the happy news that Tim was courting Clover and preparing to build a cabin in the spring.

"Good morning Orville." When Orville tapped at the kitchen door, Ben quickly made a decision. "I thought it might be a good idea if you spent the day in my old barn with the thoroughbred mares. Make sure they are staying gentle and then if that isn't enough to keep you busy you can work with the white ones."

"Hey, I'm good, but I am not that fast! I think it is a good idea to work with those ladies. They may get it into their heads that all they need to do is stand around and take care of those beautiful babies. It will be a pleasure, Ben. Thanks for the honor."

"Have a cup of coffee with us before you go, Orville. Did you have something to eat?"

"Yes, thanks, I am all set. I may as well head on over there and remind those ladies that we like a ride now and then."

He left with a smile and swung up on Tinkle with a feeling of pleasure. It is nice that they trust me with their finest animals. He didn't know that Ben had been trying to think up a chore that would take Orville to the other side of the ranch, while they dug up Chum and removed enough gold for Tim's bride price. It took a pick and hard work to open the cache. Putting it back was equally hard. No matter what they did, anyone could see that they had been digging there. With a last effort they all started piling snow on the area and rode their horses back and forth over the entire hill.

"I think we are just making it worse. I sure hope it snows tonight," said Jed with a chuckle. Father Bob stayed longer than he intended because it did snow that night and all the next day. It took two days for the sun to make the trip back less of a struggle. As Father Bob prepared to leave, Ben brought one of the white mares out of his barn. She was saddled and ready to go.

"Orville tells me that she is gentle. Her name is cotton. Tell Lori to bring her back carefully. They are both worth a lot to me."

"I will Ben. I think it is important that she hears that from you just now. Oh, and keep those kids out of Sarah's packages until Christmas morning." He laughed as he gently led the mare across the river and out onto the pristine white prairie. Cotton pranced along happy to be out where she could move along easily. Father Bob was missing Macho. The pack horse didn't have the smooth gate or movement that made for a comfortable mount. Many bundles were stuffed behind him and again the warning was given.

"These are not to be opened until Christmas," said Beth as she tied the last small package on tightly.

Father Bob was glad when the two young men greeted him and escorted him across the river. It had seemed like a long trip. It had been cold and uncomfortable. He gladly yielded the pack horse to them and they returned him to the herd and Gray Cloud's watchful eye.

Tim had helped him put the packages safely away in the cave and then he walked Cotton to meet Lori. She squealed with delight when she saw her, but her face grew serious when she heard Ben's message.

"Thank you Father Bob, I will take her back in the morning." Lori took the lead in her hands and followed David out to the shelter where he made room for her and fed her.

"She is beautiful, isn't she David? Maybe someday, God will give me a horse as nice as she is."

"Yes, Cotton is pretty, but what you learned is more beautiful. Lori, Jesus died for you, but he lives now and if you believe that and trust him, you will always have his Holy Spirit on the inside to comfort you and counsel you. You are a child of the Most High God. You will have a worthy animal and anything else you need if you ask, believe and trust."

Sarah had started at the beginning and given Lori the knowledge that she needed to receive the gift of faith. She realized now that she had a lot of apologizing to do, but she also had a marvelous story to tell.

She left after breakfast with a large water bag and waterproof basket with her. She didn't want to take this horse anywhere near the river. She stopped mid-way and saw the spot where she had taken Fancy to the edge of the river. Forgive me Father, please forgive me. I have so many things to say that I am sorry about. It will take me a long time. I have been thinking only of myself. Now I am ashamed. I don't have enough gifts made for my family for Christmas. I have to make them something, but I can't imagine what it will be. There are only a few days left. I hope Mary will forgive me for taking Fancy. I am so glad that she is getting better. Sarah said that she will be fine by spring and not limping at all. I hope she is right.

Lori approached the crossing and stopped. She couldn't believe her eyes. Everyone was there to greet her, smiling and talking and waving. Ben had cleared the ice from the river on both sides of the crossing. He came to meet her on Sundown. He leaned over and gave her a hug and they walked the horses across together.

"I can't believe you all came out in the cold to meet me. Mary I am so sorry I took Fancy and got her hurt. I am so sorry and I love everyone so much. Please forgive me Sylvia. You were totally right and I was wrong." She slid off the white mare and thanked Ben for letting her use such a wonderful horse. "Cotton is so good." Ben smiled broadly and walked her to the barn door. Cotton trotted to her stall and nuzzled her foal.

"Your foal is fine, but I am sure you missed each other."

Mark was the only one that had not looked joyous at her return. He was angry with her. His face showed his attitude.

"Mark, I am sorry that I left like that. I know that you were worried about me. Forgive me. I have learned so much while I was gone. Sarah and David are amazing people and they told me about the Lord. Mark maybe we can all talk and you will understand and feel as I do."

"That's right Lori tell us all about how you feel. Did you think for one minute how you made us all feel and worry?"

"I said I am sorry. I don't know what else to say. Mark, please don't walk away." He had turned away from her and headed to the cabin where he and Orville lived. He didn't look back. "I want him to have what Sarah helped me to have." Sylvia put her arm around Lori's shoulder and took her to Beth's house. Everyone else followed.

"Do you all realize that Christmas is just three days from now?" Beth asked them as she offered sandwiches and cocoa after the cold wait and walk back from the river. I have all the decorations we have made through the years and maybe we can get together tonight and make some more."

"We will be glad to help, won't we Sylvia?"

"That will be fun Mom," said Lily. "When are we going to put up our Christmas tree?"

"That's up to the men. They haven't found us a tree yet. Jed, are you and Johnny going to hunt for a tree today?"

"I have spotted a nice one. We can cut it this afternoon and put it in the barn so the snow will melt off of it. If anyone needs to work on gifts, this is probably a good day to do it. I will be in the loft after we get the tree, so no one can peek," he said laughing.

"I wish Sarah and David would bring Pili here for Christmas. I miss her when she isn't here no matter what day it is," said Ben. "I have an idea. Do you think we could all be ready early on Christmas Eve morning? If we all piled into the middle sized wagon with our presents and some goodies, we could surprise them and stay a few hours and still be back here by milking time. What do you think?"

"Let's do it!"

"Yes."

"Sure." Everyone was in agreement. They hurried to finish their lunch and rushed away to do whatever they needed to. Lori and Sylvia asked if they could use three bars of the scented skin soap that Beth had made and then they asked Mary if she had any of the paraffin wax left from sealing the jam jars. We will also need three bars of the men's hand soap. They hurried to their cabin and checked the basket in the back storage room, making sure that it still held several bars of each of the soaps.

"With those we will have enough," said Sylvia. "Lori if you will help me, these can be from both of us." She described what she wanted to make. The girls worked intensely all afternoon.

"All we need to do is moisten the top of the bar so that it gets sticky. Then we can press the dried flowers on to it. When it dries we can dip them in the melted paraffin wax. They will be pretty and can still be used."

"That is a good idea, but what about the guys?"

"Let's draw leaves and bugs and cut them out. We can stick them on the same way, only on the gray work soap."

"This is fun. I can't wait until we can show them their gifts."

Mark was still fretting and finally decided to find Ben and talk with him. He found him working in his barn on something that he hastily tucked under the hay he was sitting in.

"Ben, I need to talk to you. Have you got a minute or two?"

"Of course Mark, I am glad you came. Sit down with me. What's on your mind?"

*****

Father Bob had inspired the people to prepare for Christmas. The beautiful stars the women had made that first year were repaired and once again hung in the big tent. A perfectly shaped small pine stood in the back of the tent, safely placed so that it could hold candles. The Madonna and Child paintings graced both sides of the tent and hung high enough so that they could be seen with the people inside sitting down. He had used Sarah's oven and once again the special box of sugar cookies was placed under the tree and the altar stood near the tree covered in white linen and dried wild flowers. Willow had protected them and carefully transported them during the move. Father Bob was amazed when she brought them in and placed them there.

David and Sarah had also put up a tree and Pili was learning about the Christ Child and the real Christmas story. Sarah made a special effort to make an abundance of treats, thinking that some of the people might come to her cabin to see the tree. Growling Bear surprised them Christmas Eve morning and asked if they wanted to come to the village to help make a man of snow. The soft snow had fallen during the night and the children were out playing in it. Sarah quickly bundled Pili and David scooped her up and carried her to visit the people and enjoy her first big snowman. Several people were rolling big balls of snow and David helped Pili to start hers. When she could no longer move it, he helped her start a second ball.

After a little time and much happy laughter and comments, an entire snow family stood in the center of camp. They had all had a wonderful time. Pili hugged her grandparents and several others before they headed back to the cabin. Growling Bear had told everyone his version of how he had helped to make the first man of snow.

Just as they walked through the trees toward their back door, David spotted the wagon and the family from the ranch coming. They were singing a carol and laughing. They helped ferry the people and gifts across and David took the horses to a sheltered area in the trees and made sure they had what they needed to be comfortable. The bundles of Christmas gifts that Sarah had sent with Father Bob had returned unopened and were placed under the beautiful little tree along with many more. David and Sarah found that their little cabin was full of people and more came. Father Bob and Tim, Moonflower and Chief Dark Wolf stepped in each carrying a big kettle. Snow Star and Flying Eagle each entered carrying gifts of food and packages and bringing Watching owl. Sarah and David were overwhelmed.

"Please just make yourselves comfortable. I haven't enough chairs but I have blankets and quilts and pillows. She brought out what she had and it was enough. Mary and Ben brought in blankets from the wagon and Josh and Adam brought more. Beth had a crate with stacks of plates and silverware. She had accommodated groups of workmen at the ranch and knew what would be needed. Mary had baked apple and pumpkin pies and made a huge roast with carrots and potatoes. Johnny brought in a crate with cups and big canning jars of milk, cream and butter and added them to the table. The food was tucked close to the fire and soon the aroma had drawn people to fill their plates.

Father Bob looked at Ben and asked him to say the grace. Ben grinned and begun.

"This is a day that we will always remember. Thank you, Father, for bringing everyone here so we can be together. Thank you, for the food, warmth and love. Also thank you for your Holy Son, Jesus, Amen."

"Amen." Everyone repeated it, followed by echoes of Merry Christmas." After the food had been appreciated and seconds taken and enjoyed, the gifts were distributed. Moonflower and Chief Dark Wolf were surprised to be handed a gift. It was the last thing to be handed out. Wrapped in brown store paper and a piece of ribbon from Mary's sewing basket, Ben had spent many hours on this particular gift. Moonflower held it tightly, seeming afraid to open it. Sarah read the tag to her.

"This gift is for Moonflower and Chief Dark Wolf; Merry Christmas from the S. and J."

"Open it Mother, said Sarah. She was eager to see what it was. The carefully carved plaque read "Thank You, for loving Sarah and raising her to be the woman she is." The words were surrounded with leaves and flowers. The branch of a pine tree supported one little sparrow and was positioned at the bottom of the words. The detail was amazing. Ben had poured his heart into it and it showed. Sarah was touched deeply and tearfully read the words out loud so everyone would know what it said. Moonflower looked at Chief Dark Wolf and they both stood.

"We thank you. You are an unusual man Ben Slater. I have brought no gift to give your family, but this is a gift that we will cherish always. We hold you and your people in high regard." They walked quickly to the door and left.

"Why did they leave?"

"I think they were so surprised by your gift that they didn't know what to do. Ben that was very thoughtful of you." Sarah hugged him tightly. Snow Star quickly pulled Watching Owl's coat on him and then she approached Ben.

"Mother always worried that perhaps you still felt pain and resentment toward them because they took Sarah away from you. You gave them forgiveness today. That was the loveliest gift in the world Ben." She and Flying Eagle also left quickly.

"I don't like saying it, but we all need to get back to the ranch. It is almost milking time."

Oh, Jed, I just realized that this is probably the very first time that the ranch has been left completely unattended," said Beth, "Boys gather our blankets and put them in the wagon. David, please hitch up our team. Orville, you and Josh, Mark and Ben and Jed should ride back now and we girls will bring our things and the children. Thank you Sarah and David, for the lovely gifts that you made." Pili had a new doll in her arms from her two aunts and a carved wolf that Josh had made for her. "I wish we didn't have to get going but you know we do. It will be dark by the time we get back as it is." Some of the many leftovers were transported to the wagon and the dirty plates and dishes were stacked in the crates quickly.

"Sarah, we are leaving you an awful mess. I am sorry about that. Father Bob, we enjoyed your recent visit, and you and Tim can come back anytime." Merry Christmas they said to each other as they left."

"Goodbye, God Bless you all. Travel safely. Merry Christmas!" They waved and hopped up into the hay in the wagon for the long ride home. Eli and Natty and Adam all snuggled in one of the quilts that Mary had brought. She slid up next to them. Lori and Sylvia were bundled in their new coats and cuddled with Lily under a mound of covers. Johnny and Beth were on the seat. He wanted to drive and Beth said it would be alright.

CHAPTER TWENTY
THE FUTURE

Generations later, on a day beyond today...The vehicle silently pulled up and stopped at the sprawling house. Is this really the place? Emily was amazed as she looked through the viewing panel and waved her hand over the square button on the exit. She waited as the door swung open and a carpeted step folded into place.

The beautiful red haired young woman stepped out onto the paved driveway; she was greeted by a handsome young man not much older than she was.

"Welcome to the S. and J. Ranch," he said. "May I take your cases in for you?"

"Yes, please do." She followed him up the steps of the wide porch, admiring the early flowers in beds on either side. "How long have you worked here?" She was trying to make small talk, but found that she hadn't done her homework.

"Our brochure states that the ranch is run entirely by a staff, related to the original pioneers that settled the land. I have lived here all my life except for the four years that I was away at college. I am Brian Burgess."

"Which side of the family are you related to?"

"Both, according to my father, a girl named Lily Kathleen Jones married a Parker named Adam and from that marriage came two Parker boys and a girl named Elizabeth that married a Burgess. That's how our family started. It has been so long now, that I am not sure if anyone knows for sure, but it is fun to think about."

He placed her bags on the padded bench just inside the door of her room and handed her the key.

"No one here uses the locks but sometimes I think ladies like the security of a locked door at night, especially if they are from one of the metropolis pods."

"Thank you Brian, I think I will settle in now and maybe if you have time you can show me around later."

"Miss Emily, it will be a pleasure." He left the room and closed the door softly behind him. She changed into a flowing pair of pale gray trousers and shirt that matched made of a synthetic derived from fibers gleaned from the countless vacant towns on the fringe of the radiation areas. She studied her face in the mirror and pulled off her wig. Her scalp was itching again. She smeared it with the medicated cream the doctor had given her, but it wasn't helping much. With her wig back in place and her makeup freshly applied, she walked out onto the porch and sat down in one of the large bent willow rockers.

"Welcome Emily, I am Paula Burgess. I live here, with my son Brian. Our rooms are just off the kitchen, so if you need something during the night you won't have to holler very loudly." They both laughed at the scene that the idea had conjured.

"I seriously doubt that I will need anything that can't wait until morning, but thank you for your thoughtfulness."

"Emily, I usually make tea about now, would you like some?"

"Yes, thank you so much, but how is it that you have it? There hasn't been tea in the cities since the war."

"We have many things here that are unusual for this day and age. The air currents carried the dangerous particles away from this area of the river for miles. We can still grow a garden and have healthy animals, but of course we have to use water only from the wells. Don't use the water in that fountain, not even for rinsing your hands. The last time we tested it, it was still too high to use but our guests and we like looking at it, so we let it flow. That ancient oak that you drove near when you crossed the bridge, is the oldest living tree on that side of the river that I know of. It's as if some great being put out his breath and blew fresh air toward us until all that bad stuff had gone and settled somewhere else. I'll go get the tea." She came back out a few minutes later with a tray with mugs of tea and cookies.

"Are you hungry Emily? I can make you a sandwich if you want one."

"No, this is fine. It is so peaceful here. I love the quiet."

"I forgot to tell you, that Brian put your I-Go in the big barn over there. Our hot hours are just as bad as everyone else's. Fortunately we have buildings to cover us and the animals and belongings. That little building back there near the river is our power source. The river turns turbines and we store the energy. We have cooling units in this house and the Slater house. That big barn is cooled, too. Our animals all know enough to go in about one and stay there until five."

"How do you keep your gardens from burning and drying up?" We have a wind generator that runs a timer that pulls a tarp over the frame above the whole garden and it turns on the water system from a well. If Brian forgets to check that timer, we are in big trouble, but he is very responsible. He has never forgotten."

"I thought only the cities that were hit had the hot hours, but it is getting warm out here already." Paula carried the tray in and Emily followed with her cup of tea. This tea is delicious, but I have never tasted anything quite like it."

"I am glad that you like it. I found the recipe in an old cookbook in the hut library. You probably saw that when Brian showed you around."

"He didn't have a chance to yet."

"Well you won't want to do that now, but maybe this evening. Emily, look out at the back of the barn. Brian is out there and has started their fans and the cooler." Several horses and six cows strolled in a row and disappeared around the back of the barn, Emily continued to watch as range chickens ran or flew short distances and made their way in that direction.

"That's amazing. Even the chickens know to go in. I think I will go in my room and rest until the sun goes down. I have a book I am reading. Thanks for the tea, could I take the last of it from the pot with me?"

"Yes, of course. Do you need me to make more?"

"No this is just right."

"Enjoy your peace while you can. This weekend it will be crowded with young adults from all over. They stay here during the break from studies and go into the nearby pods for excitement. So far I have put all the young guests in the Slater House. I have only one other room booked in here and it is down at the end of the hall."

"I am sure that I will be fine."

Emily read the last page of her book and put it on the table beside the bed. She walked to her window and peeked out. The shade held a layer of heat. She stepped back from it. I wonder how long it will be before people can live the way they did before the missiles started coming. All the big cities are either ruins, burned completely or uninhabitable. They probably will never be totally clear of the radiation. If they are I won't live to see it. The ozone layer was nearly destroyed. They say that's why we have the hot hours now. She was tired and feeling depressed.

The sun had dipped down behind the trees near the river and Paula tapped on her door just as Emily had decided that she wanted to go out to explore the ranch.

"Dinner will be at seven. It is nearly six now. You can walk around if you like. The ground is still hot but it will cool off quickly. It gets cold here at night. I hope you brought some warm clothes. We have one family staying in the Slater house right now but we will be getting more guests closer to the weekend. Dinner will be served there each night at seven. Brian will find you and bring you down when it is time, if that is alright."

"Yes, it sounds like fun and I did bring some warmer clothes."

Emily walked along the drive and noticed a green hill with a door in it. A little sign read, "Hut Library." It is strange that they have green grass here and trees. These must have adapted to the hot and cold temperature changes. That's odd, she thought. Those trees look like pine trees. How do they take the hot hours and they are standing near water that tests high for radiation? She tapped on the wooden door and opened it slowly. It was dark inside. She felt around for a light switch and then realized that this building had never been wired for electricity. She pushed the door wide open for light. Everywhere she looked, were books, the shelves lined the walls from floor to ceiling. A heavy wooden table sat in a side room. On it was an old fashioned oil lamp. Beside it a glass jar held matches. A strip of sandpaper was wrapped around it and held with a piece of twine. I wonder if I dare light this. She hesitated for a moment and then lifted the glass chimney. She was surprised at the amount of light it produced. She enjoyed old books, the older the better. Her hand slid over the bindings lovingly.

A soft cool breeze reminded her that the door was open. She closed it. Above her head was a leather bound book and beside it rested journals. She pulled down the leather bound book and the first journal and sat at the table near the lantern. She found herself looking at a very old, worn Bible. This is marvelous. I better be gentle with this. She opened the cover and read the inscription. "This sacred word is given to Josiah and Mary Slater on the occasion of their marriage, on September tenth, in the year of our Lord, Eighteen Hundred and Forty Four."

Emily drew in a quick breath, knowing that she had discovered something important, without really intending to.

She turned to the center pages seeing the separation of the Old and New Testaments. Handwritten names and dates, neatly recorded until there was no space left. She turned to the back and saw more names and dates, indicating marriages, births and deaths. Closing it carefully, she opened the journal.

†Journal   "This is the journal of Mary Parker Slater. This is written to record the things that God has done to affect and bless our lives here at the Slater and Jones Ranch."

She sat and read until her eyes were burning. It must be well past seven. Brian was supposed to come get me. I think I can find my way in the dark. I'll take the lantern and these books with me. She had trouble picking up the lantern. It had no handle. Finally she stuffed both books inside her blouse and held the lantern by its base with both hands. The door posed a problem but she managed. Once back in what she thought of as the main house, she set the lantern on the table and listened. It was very quiet. Where are they?

Just then the front door opened and Brian came in looking relieved.

"There you are! Where have you been? I have been looking for you. I was afraid you had gone out in one of the fields and had gotten lost or hurt or something. Are you alright?"

"Yes, of course, I am sorry if I worried you. I was in the Library. It got dark and I had to bring this lantern to find my way back here. I just got here. Look Brian. Look at these books! Did you know they were in there?" She was embarrassed as she pulled them from her blouse.

"Yes, I saw them when we moved all the books. Some were in the Slater House. We moved them here. There aren't many of those around. It is probably worth a lot of money to the "Under Grounders". You know the "One World Union Leader" ordered all the Bibles burned when he came into power. I should get rid of it."

"No! Brian, do you have any idea what you have here? It has your whole family history with dates and names. The journal has handwritten accounts of happenings and hardships during their lives. You should take time to read it all."

"The One World Union Soldiers would kill me on the spot if they catch me reading that Bible. I forgot we had it. Give it to me."

"Brian, would you mind if I keep it for a while? I want to read some of it. I promise I will hide it if they come. Please, Brian," she smiled teasingly.

"Alright, but just remember, I warned you! It's your funeral. As far as we are concerned that book doesn't exist."

"That's fair enough." I will be dead in a few months anyway, she thought. Emily shoved the two books back in her blouse as she followed him out the door. He grinned at her clumsy attempt to conceal them.

Brian flipped a switch and lights came on causing a sparkling edge for the path she had just used.

"Hey, you must be starving. Have you ever ridden a horse?"

"No," she answered as she backed up hesitant to approach the large animal. He scooped her frail body up in front of him on the brown mare and wrapped a soft blanket around her that had been fastened in a roll behind him. The primitive form of transportation amused her. Emily had never been near a horse, but now she felt safe with him holding her tightly against his chest as the horse walked, following the way to the "Slater House."

"It will be really cold soon." He gently helped her down in front of the steps of the beautifully lit, decorated and grand, "Slater House."

"This place is magnificent!"

"Just wait until you see it in the daylight. It's been renovated several times.

Mother has been keeping a meal warm for you." They entered the foyer and could hear conversation and laughter coming from the dining room.

"Paula, I am so sorry to cause you concern and extra work. I was having a wonderful time in the library."

Brian wrapped a bulky sweater around her and helped her into it, suggesting she tie the belt tightly. She nodded, realizing that as well as comfort it offered a cover for the shape and sagging blouse from the books. A girl in her late teens sat at the table sipping a pink concoction and nibbling on a yellow cookie.

"I want what she is having," laughed Emily.

"Not until you wrap yourself around this first. Be careful, the plate is hot. It has been in the oven." Paula put down a thick placemat and then the sizzling plate. She brought out a glass of milk and poured her a cup of coffee and filled the others. "Let me introduce you. Miss Emily Baker, this is Janet and John Pariah and their children, Mason and Amber."

"It is nice to meet you. I apologize for disturbing your evening."

"Not at all, we were just concerned for your well-being."

"What were you talking about when we came in?" asked Brian.

"I was just saying that it is so nice now that every member of our family has their own I-Go. We program them and off we go. Everyone can do what they want inside and we all arrive quickly and safely without being subjected to each other's preferences on the journey."

"Yes, I enjoy using mine. It makes travel so much more comfortable. I like that they have viewing shields and other sensory protections," replied Emily.

"What do you mean?"

"I always close my shields until I am close to my destination. Seeing the devastation and the Under Grounders when they come out, it makes me sick."

"Yes, I know what you mean. We were stunned when the aliens took all the hundreds of thousands of people from the earth. They pulled people right out of their graves, too! My father kept some of the news cores from those days," said Mason.

"It was horrid. Most of the devastation still remains and has been vastly added to by the missiles and bombs."

"Now Mason and John, this is not suitable dinner conversation."

"You are right dear, I apologize."

"What aliens Father? Where did the people go? Are the aliens coming back here to get us?" Amber looked frightened. She hadn't heard that story.

"No Honey that was more than a year ago and our great world Leader says we will always have peace now under his leadership. You haven't a thing to worry about with him in control." He tried hard to protect his family from most of the news laced with propaganda.

"Dad, you know that some people don't believe all that he says."

"Mason, shut up! Don't you dare ever say that again! If his soldiers hear you they will punish you!"

"Sorry Dad. May I go to my room now?"

"Go! When kids reach sixteen, they think they know everything!" Emily pushed her chair back and asked to be taken back to her room.

"I enjoyed the food Paula. I think next time, I should have smaller portions." She had eaten very little.

"Thank you, Brian, for bringing me back. I can find my way from here." Brian followed her into the house and turned on a light in the hall. He took the lantern from the table and returned it to the library.

Emily's hand shook as she took her medicine and then removed her clothes. She placed the Bible and journal under her pillow for temporary, out of sight, keeping. When she finally went to sleep the nightmares returned. She heard the bombs and her mother scream and then a roaring and heat that burned her skin and hair. Even in the bathtub full of water she had not been protected. She woke with a start. She could hear men's voices in the hall.

"She is sick, you shouldn't disturb her." Emily knew that Paula was trying to dissuade the O.W.U.S. from entering her room. She jerked her sleeping gown off and pulled on her clothes from the day before. The books, I must hide the books, she thought. She stuffed them back into her blouse and pulled on the thick sweater tying it tightly. She stood at the mirror when they burst into the room without knocking. She slowly smeared the cream over her bald scalp and neck scars before turning to face them.

"Good morning gentlemen, I haven't made myself beautiful for you yet today. Please feel free to do your inspection." She pulled the red haired wig on at a rakish angle and stepped close to the double breasted uniform of the nearest soldier invading his space. She put her palms on his chest leaving smudges of the medicinal cream as she looked up impishly.

"Do you think I'm beautiful?"

"Get away from me woman. You are ugly!" He turned and stomped his way out of the house. Paula started to bounce as she tried for dear life to suppress a giggle that wouldn't stay quiet. She was glad to see that the three "I-Goes" that had parked at the bottom of the house steps were leaving the property and on their way to inspect some other unsuspecting citizen. The women enjoyed a hearty laugh together.

"That was some performance. You are a brave girl. He could have arrested you!"

"Yes, I know, but what would it matter?"

"Paula would like to have discussed it but with so many guests soon to arrive at the "Slater House," she had many duties to take care of and jobs to assign to the also arriving, temporary help. That poor girl is so depressed. I wonder if she is in pain, she thought.

Emily had taken her shower and was dressed for a day of exploration when Brian met her on the porch.

"You showed an interest in this last night. I thought you might like to try it with one big yellow cookie." He laughed as he handed her a glass of pink liquid with ice in it.

"This is delicious! What is it?"

"We make barrels of it in the fall when the cherries ripen. It has sweetener and preservative and then it is sealed. Basically it is just juice and water."

"Cherries, it isn't possible that you can keep cherry trees alive here."

"Not here, but there is an area we found upriver behind the bluff that looks like there was never a war at all. I wanted to live there but then Mom said that we should stay on the land that our ancestors homesteaded."

"How far is it? Will you take me there?"

"I probably won't have time this week, but after this mob leaves, we can go."

"Thank you Brian, for the best breakfast ever. I will wander around a bit but I will be careful and not get lost. I know now, dinner at seven and I know where." She smiled and went in her room to retrieve the journal. Paula offered her breakfast but she said she was satisfied for now and held out the last bite of her cookie.

Paula laughed and suggested that Emily was a nonconformist.

Emily sat on the porch reading until she saw a group of young people heading her way with blaring scrambled sounds and ill-mannered behavior. She retreated to the quiet of her room, but the sound followed her into the house. The young people poked and nosed into every room, drawer and cupboard, turning the handle on her door. She was glad that she had locked it.

"Leave her alone Damian. Paula said she is sick. You don't want any of what she's got!" The laughter suggested that the girl had made a crude gesture.

"This place is boring! Let's get the others and blast into the dance pod." They all seemed to like that suggestion and went noisily back the way they had come taking their sound bubble with them. She glanced out and saw several I-Goes leave. Finally it was quiet again.

Brian tapped on her door a few minutes later.

"It is safe to come out now."

"Silly, I was just reading. I wasn't afraid of them. I just didn't like their noise."

"Since most of them are gone until meal time, do you want to go see the cherry tree valley?"

"Oh, yes I would. I have been reading this journal and it talks about a cave and a church and a water source that pours out of the bluff and a Lion. Do you know anything about any of that?"

"Now you are talking ancient history. There is an old church ruin there. I will show you. It will start getting warm soon. Let's take a lunch and a lot of water and we can go into the cave during the hot hours."

"This is going to be fun. Do you want to use my I-Go or yours?"

"Let's take mine," said Brian. "Mom got us the We-go so I could use it with guests. It isn't the latest model but I like it. It knows me."

"Is it alright if I bring the books?"

"Sure I guess so."

He placed the packaged lunch inside, along with a large container of water and another container filled to the brim with ice and the cherry drink.

"Grab that big sweater, and I have blankets in the hold. Get in. It's a good thing you are small. These things are built tight fitting to conserve power." Brian touched a location on the screen and tapped the shield on her side. The view opened and the vehicle began to move. He pulled his finger along a line on the edge of the screen and they slowed down. I want you to be able to see the trees and things along the river. There aren't many places like this left. Such natural beauty has not survived."

"Brian, please stop. Look, there is a fawn in the brush. I wonder where she takes him when it gets hot." Emily stepped out, enjoying the wonder of it.

"Get back in. You are going to scare him. His mother has survived so she must have found a place to go."

"Isn't it amazing that there is still wildlife left here?"

"Yes it is. Hey, have you heard about the big roaches in the evacuated cities? Talk about wildlife! Some are as long as my arm and they seem to still be getting bigger; at least that's what I have heard. I haven't seen one and don't want too. How would a person kill a roach that big? They fly too you know."

"Brian stop talking about disgusting bugs. You are making my skin crawl!" He laughed at her and slowed Babe to a stop.

"Through the trees is the old church. If you look in the brush over there, you can see what's left of the white cross that stood out here on the edge of their land. I will go slowly so you can look all you want." He pulled up the unused driveway and stopped again. "We have to cross the river and I don't trust the bridge, so we will take the wet route."

She squealed as the water sprayed over the nose of the We-Go and splashed at the top of her side viewer.

"I knew these things can do this, but I have never taken mine in or on water." As he pulled up onto the smooth slate in front of the cave, his vehicle spoke.

"Brian, do you want to stay in water mode or may I switch back to land travel?"

"Thanks Babe, for reminding me. Yes switch, I forgot."

"You are welcome Brian, I am switching now." He directed her into the dense shade of the cave opening and stopped. "Do you want to run the cooler while you are out?"

"Yes, thank you."

"Brian, you treat her as if she is human."

"She treats me better than most humans. She has learned my needs and anticipates what I want. Babe takes good care of me."

"Thank you Brian, I am going to rest now until you return."

"Babe, before you go into rest mode, there is a passageway through the bluff. Please take us through it and then return here to rest."

"I know the way, but it will be difficult. We will need to use float mode part of the way. An attempt has been made to block the pass with boulders. If you will allow me to choose the modes necessary, I will be able to go through using minimal energy."

"Thank you Babe."

"Closing all shields; hover mode engaged; programing scan for current project." They felt a slight lift and then a tilt. After what seemed like a hesitation, she spoke. "Execution is complete." The door opened and the cover on the hold lifted. Babe silently waited until they had removed everything and dismissed her.

"Thank you Babe. Please return to the shade in the cave and stay cool."

"Yes, I will do as you have instructed. The current time is eleven o'clock; air temperature is eighty eight degrees and rising." She lifted from the grass quickly and silently left."

"That is one amazing vehicle. She is a Show Go and mine is an untrained puppy!"

"I use her a lot. The more things you do with them, the more they learn what you want." Emily was already thinking that she would have to give her I-Go a name and start teaching it.

Brian put all their belongings in the shade of rocks at the bottom of the bluff.

"Are you alright? Is it getting too hot for you?"

"No, but I think I should leave the books here so I don't have to carry them. I'll put them in the fold of your blanket."

"I brought a tester, so we could be sure that the water here is still safe." His long legs quickly took him to the edge of the small lake. He filled the vial and inserted the test pin. It beeped and a blue light blinked. "It is perfect. Over there near the trees it is shallow and we can wade across to the cherry trees if you want to."

"These old willows are beautiful. I read about them in the journal. An Indian woman with three children asked the priests to bring cuttings from their old camp location when they moved their camp here. She ended up marrying a man that hadn't finished his studies to become a priest yet. Theirs was the first wedding in the church by the cave. The Apple trees on the edge of the lake near the bluff were planted by a woman named Willow. Ben Slater bought a barrel of apples at the original Trading Post in Silverville and gave them to The People of the Lion when they came and built cabins and dug wells on the ranch to meet the requirements so they could keep the homestead land that was half the ranch at that time."

"That's interesting. I should read that journal so I learn the stories. I can make it more fun for the guests that I bring here." Emily was thinking of this as being a private adventure. When he mentioned bringing others it spoiled it for her.

"I think we should go back in the shade now. My head is stinging and it is getting very hot."

"Sure Emily, do you want me to buzz Babe or should we try going up there under those old pines? It looks like they are getting a bit of a breeze.

"Let's go up there, but I am afraid you will have to carry most of our things." Once again she tucked the books inside her blouse and this time she tied the sleeves of the sweater around her waist. He placed the packaged lunch and both water and juice in the center of the blanket and carried it all with one hand.

"You go first, so if you slip, I will be right behind you to help you." Cautiously they headed up to the pines, not knowing the adventure that awaited their discovery. He spread the blanket in the shade under the ancient trees and opened the package first, handing her two cups. He filled them to the brim with water. "Bottoms up," he said and downed his. He filled it again and looked at hers. What's the matter? Why aren't you drinking?"

"I don't know. I should be thirsty and hungry, but I'm not. It is this place. It is otherworldly. How can it be here and look like this and feel like this? Now that I am sitting in the shade, I don't feel hot. It is comfortable here. Brian, I am so grateful to you for taking time to bring me here." She drank her water and held the cup up. May I have a cup of the cherry juice?"

"You can have anything that is here?"

"Does that include the wonderful peace? I wish I could take it with me wherever I go."

"Yes, silly, that comes with the absence of the noisy mob back at the house." A little bird lit on a branch and turned toward the bluff and flew.

"Brian, did you see that?"

"I saw the bird, what about it?"

"I think it flew into a hole in the bluff. It probably has a nest in there." They stood up leaning left and then right pushing the branches out of the way so they could see the face of the bluff behind them, expecting to see a crevice or deep ledge. There before them was the entrance to "The Lion's Den."

"Brian, this is a little scary. What if there is an animal in there? There could be a bear or a mountain lion. It is awfully dark. I don't think we should go in there."

"You are probably right. We should eat," he said encouragingly. He opened the package and spread its contents.

"Where are all the people? It seems with a place this productive and lovely with good water, that there would be people here taking advantage of it."

"Well we haven't exactly been telling anyone. We wanted to keep it the way it is. I bring folks here but I just show them the old church and the cave front and walk them around a little. I don't take them back here. I am the one that put the big rocks in the passageway. I used a crowbar and pried them loose from the sides and made them fall."

"I am glad to hear that. It makes it very special that you trusted me enough to bring me." Brian leaned back against the tree and yawned. I am tired today. I couldn't rest last night just knowing the morning would bring all those noisy young people."

"You are not old Brian you are just mature. There is a big difference." When he didn't respond she leaned closer to see and sure enough, he was sound asleep. It is this place, she thought. It is wonderful. I feel that if I could stay here, that I would get well. She stood up slowly, not wanting to make a sound that would wake him. She wanted to look into the cave. I won't go in, I'll just peek, she thought.

It was easy for her to slip through the branches because she was small. She stood in the opening. She took one hesitant step and then another. As her eyes adjusted to the interior; she became aware of a beautiful glow of blue-white light far in the distance. That could be Under-Grounders, she thought. I don't think I want to meet up with them. The entrance was cool and the breeze reached in to stir the air. It was pleasant seated on the stone floor with her back against a smooth gray wall. With both books beside her she decided to look at the Bible again. She randomly thumbed through the text of the Old Testament and passed all the books of the prophets without knowing the wisdom they held. The New Testament opened to Matthew 7:7 NIV "Ask and it will be given to you; seek and you will find; knock and the door will be opened to you, For everyone who asks receives; the one who seeks finds; and to the one who knocks, the door will be opened." She was puzzled by the words before her. This Bible seems to be a bound set of books, not just one book. John; strange that name is in here, she thought. The John at the table last night was not anyone I would want to spend much time with. Her eyes rested on John 3:16 NIV "For God so loved the world that he gave his one and only Son, that whoever believes in him shall not parish but have eternal life." She scanned farther down, John 3:19 NIV "This is the verdict: Light has come into the world, but people loved darkness instead of light because their deeds were evil."

Brian woke and called her name. He was concerned that she was not beside him.

"Emily, where are you?"

"I am here. I am coming. I was just sitting and reading. Inside the cave the rocks are cool."

"I am going to call Babe. I think we should head back," he said looking worried.

"What's the matter? I don't know really, I just think we need to leave right away." Babe settled beside him opening her door and hold. He packed everything inside, but once again Emily tucked the books away and pulled the sweater tight around her waist.

"Hello Brian, my current power level is fifty percent. The time is five thirty five p.m. The air temperature is dropping. It is one hundred and nine degrees."

"Thank you Babe." As they climbed in for the trip back, Emily decided to see if Babe would follow her wishes as well as Brian's.

"Babe, would you please stop in front of the cave?"

"Who is addressing me? Brian, is it your wish that I respond to this female voice?"

"Yes, Babe, this is Emily. Please do whatever she asks."

"I am not programed to accept instructions from anyone other than you or Paula. I must adjust my protocols. One moment please; very well then, we are stopping in front of the cave."

"Quick Brian, get out, the sun is dropping. I want to see if the image of the Lion appears."

"Go in the shade Babe, run on energy conservation."

"Thank you Brian." Emily hurried to the spot where a bench stood. She stopped in front of it looking up. Bits of shadows from trees that had been stripped for fuel played against the bottom of the bluff wall. Suddenly, Emily began to squeal with delight and Brian backed up as if afraid of what he was seeing.

"It's real Brain. It's all real. Everything in the journal and in the Bible is the truth. I feel it in my heart. It is just as it is written." She was holding her breath as the image faded. She turned and hurried to the vacant church. It isn't a ruin Brian, it is just empty. Look, the inside is beautiful!" She said it quietly, while slowly stepping in. The beams are all carved and I think that we are being watched. The O.W.U. has a camera up there and it is pointing right at us. Now I get why it is empty, she whispered. Let's go."

Brian was glad to leave.

"Emily, you shouldn't go poking around like that. You could get us in trouble."

"You knew it wasn't a ruin. Didn't you?"

"Yes, it had people come and go until the aliens took so many and then the soldiers came and took anything of monetary value. Everything is changed. Nothing is safe anymore. Be careful when you get back. Don't say much about our trip and don't mention that image or the church! I don't think I am going back there. That place is creepy."

"Oh, Brian, I didn't feel that way at all. I thought it was peaceful and I like the area." She didn't know that it had a beautiful sacred secret waiting for her to discover. She glanced to her left before getting in and noticed the inviting cabins. One was quite near, the other appeared larger and it was deeper in the trees. They had been well maintained.

"Who lives in the cabins?"

"They are vacant, too. Let's go."

She wrapped her arms around her chest and went to her room as soon as they got back. Brian took Babe to her energy station and after removing their food and water he gave her one last instruction.

"Babe, erase all record of our trip today, including conversational data."

"Do you want me to remove the new female voice protocol?"

"Yes Babe, do that."

"Thank you Brian. I will go rest and recharge now."

Emily wanted very much to read, but she knew that if she missed the meal at the Slater House, they would come looking for her. She showered and changed into a simple floor length, ice blue dress. When she looked in the mirror to put on her wig and makeup she was stunned. Her head was covered with a quarter inch of soft fuzz. She felt it and laughed and twirled around. It can't be that my hair is growing back after all the skin grafts and scars. How can this be? She leaned closer to the mirror grinning. When she got over her discovery, she finished getting ready and walked to the Hut Library. I think the best place to hide these books is in plain sight. She pulled two books from the floor level of the shelves and gently placed the Bible and journal there. The two from the lowest shelf she put in the space above her head, left by the removal of the Bible and Journal. The low corner shelf was dusty and dark and would remain dark even if the lantern was lit.

"I'll be back to get you after we eat," she said conspiratorially. She did go back and read half the night before giving in to her need for sleep.

In the morning, dressed in a mint green sundress and roman sandals she asked Paula for a picnic and some water, saying that she was going to take her new I-Go out for a lesson and didn't know how long she would be gone. Paula was happy to accommodate her request and included some cherry drink and one of her signature large yellow sugar cookies. She said she thought that Emily was looking like she felt better.

"Yes I think I am, a little. I am going to give my I-Go a name today, any suggestions?"

"Be sure it's something that is easy to remember!"

"That's a good idea." Emily laughed as she turned and went outside. Paula could hear her talking to the vehicle as she got in.

"I-Go, do you have a masculine voice?"

The door closed and the unit moved away from the house down the driveway and out over the bridge.

"I-Go your name from now on is Danny. You are to serve only me unless I tell you otherwise. I am Emily. I own you."

"Yes, Emily. I have been waiting for you to request my service on a more intimate level. I am full of energy and eager to do your bidding."

"Thank you Danny. When I enter for a trip, I would like you to give me the time and temperature. I would also like you to keep our interior at seventy degrees when we are active."

"The time is nine o'clock a.m. and the current air temperature is sixty degrees Fahrenheit." She could feel a gentle stream of warm air surrounding her.

"Thank you Danny. I want you to verbally list for me your abilities for transportation modes, Danny."

"I have modes for air, land and water travel. I can fly, cruise, hover and submerge. Basically I can go anywhere."

"Danny, what would you do if I asked you to go forward but the space was too small to get through?"

"I am able to make a way if necessary."

"Danny, do you have weaponry?"

"Yes, of course."

"Thank you Danny. You make me feel much safer."

"I was created to serve you and keep you safe."

"We are cruising but you have not indicated a destination. Where would you like to go?"

"Take me upriver, until you see a white cross down in the grass and a church in the trees behind it." Suddenly a screen in the panel in front of her lit with a topographical map.

"We are approaching a scene that matches your description." She watched as the area came into view.

"Good Danny, go slowly to the left until you locate a passageway in the bluff. I want to go to the other side. It is blocked. You will need to use hover mode. There that's good, now up above where that clump of pine trees are, there is an opening in the side of the bluff. Danny can you gently move through there without doing damage to the trees and enter the opening?"

"Emily, I can go wherever you need to go. With the shields up you will need to use the front screen for visibility. Please put on your harness. I will have to tilt to the right a bit. There we are through the trees and I am hovering in the entrance. This is a large cave, Emily.

"Yes, I have been here before. I didn't go in very far. I would like to explore. Please open all the viewing shields and move forward very slowly. Put your brightest lights on Danny."

"Emily, I detect an extremely strong power source ahead. Should I proceed?"

"Are there humans in the cave?"

"I do not detect normal human aura."

"Danny, continue to tell me what you are sensing, as we go."

"This is above my capabilities. My power sensor is overheating. Please allow me to turn it off immediately."

"Danny, turn off power sensor and stop. Turn off all systems except lights and rest here." Emily was frightened and yet she was undeniably drawn.

"Thank you Emily." Danny had taken her slowly down, nearly to the end of the right fork of the tunnels. The bright blue-white light glowing from the space ahead, made visibility easy. She could see the partitioned sections where the workmen had lived although she had no idea of the purpose for what she was observing. High above her head on a ledge she could see fully stuffed pouches. They appeared heavy, and old. Dust had settled into every crack and fold of their thick leather exteriors. She wondered what was in them. She quietly stepped out of her I-Go.

When she reached the back wall it had a large, rough hole that allowed her to look through to a ceiling of white salt crystals. The bottom, far below, was also white and irregular. To her right the light was brighter. She climbed several steps intending to look around a partition.

Exodus 3:5 NIV *"Do not come any closer,* God said. *"Take off your sandals, for the place where you are standing is holy ground."* Then He said, *"J am the God of your Father, the God of Abraham, the God of Jsaac and the God of Jacob."*

Emily was shaking as she removed her sandals and hid her face. She was afraid to look. Now she understood why she had been pulled to this place, why she had felt compelled to read the Bible and why her I-Go had discerned an endless power!

Still looking down, she knelt starting to weep. Revelation 5:5 NIV *"Do not weep! See, the Lion of the tribe of Judah, the Root of David, has triumphed. He is able to open the scroll and its seven seals."*

Suddenly a flood of belief strongly swept over her. She asked forgiveness for her life of unbelief. She sobbed, still not looking up. I know now that I am forgiven and healed through the blood of Jesus on the cross. I also understand the things I read and I believe that your children; those who believed your Holy Word were taken by you so they would not have to survive the things that are taking place and still to come." She lifted her eyes just a little, hoping, expecting to possibly see the edge of His sandals or His garment hem, but instead of a man's feet, she saw four, large, pure white fur covered paws and a tail that swayed as He stood near her on a floor of polished salt as shiny as glass.

"My Lord, I am unworthy to be in your presence!" Her heart was beating so fiercely that her chest was filled with pain. Emily grabbed her sandals as she dashed quickly back to Danny.

He sensed her speedy approach and opened the door.

"Are we leaving?"

"Yes Danny, take me back so I can tell Brian and Paula what has happened to me. I long to stay, but I want to help them have what I have."

"What happened? What do you have? Do I need to retaliate?"

"No Danny, I was just saved! I am a believer."

"What should I do? I do not know those words. The meaning is not in my word bank."

"That is alright. It means that I am happier than I have ever been in my life. It means that I am going to heaven and that Jesus loves me. It means that the emptiness inside me is gone!"

"I do not understand."

"Danny, I love you."

"Thank you Emily. You own me. I am a machine and I am incapable of such emotion, but if I could, I would reciprocate by saying that I love you, also."

"We have arrived at the Jones House. The time is five o'clock. The temperature is one hundred and thirteen degrees Fahrenheit."

As she stepped out she realized that she had not touched the food or water she had taken with her, but she was neither hungry nor thirsty.

"Danny it is not necessary to say Fahrenheit and you should go to the charging station now."

"Thank you Emily."

In her room she stepped into the shower and laughed at a thought that entered her mind. Lord, please baptize me with this water and your Holy Spirit. I desire to be baptized, but there is no one here to do it. You are here. I believe it. She didn't understand why she felt like laughing out loud. Her mind replayed her experience in the cave, over and over. "I feel such joy! I should have remained in your holy presence. Why did I leave? Thank you Jesus for accepting me!"

As she rubbed her head with the towel she felt the fluff. Her hair was nearly an inch long, forming little curls all over her scalp! I can't believe this is happening. I am healthy! She looked at her reflection in the mirror and smiled. She looked younger and joyous.

"Thank you God, Thank you Lion of Judah. Thank you Jesus!"

She slipped into a soft white, cotton dress that matched the white flat shoes she put on. With a simple string of small pearls and earrings to match she applied makeup and pulled her wig back on, combing and arranging the hair until she was satisfied.

She was sitting out on the porch when Brian pulled up in Babe. She looks like a beautiful bride, he thought.

"I have been looking for you. Would you like to go for a ride?"

"Yes, I would. I have something to tell you. Let's use my I-Go. He is getting so smart and he can expand, too." She was smiling.

"Danny, come here please."

"Good afternoon, Emily. It is five thirty eight, p.m. And the temperature is one hundred and one degrees."

"Danny, the instruction manual says that you have a passenger expansion. Can you accommodate one extra person?"

"Yes, of course." The sides of the vehicle made a clicking sound and in a brief moment the area beside the driver slid sideways and a soft cushion slid out from under the floor of the hold to sit on. A similar pad folded down from the ceiling and clicked into place. The entire process took less than a minute.

"I will adjust the floor space and seat height as soon as your passenger boards."

"Thank you Danny."

"I can see that you have been doing some training on this guy!"

"Yes, Danny learns fast and he has capabilities far beyond any simple transportation I expected. For instance, the gray exterior is totally coated with zirconium, which protects us against absorbing any radioactive neurons when we might unknowingly draw near an area hot with radiation. Even the viewing panels are made of it in a transparent form."

"This is nice. I am comfortable. As soon as I sat down the seat raised and the foot area expanded. I wonder if my We-Go can expand."

"Haven't you read the manual?"

"No, I just like to try things out and see if they work. I get bored when I start reading. Mom was never elated with my World Brotherhood scores," he said laughing.

"Danny, are you able to take us where we went earlier and return without a power stop?"

"Yes, I can, even with the added weight. I am at full power. I can go there and back, but if I am forced to use weaponry we may run low on power."

Let's go Danny and run on conserve power. We are not in a hurry."

Brian looked puzzled but didn't ask where they were going. His mind was wondering about the word weaponry. Soon it became obvious that she was returning to the old church and cave area.

"It is going to be dark soon. We probably shouldn't be back here. They will see us on the cameras. Mother will worry when we don't show up at the Slater House for the evening meal. Emily, are you listening?"

"Yes, Brian, I hear you. Danny, take me in the cave behind the trees and proceed slowly as before. That was smooth. Well done. Open Danny and turn on your light system."

"It is fully powered."

"Thank you Danny, please rest until we return. The time is five forty seven P.M. The temperature is ninety degrees outside and 68 degrees here. I will rest now."

"Emily, why are we going in here? It is dark. One of us could get seriously hurt. Your lights are not bright enough to show the entire area. There could be something dangerous in here. I don't like this at all!"

"Brian, something has changed. I don't understand. I was able to see in here and back there was an opening to look through into another space, but I can't find it now."

"Emily, I am not comfortable here. Let's go back. You seem to be fixated on this area. I should never have brought you here."

"Brian this is a sacred, peaceful place. What is bothering you?"

"I'm not sure. I just feel like I don't belong here!"

"Danny, we are leaving now. Please power up and cool the interior."

"It is done. Do you wish to return to the Jones House?"

"Yes, return, Danny."

As soon as they were in and comfortably seated, Danny zipped through the air, over the pass and emerged through the trees and rocks on the church property and onto the highway that went directly to the ranch. He pulled up by the Jones House.

"That is fine Danny." The driveway and grounds were busier than she had ever seen them. She looked at Brian as he stepped to the back, removing her satchel and thermos.

"You haven't eaten today."

"The food is good. I just didn't feel like eating. Brian would you let your mother know that I won't be there at the Slater House for the evening meal tonight and then if you would, could you meet me in the Hut Library after you have had something to eat?"

"Yes, Sure, but why?"

"I will explain later." She went to her room just long enough to change into warm slacks and a pullover sweater. She knew the hut would be cool inside.

*****

She lit the lantern and took the journal to the table where she sat eating a sandwich and reading the journal.

†Journal

"Sarah rode to the ranch this morning on Blackie. She was frantic. She said all of her white horses were missing! When Ben checked the far field where the white mares, yearlings and white foals were, he found that they too were gone. Josh and Jed checked all the barns and climbed the bluff so they could see the prairie. Cloud and Buddy are gone from the field by Sarah's cabin! Orville said he didn't hear any unusual sounds last night. Neither did any of us. Ben intended to ride to town to tell the new Marshall as soon as they made sure that there was no wild herd in the area but then instead, Ben picked up the Bible and it opened to Revelation 19: NIV" He gathered us all in the house and read verses 11 through 14. "I saw heaven standing open and there before me was a white horse, whose rider is called Faithful and True. With justice he judges and wages war. His eyes are like blazing fire, and on his head are many crowns. He has a name written on him that no one knows but he himself. He is dressed in a robe dipped in blood, and his name is the Word of God. The armies of heaven were following him, riding on white horses and dressed in fine linen, white and clean."

Ben said that he thinks we will not see our white horses until the end times when Christ, The King of Kings rides with His army on white horses. If Ben is right, our horses are the start of Christ's herd of mounts for the final battle. God could make them all in an instant, but maybe he has chosen not to do that. Jed and Ben are going to check to see if the army is missing their white horses. God has given us so much. We feel honored that maybe God has chosen our white horses to create his herd. I can feel it inside as if they are still near us here. It is strange.

Ben came back from town and said that the army still has white horses. I don't understand it, but I feel Ben is right.

Last night the mustang fence went down. When Orville went out to work this morning, he said instead of ours leaving, at least twice as many horses were in the field grazing peacefully. The men repaired the fence and said that every one of the extra horses look purebred! They are not white, but they are extraordinarily beautiful. We all went to see them. Their manes and tails are long, full and silky and they appear shiny and muscled as if sculpted. They are a new magnificent breed!" †

*****

Brian entered the hut and closed the door quickly and quietly.

The soldiers are looking for us. They saw us on the cameras at the church again today. They are searching the Slater House right now!"

"Why are they looking for us? That area isn't posted as off limits. I didn't see any signs. Brian, it's alright. Turn the lantern off and hold my hand. Follow me." She went to the back of the main room and pushed on the shelves. They slid open silently. "Step inside and pull the shelves back tightly in place. We can stay here while they check the hut or we can climb up on the bluff. That big boulder you can feel behind you, made this little room when it crashed through the roof. Ben Slater couldn't move it so he and Jed Jones built in front of it and left access to this space on both sides of the rock. They felt they could hide here from the Indians if they came."

"This is amazing! How did you know this room would still be here? You know things about this place that I don't."

"Quiet I hear them." The door pushed open and two soldiers stepped in searching the place with bright lights. They listened as the hard heels of the soldier's boots moved across the wooden floor of the hut.

"This lantern is still hot! They were here."

"Well they are not here now!"

Emily recognized the voice of the soldier that had been in her room. She could sense the evil in the man. She put her hand over Brian's mouth and held very still. Brian slipped his arms around her waist knowing she could not object under the circumstances and with her hand on his mouth she could feel him smiling. The men opened the door and closed it. Something inside warned her that one of the men had not left. She stepped up on the bluff behind her and pulled on Brian's hand in the dark. He felt the hand hold and toe hold chipped into the face of the back wall. They cautiously climbed up and pushed away the loose section of the roof, sliding it onto the grass and were able to silently exit the hut. Once they were outside a half moon gave them just enough light to crawl carefully to the top and lie flat. They wordlessly waited. Finally the second soldier stepped out of the hut. He had been in there waiting for them to reveal themselves. He was sure that they were there somewhere.

"What were you doing in there?"

"I thought they were in there hiding but I guess I was wrong." The silent vehicles slipped away in the dark projecting their paths with bright lights.

I'll catch them and that will be the last of their kind in my territory, he thought.

"Brian you need to read the journal. The Jones House has a hidden tunnel and I am guessing that if you check carefully the Slater House probably has a safe room or route up and out."

"Where is it?"

"What?"

"Where is the journal?"

"Oh Brian, I left it on the table! I hope he didn't take it with him!"

"You stay here and I will go check and get a porta-lamp." She stayed still enjoying the dark cool air. "Emily, I am coming back up."

"Why don't you just light a path for me to climb down?"

"I just thought that as long as they visit here so often, I should hide these up here." He looked around for a spot to put the books and noticed the same overhang that Josh had used to hide the carved gifts that he made for Christmas so long ago. "This is perfect. They will stay clean and dry and I can come up here and read when people are not around."

"You can use this as a bookmark in the Bible." She handed him a slip of paper. On it she had listed the verses that had turned her heart to Christ. "If you promise to read those, I think that when I return here next year, you will be one of the dreaded, hunted Christians, too. I will leave very early tomorrow, but I want you to know my secret before I go." She pulled off her wig and placed his hand on her new, soft hair.

"Your hair is growing back! I am so happy for you. You are beautiful in your wig but you will be stunning with your real hair." He pulled her close and kissed her gently. "Emily, I am sad you are leaving, but you have given me a reason to look forward. Promise you will return. Come back to me Emily."

"Only if you will promise to read the Bible, especially the verses that I wrote down for you and then read the journal. Suddenly you will be seeking a new route to the cherry tree valley. One without cameras; you won't feel like you don't belong there anymore. Brian, we are all God's children and the people that were snatched from the earth were not taken by aliens. They were believers taken to be with the

Lord until His return. He will return to earth soon Brian with an army of His believers. They will ride out of the clouds on beautiful white horses and He will lead them. Christ will subjugate the leader of the O.W.U. That man is evil. He is a deceiver and he is the anti-Christ. After you have read the verses on that paper, read the book of Revelation. It is God's war plan for the time of tribulation that we are living through right now."

"Emily, I don't know what to say. You sound like a radical! Where did you hear all that stuff? I read it in the Bible. I was not a believer before I came here. Didn't you ever wonder why it was the people that were good, kind, and innocent that disappeared? He took all the young children. The church is not a ruin, Brian. It is just empty. Christ will overpower the whole One World Union. Which side do you want to be on when that happens? Goodnight Brian."

"Goodnight Emily, Sleep well." She made her way down the bluff and went to her room.

Emily left very early the next morning. She left a note for Paula and Brian saying that she had enjoyed her stay and although she had paid for another week that she was feeling so much better that she should get back to her job. She asked them to hold her credit until next spring when she planned to come back.

CHAPTER TWENTY ONE
A NEW WAY

Brian couldn't wait to have the guests leave and the ranch back to its peaceful routine. After several days of cleaning and helping with laundry, he and his mother were able to relax.

"Brian, I am so tired that I don't want to use the effort to breathe. I am going in and take a long nap."

"Mother, are you getting ill?"

"No son, I just feel like I need to rest."

"Mom, I will take care of everything. You have been working so hard. I can make a sandwich when I get hungry. Just relax."

"Thank you Brian, I think I will sleep, but if I can't, I will still stay in bed, read and rest."

"I really think you should. You need it. This place is getting to be too much for just the two of us."

Brian climbed the bluff and retrieved the books. He placed them in the hidden space in the back of the hut. I should not have put these up there in the heat. What was I thinking? It seemed like a good idea at the time. I need to put a lamp in there and put a black seal around the seams where the shelves close. Do I need anything else? Yes, I need a chair.

The next day after lunch, he suggested that his mother take another nap.

"I could get used to this you know!" She said laughing. "I think I will go get a book from the hut and just lie down and read." It seemed to take her a long time to find a book that she wanted to read, but finally she had walked very slowly to the Jones house, under the protection of a large umbrella. Brian had worried that she would stay in the hut until the hot hours were over. He had lovingly placed a tray on her bedside table with a glass of the cherry drink and a big yellow sugar cookie. When she saw it she smiled. He is a good son, she thought. He does so much for me.

I hate the times we are living in and the burned ugly ruins of the cities. The scarred people, who come here like Emily, are sick and weak. I don't like the disrespectful, wild bunch we finally got rid of. I wish she had stayed. There was something special about her. I liked her right away and I think Brian did, too. He needs someone nice, but where can he find such a girl in this world?

As soon as she left the hut he entered and went to the hidden space beside the boulder. It was dark and cool. He could smell the scent of Emily's perfume. He pushed open the loose panel of sod on the roof and lit the small lantern. He began to read the scriptures that Emily had listed. He was surprised how easy it was to find them, but he still doubted until he read the book of Revelation and realized that he was living in those terrible times. He didn't understand all of it, but enough. It spoke to his heart.

"Lord, if Emily is right and this book is true, is it too late to be forgiven for not believing in your Son? Is there time for me to be saved? Please help me to believe. Help me to know what to do." He sat there thinking about all the training he had received at the Brotherhood Union Academy. Some of the things they had us do. I feel filthy. "Forgive me." Then he thought of Emily and a smile crossed his face. "She has to come back. She just has to."

Brian placed the Bible down and picked up the journal flipping through the pages rather swiftly until he came to a small slip of paper marking Emily's spot.

The woman that wrote this had faith. She writes with certainty. He turned to the start of the journal and read it all.

When he stepped out of the hut it was dark and cool. "Tomorrow morning I am going to have my mother read in there, while I make a trail to the back of the Lion's Den and the cherry tree valley! Thank you Jesus for allowing me time to learn about you. Thank you for saving me. Please save my mother and if you would, please send Emily back."

Brian rode out the next day passing Jed's barn. He rode into the field that at one time had held a large herd of horses. Now there were just a few animals. The cows shared the field with the horses. They were down on the other end. He opened the gate and closed it gently, heading across another field. This one was empty. All the beautiful horses that once graced this field of thoroughbreds were gone now. He stopped and looked back at the old barn, remembering the pages in the journal that told of the gold that God had provided. Mary had outlined its use telling about the purchase of beef cattle for The Blue Stone People when their hunting grounds held too many pioneers and not enough wild animals for food. They had buried some of the gold. I wonder if it is possible that there is still gold buried somewhere behind that old barn. He rode back to that area walking his horse back and forth.

I am kidding myself. They probably had to use that gold long ago. He headed for the shade of the woods and thought how blessed they were to be here on this ranch where things were still natural. No, he thought, compared to all the rest of the world, they are supernatural. He wondered how people managed to live in the big pods with synthetic furniture, walls and floors. I wonder how Emily feels about it. She lives in one of them. It must feel like a web full of trapped people. Poor Emily, she works for United Creations. She is in the office of a place that makes those plastic housing units. It must be horrible.

He looked up to realize that his horse was following what appeared to be a game trail. It meandered through the trees and headed in the general direction of upriver. If you are happy old girl, this works for me. He stopped for a while giving the horse a chance to rest and drink from a small pond. I should have brought you tested water. I sure hope that pond is useable. He sensed movement around him, but each time he looked up he couldn't see anything moving except the leaves of the trees.

They followed the trail and finally it came out in the wide pastureland that had at one time held the camp of The Blue Stone People and The People of the Lion. As his eyes searched the back of the bluff and the grass at the bottom of it, he became aware of distinct lines in the grass forming many squares. He saw the pass they had used and noted more square patterns in the grass. That is where they built small cabins here at one time, he thought. He slid off and pulled his saddle and bridle off.

"Do whatever you want to girl. We are going to be here for a while." He knew she would come to him when he called her. She walked into the lake and drank. Looking up and into the trees she called loudly as if coaxing a new friend to join her. Brian watched as thousands of white horses came out of the trees and approached the lake. They surrounded him and covered the edges of the water and all the grass in both directions. He stood stone still. What am I seeing? Is this real or is it a vision of some sort? He wasn't sure.

Suddenly he realized how hot it was becoming. The horses withdrew after drinking and little by little they entered the trees and moved out of sight. He looked up toward the bluff thinking he should seek the shelter of the cave entrance. When he looked back his horse was the only one left. She still stood in the water looking in the direction of the trees. He watched as she strolled to the shade and tall green grass just inside the tree line where she laid down.

Brian discovered that his heart was beating very fast. He climbed up to the clump of pines and crawled through their branches and entered the cave. Instantly it felt cooler. The cave was not as dark as it had been when he was here with Emily. He became aware of the light radiating far in the back.

*****

"Brian, are you here? Brian where are you?" Paula and Emily came up beside him in the We-Go.

"How did you find me? Emily you are here! I don't understand."

"Emily came just as I was coming out of the hut. She is here to stay Brian."

"This is wonderful." Without thinking about it he wrapped his arms around her and held her close. "Emily, I asked God to bring you back to me and he did." Paula was laughing and crying at the same time.

"I didn't think it was possible for Brian to find someone with things as they are in the world, but he did. Emily we both love you and we do want you to stay with us for as long as we have," Paula said.

"Yes, Emily, I love you. Will you marry me?" Brian still had not let go of her.

"Well I would, but we are rather short on ministers to perform the ceremony." She said laughing. The light in the cave grew brighter as the three people turned to the left to see its source. The man in a simple white robe and leather sandals carried a lantern as he walked up the left tunnel toward them.

"Did I hear someone say they wanted to get married? I can perform a simple ceremony right here, right now. Are you all believers?"

"Yes," they said together. Brian smiled a big smile at his mother, pleased with her instant response.

"Come, follow me." He walked out of the cave and down the bluff as if it were level ground. "Come to the water." He placed the lantern on a rock and left it burning. The sky was dark with clouds and the heat could not penetrate them. It was mild. He walked out until he was chest deep in water. They looked at each other and followed grinning. Each in turn was baptized and then there in the flowing water he led the ceremony that made them man and wife. Paula was crying tears of Joy. The man moved slowly to the edge of the water and slid up onto a white horse that none of them had seen until that moment. Emily looked at Brian and smiled broadly.

"That was a marriage straight from heaven. Who do you think he is?" Paula asked.

Neither of the young people had an answer for her. They were still looking in the direction he had gone.

"This was so strangely spiritual and beautiful that the biggest, fanciest wedding in the world couldn't come close. Brian I love you so much, let's go home."

"Do you think he is one of the army that will ride with Christ?"

"Yes, definitely and I think it will be soon and maybe we all three will get to ride with them. This is "**Just the Beginning**!"

AN INVITATION

If you do not know Jesus, as your Savior but you would like Him to be, please pray the following prayer. Invite Him into your heart. Commit your "New Life" to Him. He will be your constant companion, counselor, comforter, and protector. The Holy Bible tells us that He will never leave you or forsake you.

"Dear Jesus, please forgive my sins. Give me grace and strength Lord, so that I will not commit them again. Come into my heart so that I can start a "New Life" with you as my companion. I want to live according to your will and commandments. Bless me Lord and lead me in a life that is pleasing to you. In Jesus' Holy name I pray. Amen"

If you sincerely prayed that prayer, you are saved. You are born again. Your soul is whiter than the snow that caps the highest mountains. The angels in heaven are singing with joy as they write your name in The Lamb's Book of Life.

Get a Holy Bible and begin to read it. Find a good Bible believing church and start attending, so that you can learn more about Your Heavenly Father and talk to Him. Tell Him what you are feeling. What a wonderful God we have. Tell someone about your new life in Christ.

If you wish, you can sign and date your Bible as an outward sign of your salvation and that you have committed your life to Christ.

I will pray for you. God bless you. Louise Bouck

BOOK TITLES IN THE NEW LIFE SERIES

- 1 More than Survival

- 2 Life's Many Journeys

- 3 The Land's Heritage

- 4 The Story of Sarah

- 5 Together

- 6 The Blue Stone People

- 7 Teewahpanee the Boy, Two Feathers the Man

- 8 The People of the Lion

- 9 The Lion's Den

- 10 Just the Beginning

Watch for a bit more about the S. and J. Ranch in:

"Little Man of My Dreams, a love story."
Subtitle,   "The story of KOZA"
Coming Soon.....................

ABOUT THE AUTHOR

Louise Bouck is a follower of Jesus Christ. She has been married to her husband, Dale, for more than fifty seven years. Together they have raised six children.

Until an early retirement from her fulltime job in December of 1999, very little time was available to allocate to writing or art. One of the many interests that Louise enjoys is painting on location. The lush greenery of Michigan, her home state and the abundant flowers in her grandmother's greenhouses and flower shop all encouraged her eye to appreciate the colors and beauty of nature.

Later after moving to Arizona, the rugged landscape of the mountains and desert stole her heart and took her artistic soul in a new direction.

Paintings in many media cover the walls of her studio as she has deliberately turned her creative side more to the written word. Hesitantly she withdrew from the art gallery where her work was sold and left the position of resident artist at the local Historical Society Museum in Show Low, Arizona. Louise has written ten books in a series of Christian; Bible based stories that she is now starting to release for the first time as she works on still another story and another painting.

www.ingramcontent.com/pod-product-compliance
Lightning Source LLC
Chambersburg PA
CBHW050918250626
47155CB00001B/285